SWEET SEDUCTION

When her face was cleaned of the mud, Stephanie spun around to gauge Cole's reaction to the transformation. "I hope you are not too disappointed with my face. Plain though it is, 'tis the one I was born with," she declared saucily.

Mesmerized, Cole strode toward her. His tanned finger brushed over her satiny cheek. "M'lady," he murmured, "no plain maiden this but rather a glittering diamond in the rough . . ."

Stephanie was impressed with Cole's direct manner —until his head made a slow, lazy descent to plant a kiss on her lips. The warmth of his arms engulfed her, and his lithe, virile body made intimate suggestions as it brushed against hers. His hands moved over her back and down to her hips. Pulling her even closer to him, his mouth expertly caressed hers, kindling a fire within her that left her wanting him, needing him as she had never needed a man before . . .

SECRET SPLENDOR

GINA ROBINS

ZEBRA BOOKS
KENSINGTON PUBLISHING CORP.

ZEBRA BOOKS

are published by

Kensington Publishing Corp.
475 Park Avenue South
New York, NY 10016

First printing: January 1988

Printed in the United States of America

This book is dedicated to:
Glee Walker and Letha Hutchinson
For all the years of caring and
sharing and love . . .

Part I

The kiss I stole, when thou and I,
  Dear girl, were romping in the glade,
Did nectar in its sweet outvie,
  But oh! how dear for it I paid!

Catullus

Chapter 1

Cole Hollister sat his satchel on the end of his bed. His scrutinizing brown eyes circled the clean but plain quarters he had rented at Reynolds Inn. Cole's thick chest rose and fell in a gesture of weariness. The past few months had been hectic ones. After setting sail from his plantation near Annapolis, Maryland, he had cruised to the West Indies with a shipload of goods. He and his crew had narrowly escaped two violent storms at sea and he had limped into port in Mystic to trade the sugar, molasses, and cloth he had purchased from the French and Spanish colonies in the Caribbean. Because of the tropical storms, Cole found his schooner in irons. The fierce gales had damaged the ship. The only way he had been able to make progress was to sail backward. And so he breezed into port on the winds of another storm that had drenched the coast of Connecticut.

There were several reasons why Cole had weighed anchor in Mystic to sell his West Indian imports. He had his business and personal motives, but he had also come to elicit the assistance of one of New England's most noted shipbuilders. Dyer Wakefield had been working on some revolutionary new ideas in shipbuilding and Cole found himself in need of a swift, agile vessel to replace the one damaged in the storms.

The other purposes for cruising into this port were ones Cole was not inclined to discuss with just anyone. The colonies were in an uproar after hearing that Parliament intended to impose the Stamp Act on its colonial holdings, forcing the inhabitants to compensate for the debts caused by the war with France. The Sugar Act and various Navigation Acts had already crippled the colonies' economy. The proposed law, which was to go into effect the first of November, had already set Americans to grumbling. This latest tax on legal documents, college degrees, playing cards, and dice was considered outrageous. Cole shared the opinion that England was becoming a mite too presumptuous by taxing colonies without granting them representation in Parliament.

The depression of the economy and trade in the colonies and the loss of his schooner annoyed Cole. But that was not all that rankled him. As much as he hated to admit it, Rachel . . .

The young woman's face popped to mind and Cole's bronzed features turned to stone. The image of dark silky hair and an ivory complexion had Cole scowling under his breath. Rachel Garret was the belle of Maryland society, but Cole considered her to be a witch in elegant silk. She was the daughter of one of his father's closest friends. Cole had deluded himself in thinking Rachel possessed all of her family's personable qualities. Most of the Garrets were saints but Rachel . . .

"Women," Cole grumbled as he dragged a fresh shirt from his satchel. He shook the wrinkles from the garment so vigorously that he very nearly snapped off its whale bone buttons.

The next time he thought he was about to fall in love

he would catch himself before he landed in a bruised heap! He had been a fool to think he could marry for love. And it was a good thing he discovered how promiscuous Rachel was before she put a ring through his nose. The joining of the Hollister name with that of the influential Garrets would have made a fine match . . . if Rachel hadn't been so fickle, so deceitful. Cole swore that even if he lived to be one hundred he would never forget how it felt to be betrayed by a woman. Perhaps that was what he deserved for taking women for granted all his life, he told himself resentfully. When he decided to put down roots and devote himself to one woman . . .

A piercing female voice sailed through the open window, shattering Cole's contemplative musings. Curiously, he ambled over to see a young woman being dragged toward the ducking pond on the outskirts of the village. Obviously, some contrary servant was about to pay penance for a disrespectful outburst, Cole speculated as he absently shrugged on his shirt.

A public ducking always drew a crowd of spectators and Cole was eager for a diversion from his frustrating thoughts. By the time he descended the steps and rounded the corner of the inn, a sizable congregation had gathered to see justice served.

Any female found guilty of cursing, scolding, or gossiping in public was sentenced to a ducking. And it should have been the fate of every female on the face of the earth, Cole thought on a cynical note. Women everywhere should be tied on the stool that set on the end of a pole and thoroughly ducked in a pond of muddy water.

Cole tromped through the mud and elbowed his way through the cluster of onlookers to survey the wench who had already had her first taste of stagnant water. The gadget upon which she sat served as an oversized teeter-totter that raised and lowered her into the murky depths. Cole had viewed this prodecure on several occasions and had frowned upon it until he had become so cynical of women.

Although Cole didn't know which crime the wench had committed, he presumed the girl to be guilty of vocal outbursts. And she had not let up, even while she was receiving her punishment. Indeed, each time the wench was raised from the pond she spouted furiously at the smug-looking aristocrat who was poised beside the sheriff.

"Pompous, deceitful viper!" Stephanie spat as she exhaled the breath she had been holding while she was submerged in the ducking pond. "*You* should be the one tied on the end of this blessed pole! You used your influence with the—"

The last of the young woman's sentence emerged in bubbles as the sheriff lowered her back into the cloudy depths. Although the recipient of Stephanie's slanderous comments was further outraged by her daring, Cole was amused. The girl was brimming with spunk. Even while she was being punished in this degrading manner, she refused to submit.

Mud clung to Stephanie's gown and the color of her hair was indiscernible when it was caked with pond slime. But there was no disguising those fiery green eyes. When she glared at the man who was responsible for placing her on the ducking pole, flames sizzled around his feet.

"Brice Reynolds, I will never forgive you for this!" Stephanie spat. "You used your position with the Crown to have me punished, but you stooped to name calling long before I called you a—" She attempted to point out the injustice of the charge against her but Brice's loud gasp drowned her words.

Brice glowered at the soggy female who was tied to

the end of the pole. "Dunk her!" Brice growled at the sheriff. "I will not have that she-cat smudging my character in front of these good citizens! And you can hold her under water until she drowns for all I care!"

Again bubbles drifted across the surface of the pond and Cole fought to keep a straight face. A wave of murmurs rippled through the crowd when the girl was left in the pond for a full minute.

"I think she has had enough," the sheriff declared.

Apparently, Brice Reynolds didn't agree. When the sheriff tried to hoist the girl upward, Brice attempted to hold her in the pond.

"I said that is enough!" the sheriff grumbled, nudging Brice out of the way. "You have disgraced her. If you drown her, the punishment will no longer justify the crime."

Begrudgingly, Brice backed away and Cole squeezed through the crowd to stand beside him. Reynolds was only two or three years older than Cole but he was behaving like a five-year-old throwing a temper tantrum. Brice was puffed up with so much indignation that he looked as if he might pop. His powdered wig and the severe frown lines that marred Brice's face made him appear fierce and unapproachable. Although Cole had never met Brice, he disliked the well-rounded aristocrat on sight. There was just something about the man that immediately alienated Cole.

Cole's gaze shifted to the woman who was being untied from the opposite end of the ducking pole. It was impossible to tell much about her when she resembled a creature that had emerged from a swamp. But whether she was beauty or beast, guilty or innocent, she was by far the most headstrong, incorrigible female Cole had ever encountered. Even while she was sputtering to catch her breath she was ranting at Brice Reynolds at the top of her lungs. (The

13

bottom half was still filled with water.)

The moment Stephanie was free, she scooped up a handful of mud from the pond bank and charged at Brice like a provoked bull. Brice's pale gray eyes widened in disbelief when Stephanie cocked her arm to sling mud. Although Brice was round as a barrel he could still dodge trouble when it was hurled at him.

Cole, however, was not so fortunate. He didn't see the glob of mud coming until Brice squealed and ducked away, leaving Cole's shoulder as the target. Cole flinched when the slime ricocheted off his jacket and splattered on his face.

"Tie her back on the ducking stool!" Brice growled poisonously. "Now she has assaulted an innocent bystander. The woman ought to be locked away. She is utterly mad!"

Stephanie did not take time to apologize to the swarthy gentleman who had been on the receiving end of her handful of mud. She was too busy glaring arrows at the conniving businessman who had whisked her to the British magistrate's office for a trial without a jury. Brice Reynolds was the kind of man who loudly proclaimed his noble sentiments and then proceeded to lie and cheat his neighbors, as thoroughly as possible.

"You are the one who should be herded off to the state prison at Newgate," Stephanie spewed venomously. "If the decent people of Mystic knew what you were about they would have you ducked, stoned, and then tossed in prison! First you *bought* your position as tax collector and customs agent from the Crown and now you have taken innocent—"

A livid hue worked its way up from the base of Brice's throat to the edge of his powdered wig. "Hang her!" Brice interrupted before Stephanie could disclose his underhanded dealings to the public.

When Stephanie doubled her first in angry frustration, Cole insinuated himself between her and the sputtering Brice Reynolds. If Cole didn't think the girl would receive another round of punishment for assault and battery, he would have let the sopping wet wench eat Brice Reynolds alive. Tax collector and customs agent, was he? No wonder Cole disliked this weasel on sight.

Just as Cole reached out to snag Stephanie's wrist in midair, she came uncoiled like a striking rattlesnake. Cole had lingered too long in thought. The blow intended for Brice Reynolds caught Cole in the jaw. Never in his wildest nightmare did he imagine such a petite bundle could pack such a whallop!

Stars encircled Cole's head as he staggered back, slamming Brice broadside. His abrupt movement threw Brice off balance. When two hundred and twenty pounds of solid muscle collided with him, Brice went down before he could even think to catch himself.

Although Stephanie wasn't the direct cause of Brice's fall, she was pleased with the end result. She watched and listened in spiteful satisfaction as Brice rolled down the slippery pond bank, squealing like a stuck pig.

"Shoot her!" Brice screeched in outrage. Slipping and sliding, Brice clambered back to his feet to survey the damages to his expensive waistcoat and breeches. "I demand another trial before the magistrate! She has already been convicted of cursing in public. Now she has struck an innocent man! We will try her and then have her stabbed, hanged, and shot!"

If Brice was attempting to sway public opinion to his side of the dispute, he failed miserably. Brice had lost a great deal of his popularity after he had taken the office of stamp agent. No one stepped forward to second Brice's suggestion. None of the bystanders had much regard for the tax collector. The silence that followed his demand was like a calm that pursued a thunderstorm, as if Mother Nature had paused to catch her breath.

But amid that temporary calm Stephanie's temper was brewing. She was not the kind of woman who buckled beneath a threat. If anything, it made her all the more determined and furious. As Brice waddled up the slope with all the grace of an overstuffed duck, Stephanie launched herself at him in another burst of fury. It was her intention to kick the blackguard into splinters. But to her dismay, Cole hooked his arm around her waist and hauled her resisting body against his.

"I am the victim of this woman's accidental assault," Cole insisted, clamping a tighter grip on the wriggling bundle. "And I do not wish to press charges. The wench has seen enough punishment and public humiliation for one day. She will remain in my custody until she simmers down."

"Let me at him," Stephanie hissed as she continued to squirm for release. "They can hang me *after* I claw out his eyes. . . ."

Cole laid his hand over Stephanie's mouth to shush her and then whisked her from the circle of bystanders before she could do as she promised.

"Will you calm down, woman," Cole growled down at her. "I am trying to save your neck. If you don't get a hold on yourself you *will* be swinging from yonder tree."

Stephanie was furious enough to bite the hand that silenced her, but she resisted the temptation. It would have served no purpose to inflict more pain on the handsome stranger who had intervened. She was itching to have Brice Reynolds's head on a silver platter, but it seemed today was not the day for her to receive her sweet revenge.

16

By the time Cole carried Stephanie to the inn, his garments were as wet and muddy as hers. Heaving an annoyed sigh, Cole set his captive to her feet. His dark eyes swept down his torso to survey the splotches of mud that clung to his velvet waistcoat and breeches. Then he inspected his tender jaw with his fingertips.

Still simmering, Stephanie combed her hand through the muddy tendrils that tumbled around her face. But the fire went out of her when she stared up at the tall, sinewy rake who towered more than a foot above her. Ruffled raven hair crowned his head. Golden brown skin and distinctly carved features claimed his face. Eyes as dark and shiny as melting chocolate bore down upon her—intelligent, perceptive eyes that were surrounded by a fan of long, thick lashes any woman would envy. His eyebrows were heavy, making a perfect arc over those fathomless lakes that suggested he was keenly aware of all that transpired about him. His mouth was rimmed with full lips that could stretch into a tight frown or curve upward into a disarming smile. His jaw was square and denoted strength, as did all his commanding features. Confidence was revealed in distinct lines that enhanced his face, and Stephanie could almost feel the strength and self-assurance that formed an invisible shield around him.

Stephanie's assessing gaze dipped to the mud-splotched shirt that strained sensuously over the wide expanse of his shoulders and chest. Though she couldn't say for certain, having never seen him without his shirt, Stephanie estimated that the man was a mass of rippling muscle. When he had carted her away from the ducking pond, she could feel his firm, unyielding flesh mashing against her, giving not an inch. It was as if she had been pressed into the bunching cords and tendons that formed the meaty contours of a lean, powerful lion. And he had carried her with effortless ease, expending only the minimal amount of energy. Why, come to think of it, the stranger had not appeared the least bit out of breath when he stood her upright.

Her curious green eyes drifted at will, each glance confirming her speculation that this dashing stranger had not an ounce of flab on him. Aristocrat though he appeared to be, this man kept himself physically fit, Stephanie surmised. His fashionable garments were filled to capacity . . . and in the most arousing sort of way. He needed no padding to make him appear masculine in dandy's clothes. This stranger could undoubtedly make even the shabbiest garments stunning because the muscles and flesh beneath them would compliment any attire.

As her attention swung upward in a second evaluation, she noticed the pulsating red welt on the stranger's striking features. Stephanie broke into a sheepish smile, ashamed that it was her temper tantrum that had marred his otherwise flawless cheeks.

"Forgive me, sir. I did not mean for your face to get in the way of my fist," she apologized on a soft chortle.

Cole regarded the dripping wet wench and then grinned out the right side of his mouth—the side that had escaped the woman's teeth-rattling blow. "Where did you learn to throw such staggering punches, woman? On the docks with brawling sailors?"

Suddenly distracted, Cole's penetrating eyes wandered over Stephanie's scoop-necked gown. With all the commotion he had failed to take inventory of this wench's shapely assets. The garment clung to her full breasts and trim waist like an extra set of skin. The daring décolletage exposed the generous swells to his all-consuming gaze. Although it was next to impossible to tell much about the girl's face since it was splattered with mud, Cole found the wench possessed an arresting

18

body. For the life of him he could not help staring down at her heaving bosom.

Stephanie's chin tilted when she realized what had drawn the stranger's undivided attention. A teasing grin dangled on the corner of her mouth as she elevated a muddy brow. "'Tis impolite to stare so boldly. You are behaving as if you have never seen a woman before, sir. Surely, at your age, you have already noticed that men and women are built differently," she mocked. "And if this is indeed your first offense, I feel compelled to warn you that if you continue to gawk, *you* might find yourself on the end of the ducking pole."

The taunting remarks were meant to shock Cole to his senses. Stephanie had a tendency to speak frankly, if only to draw a reaction. In fact, she delighted in shocking others and provoking a rise in their blood pressure.

This wench was a firebrand, Cole realized as he reluctantly dragged his eyes upward to stare into those mischievous pools of emerald green. There was nothing shy or meek about this pixie. Her refreshing candor was a welcome change from Rachel Garret's sly deception.

Biting back a grin, Cole clasped the woman's arm and shepherded her toward the front of the inn. "Come along, little nymph. We must clean you up and see if there is a comely face attached to this seductive body."

Stephanie refused to stir a step. A stubborn frown clung to her muddy brow as she glared at Brice Reynolds's establishment. "I am not about to set foot in that den of iniquity!" she told him crisply.

Cole glanced down, his expression puzzled. "There is nothing sordid about the inn," he contradicted. "You can clean yourself up in my room and then be on your way, if that is your wish. I do not expect, er, sexual favors for coming to your rescue."

19

An incredulous laugh burst from her lips. "I would guess such lurid thoughts of physical compensation had *at least* crossed your mind or you would not feel compelled to deny them," she taunted impishly.

Cole had the uneasy feeling he had been picked apart, analyzed, and reconstructed in a matter of seconds. The wench had pegged him as a rogue who usually took pleasure where he found it, no matter what the circumstances. And amazingly enough, she was correct in predicting that he was entertaining lusty thoughts. While Cole had been standing there, staring at her with masculine appreciation, it had occurred to him that this feisty chit would make an interesting bed partner. Once she had bathed and washed her hair, he silently stipulated.

Another irrepressible smile curved Cole's lips. My, but he had grinned more in the past half hour than he had in months. And all because of this rambunctious elf who was as limp and soggy as a wet mop.

"Very well, Miss . . ." He paused, waiting for her to attach a name to her camouflaged face.

"Stephanie," she supplied without hesitation. But she purposely withheld her surname. There was no reason to give it. She and this handsome stranger's relationship would go no further.

"Very well, Stephanie. I must admit I did toy with the idea while I was surveying your alluring assets." His cocoa brown eyes made another critical sweep of her curvaceous figure, finding not one flaw. "I find you extremely attractive from the neck down. I further confess that I am not a stranger to women's beds." The comment was not a boast, but rather a bland statement of fact. "But I assure you I have never found it necessary to force myself on a female and I see no reason to begin at this late date." Playfully, he flicked a glob of mud from the tip of her nose. "If you wish to use

20

my room to scrape off a few layers of grime I will expect no more than a verbal thank-you."

Stephanie liked the stranger's straightforward manner. Beating around the bush frustrated her. She had no use for coy games of coquetry. If she liked a man, she told him so. And if she didn't, she told him that too. Her ordeal with Brice Reynolds was proof of her policy. She found Reynolds to be a scalawag and a scoundrel and she had proceeded to tell him so.

After a moment, Stephanie nodded thoughtfully. "I appreciate the use of your room, Mr. . . ." One mud-coated brow lifted inquisitively.

Cole struck a sophisticated pose and swung into a bow. "Coleman Douglas Hollister the Third at your service, m'lady."

Mischief flared up in Stephanie's emerald eyes. Astutely, she assessed the virile specimen whose expensive garments were splattered with mud. "Coleman Douglas Hollister the Third?" Soft laughter bubbled from her heart-shaped lips. "It seems your family lacks originality. Why else would they have stuck you with such a long, stuffy name? No doubt there is a Coleman Douglas Hollister the Fourth toddling about somewhere—the product of *his* father's lack of imagination."

Despite his attempt to maintain a deadpan expression, Cole broke into a snicker. Giving Stephanie an abrupt tug, he shuffled her along in front of him. "You are sorely mistaken, m'lady. I have no son. Perhaps we shall make one, you and I. Then *you* can name him and my family's curse will at last be lifted."

Stephanie allowed herself to be hustled along beside Cole's long, light strides. Her expression mellowed and a faraway look glazed her eyes. "But our child would not be neglected," she murmured half-aloud. "No child should be subjected to his parents' total disregard. . . ."

21

Her words trailed off and her step quickened when she noticed Brice Reynolds striding across the open field toward his business establishment. Stephanie had had enough of Brice for one day. But she was not relinquishing her crusade against that conniving weasel. If her suspicions were correct (and she was sure they were), Brice was more the liar and cheat than anyone suspected. A humiliating ducking only made her more determined to expose that bastard for what he was!

While Stephanie was coveting vengeful thoughts, Cole was contemplating her last remark. He had been caught off guard by Stephanie's response to his teasing comment and by her quick change of mood.

Demons of curiosity were dancing in his head, wondering who the girl was and why she held such firm convictions about a child's upbringing. But by the time he attempted to put the question to tongue, Stephanie had bounded to the top of the stairs and her mood had reversed itself. As she veered into the room Cole had indicated to scrub the mud from her face, his thoughts were in a whirl.

Cole was stung by the odd premonition that he had fallen into the eye of a hurricane before being thrust back into the winds of the tempest. Indeed, being with Stephanie whoever-she-was was like riding an emotional carousel. In a matter of minutes he had experienced more sensations than he usually felt in a day!

"I really do appreciate your assistance, Mr. Hollister," she enthused as she took cloth in hand to wash her face.

"Cole," he corrected. Carefully, he removed his soiled jacket and laid it over the back of a chair.

Stephanie noticed the methodic procedure and smiled to herself. She guessed Cole Hollister to be a very meticulous, organized man. He didn't fling the stained garment aside. His satchel wasn't overflowing with wrinkled clothes that had been hastily stuffed inside it. That simply wasn't his way, she surmised. Cole was confident and poised to a fault. He was not prone to impulsiveness or recklessness as she was. Cole was a calm, calculating man who deliberated his actions before he set them into motion. He seemed very self-contained, as if no outside influences could upset him. Aye, Cole Hollister owned himself and she predicted he would be possessive of his private feelings.

When her face was devoid of mud, Stephanie spun around to gauge Cole's reaction to the transformation. The lustrous locks of red-gold hair were so caked with mud that the strands appeared almost black. Although there was little Stephanie could do about the condition of her mop of hair, her cheeks were freshly scrubbed and her features were partially discernible. "I hope you are not too disappointed with the face that sits above this body. Plain though it is, 'tis the one I was born with," she declared saucily.

Cole's breath stuck in his throat when he stared into Stephanie's lively features. Plain? One could hardly call this angel plain-faced. She had it all—the elegant bone structure, oval face, long, thick eyelashes, and a flawless complexion. Her almond-shaped eyes sat beneath perfectly arched brows. Her high cheekbones were wrapped in creamy flesh that begged to be touched. Her lips were full and luscious, the kind that silently invited kisses. Her green eyes sparkled with living fire and they dominated her comely face when she broke into a dimpled smile.

Mesmerized, Cole strode toward her. His tanned finger brushed over her satiny cheek to wipe away a lingering speck of mud. "M'lady, you are much too modest," he murmured, his voice like rich velvet. "No

23

plain maiden this. . . . But rather a glittering diamond in the rough."

Stephanie had been impressed with Cole's straightforward manner—until his head made a slow, lazy descent to plant a kiss on her lips. She had been kissed for one reason or another by a variety of men . . . or at least she *thought* she had. But in no way did kisses of the past compare to this embrace! The muscular warmth of his body engulfed her and Stephanie felt as if she was being skillfully seduced from the moment his sensuous mouth drifted over hers. His lithe, virile body made intimate suggestions as it brushed against hers. His mouth moved expertly over hers. His tongue traced her lips and then probed deeper to explore the sweet recesses that had remained unchartered territory . . . until now.

Sweet mercy! This bold stranger had probably forgotten more about kissing than she would learn in a lifetime. He had not begun with a light inquisitive kiss. Indeed, breathless passion would have been nearer the mark. Cole had discarded formality, leaped over proper procedure, and plunged headlong into intimate familiarity!

All this from a man she had presumed to be a perfect gentleman? Stephanie asked herself bewilderedly. If Coleman Douglas Hollister the Third was *all* polish and propriety, she was a royal princess! She had obviously misjudged this sophisticated rake. There was something utterly intriguing about him, something beneath that civilized veneer that caused Stephanie's heart to lurch in reckless pleasure. Now she knew why women never refused him. There was an aura of masculinity about him that no female could resist. Why, he would probably even have a devastating effect on a ninety-year-old man hater! Cole had an uncanny ability of kissing the breath out of a woman and stripping her of her inhibitions. While a female was under his seductive spell, her will was his own. How could a woman say *nay* when Coleman Douglas Hollister the Third rendered her speechless?

It rattled Stephanie to realize that this sizzling kiss did not fit the image of a man whose life was most likely an orderly chronicle of calculated events! She was receiving conflicting vibrations from this suave, debonair stranger.

Stephanie possessed a childlike quality, an intuitiveness that enabled her to form accurate impressions at the onset of friendships. But that ability had obviously malfunctioned when she encountered this dark-eyed devil and she wasn't certain what to make of him. There was an earthy sensuality about him that had not been there moments before. It was like peeking between the cracks of stone. Beneath the polish of elegance was a man capable of losing complete control. Cole could doff his sophisticated air and become the kind of rake who could arouse a woman's slumbering passions.

Aye, there were two men lurking inside the rock-hard flesh that was pressed familiarly against her, Stephanie decided. One was a dignified gentleman, but the other Coleman Douglas Hollister the Third could knock the props out from under the stablest of women if he had a mind to! And it certainly felt as though he had. Stephanie's legs had turned to rubber the moment Cole enfolded her in his powerful arms to teach her things she had never known about kissing.

Was a kiss supposed to kindle fires? Stephanie asked herself breathlessly. Were her ears supposed to be ringing like this? Nay, it must have been the aftereffects of her dunking, she diagnosed. She was probably coming down with the grippe after being half-drowned in the pond. Once she stepped into dry clothes she would be feeling her old self again, she reckoned.

When Cole had the decency to withdraw, Stephanie wobbled backward to clutch a nearby chair. Her lashes fluttered up to study the man who had caused a herd of goose bumps to stampede across her skin. Her gaze lingered on those dark, deepset eyes that twinkled in quiet amusement. Her attention focused on the fringe of jet black lashes that laced those spellbinding depths, luring her deeper into his spell.

There was something hypnotic about those eyes. Stephanie almost jumped at the impact of his penetrating stare. It was as if Cole could look right through her and pluck out each secretive thought. And before that happened, Stephanie shifted her attention to the crow's-feet that gathered and then fanned out from those chocolate brown eyes. Nobility was stamped in his chiseled features, ones she had earlier described (and most accurately) as angular and distinct. The good Lord had collected all the handsome characteristics for a face and blessed Coleman Douglas Hollister the Third with nothing but the very best.

Her gaze settled on the crop of naturally curly hair that framed his ruggedly attractive face. Stephanie approved of the fact that Cole chose to wear his own hair instead of resorting to the powdered wigs that cropped many a colonial head. Hair as black and shiny as a raven's wing absorbed the sunlight that splintered through the open window and Stephanie marveled at the thick strands that capped his head. Impulsively, her hand moved upward to spear her fingers into those crisp, blue-black curls.

One bushy brow elevated in response to her inquisitive touch. It pleased him that Stephanie was as curious about him as he was about her. He stood stock-still while her eyes roamed over him, scrutinizing him as if he were a statue on public display.

Unable to control the brazen wanderings of her eyes,

Stephanie's attention descended to the broad expanse of Cole's chest and then wandered over his tapered waist. She was, quite frankly, in awe of the way his tailor-made clothes accented his well-sculptured physique. For such a large, muscular man he moved with extraordinary grace, she recalled. And after feeling his lithe body pressed closely to hers on two occasions, she was absolutely certain that strong vitality lay just beneath these elegant garments of velvet. It left Stephanie to contemplate how it would feel to allow her fingertips to drift across his masculine flesh on an uninhibited journey of discovery, to explore his lean, hard muscles and watch them flex and relax beneath her inquiring touch. It left her wondering if the rest of his masculine body was as tan as his face and hands. . . .

The wicked thought caused Stephanie to flinch as if she had been scorched. It startled her to realize how strongly this man affected her. Cole Hollister had her pondering lurid thoughts that should never have entered her head. At the age of twenty, Stephanie *thought* she knew what transpired between a man and woman when they made love. But she had the odd premonition that, with a man like Cole, there would be a vast difference between appeasing sexual curiosity and experiencing passionate lovemaking. His touch was explosive and his kiss was the fuse. No doubt, his brand of lovemaking would be . . .

A hot blush stained Stephanie's cheeks. It was suicide to even imagine what it would be like to lie in Cole's arms. If she gave way to such sinful speculations, she might not be able to walk out of his room as pure and innocent as she had been when she breezed in!

Defensively, Stephanie raised her proud chin and bolstered her sagging integrity. "You really shouldn't have kissed me," she scolded him, her voice two octaves

27

higher than normal. "We barely know each other."

His cocoa eyes drilled into her, crumbling the barriers she had attempted to reconstruct. "Nay, I shouldn't have," he confessed. His resonant voice was caressingly husky and his gaze began to devour her. Cole closed the narrow distance between them, making Stephanie all too aware of his male magnetism. "Touching you is like throwing sparks on kindling. Your kiss creates a fiery craving that provokes me to do this. . . ."

His hand glided around her waist and then slid to her derriere. Before Stephanie could formulate a protest, Cole drew her full length against him. Stephanie could feel her breasts brushing against his chest, feel his bold manliness pressing against her thigh. The musky fragrance of his cologne swarmed her senses. Before she could clear the aromatic haze from her mind, she found herself enveloped in his arms. His lips slanted across hers, savoring the taste of her, promising things Stephanie wasn't sure she wanted to experience. But as his roaming hands discovered the sensitive points on her naive body, strange, quivering sensations began to migrate through her nerves and muscles. They were startling feelings, ones Stephanie was at a loss to comprehend. They made her want something, but for the life of her she didn't know exactly what!

A quiet moan bubbled in Cole's chest. Sex had always been second nature to him. He exercised his needs and desires when an attractive woman aroused him. But in all his thirty-one years he could not recall experiencing such a volatile reaction to a woman. There was a natural warmth and vibrance about Stephanie that drew him like metal to a magnet. And once he dared to kiss and caress her, there seemed no way to stop himself. Even when Stephanie whoever-she-was looked her worst, her radiant beauty shined through. Limitless energy exuded from her and Cole found himself wanting to share it, to become a part of it. She reminded him of a feisty little pixie with those dazzling green eyes and that saucy smile. She was like a dose of spring sunshine—so exhilarating, so refreshing.

Cole's calculating brain began to malfunction when Stephanie melted in his arms. Her surrender was *his* captivity. This emerald-eyed leprechaun had entrapped him. Her innocent kiss set off a chain reaction inside him and his body trembled with the hunger she aroused in him. His heart was galloping around his ribs and his breathing came in ragged spurts.

The sensations that channeled through his body made him feel young and reckless and not at all in control of his emotions. And that was highly unusual! Coleman Douglas Hollister, ship captain, lord and master of his plantation, was never out of control, not even when he deluded himself in thinking he had fallen in love with Rachel Garret! Rachel had satisfied his primal needs and Cole told himself that he could devote himself to her for the remainder of his life. But judging by his reaction to this sassy firebrand, he had only been fooling himself. His response to Rachel was no more than second nature, but his reaction to Stephanie was an altogether different matter. There should have been a warning posted on this high-spirited beauty that alerted a man to the dangers he faced. This lovely little sprite could set a man on fire with her first kiss and cause him to misplace the good sense he had been born with!

My God, have I been too long without a woman? Cole asked himself shakily. Had his two months of celibacy at sea caused him to react like an erupting volcano? That had to be the reason he was being swamped and buffeted by these turbulent sensations, he decided. If his sexual routine hadn't been interrupted during his cruise . . .

Cole intended to pursue that logic. He truly did. But just as he began to turn the thought over in his mind, Stephanie kissed him back. Suddenly, broken syllables were bouncing off the corners of his brain and Cole couldn't think straight. The room grew dark; the walls shrank.

All thought processes malfunctioned and his mind became a stage. He could see the bewitching green-eyed minx hurling mud. He could see her doubling her fist to level a brain-scrambling blow. He watched in amazement as the muddy little face transformed into the features of a radiant nymph. Her eyes were boring into him, spreading inner fire, making him want things he really shouldn't take from her. Ever so slowly, he could feel himself backing toward the edge of reality, dangling from a towering cliff. And as long as this mystical sprite was in his arms Cole didn't fear the fall. Ah, she would provide him with a world of pleasure on their way down. . . .

Stephanie choked on what little breath she had left when she felt Cole's hands taking improper liberties. His fingertips had dived beneath the sleeves of her gown and then followed the drooping neckline to the taut peaks of her breasts. Wildfire sizzled across her skin as his lips abandoned hers to whisper over each roseate bud. He was making her throb all over. He was making her ache in places she never realized existed! Flames were flickering beneath her flesh. Desire was uncoiling, demanding fulfillment. And to her shocked amazement, Stephanie was pressing closer, permitting Cole to have his way with her.

A soft moan bubbled from her lips as his adventurous hand glided beneath her petticoats to make arousing contact with her sensitive thighs. And as his fingertips mapped her soft, inviting curves, his moist lips returned to hers. While his tongue darted in and out of her mouth, his hands teased and excited her, causing another knot of longing to uncoil inside her.

She felt herself melting, surrendering to his expert fondling. But the split-second before she abandoned all thought, the voice of conscience whispered in her ear. It was a halfhearted, feeble warning, but it was just enough to jolt Stephanie back to reality.

Mortification flushed her cheeks as she twisted away to readjust her gaping gown. She struggled to draw a ragged breath. Wide green eyes blinked up at Cole. She was confused and ashamed of her reaction to a total stranger. Stephanie could count, on one hand, the number of times she had been left dumbstruck and addle-witted. Two of those incidents had occurred in the past half hour. Stephanie, who had always prided herself in startling her friends and acquaintances, who was rarely at a loss for appropriate words, could not have uttered an intelligent sentence if her life depended on it. Her tongue was frozen to the roof of her mouth!

Sweet mercy! She had allowed Cole to kiss her and caress her as no man had. She had yielded to him like a common strumpet. Lord, what must he think of her? But even what *he* must be thinking couldn't hold a candle to what Stephanie thought of herself.

Conflicting emotions were playing havoc with her self-control. She was hot and cold and jittery. With a strangled squawk, Stephanie shot toward the door like an exploding cannonball. She did not spare Cole so much as a backward glance. Cole stood there as if his boots were nailed to the floor. His jaw sagged on its hinges while he listened to the swish of damp skirts and watched the mysterious green-eyed leprechaun spirit away.

Cole shook his head to shatter the spell that loomed

over him. His keen eyes swung back to the closed door and then scanned the empty room. Absently, he wandered over to stare out the window at the abandoned ducking pond. Deafening silence clung to the breeze that drifted into his room.

Giving himself an inward shake, Cole spun around. He hadn't *dreamed* that he had been visited by a high-spirited nymph . . . had he? She really had been there and he really had lost himself in a sensual fantasy. . . .

A faint tap at the door drew Cole from his perplexed musings. When he ambled over to the portal, he found himself staring down into a woman's face—but not the one that was clogging his thoughts.

"Captain, is there anything I can do to make your stay at the inn more comfortable or enjoyable?" a timid voice questioned.

Cole surveyed the frail servant girl and he frowned at the provocative blouse that fell over one pale shoulder. He couldn't be certain, but he had the feeling he was being meekly propositioned. The wench did not seem overly eager to accommodate him, even though she voiced the subtle suggestion. Yet he doubted she would resist if he approached her, requesting more than a pail of fresh water.

"I—I am here to serve you, sir," Elizabeth Marrow reiterated, her gaze lancing off Cole's muscular frame. "You have but to voice your whim and I shall see it done."

It was obvious the wench had mentally rehearsed her lines and it was also apparent that she lacked enthusiasm. So why was she propositioning him when she sounded as if she would have preferred to be anywhere else?

"My thanks, miss, but I have business to attend at the moment," Cole replied with a faint smile.

As Cole turned away he swore he saw the girl breathe

a sigh of relief. He might have pondered Elizabeth's odd behavior but the moment she disappeared his mind wandered back to the muddy pixie who had left puddles on his floor, puddles he was presently standing in.

She *had* been here, Cole reassured himself as he shook off the drippings of mud and water. He hadn't imagined it all. As he rapidly paced about his room, changing into a clean set of clothes, he kept rehashing his encounter with hurricane Stephanie. Damn, he had been so distracted by that little elf he never got around to inquiring about the reasons she had been ducked. Why had Brice Reynolds, proprietor of the Reynolds Inn, tax collector for the Crown, demanded that Stephanie whoever-she-was be punished . . . and for what?

Finding no answers, Cole determinedly shoved all thoughts of Stephanie from his mind and turned his attention to the business at hand. He had sailed into Mystic to locate Dyer Wakefield and to attend several duties requested of him by his associates. When he completed his transactions with Wakefield and fulfilled his other obligations in Connecticut, he would return to Annapolis before making his journey to Boston. And if he knew what was good for him, he would make it a point never to cross paths with the mysterious mermaid of Mystic, Cole lectured himself sternly. But if the manner in which Stephanie had fled out the door was any indication of how *she* felt about their passionate encounter, he wouldn't have to fret. Things had gotten completely out of hand and they both knew it. She wouldn't be back and he wasn't going to turn the town upside down looking for her. She had affected him physically as well as emotionally and Cole was not prepared to deal with such complications just now. He and Stephanie would both be better off if they left each other alone. When a man and a woman provoked such devastating sensations from each other, they would only be asking for trouble.

Cole couldn't very well drag home some feisty serving maid just because she had kissed him and he had gone up in smoke! There was no sense toting home an import when there were plenty of native trouble-makers in Maryland already. His father would kill him, Cole reminded himself. Coleman Douglas Hollister the Second had been needling Cole for two years to marry and to marry well. The old man would fly right through the ceiling if Cole showed up on the doorstep with a serving wench in tow, no matter how irresistible and dynamic she would have been.

Nay, that would be insane, Cole lectured himself. Mysterious Stephanie had breezed in and out of his life like a misdirected cyclone and he wasn't going to make one attempt to locate her. When he took a wife to satisfy his father's wishes, the chit would be of good standing. That was the way it had to be. A man of wealth had certain obligations to his family, and like it or not, Cole was obliged to comply with his father's request.

After delivering himself that sensible sermon, Cole checked his appearance in the mirror. Satisfied that he had recovered from his momentary lapse of sanity, Cole aimed himself toward the door. But as he rounded the corner to descend the steps, he noticed the path of puddles that led to and from his room. A quiet smile caught the corner of his mouth. Stephanie may not have had blue blood flowing through her veins, but she was the kind of woman who could kindle *fires* in a man's blood. And when she left a man simmering, the taste of her kiss continued to linger on his lips.

Stop this nonsense, Cole scolded himself. Don't give that leprechaun another thought. You don't belong in

34

each other's lives. She's gone and you should be thankful she is. If you have any sense at all, you will remember that!

Humming that determined tune, Cole strode onto the street to ask directions to Dyer Wakefield's office. But to his chagrin, visions of a green-eyed pixie danced in his head all the while he was riding to the shipping yard that lay to the northwest of Mystic.

Chapter 2

Dyer Wakefield surveyed the tall, handsome captain who sat across from his desk. After visiting with Cole for more than an hour, Dyer was extremely impressed with the young man's credentials. Not only did Cole manage a fifty-thousand acre plantation but he also transported colonial products to the West Indies. It was apparent that Cole Hollister was a competent, capable man who had often tested his abilities and who was no stranger to success. Dyer and Cole shared many of the same views on the political and economical situation in the colonies. And although they had only met, Dyer was most anxious for the two of them to become friends.

Dyer also had an ulterior motive for endearing himself to Cole Hollister. He was eager to design a schooner to Cole's liking, yet he was even more anxious to match his eldest daughter with this eligible bachelor. Natalie Wakefield was Dyer's pet, his protégée. She had a head for business and she had been assisting Dyer with his book work for more than four years. It worried him that, at age twenty-four, Natalie had yet to marry. It was disgraceful that his pride and joy had no husband and no family of her own. The past two years

Natalie had shunned one beau after another. She had shown no interest in the men Dyer steered in her direction. Although Dyer was aware that Natalie was timid and shy, he was beginning to fret over her cool, standoffish attitude toward men.

Dyer's perceptive cobalt blue eyes scanned Cole's striking features and masculine physique. Surely Natalie would find no fault with this elegantly dressed gentleman, he mused pensively. What was there not to like? Cole was attractive, intelligent, and wealthy.

"Dyer?" Cole prompted, having received no answer to his question.

Dyer jerked up his head and smiled apologetically. "Forgive me, Cole. I fear my mind was wandering. A hazard of age, I suppose."

"I asked if you have a ship near enough to completion that I might transfer my merchandise within the week. I have several other stops to make before I return to Maryland and I am most anxious to reach my final destination," he repeated patiently.

A week! Dyer inwardly groaned. That would hardly be sufficient time for Natalie to become acquainted with Coleman Hollister. Why, it would take her a full week just to warm to the idea of courting the man Dyer had selected for her!

While Dyer ran that frantic thought through his mind, Cole was eyeing him carefully. Still holding Dyer's unblinking gaze, Cole leaned over the desk to retrieve a piece of paper. "I have some specific designs I wish for you to add to my new schooner." Meticulously, Cole sketched the sailing vessel and made note of his unusual requests. And then, at the bottom of the parchment, Cole printed three words in bold letters. His somber gaze swung back to Dyer. "Can I count upon you to meet my requirements?"

Dyer's brows shot straight up when he read the

37

message and surveyed the alterations for the schooner. When he recovered from his surprise, a sly smile pursed his lips. "Well, I'll be damned."

Chuckling, Cole reseated himself. "Perhaps," Cole agreed. "Are you willing to take that risk?"

The expression on Dyer's face spoke volumes. "You have but to ask and I will do what I can to assist you," he insisted.

Cole drew a gold medallion from his pocket and placed it in Dyer's hand. After Dyer accepted the gift, Cole gestured toward the medal that hung on his neck. "I'm greatly relieved to know you share our opinions and philosophies. We need the support of every citizen if we are to succeed. 'Twas *John* who suggested I seek you out."

"You shall have my support, spiritually and financially," Dyer promised faithfully. A wry smile pursed his lips. "I think I know the associate to whom you referred. Perhaps friend *John* in Boston?" His speculation proved correct.

Cole nodded positively. "Aye, he is the one who boasted of your talents in shipbuilding and complimented your moral fiber."

Dyer eased back in his chair, his smile as wide as the Atlantic Ocean. This surprising new twist made Dyer all the more determined to see Natalie wed to Cole Hollister and one week was simply not enough. Since Dyer held the trump cards he full well intended to play them to his advantage.

"It won't be difficult to add the designs you have sketched and I have one such vessel under construction," he said carefully. "But I would estimate that it will take three weeks to complete the ship to your satisfaction and to ensure that 'tis seaworthy. In view of what you have just divulged to me about your worthy mission, I would not think of cutting corners or risking

38

the safety of you and your crew."

Three weeks should be ample time, Dyer decided. In that span of time he could think of a million excuses to throw Natalie and Cole together.

"Three weeks!" Cole croaked. "Surely you realize that I have obligations to meet, as well as a plantation to run."

"Two and a half?" Dyer elevated a hopeful brow. "I can keep my employers working round the clock," he baited. "Haste could cause careless mistakes. I do have my reputation to uphold, Cole. I would never forgive myself if you opened sail and promptly sank in the middle of the harbor." A wry twinkle lighted his eyes. "I'm sure you can find some sort of diversion to occupy you during your extended sojourn in Connecticut. My own sloop and carriage will be at your disposal."

Cole expelled an exasperated breath. No doubt, he could make good use of his time in Connecticut but he had hoped to return to the plantation *before* he sailed to Boston to see to his secretive business. Oh, what the hell, Cole told himself. The extra weeks away from the plantation would provide the time needed to strengthen his dislike of Rachel Garret. The next time he laid eyes on that scheming witch he intended to hate her—thoroughly.

Finally, Cole nodded his consent. "Very well, I will wait."

Dyer was so delighted that he had to resist the temptation of jumping up and down. "And you will do your waiting in style," he enthused as he pushed out of his chair. "I insist that you stay at my manor."

"I couldn't impose," Cole insisted, rising to full stature.

"'Tis no imposition. We have a grand guest room, complete with its own balcony and private entrance to the house. The spacious suite overlooks the bay and

39

you can come and go as you please." When Cole looked as if he were about to demur, Dyer graced him with a bright smile. "I shan't take nay for an answer. As soon as you journey back to Mystic to retrieve your belongings, I will have Natalie take you to the house to unpack."

Before Cole could argue, Dyer latched onto Cole's arm and herded him into the adjacent office. "Coleman Douglas Hollister, I want you to meet my daughter—Natalie," he announced proudly.

Cole's eyes widened in pleasant surprise when Natalie came gracefully to her feet to offer him a shy smile.

"'Tis my pleasure, Mr. Hollister," Natalie murmured in her soft, husky voice.

The first thought that breezed through Cole's mind was—why hasn't this beautiful beauty been snatched up? She was curvaceous and attractive. Her hair was the same shade of auburn as her father's, her eyes the same dazzling shade of blue. Her olive complexion was flawless and Cole was thoroughly impressed.

My, this might turn out to be a very enjoyable few weeks after all, Cole decided. His assessing gaze worked its way over Natalie's striking figure, finding not one imperfection. No wonder Dyer was beaming with pride. Natalie was stunning and she was obviously intelligent or her father would not have placed her in charge of his ledgers.

"The pleasure is all mine, Miss Wakefield," Cole replied as his eyes made another thorough survey of Natalie's attractive assets.

"I think the two of you should call each other by your first names since we will all be sharing the same house for the next few weeks," Dyer suggested.

Dyer was pleased with Cole's reaction to his daughter. His attention shifted to Natalie, whose downcast gaze silently conveyed her shy reserve. "As soon as Cole returns from town I want you to escort him to the manor. I promised him the guest suite overlooking the bay. Once he is settled in you can take him on a tour of the estate."

Natalie's blue eyes shot open wide. "But, Papa, I have stacks of papers to file and ledgers to complete," she chirped. "Surely Adeline would better serve as a hostess for—"

Dyer waved away his daughter's excuse. "Adeline isn't home. And as far as your work is concerned, there is always tomorrow," he proclaimed. "But if there isn't, it will make little difference how great the amount of book work."

"Aye, Papa." Natalie forced a tremulous smile and then reseated herself safely behind her desk. "I will be happy to acquaint Mr. Holli—Cole," she hastily corrected herself. ". . . with our estate."

After Cole closed the door behind him, he glanced down at Dyer. "You have a very lovely daughter," he congratulated. "She looks a great deal like you."

Dyer closely resembled a strutting peacock. "Natalie is my pride and joy," he confessed. "Since she was a little girl she has followed me like my own shadow. Nattie has a head for figures." A low chuckle rumbled in his chest. "And if I may be so bold to boast, she has an enchanting *figure* as well. Indeed, I am very proud of my daughter. She will make just the right man a fine wife. You well could be the right man, Cole."

Cole broke stride when Dyer openly admitted his intentions. So that was what this delay was all about, Cole predicted. Dyer Wakefield had matchmaking in mind. Wouldn't that devious Rachel Garret be shocked out of her slippers if Cole sailed home with this heiress in tow? It would serve that promiscuous witch right. And it would also save Cole from listening to his father's constant nagging about taking a wife.

A marriage to this bright, attractive young lady wasn't the worst thing that could happen to him, Cole consoled himself. Natalie was the shy, retiring type who would cause him little distress. She would also be an asset to the financial management of the plantation with her ability with numbers. The gracious lady would make a fine hostess and a suitable escort for social gatherings. And Rachel would be seething, Cole's injured pride spitefully reminded him.

The thought provoked Cole to grin slyly. Aye, perhaps a marriage agreement between the Wakefields and the Hollisters would be a fine match. Cole's calculating mind began to list all the advantages. He was tired of the hectic life he had been living. He was thirty-one years old, after all. It was time he settled down to raise a family. Natalie could give him handsome children and Cole might even come to feel something for her in time—after he fully recovered from his bout of humiliation with Rachel. But even if he couldn't fall in love with his wife, he would treat her with utmost respect and he would give her no cause for complaint.

Cole seriously doubted he would ever allow himself to love again, not after he found Rachel in a carriage with one of her secret lovers. He had become too cynical after he had come upon the two of them in a clench in the forest. Even when she knew Cole was furious, Rachel had the nerve to insist that she had the right to one last fling before their wedding. One last fling? Cole had burst out in a bitter laugh. The way the two of them were carrying on Cole doubted that Rachel had any intention of sacrificing her trysts with other men. The challenge of cuckolding a husband was something that fickle minx would never be able to resist.

Aye, Natalie Wakefield was the kind of woman he needed, Cole assured himself as he rode back to Mystic. It was for damned certain he didn't need a minx like Rachel or a feisty leprechaun like Stephanie, who could cause him to lose complete control of his mental facilities!

Stephanie. Cole battled the name that popped to mind, but he couldn't smother her image. The mere mention of her name brought the rollicking episode into his thoughts. He could see that mysterious pixie with the fiery green eyes staring up at him. He could feel himself getting carried away when he drank the addicting wine of her dewy lips and caressed her shapely body.

Cole frowned puzzledly. Was she one of Brice Reynolds's servant girls? Why had Brice ducked her in the pond?

Why are you still fretting over that high-spirited nymph? Cole asked himself. Stephanie had come and gone and he was better off never becoming involved in another fleeting affair. He should concentrate on harmless Natalie Wakefield, not Stephanie whoever-she-was. That green-eyed minx *looked* like trouble. She was saucy and sassy and full of fire.

A woman like that would upset Cole's carefully organized routine. Accuracy and method were important to Cole. He rose at the same early hour each morning. He sipped two cups of tea and mentally listed the duties he was required to perform. Then he executed his tasks with expedience and efficiency. In the evening he courted females who caught his eye . . . or at least he had until he made the foolish mistake of offering Rachel Garret an engagement ring. The damned wench had considered it an invitation to carouse with everything in breeches. The nerve of that woman! The night he confronted her and her lover she

43

maintained that since Cole dallied with every available female at every port that she could exercise the same rights.

In the first place, Cole hadn't caroused with another female in any port since the day he offered Rachel the engagement ring. And second, he had resolved to remain loyal to one woman. Unfortunately, he had vowed to remain faithful to the wrong woman. Cole had informed that little snip of just that before he thundered off, seeing red trees, red stars, red everything! The following morning he had set sail for New York, Boston, and then the Caribbean. His only mistake was forgetting to demand the return of his ring. But, by God, that would be his first order of business when he set foot in Annapolis!

That incident was reason enough for Cole not to moon over mysterious Stephanie. As ornery as she was, she might pull the same stunt. With her feistiness she would probably steal off with another man, just to get Cole's dander up. High-spirited women were like that, Cole contended. And even if he dragged a woman like Stephanie home to spite Rachel, his father would have a heart seizure. Aye, Stephanie had set him ablaze with her first kiss but she was not the kind a man could safely marry. She could make a man laugh with her unconventional antics but she wasn't wife material. She would put her husband in a tailspin and keep him there—permanently.

Cole had carefully thought it over. Natalie Wakefield was what he needed if he was to consider matrimony. He had no time for firebrands like Rachel or Stephanie. Cole could sail off into the sunset, knowing that when he returned, Natalie would be there to greet him with that timid little smile of hers and she would pose no probing questions.

When Cole lifted his raven head, he blinked

44

bewilderedly. He had contemplated all the way back to town. Well, at least he had made his decision, he consoled himself. Although he had just met the bashful Natalie Wakefield, he knew his father would probably approve of the match. The marriage would remedy his disastrous engagement to Rachel. And perhaps when he dared to kiss the shy brunette, she would set him afire the way Stephanie . . .

"Will you forget that mischievious chit, for God's sake!" Cole muttered half-aloud. "If you want to ignite a flame, so build yourself a campfire! You are not going to get involved with that feisty imp. Concentrate on Natalie and be satisfied with what she can offer."

This was the very last time he was going to allow that green-eyed pixie to sneak into his thoughts, Cole lectured himself as he gathered his belongings. He had resolved to pose no questions about Stephanie and he was going to stand firm in that vow. His preoccupation with that rambunctious hellion would bear no ill-effects on his courtship with Natalie Wakefield. Besides, Stephanie had stirred something in Cole that he found too difficult to control. She was not the ideal companion for a man who desired method and order in his life. Stephanie was one of those unique females who could turn a man's world upside down like a cyclone on its way to uproot a few dozen trees. She made him feel young and reckless and too much alive.

Cole frowned puzzledly. Was there such a thing as *too much* alive? Well, of course there was. The affliction was commonly known as living dangerously. His father had preached on the subject until Cole relinquished the life he had known before he returned to manage the plantation. The reckless life was behind him now—a closed chapter of his existence. Cole had returned to civilization to assume his position of responsibility. What he had been in that other lifetime was a forbidden memory of the past. He could savor brief tastes of that other life during his secretive duties in the months to come. But the man of his past *could not* and *would not* replace the distinguished, practical Coleman Douglas Hollister the Third of the present. Each man had his own separate identity and they were far too different to ever become entangled in one body.

Cole suddenly swallowed hard. All this soul-searching had finally brought him around to the real reason he was afraid to seek out Stephanie and discover more about her. It was because she aroused those savage feelings that had once ruled his life. She released those long-restrained emotions and caused inner conflicts.

Damnit, he had made a commitment to himself and to his father. Cole had vowed that he would never revert to his old ways. And yet, the moment he touched that bundle of fiery energy he had been transported back in time. He was experiencing those reckless sensations he thought he had learned to control.

Cole *had* to keep his priorities in perspective. First and foremost were his civic duties to the colonies, then his obligations to his father and the plantation, and finally the woman in his life. Men who allowed their hearts to rule their heads usually found themselves stewing in their own juice. Coleman Douglas Hollister the Third learned to be deliberate and methodic. He couldn't go chasing off after some mysterious green-eyed leprechaun, just for the pure pleasure of it. It was tomfoolery!

Nay, Natalie Wakefield fit the mold. She was quiet, reserved, and uncomplicated. Cole could keep his business and personal life separate if he married a woman like Natalie. And in these trying times a man needed to keep his wits about him. He couldn't entangle himself with a feisty female who would

46

preoccupy his thoughts and keep him on his toes to stay one step ahead of her. Cole needed stability, not frustration. He had enough trouble already. Rachel had exasperated him and he had the odd premonition that a whirlwind fling with that feisty servant girl would leave his life in shambles.

Mentally patting himself on the back for relying on common sense, Cole retraced his steps to the shipyards and the sprawling estate that lay to the north of Mystic. Now that he had his emotions in hand he could proceed in a calm, deliberate manner.

Cole plodded along on the gelding he had rented at the stable, feeling quite pleased with his ability to organize his thoughts and plot his future. But suddenly, a disconcerting sensation buzzed down his spine and splintered his confidence.

All that is fine, well, and good, a quiet voice whispered to him. *Now how do you intend to wash away the taste of a kiss that has been lingering on your lips since this morning?* Cole wrestled with that question while he retraced his tracks, but he hadn't puzzled out the answer when he reappeared at Dyer Wakefield's office. With any luck at all, Natalie would distract him and he would forget he was still wanting something he couldn't have—an emerald-eyed leprechaun who could blossom into a dimpled smile and make the sun shine twice as bright.

After a full afternoon of touring the shipping yard that lay on Wakefield's private harbor and examining the huge estate, Cole decided Natalie's companionship was just what he needed. She was lovely and knowledgeable. There was only one peculiarity about her that bothered Cole. Each time he attempted to take her hand for one reason or another, she shied away like

47

the wary thoroughbred colts that grazed Dyer's pasture. Cole was aware that Natalie was bashful, but she avoided physical contact as if he were plagued with leprosy. He was beginning to understand why Natalie was twenty-four years old and still unwed. She never allowed a man within five feet of her unless a close encounter was completely unavoidable.

How could they ever hope to produce children if she insisted on no physical contact? Would she beg for separate beds as well as separate bedrooms? There were times when a husband and wife had to be close even if they weren't in love. But judging by Natalie's standoffish manner she was horrified of intimacy—either that or she simply didn't kin to men in general.

That particular thought caused Cole to peer even more closely at his blushing escort. Was Natalie more interested in spending time with—

"Supper will be served promptly at six o'clock," Natalie informed Cole, refusing to make direct eye contact. "Mother insists that we dress for dinner. She believes in making our meals a social affair."

Before Natalie could squeeze past him and slip inside the manor, Cole grabbed her arm to detain her. He strategically cornered her on the stoop, forcing her to endure his light touch. "Thank you for an enjoyable afternoon, Natalie. You make a wonderful escort . . ." His head came toward hers, focusing on her rosy lips, determined to eradicate the speculation that had begun to hound him.

A startled yelp burst from Natalie's lips. She wasn't sure if she were more distressed over the handsome captain's intentions or the sight of the young woman who was galloping toward the rear of the stables. But one thing was certain: Natalie had no intention of being kissed on the stoop. As quick as a cat leaping from harm's way, Natalie ducked under Cole's arm and

48

sailed off the porch.

"I will see you at supper, Cole. There is an urgent matter I must attend."

To Cole's dismay, he watched Natalie scurry along the path that led to the stables, her satin gown and petticoats swishing about her. It was obvious Natalie had no wish to suffer a man's kiss, no matter how harmless it might have been.

The chit had been as jumpy as a grasshopper since the moment they met. What was there about him that Natalie found so offensive? Cole asked himself earnestly. He had bathed and generously splattered cologne all over himself. He had shaved and donned fashionable clothes. He had been on his best behavior— Well, until the previous moment, Cole amended.

So he attempted to steal a little kiss. What was the harm in that? He was curious to know if bashful Natalie could kindle even the smallest fire of desire. He had only meant to satisfy his curiosity, for Pete's sake! It wasn't rape on the front porch that he had contemplated!

It was growing ever more apparent to Cole that Natalie did not appreciate any member of the male species. Well, that would certainly explain why Natalie was twenty-four and unmarried.

Stop leaping to drastic conclusions, Cole scolded himself. Just because Natalie hadn't melted beneath his charm was no reason to assume that she preferred female companionship. Cole decided to give the girl the benefit of the doubt since he might find himself maneuvered into a wedding before the month was out.

Maneuvered? Cole smiled wryly to himself. No one was going to manipulate him into taking a wife unless he decided it suited his purpose. Cole certainly didn't need Natalie's staggering dowry as temptation. Money was the least of his considerations. Cole could live out

49

his life quite comfortably without depending on wealth from his future wife's family. All he wanted was a respectable female to serve as mistress of the plantation and a thorn to jab in Rachel Garret's side. Natalie could go her own way and Cole would go his—no questions asked. Many of his friends had survived quite nicely in loveless marriages and so could he.

Cole had allowed himself to believe a marriage to Rachel would have been different, special. But now that his eyes were wide open he realized they would have shared the same space until Rachel's roving eye embarrassed the both of them.

"Love, bah," Cole muttered cynically. He would have tried to remain devoted and faithful to Rachel. But with her, he could never have been certain if he were the father of her children. Rachel prided herself in her beauty and her ability to attract men. Why, he probably would have found himself standing in line on his wedding night!

Annoyed, Cole shook off the thoughts of Rachel and concentrated on the shapely brunette who had just disappeared around the corner of the barn. Maybe Natalie was just extremely timid around all men. Maybe she was a bit insecure and unsure of herself. He shouldn't condemn her just because she was as nervous as a gun-shy rabbit.

Deciding to give Natalie a second chance, Cole reevaluated her reaction to him. Lost in pensive contemplations, Cole pivoted on his heels and ambled into the foyer. Perhaps he was moving too swiftly for the shy, innocent Natalie. Maybe she was the kind of woman who refused to dole out samples of affection until she felt she knew all there was to know about the man her father had dragged home to court her. Surely a man could find no fault with that, Cole reminded himself. Once they became better acquainted Natalie would respond to his advances. He would simply have to proceed at a slower pace.

Mulling over those contemplations, Cole ascended the steps to the spacious suite in the south wing of the mansion. Even if Natalie couldn't tolerate men, he should marry her, Cole decided. Then his problem would be solved. Bold adventuresses would no longer see him as a fine catch and Rachel would be out of his life forever.

That was one of the drawbacks of wealth, Cole lectured himself as he shed his jacket and eased into the alcove bed that was built into the wall. Since Cole had returned to civilization he was never quite certain if the women who pursued him truly cared about him or if they were attracted to his money. There had been one or two bold wenches in his past who could hear a man's coin purse opening and closing. They gushed with affection when they were showered with costly trinkets and they were as cold as icebergs when they received no gifts.

Natalie was accustomed to money, Cole mused as his dark eyes appraised the elaborate suite. Dyer had furnished his mansion with every convenience and luxury known to man. Natalie wasn't hungry for wealth. She could probably pick and choose her beaux—*if* she desired them. Cole chided himself for tacking on that suspicious thought.

He really was trying not to question Natalie's apparent lack of interest in those of the male persuasion. But it was damned difficult not to speculate on her preferences when she flew off like a frightened pigeon the instant he tried to plant a harmless kiss on her lips.

As the bumfuzzling thoughts chased each other through his head, Cole closed his eyes. But the moment he did, Stephanie's lively features materialized before

51

him. My God, how could such a wild, uninhibited misfit make such a strong impression, he wondered. When he wasn't guarding his thoughts Stephanie's expressive face and enormous green eyes appeared to torment him. He could see that radiant sparkle in those rippling pools of emerald. He could feel her firm, ripe body beneath his inquiring caresses. He could still taste the honeyed softness of her lips.

If Cole had been aware of the dreamy smile that quirked his lips as he drifted off to sleep he would have given himself a hard shake. The free-spirited pixie had no place in his well-organized life. He did not make it a habit of mooning over females who slung mud at him, punched him in the jaw, and then kissed him until he caught fire and burned.

He knew she was trouble with a capital T. He knew she would never be accepted in his world. He knew his father would be appalled if he toted home a feisty serving wench to appease his lusty passions. Aye, Cole had reasoned all that out. But deep down inside, beneath the veneer of polish and civility, a small flame continued to burn. Stephanie set off emotions Cole no longer wished to experience, could *not* experience if he were to keep peace in the family. She reminded him of another time, another place, another personality—the man he had been. And it was that *specter* of his past that had responded so wildly, so uncontrollably to that fiery vixen. It wasn't Coleman Douglas Hollister the Third. And for that reason alone, Cole knew he had to avoid the mysterious elf at all costs.

Chapter 3

Horrified, Natalie peered at Stephanie's stained gown and the mop of mud-caked hair that was draped around her shoulders. The young girl looked as if she had been trampled by a herd of wild horses during a thunderstorm.

"What happened to you?" Natalie chirped.

Stephanie hopped from the chestnut stallion's back and surveyed her appearance. "I did as you suggested," she grumbled as she tugged at a clump of dried mud that clung to the hem of her gown. "Unfortunately, Brice Reynolds and I got into a shouting match. That miserable scoundrel hustled me off to the magistrate's office, saw to it that I was tried and found guilty of verbal abuse, and then had me ducked!" she spewed furiously.

Natalie's face bleached white as she swayed back against the barn. Her long lashes fluttered down, squeezing out the dreadful thought of such public humiliation. "'Tis all my fault," she choked out. "You are the one being punished because I don't have the nerve to speak up and announce myself to the world."

Stephanie suddenly found herself in Natalie's bear hug. The comely brunette was sobbing all over

Stephanie's grimy gown, turning caked dirt back to oozing mud.

"For heaven's sake, Nattie, you will look as hideous as I do," Stephanie reminded her. She wiggled free and then brushed away the clinging dirt from Natalie's shoulder. "I survived the ducking and Brice will sorely wish he hadn't dragged me to that public embarrassment." A wicked smile pursed Stephanie's lips. "I stashed a family of rats in his bed. And then I replaced his cologne with kerosene." The mischievous grin faded when Natalie wrung her hands and nervously paced back and forth. "But nothing has changed except that I was allowed a small taste of revenge for my persecution. Brice Reynolds won't budge. I offered him the full purse of coins you gave me and still he refused to agree to the request."

Natalie's slim shoulders slumped defeatedly. "What am I to do? If I tell Papa the truth he will be furious. And if Papa keeps throwing eligible bachelors at me I will go stark raving mad!"

A tired sigh tumbled from Stephanie's lips as she watched Natalie wear a path and stew over her predicament. Her heart went out to the shapely brunette. If Brice Reynolds had his way, Natalie would be ostracized. Brice was no kind, compassionate individual who would take the money and promise never to break the silence. Nay, the proprietor of Reynolds Inn was a selfish rat who had too many skeletons in his own closet to care what was rattling around in Natalie's wardrobe.

It was apparent that the disheartening news had upset Natalie. She was buzzing back and forth, muttering to herself, struggling to find a solution to her problem.

"What am I to do now? If Brice won't cooperate, Papa will learn the truth about me. And heaven help

54

me when he does!" she wailed.

Stephanie heaved an exhausted sigh. There was nothing she wanted more than to return to her quarters and shed this limp gown. But she couldn't leave Natalie to suffer through this dilemma all by herself. "Fetch me a clean set of clothes and something to eat," Stephanie requested. "And please stop fretting, will you? You are going to make yourself sick. This will all work itself out if you don't panic." A spiteful gleam glistened in Stephanie's eyes. "I am not finished with Brice Reynolds. If he keeps refusing me, I will expose him for the slimy snake he is and he will sorely wish he had taken the money offered him."

Natalie's eyes were wide with apprehension. "Expose him for what?" When Stephanie shrugged evasively, Natalie let her breath out in a rush. "If you don't watch your step you will be caught in the middle again. Have you stopped to consider what might—"

Stephanie waved Natalie to silence. "You mean a great deal to me. I agreed to help you solve your problem and I will not be satisfied until 'tis resolved . . . one way or another. Just fetch the food and clothes, Nattie." A devilish grin settled in her features. "I should like to pay Brice Reynolds another visit. He may as well know that *I* know exactly what is going on in his seemingly respectable establishment."

"I wish I had been born with such courage," Natalie sighed wistfully. She grasped Stephanie's hand, giving it a fond squeeze. "But, 'twas my lot in life to be a coward. Even when I try to be bold and speak up for myself my knees go weak and my tongue becomes entangled in knots."

A bittersweet smile traced Stephanie's lips. "At least you are not plagued with a tongue that runs away with itself," she consoled as she nudged Natalie on her way. "I care not what kind of clothes you can find to replace

55

this spoiled gown. But bring something quickly. I swear there are lizards and snakes crawling around inside this garment with me."

Spurred into action by Stephanie's words, Natalie hurried around to the back of the manor to replace the grimy gown. After she had found suitable clothes she sneaked into the kitchen to fetch food. When she veered around the corner of the stables a feeble smile hovered on her lips. Natalie extended her arms to unload the supplies Stephanie had requested.

"I could go with you . . ."

Stephanie gave her tangled hair a negative shake. "'Tis better that I handle this myself," she insisted as she tied the supplies behind the saddle.

Natalie hadn't really wanted to go along, but she felt obliged to offer. As Stephanie thundered off in all directions at once, Natalie wheeled around to return to the mansion. She breathed a quiet sigh of relief when the carriage carrying her mother and her sister rumbled up the path. At least Eileen and Adeline hadn't seen Stephanie's arrival and departure. Natalie didn't want to answer any prying questions until she had time to gather her wits. Indeed, the purpose of Stephanie's intervention was to spare Natalie any embarrassing explanations. But this business with Brice Reynolds had her walking on needles and pins. The mere mention of the man's name wrought havoc with her emotions.

"Ah, Nattie, I am happy to see you have emerged from that stuffy office at a reasonable hour," Eileen Wakefield remarked to her eldest daughter. "You spend too much time assisting Dyer. I do wish you would socialize more. The Stovers asked why you didn't join Addie and me when we paid them a call this afternoon."

Natalie followed her mother and sister through the

front door. "Papa asked me to show our houseguest around the estate and shipping yards," she explained. "He will be joining us for dinner and I believe Papa said he would be staying for several weeks."

Sporting a wry smile, Eileen pirouetted around to confront Natalie. "And just who is our distinguished guest?"

"Coleman Douglas Hollister the Third is a ship captain and plantation owner from Maryland," Natalie announced, averting her eyes from her mother's knowing grin. "Papa has sold him a schooner but it will not be ready to sail for a few weeks yet."

"Mmmm . . . he sounds impressive. But is he handsome?" Adeline questioned as she peeled off her bonnet and handed it to the butler.

"Very," Natalie affirmed with a blush.

"Another of your father's attempts to marry you off?" Eileen cast Natalie a disapproving frown. "Really, Nattie, you should take an interest in the men your father steers in your direction. There have been several to whom I would have given my stamp of approval. But you have rejected them, one and all."

"Is there anything wrong with being particular, Mother?" Natalie questioned, failing to meet her mother's probing stare.

"Nothing, my dear," Eileen assured her breezily. "But you are far past *particular*. You have been behaving as if all men suffer the plague and you fear contracting it!"

Adeline thoughtfully studied her sister as they ascended the staircase. "Were you truly impressed with Mr. Hollister?" she questioned point-blank.

"He seems more your type," Natalie informed the sultry blond. "And I will not take offense if you turn your wiles on him."

Adeline tittered softly in response to Natalie's

remark. "Perhaps I would if I hadn't become so fond of Richard Stover. He has invited me to the ball Papa is giving and Mother has given her permission. I have become, er, rather attached to Richard of late."

"Then what shall we do about Coleman Douglas Hollister the Third?" Natalie mused aloud.

"We will tolerate him just as we do all the other beaux Papa totes home for your inspection. But I do wish you would resolve your problems," she sighed heavily. "You know Papa will not permit me to marry until you have wed first and you never . . ." She compressed her lips to smother her words when she realized her careless comment had upset her older sister.

Natalie looked as if she had lost her last friend. Her eyes took on a misty haze as she stared straight ahead, seeing nothing. "I wish you had been the first born, Addie. I did not wish to complicate your life with my problem."

As Natalie ambled down the hall to her room in the north wing, Adeline pushed open the door to her boudoir and frowned thoughtfully. She sorely wished Natalie would go to Dyer and tell him the truth. Since Dyer had specified that his daughters had to be married in chronological order, Adeline was forced to sit and twiddle her thumbs until it was her turn to leave the nest. Only God knew how long it would take Natalie to work up enough courage to face Dyer and blurt out the truth!

Confound it, Adeline was already twenty-two. In another two years the town gossips would be referring to Adeline as a spinster or a— Adeline flounced on her bed. Damnation, there were times when she wished she were an only child. It would certainly make it easier for her to resolve *her* problems. Aye, Natalie had colossal troubles, but she wasn't the only one in Wakefield manor who was traipsing around on thin ice! And if Dyer knew what Adeline had done without his consent . . .

Adeline shuddered uncontrollably. It was little wonder Natalie hadn't found enough nerve to tell Dyer the truth. He would be furious with the both of them if he knew what was going on in his own household. Adeline wasn't sure she could muster enough bravado to make her own confession! And aware of her own inability to gather the nerve to confront her father, Adeline could not truly condemn Natalie for being such a coward.

After double checking his appearance, Cole ambled down the hall and descended the stairs. He was about to meet the rest of the family that might eventually become his in-laws. The moment Cole entered the dining room, Dyer clamped a hold on the younger man's arm and steered him toward the chair beside Natalie.

"I trust you and Nattie made the grand tour of our estate," Dyer commented as he dropped into his seat at the head of the table.

"I was . . ." Cole's voice trailed off when Eileen and Adeline swept into the room.

Eileen came to a screeching halt when she laid eyes on the muscularly built gentleman who was seated beside Natalie. The cut of Cole's clothes and the broad expanse of his shoulders gave him a striking appearance. Cole looked the part of a nobleman who had kept himself fit and Eileen was immediately impressed.

Dyer may have thought the swarthy rake was the perfect match for Natalie, but Eileen considered the wealthy aristocrat to be the ideal mate for *her* pride and joy—Adeline.

Adeline's alabaster skin and pale blue eyes would make a dazzling contrast to Cole's deep tan and jet black hair. Dyer had briefed his wife on Cole's redeeming qualities, but Eileen assumed that her husband had exaggerated. If anything, Dyer had modestly described their houseguest. Cole Hollister was everything a well-bred woman could possibly want. Why, even Richard Stover was a dim shadow in comparison to this tall, muscular mass of masculinity.

With Adeline's poise, charm, and knowledge of the social graces, she would make the perfect hostess and wife for this plantation owner. Although Eileen was most anxious to see her eldest daughter properly married, she continued to picture Adeline standing next to Coleman Douglas Hollister the Third.

"Dyer, won't you introduce us to your guest," Eileen prompted her husband.

After a quick round of how-do-you-dos, Adeline was hustled into the chair directly across from Cole. It did not take a genius to realize that Eileen had her own ideas about *who* should marry *whom!* Eileen bragged on Adeline from the moment the main course was served and she didn't let up until after dessert. The meal became a contest to determine which one of them, Dyer or Eileen, could dominate the conversation and boast about his or her favorite offspring.

Cole found himself in a ticklish situation. It was evident that Dyer favored a match with shy, quiet Natalie while Eileen had her heart set on seeing him attached to the comely, sophisticated blond. Cole found no complaint with either of the Wakefield daughters. Each one had charming, though very different, qualities. Natalie would prove to be an asset to the business facet of a marriage. But Adeline would be the epitome of proper etiquette.

His gaze strayed from one lovely face to the other,

comparing two very different personalities and finding no visible fault with either Natalie or Adeline. If Cole decided to take a wife and seal a permanent business venture with the Wakefields, he would be satisfied with either Natalie or Adeline. After all, his marriage would be a practical one, Cole reminded himself. He had become too cynical to think he could completely devote himself to either woman—whether she be blond or brunette.

"I must compliment you on your family," Cole murmured as he sipped his wine. "You have two very attractive daughters. You must be proud of both of them." Of course, they were. Eileen and Dyer had been rattling nonstop since the meal commenced.

"We are," Dyer replied before touching his napkin to the corner of his mouth. "Natalie has chosen to assist me with the family business, Adeline prefers to help Eileen manage the household, and—" Suddenly, Dyer glanced around the table. He had been so busy competing with his wife that he hadn't realized there was an empty seat at the table. "Eileen, where the devil is your youngest daughter?"

Eileen was suffering from the same affliction that plagued Dyer. She had been so immersed in centering the conversation around Adeline that she had forgotten about her youngest sibling.

"To be perfectly honest, I don't know," Eileen answered sheepishly.

"You have been blessed with three daughters?" Cole interjected in surprise.

He glanced back and forth between Dyer and Eileen, wondering how parents could overlook the fact that one of their children had not shown up at the dinner table. Cole almost pitied the poor chit. No doubt she was the ugly duckling, the one Dyer and Eileen preferred to forget. They each had a child who favored them in looks and interests. The third daughter obviously ached for attention from her mother and father. But there was none left to give. Natalie and Adeline were showered with affection, leaving not a drop for their ugly duckling to wallow in.

Cole promised himself, then and there, if he had children he would have himself kicked if he neglected any one of them! It was shameful to pour so much love on two children and deny the one who probably needed family affection most.

The silence in the dining room was as thick as hasty pudding. Finally, Dyer exhaled his breath and smiled, shamefaced. "I am afraid our youngest daughter is very unlike her sisters. I believe the proper label for her is *misfit*. She is rowdy and unruly and she takes after Eileen's father. He was a most colorful Irishman whose free spirit is a source of many legendary tales."

"I should have known you would blame that child off on *my* side of the family," Eileen snapped huffily. "My father was adored by all who knew him. He livened up every social gathering he ever attended. And if you hadn't neglected *your* youngest daughter, we would not have found it necessary to pack her off to London for strict schooling." Eileen silently cursed herself for blurting out the mocking rejoinders that gushed from her lips. But blast it, their young daughter was a sensitive subject that always provoked an argument between husband and wife.

"That was *your* idea and it didn't help a whit," Dyer said with visible restraint. "I wasted my money attempting to civilize that willful, rambunctious child. Indeed, she is more independent and headstrong than she was when we shipped her off to England. What that girl needs is a private tutor who has been apprenticed as a prison warden!"

Eileen sliced her husband a silencing glare and then

smiled sweetly at their guest, who was on the edge of his seat waiting to hear who would take the blame for the black sheep of the family. "Forgive us, Mr. Hollister. My husband and I have created a breech of etiquette. 'Tis unforgivable to allow you to be caught in the cross fire of our domestic squabble." Nervously, Eileen toyed with her napkin and then replaced it in her lap. "When you finally meet our youngest daughter—*if* she returns to the roost at a reasonable hour—I hope you will be tolerant of her. She would try the patience of a saint."

Dyer smiled ruefully. "I'm afraid Eileen and I have failed her miserably. Once Natalie and Adeline have made a place for themselves in this world, I hope we can devote ourselves to our youngest daughter's upbringing."

"*If* we haven't damaged her permanently," Eileen grumbled, more to herself than to their guest.

Setting the controversial topic of conversation aside, Dyer rose to his feet and gestured toward Natalie. "Why don't you and Cole take a stroll through the gardens. They should be lovely in the moonlight."

"And Adeline can join you," Eileen enthused. "You young people run along and become better acquainted. It will give Dyer and me the opportunity to discover how and why we have misplaced our youngest daughter."

The moment Cole swaggered out the door, bookended by a blonde and a brunette, Eileen muttered under her breath. What would Cole think of them now? They had made a respectable impression on this eligible bachelor until they landed on the ultrasensitive subject of their renegade daughter.

"Where do you suppose she could be at this hour?" Dyer questioned, drawing Eileen from her contemplative deliberations.

Eileen's shoulder lifted in a helpless shrug. "I haven't the slightest idea where she is or what she is up to." Tears misted her pale blue eyes. "We have failed her miserably, Dyer. You doted over Natalie and I have pampered Addie."

Dyer nodded in silent agreement. They had neglected their youngest daughter and now they were paying for that tragic mistake! She came and went as she pleased and her reputation was one that left a black splotch on the rest of the family. No one knew what that feisty sprite was going to do or say next. Indeed, the entire family held their breath and hung on her every word, waiting and wondering. . . .

Determined to learn his young daughter's whereabouts, Dyer snatched up his jacket and headed out the front door. Surely someone on the estate had seen the girl. Her disappearing acts were becoming a constant frustration and Dyer decided it was time to take the girl in tow and lead her down the straight and narrow path instead of allowing her to gallivant all over the countryside, dressed like a lost orphan!

Chapter 4

It was with frustrated tension that Cole shrugged off his clothes and climbed into the alcove bed. He grasped the shutter doors and tucked himself in the feather-soft niche that was built into the wall. Suddenly, he had a change of heart. The idea of being closeted with his thoughts held little appeal.

Cole threw open the doors to survey the shaft of moonlight that spilled into his suite. Pensively, he studied the silver-rimmed shadows that drifted across the far wall.

Accepting this invitation from Wakefield left Cole between a rock and a hard spot. Both Natalie and Adeline would suit his purposes after he had become disillusioned with marriage in general and love in particular. Since he was doing business with Dyer Wakefield it would suit Cole's long-range plans to ask for Natalie's hand, even if she purposely shied away from him. But it would be to Cole's disadvantage to rile his future mother-in-law by rejecting Adeline, the daughter who had been reared and groomed in the image of Eileen.

Hell, maybe he should save himself a great deal of misery by withholding the proposal Dyer anticipated.

After all, there were other shipbuilders in the colonies he could deal with. Perhaps none of them equaled Dyer's abilities, but hopefully the others didn't have *three* eligible daughters to contend with!

A muddled frown creased Cole's brow when he reflected on his conversation with Natalie and Adeline. Neither of them offered a smidgeon of information when he cross-examined them about their uninhibited sister. Cole could have sworn both women had been given strict instruction to avoid the subject, no matter what. Each time he mentioned their youngest sister, Natalie and Adeline became as tight-lipped as clams.

What was she like? Was she as homely as Cole was beginning to imagine? Was she like Rachel, who had a penchant for men? Was that why she was followed by an unseemly reputation? Was she, at this very moment, having a tryst with one of her many lovers?

A myriad of questions clouded Cole's mind. Finally, he climbed down the small step ladder attached to the bed and pulled on his breeches. The silver moonlight drew him through the terrace doors to the balcony. Cole peered across the glistening bay, mulling over his alternatives. Perhaps he should dream up several excuses as to why he should return to his cabin on board the schooner. He certainly couldn't go back to the inn, not when he might chance to meet that green-eyed sprite. If Cole made the schooner his base, he could still meet Dyer in his office or at his private dock just beyond the estate. Aye, that would be wise, Cole decided. His presence was causing conflict between Dyer and Eileen and throwing Natalie and Adeline into competition.

An amused smile replaced Cole's pensive frown when he remembered the distressed expression on Dyer's and Eileen's faces. Their youngest daughter must be a handful, Cole reckoned. No doubt, she and that bright-eyed, hot-tempered servant girl were cut out of the same scrap of wood. But it was a pity that the youngest Wakefield didn't possess Stephanie's stunning looks.

Cole trolled through the sea of incidents that had taken place during the day and fished out one magical moment. *Magical madness,* Cole quickly amended. He was still distressed by his volatile reaction to Stephanie. He had taken incredible liberties with her. Indeed, he had abandoned common sense!

"Stop this nonsense," Cole growled at himself. The Wakefield's promiscuous daughter was none of his concern and neither was that feisty serving wench.

Cole was annoyed with himself for dwelling on the devastating whirlwind who had breezed in and out of his life that morning. Grumbling, he wheeled back toward his suite. Fumbling his way through the dark, unfamiliar room, he finally flounced into bed, determined to sleep.

Damn, wouldn't the world be a delightful place to live if the good Lord had thought to place females on another planet? They gave men fits. If Dyer hadn't had daughters, Cole wouldn't have been grappling with an alternative course of action. He would still be at the inn, sipping a brew, afraid he might bump into Stephanie.

My, but Stephanie was the most exhausting female he had ever met. He didn't want to give her a second thought and yet he was wearing himself out trying *not* to think about her! Although he had only met Stephanie. It was as if he had known that high-spirited firebrand forever. She was a part of his past, a memory he had hoped time would erase. She was the living reminder of what *he* had been, his sacrifice. Touching her was like reaching back through time and space to grasp emotions he had once allowed to rule his head.

A man who resolved to bury his past couldn't very well go around excavating old feelings, now could he? Cole asked himself solemnly. Nay, he could not. Expelling an exasperated breath, he closed his eyes and begged for sleep. He had made a commitment several years ago and, by God, he was going to live by it. That was all there was to it!

Stephanie Wakefield sank down on the edge of her canopy bed to breathe an exhausted sigh. Absently, she raked her fingers through the renegade curls that dangled about her face. Her green eyes had taken on a pensive hue as she stared at the far wall. The usual vibrance that claimed her features had evaporated after the long, frustrating hours she had endured. Weary though she was, her petite body was still a bundle of nerves, a bottle of pent-up energy searching for release.

The entire day had been a frustrating nightmare. She had approached Brice Reynolds, determined to proceed in a peaceful, logical manner. But their confidential conversation had become a trenchant argument. There was no reasoning with Brice. The man would attempt to argue with a stone wall. Stephanie had lost what was left of her temper when Brice refused the compensation of gold and began insulting her. Insulting *her,* mind you! The lowest form of life on earth was cursing *her* with words she had never even heard before! What was she supposed to do? Stand there and endure a verbal lynching when it was Brice who should have been swinging from a rope?

I should have endured his tirade, Stephanie mused in retrospect. Vigorously, she brushed her freshly washed hair. It would have saved her a near drowning if she would have grasped the trailing reins of her temper. But Stephanie had countered Brice's insults with a barrage of accusations that were sprinkled with a few unprintable curses.

Damn that man! He had dragged her off and had her tried and found guilty so quickly it left her head spinning. And to make matters worse she had wound up assaulting an innocent bystander after her ducking!

A reluctant smile trailed across Stephanie's lips when Coleman Douglas Hollister the Third materialized from the shadows. He had every right to demand retribution after what she had done to him, but he had remained calm and collected. Cole had even offered her his room to wash the grime from her face.

A strange tingle sailed down her spine, remembering what else the bold rogue had done. She could feel his sensuous lips exploring hers, feel his muscular torso brushing intimately against her. Those fire-laced kisses and caresses had lingered on her mind throughout the trying day. And for the life of her, Stephanie couldn't fathom why she had responded so recklessly. She had had no right to feel such a sizzling reaction to that handsome stranger.

Perhaps her response was the result of her fiasco with Brice. Or maybe it was just Cole Hollister himself. She had stared too long into those magnetic chocolate brown eyes and listened to the low, husky resonance of his voice. Then she simply forgot everything else— Brice Reynolds, Natalie, Wesley Beacham. How on earth could she have forgotten Wesley?

Stephanie tried to conjure up Wesley's face but Cole's ruggedly handsome features kept getting in the way. And why was she sparing Cole a thought in the first place? He was her exact opposite, she told herself as she wandered to the window to stare up at the night sky. Cole was all polish and sophistication and she was the personification of quick temper and impulsiveness.

There were times when Stephanie wished she could

react as precisely and decisively as the charming stranger. Perhaps then she wouldn't be followed by such a notorious reputation.

Dyer had sent her to school in London, hoping to iron the wrinkles out of her rebellious soul, but it was permanently creased and the schoolmaster immediately sent her home. Stephanie had sorely resented the finishing school's rigid set of rules. It was like being sentenced to prison after she had been allowed to run wild for the first seventeen years of her life. A free-spirit couldn't be confined to captivity for too many months before she was overwhelmed by the urge to spread her wings and fly. And fly she did—each time temptation lured her to roam into the darkness, away from the cramped spaces of her room. That is, until the schoolmaster caught her sneaking out at night.

Aye, Stephanie was everything Coleman Douglas Hollister the Third was *not*. But still he had made a lasting impression on her, even when he had no right to make any type of impression at all. But Stephanie simply could not toss their romantic encounter aside. It nagged at her all day, even when the incident had no right to prey on her mind.

Nothing could ever come of a relationship between her and a rudderless sea captain. It was too late for any relationship, Stephanie firmly reminded herself. She was already committed and she had made her vow. Besides, Cole wasn't her type. He was a part of the structured, rigid society Stephanie could never fit into. She had always held a different perspective of life. And the pitiful part was that Stephanie didn't want to change her ways. Her entire life had been an adventure. She had never been satisfied to trudge through the paces of living, following every rule and regulation that had been laid down since the beginning of time.

Stephanie had never done anything halfway. She

70

thrust herself, body and soul, into a day's living and milked every moment for all it was worth. Even now, while she was staring at the array of twinkling stars, she was reveling in the serenity of the instant and employing the moment to sort out her cluttered thoughts.

Suddenly, a flickering light in the gardens below caught her attention. Stephanie chided herself for her forgetfulness. She was supposed to meet Wesley! Lord, how could she have forgotten about him again? My God, the morning's disaster had partially evolved around attempting to set *him* free!

Hastily, Stephanie snuffed out her lantern and padded across the room to the door. With the silence of a cat, she crept down the hall to the guest room that held the only private exit from the manor. Stephanie had used the room as her escape route for a dozen years. She could come and go without alerting her family that she had taken flight for one whimsical reason or another.

Stephanie kept her unsightly garb of men's breeches, shirt, and cape stashed in the unused drawers beneath the alcove bed. Thus far, no one had discovered the garments and questioned them. The guest suite had proved to be a perfect hideaway. Stephanie could slip into the dark room, peel off her nightgown, and step into her unconventional garments. Without being detected, she could stroll across the balcony, descend the spiraling steps, and become one of the midnight shadows.

There had been many a night when her nervous energy refused to grant her sleep. On those occasions Stephanie had wandered to the stables for a late-night ride—the kind that would have given Dyer heart failure. Dyer only allowed his trainers to exercise his prize thoroughbreds at swift speeds. But Stephanie thrilled to the sound of powerful hooves pounding the ground, the feel of the wind lifting her long hair and sending it trailing wildly about her.

Since Dyer announced that he had better not catch any of his daughters racing at breakneck speeds on his expensive horses, Stephanie honored his requests. Not once had he *caught* her. She spared Dyer an inevitable stroke by restricting her wild rides to those times when Dyer was fast asleep. Actually she was doing him a favor, Stephanie mused mischievously. He truly should thank her for sparing him bouts of anger and frustration.

Chewing on that impish thought, Stephanie tiptoed down the corridor toward the guest suite, unaware that the room was occupied. She had no way of knowing that Coleman Douglas Hollister the Third was tucked in the alcove bed. Her only conversation with any member of the family had been her hasty encounter with Natalie. At the time, there had been too much on either of their minds to concern themselves with the distinguished Captain Hollister. Stephanie had been trying to free Wesley from his obligations and Natalie was attempting to save herself from public embarrassment.

The creak of the door stirred Cole from sleep. He blinked drowsily, attempting to get his bearings. His gaze snagged on the trim silhouette who floated through the shaft of moonbeams and silently approached his bed. For a moment Cole swore he had awakened in the middle of a dream. The specter's features were unrecognizable in the darkness, but her enchanting profile drew his unblinking gaze.

Cole watched in mute amazement as the young woman knelt before the alcove bed to pull open the

72

drawer beneath it. He heard the rustling of clothes and then saw her rise and walk back to the meager source of light. And to his bewilderment, the curvaceous apparition paused in the silver path of moonlight that flowed across the carpet and then proceeded to discard her flowing gown!

His jaw dropped off its hinges when the woman tossed her garment toward the alcove bed, leaving her silhouette bathed in splinters of moonlight. Cole's wide eyes swept over the gossamer gown that drifted across the room to tumble into *his* lap. He scolded himself for all of a tenth of a second for peeping at her. But then he consoled himself by rationalizing that it was human nature to gawk, just to see what one could see. And gawk he did!

The woman's well-proportioned physique was like a Greek statue—exquisite, flawless, incomparable. She was breathtaking—the shadowed picture of femininity. Long flowing hair tumbled over her shoulders. Its color? Cole couldn't tell for certain in the darkness. Was it Natalie? Adeline? Or one of Dyer's many servants? Cole didn't know, but the wench was having a disturbing effect on his blood pressure. He felt like a schoolboy hiding in the darkness, spying on a young woman who seemed oblivious to his presence.

Cole quickly ruled out Natalie or Adeline. They both knew he had taken up residence in the guest suite and so did most of the servants. Deductive reasoning led him to the conclusion that this vision of loveliness must be Dyer's youngest daughter. Her face may have been a ghastly sight to behold but her body was the stuff dreams were made of!

While Cole lay there, moonstruck, Stephanie shrugged on her black linen shirt and fastened herself into her black breeches. When she had tied the cape around her neck to disguise her gender to anyone who might inadvertently spot her while she made her escape, she moved swiftly toward the terrace door and disappeared into the darkness.

For a long moment Cole lay in his niche in the wall, waiting for his altered breathing to return to normal, staring after his mysterious midnight visitor. Finally, he pinched himself to ensure that his imagination hadn't been working overtime. But he *was* awake and the crumpled silk gown lay across his loins. After all, he didn't make it a habit of sleeping with a woman's negligee, *not* unless there was a woman in it.

When Cole inhaled a steadying breath, the scent of jasmine invaded his nostrils. The fragrance didn't belong to Natalie or Adeline. Natalie was partial to the scent of lilacs and Adeline smelled of roses.

This alluring fragrance must belong to the youngest Wakefield, he surmised. Had he been visited by the black sheep who came and went when it met her whim? Cole's deductive mind was buzzing in attempt to link logical questions with reasonable answers. Surely no servant girl would stash an extra set of clothes in the guest suite. There could be only one person who was unaware that the quarters were occupied. Cole would have bet his fortune that he had just encountered the youngest daughter, the misfit who breezed in and out of the manor on her way to only God knew where.

A wry smile pursed Cole's lips as he fluffed his pillow. Perhaps the Wakefields had attempted to protect him from the black sheep of the family, but he already knew a great deal about her. As a matter of fact, he had *seen* a great deal of her in the span of a few minutes. She may have been plagued with a hideous face but the rest of her was perfection! Cole preferred to remember her as she had been in the scant moonlight—a mysterious witch-angel whose reputation preceded her wherever she went.

That tantalizing thought followed Cole into a strange dream. In his fantasy the forgotten Wakefield daughter spirited not only into his room but into his enclosed bed as well. The savory scent of jasmine swirled about him, adding credence to his arousing dream. Cole could almost feel her luscious moonlit body brushing provocatively against his, taste the moistness of her lips.

All of his speculations about the kind of woman Dyer's youngest daughter was, formed the dimensions of his erotic fantasy. Cole imagined himself making mad passionate love to the mysterious misfit. She was a temptress, a seductress who was no stranger to a man's arms. She loved for the pleasure of it, giving and taking in moments of reckless abandon. There were no strings to bind such a wild, free spirit. Cole didn't have to fret about allowing his desires to run rampant. He could emerge from his constricting shell and respond to this love goddess for one night, fearing no repercussions. . . .

And what a dream it was! A fantasy to end all fantasies! He was imagining himself in the arms of a nameless, faceless angel. She was stripping him of his inhibitions, just the way Stephanie had that morning. She was pleasing him, weaving her magical spell about him. . . .

While Cole was dreaming that he was making love to her, Stephanie was darting through the maze of flowers and shrubs to meet Wesley Beacham, the indentured servant who assumed the bookkeeping duties and managed the inn for Brice Reynolds.

Wesley was a bright but misfortunate young man who had been enrolled in Dublin's Trinity College until he depleted his funds. When his father died suddenly, Wesley's older brother inherited the small estate and Wesley was left penniless. His brother offered to help with the expenses of his education, but Wesley did not have the heart to take the meager amount of money when his brother had a wife and several small children to support.

Seeing no alternative, Wesley boarded a ship bound for the colonies and sacrificed four years of his life as a redemptioner. It was his misfortune that Brice Reynolds paid his passage from England and put him to work managing the inn. Brice had profited from Wesley's intelligence and education and he was not the least bit anxious to see Wesley become a free man. But Wesley's four years of service would terminate in six months and Brice was scheming to find a way to keep Wesley under thumb.

The moment Wesley spied Stephanie in the shadows, he started toward her. Stephanie was swept off the ground to receive Wesley's overzealous hug. When he finally set her to her feet, Stephanie inhaled the breath Wesley had squeezed out of her.

"I'm sorry I'm late," she apologized. "I almost forgot our meeting."

"I was afraid you wouldn't come," Wesley murmured as he wrapped his arm around her and led her farther from the mansion. "After what happened today I just had to see you, to express my appreciation, and to apologize for getting you into so much trouble."

Wesley grabbed Stephanie again, very nearly squeezing the stuffing out of her. "Oh, Steph, every day that passes brings even more torment. I ache to be free to live as man and wife. I want to declare to the world that I am in love, that I am married to the woman of my dreams!" A deflated sigh escaped his lips as he cuddled Stephanie against him. "I am sick of this pretense, afraid of what is going to happen when Dyer learns the truth. He will kill the both of us!"

Stephanie offered Wesley a comforting pat. "You fret too much. Papa isn't going to kill anyone. If he were prone to violence, he would have had me shot years ago."

A soft chuckle rumbled in his chest. "And if he had, too late he would have realized he had lost a priceless treasure."

"I'm sure Papa would vigorously debate that statement," she sniffed in contradiction.

"Sometimes I think I am the only one who appreciates your true worth. And 'tis a pity, love," Wesley whispered back.

Stephanie leaned back in the circle of his arms to stare into the refined features of his face. Although she and Wesley were also as different as dawn and midnight, they shared a special bond. Wesley was the only man who truly understood her, who loved her the way she was without trying to change her. And for that reason Stephanie had made a commitment to him, one she was prepared to defend with her life, if need be.

"Methinks you have endeared yourself to a black sheep, Wes," she teased with an impish grin.

"Nay, an angel," he parried. Unable to resist her radiant smile, Wesley bent to press a fleeting kiss to the tip of her nose. "I adore you, Steph."

His arms dropped away as the cloud of doom settled about him, dampening his mood. "If only Brice would have accepted the money to pay off the last six months of my indentureship and spare Natalie embarrassment, none of us would be in such a scrape." Wes muttered under his breath. "Damn that man. He will never let me go or sympathize with Natalie's plight. I know too much about his business. I am a threat to him and I will be even more of a threat when I am free to exert my civil rights. Brice knows I cannot voice charges against him

77

while I am his indentured servant. And after what happened today he has suggested that I marry Elizabeth Marrow. If I promise to make her my wife he will dissolve *her* four years of indentureship and the last six months of *mine.*"

"What?" Stephanie choked on her breath, her eyes wide as saucers.

Wesley nodded grimly. "The catch is that we would not truly be free. I would have to promise to remain in Brice's charge until Elizabeth's four-year term is truly up. Since Brice is on such friendly terms with the British magistrate, he can offer me my precious freedom, but I won't be free at all. 'Tis just another of his attempts to keep me tied to him." Wesley threw up his hands in exasperation. "He is willing to do most anything to ensure that I keep silent about his business dealings."

Stephanie's exquisite features puckered in genuine concern. Like a homing pigeon coming to roost, she flew into Wes's arms. "Then Papa *will* be furious when he realizes his daughter has married without his permission and that her husband is about to be forced to take another wife!"

"That is what I have been trying to tell you, Steph," Wesley groaned as he held her close. He felt the need to go on holding her, afraid his world was about to crumble around him. "We both know the marriage was illegal. A redemptioner has no right to wed. But we defied the law and now Brice is going to find a way around that law and force me into a marriage of *his* making. Damnit, what are we going to do? We cannot allow Natalie to go forward in my defense, Brice will crucify her! Her reputation will be ruined and she is not strong enough to deal with that sort of frustration. She has to protect herself from her shame."

Stephanie suddenly felt very tired. It was as if the weight of the world were draped on her shoulders. Everything had become so entangled and complicated and the marriage was in jeopardy. Wesley was about to be forced into another wedding ceremony, one that was only a smidgeon more lawful than the first. Natalie risked being exposed and Dyer would be beside himself. Sweet mercy, what were they going to do?

She needed time to think, but there was so little time! Her attempt to buy the last six months of Wesley's indentureship and Brice's silence for Natalie's sake had seemed the perfect solution. But Brice adamantly refused and then set about to bind Wesley to him for another four years. Damnation, they all would have been better off if they hadn't been so impulsive. This secret marriage was going to cause heartache and the repercussions would affect the entire Wakefield family!

Slipping from Wesley's arms, Stephanie paced the garden for several minutes. Finally, she swung around to face Wesley. "You must make a copy of Brice's ledgers," she insisted. "Perhaps we can use them to expose Brice's underhanded dealings. He may find it wiser to set you free than to face accusations in court—even the prejudiced court held by the British magistrate."

Wesley nodded in agreement. "But it will take time to make the copy. Brice has been watching me like a hawk. And if he learns I have handed them over to you, he will—"

Stephanie pressed her index finger to his lips to shush him. "We will worry about that when the time comes."

"But what will we tell Natalie?" Wesley mused aloud. "She will be curious to know what we are contemplating."

"Concoct a lie," Stephanie muttered more harshly than she intended. "It should fit in quite nicely with all the other secrets we are forced to keep! But for heaven's sake, don't tell her what we are planning. Her emotions are already in turmoil."

Wesley looked hurt that Stephanie had raised her voice to him and Stephanie could have kicked herself for being so irritable. "I'm sorry," she relented. "I didn't mean to be so curt. 'Tis just that I am as frustrated as you are."

A tender smile bordered Wesley's lips as he gathered Stephanie close. "Do you know how very much I adore you, Steph?"

The tension fell away and Stephanie smiled as she rearranged the tuft of dark hair that lay across his forehead. "If I didn't love you so, I would never have stepped so far out on a limb." Quiet laughter filled the small space between them. "Even the ducking was worth it. I would do most anything to see you free."

"You are a rare gem, love," he murmured sincerely. "And one day I am going to compensate for all the trouble I've put you through."

A saucy twinkle glittered in her green eyes. "And when that day comes I think I will be anxious for that compensation," she teased mischievously. "I only hope you can meet my every whim."

Wesley playfully flicked her upturned nose. "You have but to ask and your wish will be my command, little elf."

"I will hold you to that promise," Stephanie assured him as she spun on her heels to vanish into the darkness.

"Stay out of trouble," Wesley called after her.

The smile evaporated from her lips as she left Wesley in the shadows. How could she stay out of trouble when she was born to it? No matter what she did, it always backfired in her face. And now her world was an entangled mess and it was all Brice Reynolds's fault. She was going to pester that man until he made a wrong move and exposed himself for the devious varmint he was.

Mulling over that thought, Stephanie ambled in the darkness like a lost soul. The cool fingers of the wind drummed on her spine and she shivered involuntarily. With a dispirited sigh, Stephanie clutched her cape tightly about her, wondering if the chill that trickled down her backbone was provoked by the damp night or apprehension.

At the moment the situation appeared so bleak. But perhaps after she rested, the obstacles wouldn't seem so insurmountable. She was going to find a way to release Wesley from his indentureship. She just had to! A man couldn't keep two wives, for God's sake! Dyer would be fit to be tied if he found out what had transpired behind his back. Lord, Stephanie didn't want to have to be the one to explain to Dyer if Brice had his way in this matter. It would be so much simpler if Wesley could be freed and they could repeat the vows in public. Then no one would ever have to know about the illegal marriage.

Both of them should have had more sense! Stephanie thought bitterly. They should have known their romantic whims would collide with disaster. Love! That complex emotion had a way of complicating everything. Stephanie was a walking example of how impulse could entangle life. They should have profited from her past mistakes. But nay, they had stumbled headlong into a marriage that was not recognized by the British court and they could not live as man and wife. Instead they met in the darkness, sharing a few private moments, pretending they were only acquaintances when they happened to meet on the street.

What kind of life was that? Stephanie grumbled under her breath. There were times when she wished she could turn back the hands of time and change the events that had led them into the dark tunnel of despair. And this was one of those times!

Chapter 5

Cole awoke in a cold sweat. His lifelike dream had tormented his body into believing he was engulfed in a moment of passion—something he had done without for two months. Some men reacted to a woman's betrayal by bedding every female who crossed their path, by replacing bitter memories with new ones. Cole, on the other hand, had chosen celibacy to forget Rachel's betrayal. He had allowed the bitter memories to burn in his mind until they poisoned every pleasant thought about Rachel Garret.

But there were serious consequences to face when a man refrained from exercising his animal desires and Cole was feeling the full effects of doing without a woman. His brief encounter with Stephanie had whetted his appetite for passion. The appearance of Dyer's youngest daughter in his room had added fuel to smoldering coals. His arousing dream had intensified the gnawing hunger and left him wanting in a maddening sort of way.

It was the youngest Wakefield's fault, Cole thought sourly. If the minx hadn't stripped naked in the middle of his room, unveiling her comely figure, Cole wouldn't be dreaming wild, erotic dreams! Damn that tigress.

He didn't even know her and he disliked her already. No doubt, she was a great deal like Rachel. The girl had probably been on her way to rendezvous with one of her many lovers. Cole may as well have been one of them. That promiscuous vixen probably didn't care who warmed her bed, as long as she satiated her feminine desires.

It was at that moment, while Cole was cursing the woman he had yet to meet formally, that Stephanie blundered back into her secret hideaway. Employing Mother Nature's night light to disrobe, Stephanie unclasped her cape and tossed it on the floor in her usual reckless fashion. Next came the breeches, joining the cape in a crumpled heap.

Cole swallowed the lump that had collected in his throat when Stephanie exposed her long shapely legs to his attentive gaze. Her fingers moved swiftly over the buttons on the black shirt. As she shrugged off the garment, Cole gulped a roomful of air. His eyes had not betrayed him the first time, he quickly realized. This mischievous witch was perfection, every exquisite inch of her. Her breasts were full and her waist was so trim that a man could easily wrap his hands around her. Her hips held a delicately inviting curve and . . .

Cole inwardly groaned. He had not hopped into bed with a total stranger since he had stepped into his respectable position of lord and master of the plantation. He had become cautious, an escape artist no woman had captured. Instinct and habit warned him against tossing aside his policies. The last thing he wanted was to be entrapped in a marriage after a woman passed out favors and then screamed that *she* had been compromised.

Yet all that wise sense of self-preservation flew out the window when Cole was treated to this unique display of bare flesh. His body was well warmed and ready for passion and his brain was malfunctioning.

He couldn't think past the moment to contemplate the consequences. After all, he rationalized, his eyes still glued to Stephanie's luscious figure, this witch had probably bedded more than her fair share of men if she was as wild and uninhibited as the Wakefields implied. Her brand of woman would have no qualms about a reckless tumble in the darkness. It would probably excite her to wonder who was making love to her . . . or perhaps she had known he was there all along, he told himself, half dazed, half wanting to believe that theory. Maybe this vixen delighted in taunting men with her curvaceous body. Perhaps . . .

Cole's thoughts dispersed when Stephanie walked toward the alcove bed, as naked as the day she was born. He still could see no more than the dark shadow of her face, but it really didn't matter what she looked like from the neck up. From the neck down she was every man's dream—trim, shapely, voluptuous—and he was on fire for the want of a woman!

Unaware there was a man in the guest bed, Stephanie stepped onto the ladder to grope in the darkness for the nightgown she had recklessly thrown aside. Her search for the missing garment led her right onto Cole's lap—a lap that was not supposed to be there at all!

A shocked gasp gushed from Stephanie's lips when she confronted the dreadful realization that her hand had collided with a body. And it took less than a split-second to determine which gender that body was. It was a man, for crying out loud!

There is a man in my private hideaway! her mind screamed in panic. And she had touched the most private parts of his anatomy!

Stephanie would have leapt off the stepladder to make her hasty exit, but strong fingers shackled her wrist. Like a defenseless fish being dragged into the engulfing arms of an octopus, Stephanie was pulled into the bed in the wall and pressed full length against the stranger's iron-hard body.

She would have squealed at the top of her lungs if Cole's all-consuming kiss hadn't deprived her of every ounce of oxygen. She couldn't breathe. She couldn't think. Her body was being assaulted by tantalizing caresses, ones that flooded over her, doing the wildest things to each sensitive point on her bare flesh.

A gutteral groan erupted from Cole's chest as the unidentified woman's satin flesh made a searing imprint on his. He could feel the taut peaks of her breasts, the supple curve of her hips. She felt as delicious as she looked in the moonlight and Cole's male body roused by leaps and bounds. He wanted her as his possession—no questions asked. He wanted to appease this insane craving that was provoked by his erotic dream. He was far past contemplating what was right or wrong. Cole didn't care if he had to walk through fire, or if he had hell to pay in the morning. If he didn't feed his hunger tonight, he would surely reduce himself to a pile of frustrated ashes.

With his lips firmly planted on hers, he reached behind him to clasp the shutter door, filling the niche with total darkness. He could see nothing, hear nothing except the frantic beat of his heart. And for a tenth of a second he hesitated, thinking he should be ashamed of himself for what he intended to do. But then he quickly reminded himself that he didn't know exactly how he should react in such unusual circumstances because he had never before experienced a moment quite like this one.

Conscience be damned, Cole mused as the muscular column of his leg insinuated itself between Stephanie's thighs. Every man was entitled to one or two reckless mistakes. He might as well enjoy this one. He certainly hadn't enjoyed his blunder of falling in love with Rachel. There should be some sort of compensation for being humiliated by a witch, he contended. This mysterious apparition, the Wakefield's wildest daughter, would become his consolation.

And that was the last sane thought to cross Cole's mind (or as close to sane as a man could get when he found himself in bed with a shapely black sheep of the Wakefield flock). The moment his lips slanted over Stephanie's to drink the intoxicating taste of her, the reasoning processes of his brain bogged down. His sense of touch and smell took command, leading him deeper into the sensual world of desire. This mysterious vixen was bathed in jasmine, and the lingering scent of the whole outdoors clung to her. The feel of her skin sharply contrasted his hair—roughened body, reminding him how long he had been without a woman. She was like silk and satin and she tasted like the sweet nectar of a wild flower.

Cole could not get enough of her. In some strange, unexplainable way, this encounter reminded him of his uncontrollable attraction to Stephanie, one of Brice's serving maids. Again he resembled a wayward traveler who had been stranded on a barren island and had, at last, been rescued. He wanted to devour and savor her all in the same moment. He wanted to touch her, to ensure that this wasn't another tormenting dream. He wanted to possess her, to become a living, breathing part of her, to give and share the pleasure of this incredibly reckless moment.

It was just that he had been months without a woman, Cole assured himself. His wild response to this unknown woman was the result of his celibacy and the arousing effect of watching this curvaceous specter disrobe before his eager eyes. Any man in his situation would have reacted the same. No man would think to resist this luscious temptation when she practically crawled into bed with him without invitation!

Stephanie lay stiff as a corpse, horrified by what was happening, what would inevitably happen if she didn't regain control of her senses and find a way to escape. Escape? She laughed bitterly at herself. There was no retreat from this dark abyss. She hadn't known the alcove bed was occupied, but her blundering mistake had thrust her into a most unusual situation from which there could be no honorable retreat. Though she was innocent of scheming to seduce one of her father's distinguished guests, no one would believe her guiltless. She was like the unsuspecting fly entrapped in a spider web. She was tangled in a stranger's arms, a man who wanted only her body for his lusty pleasure . . . after *she* had unknowingly tempted him by stripping naked and crawling into *his* bed. He didn't know her and she didn't know him, but they were learning things about each other that Stephanie didn't really want to know!

She had been saving herself for her husband, the man of her dreams. But this bold stranger was depriving her of that precious gift that was hers alone to give. How would she explain that she had lost her virginity to a total stranger, a rogue who saw her only as an object of lust? How could she possibly explain that she hadn't planned the seduction when she was the one who crawled, naked, into bed with a stranger? Even a man who professed to love her would not understand how and why she had allowed this to happen! What she could say in her own defense except that circumstances beyond her control had evolved into this intimate encounter?

The dreary thought caused Stephanie to whimper in frustration. She tried to push the bold stranger away but there was no stopping him, not when he possessed the strength of three men. He held her tenderly but firmly against his swarthy length. There was no forcefulness in his embrace, only the soft whispering of hands over her quivering flesh, as if she were a treasured gift he was reverently examining. His husky whisper coaxed her, as if she were a skittish colt. His moist kisses tasted rather than devoured her, as if she were a long-awaited sip of thirst-quenching wine. All of her reeling senses came to life, as they never had before. The taste, the feel, the masculine scent of this faceless stranger sent logic spinning in a mindless whirl.

Muscles and nerves that had been taut with fearful apprehension began to melt beneath his deliberate, masterful touch. Over and over he whispered how he delighted in caressing her exquisite flesh. His patient hands seemed to tremble, as if he were in awe of the titillating contrast between his steel-hard flesh and her soft, supple curves. What he intended was not a hurried, hungry assault, she realized. This was languid lovemaking, the discovery of sensuality, an expression of physical communication.

When his skillful hands began to drift across the taut peaks of her breasts, embroidered with amazing gentleness, strange, tingling sensations invaded her chaotic thoughts. Her body began to respond on its own accord, yielding to his practiced seduction. This man knew how to melt a woman and make her will his own. It was a tormenting reminder of the incident at Reynolds Inn that morning. Stephanie had been caught up in sensations she was helpless to defy.

Her naive body instinctively arched toward the butterfly caresses that fluttered across her abdomen to seek out the sensitive flesh of her thighs. He was doing incredible things to her body while he continued to kiss her senseless. He was discovering every inch of her flesh, setting her nerves to tingling.

Had she been a trollop in another lifetime? Would she respond to any man who touched her so familiarly? Hadn't she wilted like a witless fool in Cole Hollister's arms?

Wesley had never concerned himself with her notorious reputation. He had accepted her as she was. He had been kind and understanding. But would even a man as compassionate as Wesley tolerate a woman who had been tainted by a seductive rake she didn't even know? Stephanie thought not! Heavens above, even *she* didn't know why she was feeling pleasure when she should have felt repulsion. She felt the odd compulsion to investigate the physical phenomena she was experiencing. None of this made sense unless she shamefully admitted to herself that she was all the terrible things her parents thought she was!

Stephanie sucked in her breath when Cole guided her legs apart. His fingertips aroused and explored, setting off another chain reaction of indescribable sensations. Stephanie felt her heart leap into her throat to strangle her, felt her body warming from inside out. Over and over again, her mysterious lover's hands flooded and receded across her breasts and then swept over her thighs. His skillful seduction erased her inhibitions, her defenses, leaving her pliant and unresisting.

How could any woman resist this skillful stranger, she asked herself deliriously. He didn't roughly assault a woman. He worshipped her body, made her want what she knew she shouldn't have.

And then her overworked heart stopped beating. Stephanie felt hair-matted flesh intimately molding itself to her. His muscular body covered hers, making her vividly aware of the differences between a man and a woman. She was being enveloped in strong, capable arms. She could feel his male hardness invading her

90

feminine softness. His voice was no more than a hoarse whisper, assuring her that touching her pleased him, promising to return the rapture he was experiencing.

The dazed splendor became a sharp pain and Stephanie bit her lip until it bled. Fighting him now would only induce greater pain, she reasoned. It was too late to scream for all she was worth. If some member of her family came to her rescue, she would be forced to explain what *she* was doing in this man's room in the first place. How could she successfully lay the blame where it belonged when her garments of black were strewn all over the guest suite? Who would believe that she was innocent of encouraging this man to make love to her? Sweet mercy, if she weren't the victim, even *she* wouldn't have believed such an illogical story!

As the faceless stranger made her his possession, Stephanie felt the pain ebb, to be replaced by sweet, tantalizing sensations she hadn't imagined possible. Her body was drifting just beyond the perimeters of reality. He was taking her so gently, lifting her onto a sensuous plateau, leaving her to chide herself for enjoying his tender brand of lovemaking.

It wasn't fair. There was no justice in this world, Stephanie thought as her arms involuntarily drifted over his broad shoulders. She should be cursing this man with every breath she took. But how could she when he was loving her in ways that awoke the feminine longings within her? He had taken a nightmare and transformed it into secret splendor. He was teaching her things that instilled wonderment and provoked her to discover where these delicious feelings would ultimately lead.

The most incredible sensation unfurled inside her as his virile body moved skillfully upon hers. Stephanie could feel herself losing her grasp on reality. She was letting go, falling helplessly through space, caught in what she dared to define as rapture in its pure, raw form. Her innocent body was moving in rhythm with his as pleasure built into a hauntingly sweet crescendo.

And then, each separate sensation she had experienced in those timeless moments began to recoil on top of her like thick, congested fog. Stephanie gasped for breath as the feelings deep inside her filled to overflowing. Previously inexperienced emotions began to flood over her, spilling from the confines of her naive body. It was as if those feelings had just been created to suit this moment. It was as if this stranger were a magician who could create something from nothing and transform it into the most splendorous sensations she had ever encountered.

Instinctively, Stephanie clutched Cole to her as if the world were about to explode. And explode it did, taking Stephanie with it. Thought and emotion disintegrated into a thousand unrecognizable pieces.

This was a time for feeling and experiencing, not a time to think and analyze. And what Stephanie was feeling could not be conveyed into words. She wasn't sure if she were living or dying, but she seemed to be entrapped in a dimension of time that she had never realized existed.

For what must have been forever, Stephanie struggled to find herself in this mist of forbidden ecstasy, to attach names to the incredible sensations that were assaulting her. But there was no conceivable way to describe this most intimate of journeys beyond the universe as she knew it. This rapturous experience was description unto itself, a moment that defied language.

Ever so slowly Stephanie felt the numbing pleasure ebb. But the long, tedious day had sapped every smidgeon of her energy and sleep came all too quickly. For Stephanie, it was a blessing in disguise. She had no time to ponder what had transpired in this secluded world of darkness. She became the prisoner of a dream, one very much like the one that had entangled Cole and left him with the maddening need to appease a craving that challenged logic.

Cole carefully eased away to stare down into the darkness. He was in a bewildered daze, wondering if he really had any control over himself at all. Without forethought, he had given way to his primal instincts. He had allowed them to rule his mind and body. Every inhibition and every iota of self-reserve had abandoned him the moment he felt this witch-angel's curvaceous body beneath his exploring caresses.

No wonder this high-spirited female had scores of lovers waiting to meet her in the dark hours before dawn. She was the quintessence of pleasure. She could make a man forget himself and his philosophies. Aye, she was the most dangerous kind of witch the devil placed on the planet. She was the *femme fatale* who cast her wicked spell on mortal men. The moment a man dared to touch her, he became entranced, bedeviled, and rendered senseless. He sacrificed his soul when he fell beneath this sorceress's mystical charms. The Wakefields had not exaggerated when they warned him to beware of the black sheep. She was the keeper of black magic, the devil's own temptation.

When Stephanie cuddled against him like a purring kitten curling up beside a hearth, Cole's heart melted all over his ribs. Even when he knew what kind of lair he had stumbled into, he was lured closer by her delightful response to the aftermath of love. There was an irresistible, childlike quality about this mysterious woman, a perpetual innocence that gave a man the impression he was her first experience with love.

In all his years, the wild ones and the cautious ones, Cole had never experienced anything quite like this! This vixen was incredible in bed. She responded in inventive ways that fed the flames of his passion. It was like grasping a sunbeam in his hand at the darkest hour of midnight. It was like inhaling a breath of springtime during a blizzard. Cole could not remember being with another woman who left him feeling so wildly virile and alive.

Even as pleasurable as passion had been with Rachel, it couldn't rival the strange haze of ecstasy that had settled over him. It was odd, Cole mused as he sank into the feather mattress. He still didn't feel like his old self. Even now, he was groggy with the stupifying aftereffects of this new kind of passion.

As the open arms of sleep enfolded him, Cole wondered if he would ever be the same again. He had stepped out of character. He had defied his own good sense. He had thrown caution to the wind and gave himself up to sensations he couldn't begin to control.

But ah, the immense satisfaction he had derived when he completely let go and sailed past the distant stars! Come dawn, he would button himself into his expensive, tailor-made clothes. He would resume his air of sophistication and cling to the promises he had made to his father. He *could* and *would* lead a normal life again, he reassured himself.

But deep inside, in that secluded place that this mysterious witch had touched, he would always be just a little vulnerable. The memory of this night would linger there, flickering like a tiny flame. And when his methodic, well-organized life began to crowd in on him, Cole would reach inside himself to grasp this one mystifying moment. He would remember the one time he had let go, when he had responded in mindless passion. . . .

Stephanie felt an unfamiliar presence beside her. Her eyes popped open to stare into pitch black silence. Where the devil was she anyway? Had she died sometime in the night and no one had bothered to tell her? And then it all came back to her like a crushing tidal wave.

When she heard Cole's methodic breathing she went rigid. She was still in the guest room, closeted with a total stranger! Well, no longer a stranger, she amended with an anguished sigh. They might not recognize each other on sight, but they could most certainly identify each other by touch!

Not daring to breathe, Stephanie cautiously inched her way around the inside corner of the enclosed bed. Her only chance to escape was to crawl around the man's body and ease open the doors without waking him. With her mouth set in grim determination, Stephanie felt her way around the wall. Her hand landed on her nightgown and she clutched it to her. Carefully, she scooted around Cole's feet and felt her way toward the shutter doors. Once she had opened the portal, she groped to find the rung of the ladder.

Only when she had closed the doors and wormed her way into her negligee did she expel the breath she had been holding. Quietly, she scooped up her garments and stuffed them back in the drawer. With her task accomplished, she tiptoed across the dark room and slipped out the door.

Stephanie collapsed on her bed to stare unblinkingly at the ceiling. How could she point an accusing finger and wail that she had been molested? She might have been able to live with herself if she had fought against rough abuse. But she had responded like a willing trollop when her midnight lover worshipped her body with gentle caresses. He had touched her with exquisite tenderness and alluring kisses. He had introduced her to the sensuous, mysterious world of passion with such incredible skill that Stephanie could not hold him entirely responsible for what had happened. After all, *she* had been the one to crawl into *his* bed. How was a man supposed to react when a woman put her hand in his lap? Stephanie groaned miserably. She should have fought him with every ounce of strength she possessed . . . and to the end . . . if she expected *him* to bear the burden of the blame. Unfortunately, his tantalizing kisses and caresses had been laced with persuasive gentleness and her innocent body had come alive when his practiced hands sought out each sensitive point on her flesh. It was impossible to ignore the way he kissed her, the way he. . . .

An agonized groan tumbled from Stephanie's lips. Aye, she was as guilty as he was for what had transpired between them. How could she face the man who had taken her virginity with such experienced ease, knowing she had shamelessly surrendered to his skillful seduction? And who was he, for heaven's sake? One of the many suitors Dyer had dragged home in an effort to marry Natalie off? Someone should tell Dyer that Nattie wasn't about to wed *any* of the suitors he herded home and stashed in the guest room. And why had the stranger been allowed *that* particular guest suite? Dyer usually saved that spacious room for prime candidates he wished to impress.

Whoever-he-was had obviously caught Dyer's interest, Stephanie reasoned. Dyer would be hopping up and down if he ever found out that the black sheep of the family had bedded the man he had selected for Natalie!

Stephanie groaned miserably. If Natalie would ever work up enough intestinal fortitude to tell Dyer the truth about herself, all this nonsense would cease. But Nattie had been born without a shred of nerve. Making such an incriminating announcement to Dyer would surely kill her. Poor Nattie. She truly had tried to be everything Dyer expected of her. But she just couldn't be. She never would be!

And just where did that leave Stephanie? Right where she always was—in the way. She had tried to protect Nattie, and thus far, all she had accomplished was embroiling herself in a peck of trouble. Dyer didn't have a clue about his eldest daughter's preferences, Adeline was apprehensively biding her time, Wesley was being dragged in over his head, and Brice had declared war on Stephanie.

She squeezed back the dismal thoughts. She didn't want to think anymore. If she didn't get some sleep, she would never endure the following day. She had to keep her wits about her. She was protecting so many secrets that she might blurt out one of them if she let her guard down!

Just once she wished she could endure a convenient catastrophe. They kept piling one atop the other and Stephanie was left holding the lion's share of responsibility. She felt as if she were carrying a towering stack of fine china. If she took one careless step, the entire pile would avalanche down upon her.

Determinedly, Stephanie tucked away each fretful thought in the closet of her mind. But one thought refused to be folded and neatly stored away. Try as she may, she could not blot out the memory of the man who had no face and no name. Her body quivered in response to the forbidden thought. She had never known the meaning of passion until the mysterious stranger spelled it out to her. And what price would she be forced to pay for her introduction to physical desire? Stephanie's shoulders slumped in gloomy apprehension.

"You must pretend it never happened," Stephanie lectured herself fiercely. But even while she struggled to grasp a few hours of sleep, the forbidden dream came stealing softly through her mind. It blossomed in the corners of her heart, tormenting her, assuring her that she wasn't likely to forget this night of rapturous pleasure for the rest of her natural life.

Chapter 6

As if she were trudging up the gallows to her lynching, Stephanie opened her bedroom door and stared grimly down the hall. For more than an hour she had wrestled with her thoughts, attempting to put them into proper prospective. But with all her rationalization she was still hampered by humiliation and guilt. How could she forgive herself for what she had permitted to happen the previous night? And worse, how was she going to maintain her composure when she laid eyes on the stranger who had seduced her with his practiced caresses?

Stephanie drew in a steadying breath. Well, she had to get this over with. Not only did she have to contend with the man who had stolen her innocence with a tenderness that was more potent than force, but she also had to consider the possibility that the news of her ducking had reached Dyer's ears. Damn, she would prefer to be sick in bed rather than to breeze down the steps and pretend nothing out of the ordinary had happened.

She could only pray the mysterious stranger was also having serious misgivings about what had transpired between them. Hopefully, he also wanted to forget that the night existed. Stephanie certainly couldn't blurt out her outrage over the situation, not without provoking another swarm of trouble and setting it to buzzing around her. The next to the last thing she wanted to do was explain why she was changing clothes in the guest suite before she sneaked out of the house. And the *last* thing she wanted to do was be formally introduced to her midnight lover!

Bracing her courage, Stephanie descended the steps, garbed in a form-fitting green velvet gown. She had taken particular care to dress for breakfast. Stephanie had to look the part of a poised, sophisticated heiress even if she couldn't conform to the role her parents expected of her. Perhaps Dyer would be lenient with her if she put her best foot forward and vowed never to raise her voice in public ever again.

Nay, that wouldn't work, Stephanie thought deflatedly. She had made that vow once before and now she had broken her promise. It was best not to remind her father that this was her second offense.

With all the dignity she could muster, Stephanie swept into the dining room, flashing her most disarming smile. "Good morning, everyone!" she gushed cheerfully. "I'm sorry I'm late, but I—"

Her voice failed her when she glanced around the table to see none other than Coleman Douglas Hollister the Third sitting in *her* chair. Lord-a-mercy, he was the man who had seduced her? This was Natalie's suitor? And had he also tattled to her father about the ducking he had witnessed in Mystic? That miserable rat! Oh, how she would love to clamp her fingers around his neck and shake him until his teeth rattled.

Shock, dismay, and outrage all fought to gain control of her tongue. My, but she had certainly misjudged this *supposed* gentleman, she thought furiously. Stephanie had received contrasting vibrations after her first encounter with Cole. And now she knew for certain this man was a walking paradox. Indeed, he was a wolf in sheep's wool and she could think of nothing more spitefully satisfying than to have that rascal sheared!

Stephanie would have felt hollow consolation, at least, if she could have read Cole's mind at that particular moment. She thought *she* was suffering the shock of a lifetime? Hell, she didn't know what *shock* was! Cole very nearly fell through his chair when his feisty leprechaun sailed into the room like a misdirected cyclone.

This dazzling beauty was Dyer's misfit daughter, the one who was followed by an unseemly reputation? This was the second startling revelation Cole had faced in the short course of the morning. He had awakened, feeling remorse over what he had done. For a few minutes he had even sought to place the blame for what had happened on the enticing female who had stripped naked in the middle of his room and then had placed her hand in the middle of his bare lap. But when he discovered the telltale stains on the sheets, he seriously contemplated having himself blindfolded and shot. He had remained frozen on the edge of his bed, unable to breathe for a full two minutes, staring bug-eyed at the incriminating evidence of what he had done. He had made an awkward situation even worse than it already was!

A virgin, for God's sake! He had deflowered an innocent woman and he felt as tall as a table leg. At the time, he hadn't been certain who the woman might have been, but considering the warnings the Wakefields had extended to him, Cole deduced that it was Dyer's youngest, undoubtedly promiscuous, daughter.

His startling discovery, on the morning after, had

101

shot that theory all to hell. Cole hadn't known what to believe until Stephanie swept into the dining room to untangle his muddled speculations. He was left wondering what price he would be expected to pay for a night that had been shrouded with gross misconceptions and shadowed with misleading circumstances that had flung both of them into the most embarrassing situation ever to occur at the breakfast table.

It was no wonder his mystery lover had left the impression of naive innocence in lovemaking. She had been totally ignorant of men until Cole seduced her in a moment of passionate insanity. Lord, he felt like a long-eared, cross-eyed mule! And judging by the way the youngest Wakefield was glaring at him, she totally agreed with his estimation.

Cole had never felt so uncomfortable in all his life, but he was doing his damnedest not to show it. He could only pray that this comely heiress was willing to protect their secret. If he had known it was only one of the many secrets Stephanie was forced to keep, he wouldn't have been sitting on pins and needles.

Although Cole was mentally kicking himself, he gallantly rose from his chair and pasted on a greeting smile. "Your youngest daughter, I presume, Dyer?"

His voice was calm, his manner impeccable. Only the flicker of his ebony eyes alerted Stephanie that he was masking turbulent emotions behind his charming smile.

Calling upon her acting abilities, Stephanie extended her hand and blessed Cole with a saucy grin, the kind her family anticipated from her. But the truth of the matter was she would have preferred to crash through the nearest wall to avoid further physical contact, no matter how brief or harmless it might have been. Touching Cole's warm, steady hand was like grasping live coals.

"My name is Stephanie." As if he didn't already know her name and everything else there was to know about her. The lusty scoundrel! "Whom do I have the pleasure and honor of addressing?" she questioned sweetly.

Cole slid the rest of the Wakefields a discreet glance. He almost burst out laughing when he noticed their apprehensive expressions. They were all sitting like statues in a museum. They were holding their breath and their expressions were frozen on their faces. Were they expecting this feisty renegade to make some outrageous gesture or remark that would leave them wishing they could crawl under the table?

With a flair of chivalry, Cole dropped into a sweeping bow. He took Stephanie's hand to press a light kiss to her wrist. "Coleman Douglas Hollister the Third at your service, Miss Wakefield. It seems Dyer and Eileen have graced this world with three of the loveliest females I have ever chanced to meet."

Stephanie was silently speculating where to kick the gallant galloot. It was what he deserved after what he had done. But this was no time for a temper tantrum. Her last one had cost her a public ducking!

"Why, thank you, Mr. Hollister," she purred in a sugary voice. Gracefully, she indicated the chair he had evacuated. "Do sit down and finish your breakfast." . . . Before I succumb to the overwhelming temptation of smearing your face in your plate, she thought, but somehow refrained from giving the wicked remark to tongue.

Portraying the perfect gentleman, Cole followed Stephanie to her chair and assisted her into her seat before resuming his place. "I was just telling your family how well I slept last night," Cole remarked, only to hear Stephanie choke on her tea. He knew he shouldn't be pestering her like this, but the devil was

103

sitting on his shoulder, encouraging him. "I awoke relaxed and refreshed for the first time in two months."

Of course, he did, Stephanie silently seethed. The rogue had appeased his animal lust.

"There must be something in this Connecticut air that makes a man feel born anew," Cole went on to say in a casual tone. "I trust you slept as well."

The comment was directed at Stephanie, who had selected a vulnerable spot to clobber him and who was, at that very moment forming a mental picture of how Cole would look with his nose smashed against the left side of his face.

Her green eyes fairly sparkled with deviltry. "Actually, I felt as if I had slept under a log, Mr. Hollister," she insulted through her sticky sweet smile. "Indeed, I think it was one of the worst nights of my life."

Cole winced as if he had been snake-bit but he recovered nicely. A compassionate expression mellowed his rugged features. "I am grieved to hear that," he replied with mock sincerity. "Perhaps tonight will be better."

If he was subtly suggesting there would be a repeat performance, he was utterly mad! Now that she knew there was a lecher in her hideaway, she would garb herself in a suit of armor before she breezed through the guest suite to perform her nocturnal prowling. He wouldn't stop her from coming and going as she pleased, Stephanie mused defiantly. But she would damned well ensure last night never happened again. Now that she knew there was a lion reclining in the alcove bed, she would take a wide berth around him.

Silence settled over the room like a choking fog when Stephanie's gaze landed on Dyer. He looked like an overinflated balloon that was about to pop.

"We missed you at supper last night, Stephie," he commented in a strained voice. "Would you care to explain why you did not return home at a reasonable hour?"

Nay, not particularly, Stephanie thought as she squirmed beneath her father's pointed stare. As a matter of fact, she would have preferred to crawl into a hole and pull it in after her.

Natalie shot her youngest sister an apprehensive glance and then dived into her breakfast as if she hadn't eaten in days. Wasn't that just like Nattie, Stephanie thought bitterly. At the first sign of trouble, Nattie fed her fears. Now Stephanie would be forced to fumble with some flimsy excuse to protect the both of them.

"I was visiting a sick friend," she informed her father. "We feared she was about to succumb to the grippe."

"What caused this *dear* friend's affliction?" Dyer smirked, a taunting edge on his voice. "Was she suffering exposure from the elements? A dowsing rain, perhaps?"

So he did know about the ducking pond, Stephanie surmised. Her eyes darted accusingly to Cole. Had he told her father? That scoundrel. He was giving her dozens of reasons to hate him.

"How did you guess, Papa?" Stephanie questioned with such a cherubic smile that she should have sprouted wings and a halo—tattered and rusted though they would have been.

"Mr. Hollister has enlisted Papa's talents in building a new schooner," Adeline interjected, applying the skillful technique of smoothing over prickly subjects. She had learned the tactic from her mother. There were times when diplomacy and distraction were warranted and Addie could feel the tension between her father and her younger sister mounting. "Cole will be our house guest for the next few weeks."

A few weeks? Stephanie's spirits scraped rock bottom. How was she to tolerate this man's presence while she sneaked in and out of the house for her late-night rendezvous with Wesley, as well as her other secret activities. Aye, a few days she could handle. But a few weeks? It would seem an eternity with that starved shark swimming around in her hideaway.

Stephanie managed to fumble through her meal without tearing out her hair. Cole and Dyer discussed the economic stress and political and social unrest that was hounding the colonies, the outrageous Stamp Act, and the hampering Navigation Acts. Although Stephanie was interested in the depressed condition of the colonies and their present difficulties with the Mother Country, she was in no mood to discuss national disaster when she was involved with private catastrophe.

Just as Stephanie gathered her feet to make her exit, Dyer motioned for her to remain where she was. She had seen the look of impending doom on numerous occasions and Dyer was wearing the expression. It was obvious Dyer's breakfast meal hadn't totally satisfied his appetite. He was looking to chew on his youngest daughter.

"Natalie, why don't you keep Cole company while Stephie and I have a private chat," Dyer insisted, smiling through gritted teeth.

"Aye, 'tis an excellent idea," Eileen chimed in enthusiastically. "Adeline can accompany them for a morning stroll. I'm sure she would also enjoy Cole's company."

Dyer's brows straightened over his cobalt blue eyes. "Adeline should be helping you make the preparations for our annual ball." His head swiveled around to land on Cole. "Perhaps you would be so kind as to escort Natalie to the party. I know she would be pleased."

Eileen's upper lip stiffened. "*Adeline* would be flattered to accompany Mr. Hollister," she protested.

The look on Addie's face indicated that she would be nothing of the kind. "But Mother, I . . ." Adeline clamped her mouth shut when Eileen gave her a discreet kick on the shin.

Dyer was looking more agitated by the second. It was obvious that he wanted to throw Natalie and Cole together every possible moment. It was also apparent to Stephanie that her mother thought Addie to be more Cole's type. But at the moment, Stephanie was satisfied to let her parents squabble over which of her sisters was best suited for the wealthy captain and plantation owner. It was a pity Dyer didn't know the truth about Natalie. Then he wouldn't have found himself in a useless power struggle with his wife.

Stephanie took advantage of the situation. While Dyer and Eileen were glaring at each other, Stephanie sprang from her chair and sped around the table to grasp Cole's hand, even when she was more inclined to strangle the rascal.

"While the two of you are debating who should escort Mr. Hollister to the social affair of the season, I will show him our prized stallions." Stephanie's eyes locked with those amused pools of ebony. "You do like thoroughbreds, don't you, Mr. Hollister?"

"Why, of course." Cole unfolded himself from his chair to tower over Stephanie.

"Have you ever been trampled by one?" Stephanie questioned out of the blue.

A muddled frown plowed Cole's brow as he glanced down into that bewitching face that was dominated by green eyes. "Nay, I can't say that I have."

"Well, perhaps today will be your lucky day," she countered in what sounded like a teasing remark to everyone else in the room. But Cole knew she wasn't kidding. The wicked glint in her eyes assured Cole that nothing would have made Stephanie happier than to see him lying face down with dozens of hoof prints on his back.

"What a delightful sense of humor you have," Cole declared on a forced chuckle. "Give my compliments to the cook." He directed the comment to Dyer as Stephanie clenched her fingernails into his forearm and led him away like the mule he believed he resembled.

The moment they were out of sight, Stephanie dropped his hand as if she had been scorched. Touching him triggered all those unnerving sensations that Stephanie was in no mood to deal with, not when she was angry, mortified, and brimming with unsatisfied vengeance. She flew toward Cole like a disturbed hornet. The sting of her slap caused a bright red welt to swell up on Cole's left cheek. But Cole didn't even flinch. He knew what was coming and he had prepared himself for his just and expedient punishment.

After acquainting Cole with her look of disgust, Stephanie presented her back and drew herself up to proud stature. In stiff, precise steps, Stephanie marched toward the barn, refusing to acknowledge Cole's presence.

"Where do we go from here?" Cole called after her while he inspected his swollen cheek with his fingertips.

"*You* can go to hell," Stephanie threw over her shoulder, along with a glare that was meant to slice Cole into bite-sized servings.

"Aren't we going to discuss our problem?" Cole questioned as he fell into step behind her.

"We have no problem," Stephanie snapped tartly. "I slapped you because I felt like it. I need no other reason. As far as I'm concerned, last night didn't happen."

Amusement bubbled to the surface in a smile. My, this minx was all fire, just as he had suspected. Cole quickened his step to walk beside her. "Aye, I know," he assured her, his voice rattling with barely suppressed laughter. "If you will recall, *I* was there when it didn't happen."

"You took unfair advantage," Stephanie spewed, attempting to control her temper and failing miserably. "You should have announced yourself!"

"And miss a floor-show that exceeded my wildest dreams?" Cole chuckled, bursting into a roguish grin.

Stephanie's face turned seven shades of red. She opened her mouth to interject a snide remark, but nothing came out. She had swallowed her Adam's apple.

Cole took a step closer and his shadow eclipsed the sun that had been beaming down on Stephanie's crimson-tinted features. "And how could I even have been certain you hadn't planned that entire scene to seduce me?" he questioned frankly. "It's for damned sure *I* didn't strip naked and climb into bed with *you*. It was you who appeared in my room, offering an invitation no man could resist. I merely accepted it."

Cole didn't think Stephanie's face could turn a deeper shade of red, but it did! "You thought I was a whore who spread herself beneath any man, just for the hell of it?" she spewed in outrage.

"I didn't say that," Cole hastily defended himself. Actually, the thought had crossed his mind the previous night.

"Nay, but you were thinking it," Stephanie accused with a condemning glare. "I *saw* you thinking it."

Her comment brought rise to a smile, one Cole hurriedly suppressed. He peered straight into those flaming green eyes, straining to maintain a deadpan expression. "To be perfectly honest, Stephanie, I don't know exactly what to make you," he confessed. "Not last night *or* this morning."

"Well, I know exactly what to make you, Cole

Hollister," she declared heatedly. "You are a lusty scoundrel. You may have fooled my father into thinking you are an honorable man, but I know different. I'm sure he would be appalled to know what you did." Hollow laughter filled the space between them. "Now, isn't that the crowning glory," she sniffed sardonically. "My father toted you home to court my sister and 'twas the wrong fly who stumbled into the web of the cannibalistic spider." Her eyes were oozing venom. "I hope you are proud of yourself, Mr. Tarantula."

"Nay, I can't say that I am. But you have my permission to divulge every sordid detail to Dyer," Cole graciously consented. "But do not forget to explain what *you* were doing in my bedroom suite and who you met during your midnight rendezvous."

Stephanie cursed her carelessness. She had taken the wrong approach and she knew it. Threatening Cole was not the solution. She needed his promise of silence.

Heaving a frustrated sigh, Stephanie peered up into those fathomless brown pools that were notorious for entrancing her. "I suppose I should thank you for coming to my rescue a second time. This morning could have been very uncomfortable for both of us."

A wry smile traced Cole's lips as he studied Stephanie's bewitching features. "I have been repaid more than tenfold for my silence, Steph."

His voice was like rich velvet. It sent a flock of goose bumps gliding across her skin. Resolving not to be influenced by his seductive charm, Stephanie squared her shoulders and stared up at the towering mass of brawn and muscle.

"I think we should drop the suggestive innuendos if we are to openly discuss the matter," Stephanie stated crisply. "What *didn't* happen last night will never happen again. You presumed that I am in the habit of falling into bed with every man who takes up temporary residence in our guest suite. But I assure you, nothing could be further from the truth. I am hounded by a less than respectable reputation, but I have *not* acquired it because of promiscuity."

"I realized that a little late," Cole murmured apologetically.

Stephanie blushed up to the roots of her red-gold hair. Usually, she was quick with rejoinders to any and all kinds of remarks. But Cole had the knack of leaving her fumbling for a suitable reply. It took her a moment to formulate her comment. "'Tis a pity you are not one of those experts who can recognize innocence at a glance," she sniped. "It would have saved me considerable distress."

"Where did you go last night while you were masquerading in your dark cape?" he questioned, ignoring Stephanie's scathing glare.

She met his penetrating gaze, one that bore into her to seek out the truth. "I went to meet my. . . ." Stephanie averted her eyes to stare at the herd of thoroughbreds that was grazing in the pasture. ". . . to meet a friend," she finished cryptically.

"Male or female?" Cole prodded, hating himself for wanting to know.

Stephanie puffed up with indignation. Her chin protruded in a manner Cole had come to know all too well. Damn him! Did he think he could claim squatter's rights after their tête-à-tête? The day she felt obliged to answer to him would be the same day hell was capped with glaciers!

"I hardly think I owe you an explanation just because we slept together," she bit off.

"A man," Cole decided, judging by her curt reply. Unable to resist, Cole reached out to bring her chin down a notch. "But I know for certain that he doesn't

111

know you as well as I do. After what happened, do you wish for me to marry you to salvage your pride and make a respectable woman out of you?" he had the nerve to ask.

Stephanie's ivory skin again took on a crimson hue, and Cole realized that her fiery temper was dangerously close to bursting into flames. "You flatter yourself to think I would want to marry you under any circumstance," she countered, her green eyes flashing. "I have little use for men who consider women objects of pleasure. And if I had been in the mood to concoct a reasonable explanation about your sudden demise, I would have shot you while you slept last night. But fortunately for you, I had pressing matters on my mind!"

"Such as the argument that landed you in the ducking pond?" Cole lifted a heavy brow, hoping he had made Stephanie angry enough to blurt out the details of the incident that was gnawing at his curiosity.

Stephanie turned her back on him, ignoring him and his infuriating presence. She refused to be coerced into divulging information that was none of his business.

"Did your late-night rendezvous have something to do with yesterday's fiasco or was the man just one of your many lovesick admirers?" he pried, needling her and loving every minute of it.

"You really shouldn't poke your nose in places it doesn't belong," Stephanie warned through clenched teeth.

"Have you accepted a date to the upcoming ball or do you prefer to meet your less-than-respectable beaux in the privacy of darkness?" Cole teased mercilessly.

Stephanie rolled her eyes skyward, requesting divine patience. Didn't she have enough worries without Coleman Douglas Hollister the Third pestering her? The man seemed to derive excessive pleasure in mocking her. Indeed, he appeared to thrive on it. Cole had loosened up considerably since she had met the stately aristocrat at the ducking pond. He had projected the image of a sophisticate, but deep down inside he was ornery as hell!

"Most men shy away of me because of my sordid reputation." Wheeling around, Stephanie gritted out the words through a stiff smile. "And nay, I do not have a date to the ball. Wall flowers and wild flowers usually don't." Her greeen eyes raked him with taunting criticism. "And why is it that a man of your station in life is still without a wife? Must you wander about, seeking out fathers who are desperate to marry off their spinster daughters? Is it because you have a boorish personality? Is it because the only way you can acquire a wife is to contact her father? Or is it, instead, your policy to drag unsuspecting females into your lair and use them for your lusty pleasures?"

"Touché, m'lady," Cole chuckled good-naturedly. He hadn't taken offense to the insults. After all, he had it coming. And he truly delighted in fencing words with this quick-witted, hot-tempered minx. It was like sharpening one's mental weapons. Stephanie gave as good as she got. "The truth is, I am recovering from a broken engagement. My sojourn in Mystic has proved to be an effective cure. Thanks to your antics, I have little time to lament over losing Rachel Garret."

Stephanie was caught off guard by his honesty. It took a special breed of man to confess that his pride had been wounded and that he had been jilted by a woman. "Did you love her?" she questioned candidly.

Cole half turned to admire Dyer's prize steeds. "I thought I did." He sighed. "But then I realized all we had in common was that we both thought she was someone special."

"She must have been extraordinary for you to

become so enamored with her," Stephanie heard herself say and then wondered why she had offered that offhand compliment.

His thick brows jackknifed in surprise. "Did my ears deceive me? Did you just dish out a compliment, m'lady?" he mocked lightly.

A sparkling smile cut deep dimples in her cheeks and Cole melted in his boots. "I suppose I did, although I had not intended to let it slip out. You are a strikingly handsome man, Coleman Douglas Hollister the Third. And you are a very complex man, even though you wish others to believe they can read you like an open book," she added philosophically. A pensive frown captured her features as she gave Cole the once-over—twice. "Why is that, Cole?"

Her childlike intuitiveness prompted her to pose the question. She possessed a rare gift that permitted her to see into the depths that most people overlooked. And Stephanie was right about him. His elegant clothes and polished manners could be deceptive. There were two very different individuals lurking beneath the layers of linen and velvet. Stephanie had an uncanny knack of drawing out the uncivilized side of him, the side that belonged in the pages of his past.

Like a moth drawn to a flame, knowing he might get his wings scorched, Cole approached the green-eyed pixie. Slowly, he reached out to cup her chin in his hand. The moment his gaze locked with hers, the smoldering memories of the previous night burst into flame. Damn his firm resolve, to hell with his stern lectures on why he should take a wide berth around this feisty vixen. She instilled a gnawing hunger in him that defied common sense.

Cole studied her as if she were the meal he was about to consume. He was lost to the irrational craving, the insane longing to taste her sweet mouth, to lose himself

114

in the arousing scent of her that still clung to him. She was the most exciting, most fascinating bundle of femininity he had ever encountered. Her skin was like peaches and cream, the essence of softness. Her hair shone like exquisite tendrils of silk threads. Its strands weren't yellow or blond or auburn, but pure red-gold. Her flawless face curved from elegant cheeks to those wide, dazzling, jewel-studded eyes that flickered with living fire.

He was bewitched by the sight of her, bedeviled by the tantalizing memories they had shared in passion's paradise. Again, Cole found himself wanting things he knew he shouldn't have. But damn if he could resist the temptation.

"Steph, you are like a ray of sunshine. You can warm a man's heart, even when he is determined to remain untouched by your impish ways." An appreciative smile grazed his lips as he sketched her beguiling features with his index finger. "Although you deny it, I think there are scores of secret admirers hereabout who are afraid they are not men enough to please a woman with your undaunted spirit."

Soft, irresistible laughter rumbled in his chest as he closed the narrow distance between them. "Their cowardice is their misfortune. They don't know you the way I know you. They don't realize that touching you is like a foretaste of recklessness, a daring they have not permitted themselves to enjoy. I see in you all the things I sacrificed, a part of me that time and necessity has tamed." His raven head came deliberately toward hers and his warm breath caressed her flushed cheek. "Give me back those long lost memories, little leprechaun. You are the medium who can reopen the doors of my past . . ."

His dark, hypnotic eyes were intently focused on her lips. He was studying them as if he was fascinated by

115

their heart-shaped curve. As he drew nearer, filling up her world, Stephanie's heart collided with her ribs. Breathing was an effort and thinking was virtually impossible.

His mouth was poised above hers. His breath was warm against her already flushed cheek. "I haven't forgotten what it's like to kiss you . . ." Seduction seeped from his voice, causing Stephanie to tremble uncontrollably. His full lips skimmed hers like a bee courting a fragrant flower. "You leave fires to burn. I won't apologize for what happened last night. It was spontaneous, and tantalizing, and habit forming . . ."

It was difficult to untangle her gaze from his when he was luring her into his mystical spell. Stephanie knew he meant to kiss her. He had made no bones about what he wanted. She resented her illogical attraction to Cole and she knew she should refuse him, but her body simply would not remove itself from his close proximity. Stephanie was frozen to the spot until his sensuous lips took possession of hers, melting her into a puddle of unwanted desire.

Oh, why did this powerful, sensual man have to turn up at the most unexpected moments? Stephanie didn't want to encounter the dark, compelling side of Cole's personality just now. She was too vulnerable and the memories of their night together were too fresh, too new to dismiss. Confound it, why did this man have to stumble into her life and turn her inside out? There was dear Wesley to consider . . . and poor Natalie. There was her father to deal with, and Brice . . . what was his last name? Suddenly Stephanie couldn't remember *her* name, much less Brice's. Cole's overpowering gentleness was tying her thoughts in Gordian knots.

Damnit, she shouldn't be doing this! She shouldn't be feeling this forbidden pleasure seeping through her veins. Last night was shameful enough! What if Dyer found them in the clench? He would be positively furious. But Dyer didn't know how difficult it was to resist a man like Cole Hollister. This rogue could take a woman and turn her into senseless mush.

Stephanie found herself crowded between the corral fence and Cole's muscular body. He was pressing familiarly against her, reminding her of the intimacy they had shared in the shadows of darkness, rekindling fires that should have burned themselves out hours ago. His adventurous hand slid along her hip, holding her to him, making her body sizzle in response.

Twisting away from his scorching kiss, Stephanie struggled to inhale a normal breath and overcome her brief lapse of self-control. "Please don't do that again," she whispered raggedly. "I don't want to remember. . . ."

"But you do remember what it was like between us," he murmured, his voice heavy with unfulfilled passion. "There will be other nights, sweet nymph. Sparks fly when we touch. And when the forbidden memories of what we shared begin to burn in your mind, you will come back to me . . ."

"Nay, I cannot!" Stephanie frantically protested. "It cannot happen again, I'm not fair game for your misdirected instincts of conquering hearts. I'm—"

Another searing kiss stole her breath and sent her heart thundering off like a runaway stallion. She didn't want to enjoy his embrace, but she did. God help her she did! It was like taking a sip from a magical fountain and deluding herself by thinking she could be satisfied with one drop. The potion was addictive. As much as Stephanie hated to admit it, she had kissed him back, hungry for the intoxicating taste of him!

Cole could not understand why he was making such outrageous demands on this feisty spitfire. He should have turned tail and run as far away as his legs would carry him. But Cole was compelled to stay. He was jealous of the other man she had sought out in the darkness, curious to know what he meant to her. How could she return Cole's fiery kiss with such reckless abandon if her heart belonged to another man? And why were either one of them permitting this to happen when they could be caught red-handed? Neither of them seemed to have a lick of sense!

When they came up for breath, Stephanie half collapsed against the fence, staring wide-eyed at the man who had the ability to turn her wrong side out. The sight of her sister strolling toward them was Stephanie's salvation. She drew herself up and struggled to recompose herself.

Stephanie indicated the comely brunette who was floating down the hill toward them. "It seems Papa won the debate," she got out without her voice cracking completely.

While Natalie was approaching in her graceful gait, Cole's probing gaze remained fixed on Stephanie's kiss-swollen lips. "There will be another time and place for us. I fear we have only just begun to realize how hot the fire can burn. . . ."

There weren't going to be any more fires! Stephanie promised herself faithfully. She had other obligations. "I fear you are mistaken, Coleman Douglas Hollister the Third," she said in a stilted tone. "There are no sparks and no fires. Nothing happened, not today, not last night, not tomorrow, never."

Before Cole could argue against her firm denial of what did or didn't happen, Natalie ambled up beside them. "Papa wants a word with you, Stephie," she announced, flinging her sister a sympathetic glance.

"One word?" Stephanie laughed mirthlessly as she picked up the front of her skirt and aimed herself toward the manor. "I rather think I will receive an

118

earful." Suddenly, she did an about-face to peer into Cole's carefully guarded expression. "By the way, do I have you to thank for tattling to my father?"

Cole gave his dark head a negative shake. "I'm sure you would like to hold that against me, but whatever your father knows he found out all by himself. I am not a man who kisses and tells, so to speak."

His underlying meaning caused Stephanie to go rigid with irritation. He could have talked all day without saying that! What was he trying to do, put ideas in Natalie's head, leave her thinking there was something going on between him and Stephanie? Damn that man! She had barely known him twenty-four hours and he was already giving her fits!

As Stephanie hastened toward the house, Natalie relaxed for the first time since she had been in Cole's presence. She no longer felt the need to protect herself from the dashing rake. Natalie hadn't been surprised to see that Cole had become fascinated with her youngest sister. There weren't many men who weren't.

To hear Stephanie talk, one would think men were afraid to come near her because she was forever pulling some outlandish shenanigan. But nothing could have been farther from the truth. Men were magnetically drawn to Stephie because she was so full of lively spirit. She delighted in shocking people out of their mundane existences. She had been born with a natural vitality that had a stimulating, refreshing effect on people. No one ever knew what Stephie was going to say or do next. It kept her acquaintances on their toes. Her vivaciousness was contagious and Stephie had a dramatic effect on everyone who came in contact with her. And unless Natalie missed her guess (and she doubted that she had), the gallant Coleman Douglas Hollister the Third was feeling the effects of Stephie's devastating attraction and lively charm.

It wasn't the first time one of Dyer's acquaintances had found himself helplessly drawn to Stephanie, Natalie mused as she and Cole strolled the grounds. When Dyer realized the man he had toted home to court Natalie was spending too much time with his youngest daughter, he sent him on his way. Even though Dyer seemed overly fond of Cole, Natalie wondered how long he would last. If the past was any indication, Dyer would send Cole packing the moment he realized Stephanie was the object of Cole's attention. Natalie hoped it would be soon. These cat-and-mouse games with the suitors her father dragged home were wearing on her already frazzled nerves!

Chapter 7

The instant Stephanie sailed into the study, Dyer shot an arm toward the chair, silently demanding that his ornery daughter park herself in it. "Well, are you going to tell me what that public ducking was all about or do I have to march to the magistrate's office for a full explanation?" he questioned gruffly.

Nonchalantly, Stephanie settled her full skirts about her. If Dyer hadn't know better, he would have attested that they were involved in a casual conversation about the weather. Stephanie was behaving as if she didn't have a worry in the world.

"'Twas nothing really, Papa," Stephanie said lackadaisically. "Brice Reynolds insulted me and I yielded to the temptation of retaliating with a few emphatic remarks about his lack of character. Being the weasel he is, he herded me to the magistrate and rattled off *his* rendition of the incident. Now that Parliament has suspended colonial trials by jury, I didn't have a snowball's chance in—"

"Stephanie!" Dyer barked sharply. His graying brows narrowed over his blue eyes as he glared daggers at his daughter. "And was Brice provoked into this name-calling because of your notorious reputation?"

Stephanie bit her bottom lip. She would have preferred to tell her father the whole truth. He had so little faith in her already. This incident wasn't going to sweeten their relationship. But she had promised to protect the secret, and Natalie had begged her not to divulge her name.

"Aye, Brice made several crude references about my less than respectable reputation," she lied to protect everyone but herself. "My legendary temper got the best of me, as usual. I thought it ridiculous for the pot to be calling the kettle black."

"I see." Dyer wilted back in his chair and shook his head in dismay. "What am I to do with you? Your antics shame the entire family, as well as yourself. Last month it was your outrageous horse race with Richard Stover that had gossip tongues wagging. You garbed yourself in men's clothes and humiliated Richard by defeating him while he was astride his swiftest mount!"

She couldn't tell her father what that race was really about, not without dragging a certain member of the family into trouble. "I was riding your fastest horse," she parried with a reckless shrug. "Did you want me to lose, just because I was racing against a man?"

"You shouldn't have been racing in the first place!" Dyer bellowed. "I had not given you permission to mount my prize steed."

Stephanie winced when his booming voice ricocheted off the walls to come at her from all directions.

"And it was only a fortnight ago that you shoved one of your beaux in the mud right in front of the village square," Dyer reminded her crisply. "There are more respectable ways to handle yourself, young lady."

Stephanie couldn't divulge the reason push had come to shove in that instance either, not without embarrassing another member of the family. And so she set about to rattle Dyer. "Would you have

122

preferred that I accept his proposition, Papa?" she inquired, raising a perfectly arched brow. "He wanted me to sleep with him."

Her remark knocked Dyer to his knees, just as Stephanie hoped it would. "Nay, of course not. But you could have rejected him in a more delicate manner."

"The rogue had difficulty in understanding what *nay* meant," she explained. "After my third attempt to demur, I found it necessary to gain his undivided attention so there would be no future misunderstandings about whether I intended to accept or reject his sordid offer."

Stephanie had given the partial truth. It was the best she could do without involving anyone else. The scoundrel had tried to taunt her into submitting to him by making crude remarks about Natalie. If Dyer had known what the miserable rat had said about his pride and joy, he would have applauded Stephanie for shoving that two-legged rodent in the mud!

Dyer combed his fingers through his hair and breathed an exasperated sigh. "Will there ever be an end to these shenanigans? Your mother and I have failed miserably in your upbringing and we are constantly being punished for our mistakes."

The long-harbored bitterness rose like cream on fresh milk. "Frankly, I don't remember your being there for me at all, Papa," she told him honestly. "You were too busy grooming Nattie and Mother was buzzing about, preparing Addie for her place in society. I craved your and Mother's attention. And for a time I was jealous of my sisters. I swore the world revolved around them and their whims. But I have outgrown my envy and now I wouldn't exchange places with either of them."

Dyer couldn't very well argue the point. He and Eileen were guilty as charged. They had neglected

Stephanie, thinking she would have her own special time. But then suddenly she was all grown up. She had become rambunctious and independent and Dyer had difficulty managing her. In fact, he couldn't manage her at all!

Forcing the semblance of a smile, Stephanie rose to her feet. "If there is nothing else, I will be on my way. I should hate to interrupt your busy schedule."

"There is one more thing," Dyer said quietly. When Stephanie half turned, Dyer did not have the courage to meet her quizzical stare. "I would very much like to see Natalie wed to Cole Hollister. I am not blind. I saw the way his eyes strayed to you at the breakfast table. I insist that you discourage Cole and allow Nattie a chance at him. He would be very good for her." Uneasily, Dyer squirmed in his seat, refusing to make visual contact with Stephanie. "I would appreciate it if you would accompany Cole and Nattie on a fox hunt, or some type of outing this afternoon. It will be the perfect opportunity for you to make it known that you have no interest in Cole and it will be the perfect excuse for Nattie and Cole to spend the afternoon together. Perhaps Nattie will begin to warm to the man I would like to see her marry."

Stephanie waited until her father finally raised his eyes to meet her probing stare. "Sometime, Papa, you should ask Nattie what *she* would like," Stephanie couldn't help but say. "Then perhaps you wouldn't exhaust yourself by toting home everything in tailor-made breeches. It seems to me that you are intolerant of *her* preferences."

"And what *exactly* is that supposed to mean?" Dyer queried, his tone crackling with mounting irritation.

"It means that Nattie is not your puppet," Stephanie said boldly. "You moan and complain about the loss of colonial independence and you protest England's strict

124

rules and regulations over us. And yet you grant Natalie very little freedom of choice." A faint smile graced her lips and then evaporated. "I paid a high price for my independence—my parents' attention and affection. Don't make Nattie and Addie alienate themselves from you to acquire theirs."

The moment Stephanie sped out the door she veered toward the stoop to inhale a steadying breath. A sentimental mist of tears clouded her eyes, but she forced it to dissipate. This was no time for her to lament the lost years of childhood, the loneliness of never truly being loved. She had survived and she was far better off than her sisters, she consoled herself. They had been smothered with affection and now they were terribly overprotected.

Who did Nattie and Addie run to when they faced frustrating dilemmas? Who did they turn to in request of assistance? Stephanie expelled her breath and got herself in hand. Both of her older sisters depended on her strength and she had vowed to protect every secret they had brought to her for safekeeping.

Mulling over that thought, Stephanie stepped off the porch and aimed herself toward the stable. It was time she had a private conversation with Elizabeth Marrow, the new serving maid at the Reynolds Inn who might soon become Wesley's second wife . . . even while the first one was still alive and well and living on a sprawling estate on the outskirts of Mystic.

Her gaze strayed to the couple who was absently strolling the pasture. Her heart lurched with a riptide of emotions. Cole had paused to stare at her from a distance. Stephanie could feel those dark, compelling eyes drilling into her, demanding things from her that she couldn't give.

Hastily, Stephanie walked into the barn to fetch her mount. She didn't want to think about Cole Hollister.

The mere sight of him assaulted her with too many conflicting sensations. He was a stranger who knew her far better than he should have. But Stephanie was determined not to allow their tryst to upset her. She had a commitment to Wesley. Cole's interference in her life would only brew more trouble. No one would ever know what had transpired between her and Cole the previous night, she vowed fiercely. She would bear the burden of another carefully guarded secret.

Besides, what did Cole care about her? She was no more than an evening diversion. Stephanie reminded herself bitterly as she pulled into the saddle. Cole had only wanted a woman's body to satisfy his sexual cravings. Coleman Douglas Hollister had no interest in the feelings and emotions that motivated her. And for that and dozens of other reasons, Stephanie decided to avoid contact with Cole. The less she saw of that strikingly attractive rake with the charismatic smile, the better off she would be.

Cole may have taken up residence in her private hideaway, but he was not going to prevent her from venturing in and out of the house during the witching hour. But the next time she dared to sail through the guest suite, she would not linger to change clothes. She would simply take the garments with her and find some suitable place to wiggle into her breeches and shirt. She would seek out a quiet, secluded niche that would protect her from those spellbinding ebony eyes that were already beginning to haunt her!

A mischievious smile bordered Stephanie's lips as she galloped toward Mystic. Her father had insisted that she take the opportunity to discourage Cole and thrust him into Natalie's arms. As if any of the Wakefield sisters wanted that stuffed shirt, Stephanie smirked. Aye, she would discourage Cole Hollister all right, she promised herself on a wicked laugh. When she returned from her errand she would introduce Cole to a fox hunt—Connecticut style. It would be one event he would not soon forget.

Indeed, the afternoon romp might just take some of the starch out of that impeccably dressed aristocrat. By the time she finished with Cole, he would be wishing they had never laid eyes on each other. This was one favor Stephanie had no qualms about delivering to her father. Another impish chortle brust from her lips. She would comply to her father's wishes and ensure that Cole never wanted to come within ten feet of her . . . ever again.

Cole glanced around the congregation that had gathered to participate in the riding of the hounds. Although Natalie was hesitant about the afternoon activities, Dyer insisted that she and Cole join in the fun. And so they had garbed themselves in the proper attire and migrated to the stables.

Richard Stover, a tall, gangly young man, spent most of his time drooling over Addie instead of conversing with other members of the group. Cole was sure the gentleman would be unhorsed before the pack of hounds were unleashed to sniff out their quarry. Richard appeared to be so distracted by the shapely blonde that he didn't give a whit what became of the fox. But the man whom Cole found himself disliking on sight was Brandon Michaels, the swarthy rake Stephanie had dragged home with her when she returned from her mysterious venture into town.

An odd sense of envy trickled through Cole when he assessed Brandon. He was broad, muscular, and distractingly handsome. Not that Cole spent his spare time staring at *men,* but he could not help but size up his competition.

Competition? Cole snorted at the ridiculousness of that thought. What did he care that Steph had arrived with an escort in tow? And what did he care if Brandon's eyes caressed that high-spirited firebrand each time he glanced in Steph's direction?

Even with all of Cole's careful scrutiny, he couldn't decide whether Brandon was ~~Steph~~anie's special beau or merely one of the endless rabble of admirers who followed in that pixie's footsteps. Stephanie was her usual vibrant, bubbly self, but she didn't fawn over Brandon, at least not to the same degree that Brandon hung on her every word and devoured her with his eyes.

While the stable boys contained the howling hounds that were anxious for the hunt, Stephanie led the procession of family and guests into the barn to select their mounts. After she had pointed the other riders to their steeds, Stephanie glanced speculatively at Cole.

"Do you consider yourself a competent equestrian?" she questioned, sporting a taunting smile. "If not, I can place you on one of Papa's gentler animals."

Cole returned the intimidating grin. "I appreciate your concern, Steph, but I think I can manage to stay atop a horse at full gallop." He knew she was trying to humiliate him in front of the other guests. Stephanie had not fully satisfied her revenge after the circumstances surrounding their tête-à-tête. "I would prefer not to be seated on a plodding mare."

Dancing green eyes raked Cole from stem to stern, wishing she could find one noticeable flaw to criticize. She couldn't. "Very well, Coleman, we shall mount you on an animal with lightning speed, one with a spirited disposition, if that is what you wish."

Stephanie surveyed the remaining steeds and then

led a dappled gray gelding from the stall. Returning to Cole, she handed him the reins. Another ornery smile pursed her lips as she leaned close enough to covey a confidential comment. "Do try to stay out of my way. I would be most chagrined if our mounts collided and you were accidentally trampled."

"Your concern warms the cockles of my heart," Cole countered, his tone dripping sarcasm. He could tell by her expression and by the tone of her voice that, if he happened to take a tumble, Stephanie would have planned it with malice and forethought.

"Stephie?" Natalie eyed her sister warily. "You know the gelding—"

Stephanie held up her hand to stifle her sister's remark. "The gray will be a perfect mount for Coleman," she insisted. "Our house guest has assured me that he is quite capable of controlling the most contrary or high-spirited animal. I would not think to insult him by setting him atop a slow nag that would be bringing up the rear of the procession."

"But—" Natalie again tried to protest, only to be interrupted by Stephanie's impatient sniff.

"You fret too much, Nattie." Stephanie gathered her chestnut stallion's reins and sailed out of the stables, refusing to argue with her older sister.

When Nattie and Addie shot each other discreet glances, Cole frowned suspiciously. His dark eyes focused on the dappled gray gelding, wondering exactly what odd quirk the steed possessed. Cautiously, Cole eased onto the gelding's back, half expecting to be unseated before the hunt began. The steed threw his head and shifted uneasily beneath Cole's solid weight.

Apparently, the gray had an aversion to the bridle, Cole surmised. The horse resisted the commands of his

129

rider. If Cole touched the reins to the right side of the mount's neck, he sidestepped to the left. The steed seemed determined to prance off in the opposite direction that Cole wanted him to go. While the other riders proceeded forward, Cole and his gray gelding progressed—sideways. It was obvious to Cole that he would have his hands full trying to manage this contrary horse while Stephanie applauded herself for her ornery prank.

Fighting to suppress the smile that threatened to crack her solemn countenance, Stephanie tossed Cole a quick glance to determine how well he was managing. It irked her to note that Cole appeared unruffled by the high-stepping steed that was throwing his head at regular intervals. Cole merely gave the reins a firm tug, allowing the wayward gelding the option of taking the direction Cole demanded he go or risk having his head twisted off his shoulders. Since Cole was as strong as an ox, he won the battle of wills, much to Stephanie's chagrin.

"I see you are enjoying yourself at my expense," Cole observed as he eased the steed alongside Stephanie's chestnut stallion.

Although she resisted presenting him with a smug smile, her eyes flickered with wicked glee. "Surely even you will admit I owe you one," Stephanie countered.

His gaze flooded over the brown riding habit, making no attempt to disguise the fact that he knew exactly what the garment concealed. "I still think, my dear Steph, that the scales have weighed heavily in my favor. You may follow the policy of an eye for an eye. . . ." His dark, appraising eyes lingered on the full swell of her bosom, making Stephanie fidget under his piercing scrutiny. "But placing me on this stubborn creature can hardly equalize my advantage." His attention shifted to the bulky brute whom Stephanie had selected to accompany her on the hunt. "I hope you aren't trying to make me jealous, not when your escort has only muscles between his ears."

Stephanie stiffened in the saddle. "At least Brandon isn't an arrogant ass," she sniped as she gouged her stallion in the flanks.

When she thundered off to pursue the yelping hounds that had been set free, Cole tried to nudge his steed to a canter. He had deemed that the gelding's flaw was an objection to the bridle. But it became increasingly apparent that the steed had at least one other flaw. The gray refused to stretch into a gallop. He merely clambered along at a bone-jarring trot.

Determined not to lose his temper, Cole gritted his teeth and followed the field of riders. Since Natalie refused to press her steed, Cole found himself lagging along beside her. But all the while, his eyes were glued to Stephanie, who flew like the wind. It was obvious that she was an experienced rider, along with all her other unusual talents.

"I would guess your sister has spent more time in the saddle than in the drawing room learning to become proficient with a needle and thread," Cole smirked.

"Aye," Natalie admitted. "If Papa knew how many times Stephie has taken his prize thoroughbreds through the paces required on a race track—" She clamped her mouth shut, cursing her runaway tongue. "I shouldn't have divulged that information to you, sir. Please don't mention it to Papa. He would have Stephie's head."

"He would have to stand in line," Cole mumbled under his breath. Vengeful though he was, Cole was awed by the picture Steph presented as she raced across the meadow. Cole found himself intrigued, in awe.

Stephanie was a sight to behold as she moved in perfect rhythm with her powerful steed. "Your secret is safe, Natalie," Cole murmured, distracted. "I have no intention of embroiling your sister in any more trouble. She has enough of her own making."

Natalie smiled to herself as she watched Cole ogle Stephanie from afar. He was mesmerized by the feisty lass with shiny red-gold hair who was leading the pack. Cole wouldn't last long, Nattie decided. It wasn't difficult to tell where his preference lay. Stephie had bedazzled Cole and even his well-disciplined demeanor couldn't disguise his interest.

'Twas a pity Cole wasn't Stephanie's type, Natalie mused as she rode at a leisurely pace. But it really didn't matter. Dyer would never permit Cole to pursue his vivacious young daughter. It was only a matter of time before Dyer realized Cole had no interest in Natalie. Then Cole would be sent on his way and Natalie would not be forced on this stately aristocrat who barely realized she existed when Stephanie was stealing the limelight.

The sound of Stephanie's lighthearted laughter rang in Cole's ears as he watched her jump the hedge and bound after the pack of hounds. It was insane and ridiculous and Cole knew it. But he felt the odd compulsion to display *his* expertise. Digging his heels into the gray's ribs, Cole forced the steed into a faster clip, even under protest. It took several firm jabs in the flanks, but Cole finally managed to keep the gelding at a gallop. While Natalie took the cautious, longer route around the hedge, Cole aimed himself straight at it. He found himself willing Stephanie to twist in the saddle to watch him clear the obstacle without allowing his steed to break stride.

Cole was granted his wish. Stephanie glanced over

132

her shoulder just as Cole leaned against his mount in preparation of sailing over the tall hedge. This was to be Cole's finest hour. He could envision himself sprouting wings to soar over the obstacle with the precision and grace of an eagle in flight, just as Stephanie had. He would show that ornery minx that no obstacle was too great for him to overcome. Aye, it was childish, Cole told himself. He had no reason to attempt to impress that green-eyed leprechaun. But a man had his pride. . . .

Cole made a spectacular arc over the shrubs. However, the dappled gray did not. Too late, Cole realized his steed was not a satisfactory mount for an obstacle course in a fox hunt. The horse refused to jump unless he could see what was on the other side of the hedge before his hooves left the ground.

A surprised yelp exploded from Cole's lips when he found himself catapulted over the hedge without his mount beneath him. He was launched through the air, but not quite far enough to clear the hedge. His legs became entangled in the shrubs, permitting him to view the puddles left by the recent storms long before he plunged headlong into them. His landing was soft, but thoroughly humiliating.

Swearing a blue streak, Cole pushed up on all fours to wipe the mud from his eyes. Just as he was consoling himself by thinking the other riders were out of view, a beaming face appeared before him. It was Stephanie's and she looked delighted with herself for forcing Cole to endure this mortification. Damn her!

"Are you all right, Mr. Hollister?" she questioned. Her tone suggested that she really couldn't have cared less if he'd broken his neck.

Mustering what was left of his shattered dignity, Cole dragged himself upright and stomped out of the mud. When he puckered his lips to spout obscenities with Stephanie's name attached to them, she raised a dainty hand to forestall him.

"Please consider my delicate ears," she insisted. "A *gentleman* does not offend a lady with his lightning tongue and thundering voice."

Cole's temper was at a rolling boil. Lord, how he itched to snatch this mischievious misfit off her horse and rub her nose in the mud! *"Now* we are even," he growled at her.

"I rather thought you would think so," Stephanie countered, undaunted by the snarl on his face and the gruffness of his tone. One finely etched brow tilted upward as she surveyed Cole's grimy appearance. Mud became him. He didn't look quite so starched, pressed, and arrogant. "Now we can go our own ways, equally resenting each other. You can attempt to court my older sister and I can enjoy my afternoon outing with Brandon." She reined her steed closer to brush a clump of mud from Cole's shoulder. "I fear I have removed most of the *starch* from your shirt, Mr. Hollister." Her smile grew even broader when Cole scowled under his breath. "But I dare say there was a mite too much of it to begin with."

Before Stephanie could trot off on her merry way, Cole grabbed her reins, very nearly throwing her off balance. "Someone needs to take some of the *fire* out of you, she-dragon," he snapped back at her.

Stephanie's reckless laughter was like a double-edged saw that cut deep gashes in Cole's male pride. "When you find a man you deem capable of doing it, send him around," she suggested flippantly. "But do instruct him to pack his lunch. I guarantee it will take him the better part of the day." She purposely looked down her nose at him, delighting in her advantageous position. "And see to it that he is more man than you are, Coleman Douglas Hollister the Third, or else I shall make mincemeat of him too."

That did it! Cole's temper snapped, along with his self-control. If he could have gotten his hands on Stephanie, he would have had her face-down in the mud hole, leaving her wondering if Cole would ever grant her a breath of air. Her ducking would have been mere child's play compared to what Cole had in mind for her. But before he could put his vindictive plan into action, Stephanie gouged her steed to take flight. The stallion immediately responded to his mistress's command. The fact that Cole held one side of his reins did not deter the animal. The chestnut stallion lunged into a gallop, very nearly yanking Cole's arm from its socket. The horse's momentum sent Cole spinning like a top—right back into the mud puddle.

While Stephanie darted off to chase the baying hounds that had sniffed out their quarry, Cole vehemently pronounced every curse word in his vocabulary. His ill-conceived fascination with that fiery termagant was over and done. He had come to realize why Dyer believed his youngest daughter's tutor should have been an iron-willed prison warden or some facsimile. The chit was completely unmanageable. She was also infuriatingly vindictive. She was without scruples, and Brandon—muscle-head—Michaels was welcome to her!

Angrily, Cole stalked around the hedge to retrieve his mount. He was seeing the world through a red haze. Well, at least this humiliating incident had reinforced his conviction that Stephanie was more trouble than she could ever be worth, Cole reminded himself. He may as well turn his charm on Natalie. At least she was safe. Attempting to lure Stephanie back to his bed would only breed disaster.

Stephanie was right, Cole told himself as he led the

contrary steed toward the pond for a much-needed bath. The previous night *hadn't* happened. Cole had dreamed it all, every wild, splendor-filled moment of it. What was between him and Steph was war and Cole wasn't going to be satisfied until he had the last laugh, even if they were *even!*

Chapter 8

Although Cole survived the evening meal without losing control of his temper, his disposition was still as sour as a lemon. Oh, he had portrayed the gallant gentleman for Dyer and Eileen's benefit, but on the inside he was smoldering. Cole told himself he didn't give a tittle that Brandon—muscle-brain—Michaels had been invited to stay for supper, along with Richard Stover, the lovestruck pup who had been following at Addie's heels.

Cole reassured himself that Brandon was just the kind of man who suited Stephanie. He was dim-witted and he could follow simple instructions. When Steph told him to jump, he would inquire *how high* and she could lead him around on a leash with little difficulty. Cole also reminded himself that he detested that ornery minx who had sent him plunging into a mud puddle. Yet even after he had set himself down and reasoned it all out, he was still goaded by ill-founded jealousy and an insane need for revenge.

As the family filed out of the dining room to chat in the parlor, Cole discreetly maneuvered his foot in front of Stephanie when she sailed by. A surprised gasp bubbled from her lips when she saw the floor leaping

137

up at her. Try as she may, she could not seem to untangle her feet from the hem of her gown to catch her balance. Quick as a cat, muscle-bound Brandon scooped Steph up in his arms before she fell flat on her face.

Stephanie tossed Cole a mutinous glare, assuring him that she knew he had purposely tripped her. Although Cole's expression was a carefully blank stare, she could see the mocking twinkle in his dark eyes.

Smiling in smug satisfaction, Stephanie had wrapped her arms around Brandon's neck. "Ah, Brandon, you saved me from an embarrassing moment," she cooed. "'Tis nice to have a strong, capable man like you around the house."

Cole rolled his eyes. Stephanie's tone was so syrupy she could have drowned a stack of pancakes. His attempt to make her appear clumsy afoot backfired in his face. And Brandon was beaming with so much pride after Stephanie rattled off several other compliments that Cole swore the brawny galloot would pop the buttons on his shirt.

When Brandon finally had the decency to set Stephanie back to her feet, she managed to dig her heels into *Cole's* foot in silent retribution. A grimace registered on his rugged features and Stephanie made it a point to bring it to everyone's attention.

"Indigestion, Mr. Hollister?" she purred in mock concern. "You seem to have lost the color in your face." To remedy that condition, Stephanie soundly tweaked Cole's cheeks and then stepped back to observe the two bright red splotches. It was all she could do to prevent herself from bursting into giggles when Cole glared murderously at her. The rat, he was getting exactly what he deserved, she thought to herself.

"I'm certain I will feel much better when I sit down," Cole assured her through a tight smile. Taking her arm in a vise grip, Cole herded her toward the parlor. "You would also do well to get off your feet before you stumble over them again."

Stephanie winced when Cole's fingers bit into her arm to cut off circulation. But she was determined not to let Cole have the satisfaction of knowing he was hurting her. She endured his bone-crushing grasp until they entered the parlor and then she quickly took her place beside Brandon, leaving Cole to take his usual position beside Natalie.

Thus far, Cole's attempt to have the last laugh had been thwarted. Since Stephanie was far too clever in countering his tactics, Cole made Brandon his scapegoat, especially when the man laid his arm over the back of the sofa to toy with the shiny strands of red-gold. Cole was incensed by Brandon's forwardness. The parlor was heaping with family and guests and yet he was still actively courting this petite beauty.

A relieved smile settled on Dyer's features when Brandon showered Stephanie with attention and she responded to it. His youngest daughter had obeyed his request for once, Dyer mused and then wished Cole would take the opportunity of displaying his affection toward Natalie.

Since Richard Stover was present, Eileen's attempt to push Adeline at Cole was stifled. But she had begun to realize that Dyer was determined to have his way in the matter. He was dead set on seeing Natalie wed to the wealthy plantation owner from Maryland, even if he was more Adeline's type.

Determined to expose Brandon for the handsome, but empty-headed character he was, Cole fired several questions at him during the social gathering. But Stephanie responded to the thought-provoking topics, just to spite Cole. She knew what he was trying to do, but she could not fathom why he had his heart set on cutting Brandon into bite-sized pieces.

While Cole and Stephanie were taking opposite sides of every topic, Dyer was smiling quietly to himself. It was becoming increasingly obvious that Cole and Stephanie were as different as dawn and midnight. They seemed to have nothing in common, and for that, Dyer was thankful. He kept reassuring himself that this evening would awaken Cole to the revelation that Stephanie was not the woman to serve as his wife and mistress of his plantation. and yet . . . Dyer frowned disconcertedly when he saw Cole's dark eyes sliding over Stephanie's shapely figure. It seemed that even though the two of them delighted in debating issues and held different views, there was still a physical attraction between them. But Dyer was determined not to allow anything to become of it. Cole was going to marry Natalie. She was the first-born and she sorely needed a husband!

When Stephanie accompanied Brandon from the parlor to bid him good night, Cole feigned a headache and sneaked outside to spy on them. Aye, *spy*. It was sneaky and underhanded and improper and Cole reminded himself of all those things while he wedged himself into the shrubs. The evening had not gone according to plan and his pride was still smarting. But what annoyed him most was when Brandon had declared, after listening to Stephanie counter all of Cole's theories during their conversation, that she was intelligent enough for the both of them. Shortly after Brandon made that remark, Cole had become nauseated. Brandon had also proclaimed that he admired a woman of quick wit and that she would greatly complement his life. Of course, she would have, Cole fumed as he poked his head through the bushes for a bird's eye view of the handsome couple. Stephanie would supply the brains and Brandon would supply the brawn, should they marry.

When it came right down to it, Cole realized that he didn't want Stephanie for his wife, but he didn't want Brandon to have her either. Sweet mercy! Was he out of his mind? *Just look at you,* Cole scolded himself. *That leprechaun has reduced you to an imbecile!* He was thinking and behaving like a fool. Since when had he become so namby-pamby, for heaven's sake? *Since you met that green-eyed sorceress,* a smirking voice inside him answered. Well, he was already neck-deep in the shrubs so he might as well do what he came to do, Cole decided.

Gritting his teeth, Cole watched Brandon's burly arms enfold Stephanie's shapely body. And stung by unreasonable envy, Cole saw Stephanie lift her face to Brandon's kiss. He told himself he didn't care if the powerfully built gorilla squeezed her in two, but it galled him to watch Stephanie accept another man's kiss. Cole knew exactly what emotions Brandon was experiencing when he drew Stephanie full length against him. He also knew how difficult it was to limit oneself to one kiss when this mystical leprechaun was the donor.

Brandon would have lingered all night, allowing one kiss to lead to another, if Stephanie hadn't nudged him on his way. Inhaling a breath of fresh air, she waited until his horse's hoofbeats had faded into silence and thanked her lucky stars she had managed Cole Hollister as well as she had that evening. Cole had certainly made the night a challenge. It kept Stephanie on her guard, attempting to parry his deeds and his words.

As she spun back toward the house, she pulled the pins from her red-gold hair, allowing the thick strands to cascade around her shoulders. When she veered around the corner to enter through Cole's private door, a startled gasp escaped her lips. There, leaning casually against the side of the house, was a peeping Tom.

"Have you nothing better to do than spy on people?" Stephanie sniffed when she recognized Cole's tall, lean form. It seemed Cole still hadn't had enough, Stephanie mused in annoyance. Damn, the man never let up!

Leisurely, Cole pushed away from the outer wall and swaggered toward Stephanie. He was entranced by the way the moonlight sprayed about her, reminding him of the vision who had spirited through his room the previous night. Silver light sparkled in the unruly tendrils that tumbled down her back. Moonbeams danced in those enormous green eyes and caressed her exquisite features. Starlight and muted shadows gave her an alluring, mysterious appearance that Cole simply could not resist, especially when the fireflies were twinkling around her, intensifying her mystique.

Although Cole's intention was to taunt her about her beau, reminding her that the man possessed the intelligence of a potted plant, his thoughts were far removed from Brandon Michaels. Cole was stung by the childish need to erase the memory of Brandon's kisses, to recapture the pleasure he had discovered in the confines of his alcove bed.

Without bothering to respond to Stephanie's question, Cole looped his arm around her waist and pulled her roughly against him. Before Stephanie could protest his advances, she found herself mashed against Cole's sturdy frame. His sensuous mouth was upon hers, stripping her breath from her lungs, unchaining forbidden memories of passion that she was trying so hard to forget. Warm, giddy sensations channeled through her bloodstream, eroding her resistance, shattering every promise she had made to herself.

His exploring hands tracked across the indentation of her waist and ventured to the swells of her breasts, branding her with sizzling fires. Cole pulled her closer so that every inch of their bodies touched, bringing a vivid awareness of how intimate they had been the previous night.

Stephanie detested her apparent vulnerability to this scoundrel who had deliberately tormented her all evening. She had expected him to tattle to her father about his dousing during the fox hunt. But Cole had not mentioned the incident, giving her no further cause to despise him. But how could a woman detest a man who aroused her to such dizzying heights with his explosive kisses? How could a woman resist the spellbinding web of pleasure Cole could weave about her? Did Cole derive some demented satisfaction in crumbling a woman's defenses and watching her surrender to his skillful embraces?

Even while Stephanie was mentally listing all the reasons why she should run for her life, she was reveling in the way Cole's full mouth rolled over hers, the way his darting tongue inflamed her and left her craving for more.

His hands weren't still for a moment. His fingertips applied pressure in just the right places. His palms molded themselves to her quivering flesh, draining her will and her sanity, opening a Pandora's box of desire.

She could feel his heart's accelerated pace, taste the dewy softness of his lips upon her mouth. At that moment, Stephanie couldn't remember what it was like to be held in any other man's arms. Cole had left his brand, his burning imprint, and it seared into her flesh and mind like a hot iron.

Stephanie wasn't exactly certain how Cole had maneuvered her against the side of the house, but she was there. His solid frame was pressing against her and his hot kisses were tracking a scalding path along the delicate lace on the neckline of her gown. His lips skimmed her flesh, moving steadily lower to trace the inner swells of her breasts.

Her breath was trapped in her throat, but it seeped out in a tiny moan of pleasure when Cole's tongue flicked at one dusky peak. And then his hand was upon her breast, kneading the soft mound, brushing his fingertips over the throbbing nipple before he took it into his mouth. Her legs melted beneath her and a burning ache rose in her loins. Cole was creating a hunger, one so fierce and intense that Stephanie involuntarily dug her nails into his back and held on as the ground tilted precariously beneath her.

Cole's sensuous assault was hardly one-sided. Though he was giving her pleasure, he was receiving a great deal in return. The feel of her soft skin beneath his kisses and caresses was scorching him inside and out. He wanted to relive all the wild, wonderful sensations he had experienced the previous night. He wanted to forget who he was and what his father expected of him. He wanted to lift this enchanting nymph into his arms and carry her away, to become a part of her for that one indescribable moment that haunted his dreams.

"I want you . . . here . . . now . . ." Cole breathed raggedly.

Stephanie's eyes flew open and common sense came rushing back. Although it took considerable effort to reassemble her thoughts and her composure, she braced her hands against his chest and held him at bay.

"Nay, it won't happen again," she told him, her voice quivering with barely contained passion. "I will not reduce myself to playing your whore." Inhaling a deep breath, Stephanie willed her heart to slow its frantic pace. "My father brought you here to court Natalie. He has ordered me to avoid you." Her wide eyes focused on his face. She could see, even among the camouflaging shadows, the stronger, more dominant personality that seeped out when Cole let his guard down. "Whatever you are, you are not the man for me. We are too much alike in some ways, and yet we are worlds apart in others. If you keep pressing me, you will only invite trouble."

His fingers clenched in her hair as he twisted the lustrous strands around his wrist like a rope, tilting her face to his. "Try to deny this attraction between us, Steph," he dared her. "I can feel your reaction to me, even now, even while you protest our star-crossed fascination for each other." His lips brushed over her mouth, sending an unwanted tingle flowing down her spine. "It may have been your father who brought me here to court Natalie, but 'tis my obsession for you that keeps me here, even when logic warns me to beware of your spell."

Stephanie turned her head away, avoiding what had every indication of becoming another passionate kiss, the kind that could paralyze her mind. "You don't understand and I cannot explain it," she frantically blurted out. "Even if I wanted you, I could never have you, not without hurting the others . . ."

Cole frowned bemusedly. What others? What was she babbling about? Before he could put those questions to tongue, Stephanie wormed free and darted toward the garden. In fast pursuit, Cole closed the distance between them and tackled his fleeing leprechaun who refused to grant him even one wish.

Stephanie's breath came out in a rush when Cole landed atop of her, forcing her face into the fragrant pansies. "Let me up!" she hissed furiously. Cole didn't obey and it made her all the more agitated. "I said let me—"

Before she could complete her demand, Cole lifted

himself off her far enough to roll her to her back. Stephanie found herself pinned to the flower bed, staring up into a rakish grin that fanned the fires of her temper.

"Damn you, Cole Hollister!" she spewed.

"Sh . . . sh . . ." Cole leaned down to silence her protest with a ravishing kiss. But this time Stephanie was madder than a hornet. Her body went rigid and Cole swore he had pressed a kiss to a stone post. Slowly, he raised his head to meet her fuming glower.

"You are a beast," she growled at him and then arched upward to throw him off. Unfortunately, Cole's heavy body prevented her from throwing him anywhere.

"And you are wasting your energy," he chuckled into her flushed face.

Stephanie's bottom lip jutted out in an exaggerated pout. "Very well then, have your way with me. Exert your male strength. Feed your pride of animalistic dominance. But you will derive no pleasure in it. This time I will leave claw marks all over you," she vowed vengefully.

Cole stared down into features that were alive with anger and indignation and asked himself what the hell he thought he was doing. Lord, he wasn't sure he had any right to poke fun at Brandon Michaels. At the moment Cole swore Brandon had more self-control and intelligence than *he* had. After all, it wasn't Brandon who had plopped down on Stephanie's belly, refusing to release her! Was he going to force himself on this feisty minx, right here in the garden? The thought of how ridiculous he was behaving was like a sound slap in the face. Cole was most thankful there was a mirror nowhere near him. He feared he would glance at his reflection and see himself growing long ears and a tail. It was for certain he was making an ass of himself!

Swiftly, Cole eased off of Stephanie's wriggling body and freed her wrists. "I'm sorry," he apologized sheepishly.

"As well you should be," Stephanie snapped as she brushed the dirt from her gown and rolled to her feet.

Cole rose to full stature to grace her with a faint smile. "I don't know what got into me."

"I'm beginning to think 'tis a devil far worse than the one who looms on my shoulder," Stephanie sniped as she raked him up and down. "There is nothing between us. There never will be. There *cannot* be. I have my commitments and you have yours to Natalie and my father. Papa claims that I have disgraced this family, but you will disgrace it far more unless you learn to control your lusts!" Raising an indignant chin, she glared flaming arrows at him. "The next thing we know you will be hiding in the bushes, waiting to pounce on some unsuspecting female servant to appease your voracious appetite."

Huffily, she rearranged the gown Cole had twisted about her during their scuffle and acquainted him with her glare of icy disdain. "Stay away from me, Cole Hollister. I may have to tolerate your presence in my home, but I do *not* have to like you and I don't think I do! Nor is it my responsibility to dole out favors for every male guest Papa drags to our doorstep. I think 'tis time you were reminded that you are a guest at Wakefield Estate, not the resident rapist!"

"Steph!" Cole called as she pivoted on her heels and sped around the side of the house. He stared at the swaying shadows and then shook his head in disgust. "I'm going mad," he declared to the darkness. "Stark raving, wild-eyed mad!"

147

Thoroughly distressed over his lack of self-control and his inexcusable conduct, Cole wheeled toward the house. Then it occurred to him that he couldn't march through the front door after he had pretended a headache and announced that he was retiring to his room. Neither could he risk entering through his private door without chancing another confrontation with Stephanie. More than likely she intended to change into her prowling habit of men's breeches before she sneaked off into the night.

Aimlessly, Cole wandered off to rehash his encounter with Stephanie, to analyze why that fiery female brought out the savage in him. God, if he didn't get a firm grip on himself, he was going to be waddling around like an addle-witted fool.

Chewing on that troubled thought, Cole followed whatever direction his footsteps took him. And he vowed not to return to the house until he had regained full command of his composure. Unfortunately, it was a long, sleepless night.

The sound of voices and the sight of torches blaring into his window roused Brice Reynolds from a peaceful night's sleep. A low scowl erupted from his lips when he sat up in bed to see the mob that had collected at the back of the inn. On the perimeters of the crowd rode a man clad in black, looming like a vengeful spirit. Man? Brice snorted contemptuously. He would have bet his right hand the night rider was none other than that troublesome misfit, Stephanie Wakefield.

The previous night Brice had found a family of rats scurrying around the foot of his bed when he slid into it. And this morning, when he splashed cologne on his freshly shaved cheeks he let out a roar that would have raised the dead. The kerosene that filled his bottle of cologne set fire to the nicks and cuts left by his razor— one that had suddenly become as dull as a block of wood. Seeking relief, Brice had rushed to the commode to submerge his face in water, only to find that it too had been replaced by kerosene. No doubt, the mob that was pounding at his door was another of *Stephanie's* attempts to repay him for the public ducking.

"Reynolds! Come out here before we come in after you," one of the colonial patriots ordered brusquely.

Fearing the lunatics would set a torch to his home and business establishment that sat above his sleeping quarters, Brice bounded out of bed. But before he opened the portal, he grabbed his flintlock, prepared to fell the first man who stormed his home.

"Go home, you fools," Brice barked sharply. "If you insist on badgering me, I'll have the magistrate call out the British regiments and the whole lot of you will be rotting in jail!"

Although Brice was glaring directly at the masked rider who continued to circle like a waiting vulture, it was another member of the mob who responded to his threat. "We want yer promise that you won't sell a single stamp," the man called out and then brandished his torch in Brice's face. "If you resign yer position as stamp collector, no harm will come to you or yer establishment."

Brice had never appreciated being told what to do unless it would gain him influence or position. Stubbornly, he raised his chin. "I will not be forced from my distinguished office by the likes of a peasant mob." He thrust an accusing finger at the unidentified rider. "And you can burn in hell where you belong!"

Before Brice could decide which way to point his flintlock, a surge of humanity flooded toward him and stripped his weapon from his fingertips. He squawked like a disturbed chicken when he was snatched off the ground and carried down the street to Mystic's version of the Liberty Tree. To his dismay his effigy hung from one of the limbs and Brice had the uneasy feeling he was about to be swinging from another branch.

"You'll rue this night for the rest of your lives!" Brice screeched frantically. "The British will see that you are punished, each and every one of you! I'll make certain . . ."

Brice's voice trailed off when the crowd parted to allow one of the rebels to approach with a bucket of tar. It appeared, that although he might ultimately face a lynching, he would be tarred and feathered first. Amid his loud protests and struggling, Brice's nightshirt and exposed flesh were smeared with tar. He found himself shoved to the ground and set upon by a mob of jeering rebels who covered him from head to toe with the foul-smelling black substance.

Uproarious laughter spurred Brice's short temper. He fought for all he was worth, but he was helpless to prevent the mob from caking feathers in the tar. By the time the crowd had finished with him, he resembled a molting rooster and he was crowing at the top of his lungs.

"We want your word," one of the patriots demanded as Brice was paraded around the Liberty Tree.

"I will promise you nothing after this outrageous mauling," Brice sneered. "If you think humiliation will sway me from my loyalty to the Crown, you are all mistaken!" Furiously, Brice shook a feathered fist in the grinning faces. "I will issue stamps for every document, every license, every cussed deck of cards in Mystic! And I will continue to enforce the customs on every import that arrives in this village. I will *not*

150

be intimidated!"

Even while Brice sputtered his promises, he was marched up and down the street for all the citizens to see. Mortified though he was, his temper remained his sole driving force and overshadowed his sense of self-preservation. Never once did he promise to demur his position. He only voiced another round of threats to the mob and their mysterious leader who sat so regally upon a prancing black stallion.

When Brice was finally dropped beneath Mystic's Liberty Tree to face his own effigy, he was still swearing viciously. After the crowd dispersed, Brice climbed to his feet to shake off a few of his feathers.

Damn that Stephanie Wakefield, he growled as he stalked back to his house. She had to be the masked rebel. She was the personification of defiance and rebellion. But she wasn't going to get away with this! Somehow, Brice was going to even the score with that minx. She may have incited a riot to have her revenge, but Brice wasn't through with her either! The next time he was swarmed by that mob of unruly patriots, he was going to tear that concealing mask from Stephanie's face and turn her over to the British. They would delight in catching the rabble-rouser who was brewing trouble in the community.

Tar and feather Brice Reynolds, would she! Stephanie Wakefield didn't know what trouble was. Brice would see her pay for this last mortification. A public ducking was only the beginning for that rebellious termagant, he vowed stormily. If she sicced that mob on him once again, Brice would see *her* hanging from the Liberty Tree.

Silently fuming, Brice peeled off his night shirt and began the unpleasant task of cleansing the tar and feathers from his skin. With each feather that he plucked from his body he muttered an epithet to Stephanie's name. He would never permit Wesley Beacham to go free, no matter how much money she offered him. No matter what scheme she devised to torment him, Brice would never give Stephanie her way.

Brice snarled under his breath, and then let loose with another string of curses. He would ensure that indentured servant was tied up for life! How dare she offer him money to buy Wesley's freedom. How dare she organize a mob of patriots to frighten him!

Aye, she would pay, Brice promised himself over and over again. No one could humiliate Brice Reynolds and force him to sacrifice the wealth he had spent years acquiring. No one! Especially not that green-eyed witch who lured the citizens of Mystic under her spell and instigated riots to mortify the owner of Reynolds Inn! One day he would send that bitch to the fires of hell whence she had come and the day wouldn't come soon enough to satisfy Brice.

There had been a time when Brice was intrigued by Stephanie's beauty and vitality. He had even called on her before her father shipped her off to England for strict discipline. But Stephanie had rejected his attentions and Brice had never forgiven her for that. That alone was reason enough for him to reject her offer to pay the last six months of Wesley's indentureship.

Being jilted by the likes of that defiant wildcat, compounded by their fiery confrontations, was enough to provoke Brice's hatred. And when a woman had an enemy like Brice Reynolds, one was *one* too many, Brice mused vindictively. That bitch would find out soon enough that she had made a grave error in judgment when she riled him. One day that spitfire would make a careless mistake and Brice would pounce. Nothing would please him more than to be directly responsible for that firebrand's demise. It was growing increasingly apparent that Mystic was not big enough for the both of them and Brice had no intention of leaving, even when that witch garbed herself in men's clothes and set about to turn the entire community against him!

Chapter 9

A frustrated sigh escaped Cole's lips as he paced back and forth across the guest suite. The past few days Dyer had dreamed up a hundred excuses as to why Natalie should accompany Cole to the shipping yards, to and from town, and to and from his schooner. Damnit, Cole wouldn't have been surprised if Dyer requested that the chit accompany him to bed!

But Cole didn't want Natalie in his bed. Her quiet, self-reserved disposition had begun to wear his nerves thin. He craved that refreshing feeling that swamped him each time Stephanie breezed through the mansion like the exhilarating spring winds.

After the incident at the fox hunt and their encounter that same evening, Stephanie had still dared to employ his room as her exit. Never once did she acknowledge his presence when she drew out her garments of black and then sped out the balcony doors. Cole had watched her come and go from his room, wanting her like a starving man craves a feast. But he had not forced himself on her. He had not demanded that she remain in his room instead of spiriting off to meet the mysterious man in her life. But Cole did have the odd feeling that it wasn't muscle-head Brandon she was meeting each evening. *Why* he believed it was someone else, Cole couldn't say for certain. But he was stung by the premonition that Stephanie was meeting someone she was not permitted to associate with during daylight.

It had taken every ounce of willpower not to rise from his bed and follow that elusive nymph and solve the riddle that hounded him. Cole clung fiercely to common sense, reminding himself that he would be asking for trouble if he involved himself with a woman like Stephanie. And yet he could not closet himself in a room that brimmed with enchanting memories. Each time Stephanie made her exit, Cole felt the urge to roam. But he did not permit himself to chase after her like a love-starved pup. He had his own distractions and she had hers, Cole reminded himself. What she did and with whom was her business and he had never made a habit of meddling in someone else's affairs. But Cole was still itching to know who the man was that Stephanie . . .

Grumbling at the detour his thoughts had taken, Cole raked his fingers through his hair and then dropped his arm in a gesture of exasperation. What was there about that sassy green-eyed she-cat that fascinated him? Why had she taken up permanent residence in the cluttered cavity of his head? Stephanie had avoided him like the plague since the day of the hunt. And when she graced her family with her presence during an occasional meal, she rarely glanced in his direction.

Cole found himself looking for her each time he descended the stairs. He found himself drowning in the depths of those sparkling emerald eyes and saucy smiles, hanging on the words that drifted from those soft pink lips.

Scolding himself for his irrational preoccupation

with that lively vixen, Cole strode toward the door and marched down the hall in long, deliberate strides. Dyer had requested his presence in the parlor for a late evening drink. No doubt, Natalie would be placed on the sofa beside him, wedged between him and Dyer.

Cole's predictions were accurate. The moment he appeared in the parlor door, Dyer shackled his arm and led him to Natalie's side. But it wasn't Natalie who attracted his gaze. There, poised in the corner, sat Stephanie, looking like a glorious angel in her satin gown of royal blue. And across from the sofa, Eileen had strategically seated Adeline, the comely blonde who was the graceful image of her mother.

Stephanie viewed the scene with wry amusement. Dyer had insisted that she join the rest of the family in conversation, but she found herself seated outside the family circle. Since Coleman Douglas Hollister the Third had entered the mansion, he had assumed her place at the dinner table, in the parlor, and everywhere else for that matter.

As the conversation drifted from one topic to another, Stephanie found herself studying Cole's rugged, commanding features. The man still puzzled her. He was a walking enigma that Stephanie couldn't quite figure out. Aye, he looked and behaved like a well-to-do plantation owner. But she had seen another side of him, a side he seemed to prefer to hide from the rest of the world.

"Stephie?" Dyer's voice dragged her from her silent reverie. "Have you heard of Brice Reynolds's recent misfortune?" he inquired, casting her a speculative glance.

Stephanie took an unhurried sip of her wine. "Nay, Papa," she replied nonchalantly. "But I am certain whatever calamity has befallen him is well deserved."

"It appears that public opinion has turned against

156

the proprietor of Reynolds Inn and the Crown's stamp agent," Dyer announced to his family, but mainly to his mischievous daughter. "Several of the townspeople gathered into a mob and marched to Brice's doorstep. They were led by a 'man' garbed in black from head to toe and whose identity was hidden behind a black mask. He sat upon his gleaming black stallion, directing the mob while they voiced threats and made their demands."

Stephanie raised an innocent brow, despite her father's accusing stare. "Oh? Did the crowd gather to protest Brice's unprincipled behavior or his audacity of dragging me to a public ducking?"

Dyer snorted derisively. He wasn't fooled by Stephanie's angelic expression. He was certain that Stephanie knew perfectly well why the mob had sought out Reynolds. "Nay, my dear," he patronized for the benefit of the others who were present in the parlor. "They were patriots demanding that Brice resign his position as tax collector for the Stamp Act . . . or suffer the consequences. When Reynolds refused he was tarred, feathered, and paraded about town for all to see."

Adeline sucked in her breath and glanced worriedly at her father. "I do hope Mystic does not become another Boston! I have heard that an unruly mob hung the effigy of two British sympathizers on the Liberty Tree. Then they marched through town to tear down the stamp office that was under construction."

"It seems we now have our own version of the darkly clad vigilante who stirs public opinion into action," Dyer remarked as he reached for the pastry tray and passed it to his guest. "We also have our own Liberty Tree in Mystic and it was Reynolds's effigy that was hanging upon it."

Concern clung to Eileen's brow. "News has also

157

spread that crowds of patriots laid siege to the Royal Artillery garrison in New York and then burned the official coach of Governor Colden. Do you suppose the British magistrate, as well as Mystic's tax agent, will meet with such violence?"

Dyer shrugged as he shot his youngest daughter a hasty glance. "A controlled mob will force tax agents to resign their positions. But the behavior of local patriots will largely depend on the rabble-rouser who has incited the riots. Although I favor boycotting British goods, believe in the verbal protest of British regulations, and encourage the unity of all colonies in a common cause, I do not condone the kind of destructive violence that plagues New York and Boston."

A curious frown knitted Addie's brow. "Why is the name *Joyce Jr.* given to the darkly clad vigilante who incites rebel riots?" she questioned her father. "It seems an odd name to me."

"The legendary character evolved from the traditional Pope's Day celebration in Boston," Dyer explained after he had swallowed his mouthful of pastry. "A huge wagon with a wide platform carrying paper lanterns sets the stage for Boston's ghoulish celebration of ghosts and goblins. Men masquerading as monks and friars line the float." Dyer paused to sip his wine. "And last but not least is Satan himself, garbed with horns, cape, and toting his traditional pitch fork. Somehow or another, the personage of the devil has gotten tangled up with Cornet George Joyce—the man who captured Charles the First in England and who was one of the two darkly clad, masked henchmen who were present when the king's head rolled on the chopping block. Since George Joyce became the English symbol of popular revolt against the government, the patriots have adopted the semi-mythical character and named *their* version *Joyce Jr.*"

Cole passed the pastry tray to Natalie, but his hooded gaze drifted to Stephanie as he posed his question. "Does anyone know who portrays Joyce Jr. during these riots in Mystic?"

Dyer had an educated guess as to who might wish to see Brice Reynolds run out of town, but he was in no position to make accusations, not when the mysterious rider might have been sitting in their midst. "As of yet, no one has recognized the rabble-rouser. And I'm sure 'he' wishes to keep his identity a secret to protect 'himself' from the wrath of the King's men. 'He' has been passing pamphlets among the citizens of Mystic and the surrounding communities, encouraging them to stand in defense of their rights and to unite in an effort to defy the Stamp Act."

"I, for one, applaud him," Cole remarked between bites. "Reynolds came down to the wharf yesterday to inspect the cargo on my schooner and to collect tariffs on the goods I transported from the West Indies. Thanks to a group of rowdy sailors, Brice thought better of presenting a Writ of Assistance and inspecting every nook and cranny on my ship."

"Would you have had something to hide if Brice had been allowed to present you with his blanket search warrant and confiscate part of your imports?" Stephanie questioned point-blank. "Are you, perhaps, smuggling in goods from the French and Spanish Indies, rather than purchasing legal imports from the English Indies?"

"Stephie, for heaven's sake!" Dyer snapped, glaring his daring daughter into silence. "I did not invite you here to interrogate our guest, but rather to familiarize yourself with the events that could very well mold our future relations with England."

Stephanie conjured up a most becoming smile and

presented it to Cole who looked as if he was having difficulty biting back a grin. "Forgive me, sir," she apologized, her tone denying her words. "There are times when my tongue seems to have a mind of its own. And my curiosity often gets the best of me." Gracefully, she gathered her feet beneath her to fetch another glass of wine. "I only wondered if you might have profited from the mob's actions."

"Well, you may as well have come right out and asked our distinguished guest if he were a card-carrying smuggler," Dyer grumbled sourly.

A deliciously wicked grin curved the corner of Stephanie's mouth. The entire family went as stiff as marble statues, knowing Stephanie would never resist countering Dyer's reckless rejoinder.

"Very well then, Papa, I shall," she complied. Her teasing green eyes flooded over Cole's expensive waistcoat and then returned to his handsome face. "Are you a smuggler, Mr. Hollister, as well as a sea captain and plantation lord?"

"Stephanie, bite your tongue!" Eileen gasped, looking as if she might pitch forward in a faint at any second.

Cole was the only one in the group who did not decompose the split-second Stephanie posed her bold question. Indeed, he had difficulty containing his laughter. That minx could transform a peaceful conversation into mayhem in a matter of minutes. If she wasn't presently involved in the rebel activities, she certainly ought to be, Cole decided. This lively leprechaun would make a marvelous rabble-rouser.

"Do you enjoy the wine you have been sipping this evening?" he asked Stephanie out of the blue.

Stephanie stared into the contents of her glass and then cast Cole a quizzical glance. "Aye," she admitted.

Cole's eyes twinkled with deviltry. "'Twas a gift from me to your father, a means of expressing my appreciation for his hospitality." He took a long sip of his wine before refocusing on Stephanie's bewitching features. "'Tis French, my dear Stephanie, purchased in the French Indies. And when the British authorities haul smugglers off to prison for defying their Navigation Acts, they also round up all those who have benefited from the smuggler's illegally imported goods. 'Tis possible that you could be caged in the cell beside me."

Everyone in the parlor was suddenly staring at their drinks as if they were laced with poison. It was Stephanie who broke the stilted silence with irrepressible laughter.

"Then we are close patriots, one and all," she declared, raising her glass in toast. "And if Joyce Jr., the mysterious rider who garbs himself in black, requests my assistance to his cause, I will not hesitate in offering it."

Cole's dark eyes probed into hers while he watched her from over the rim of his glass. There was the slightest hint of mischievousness quirking his lips. "My dear Miss Wakefield, I cannot help but wonder if you have not already made contact with the mysterious man in black. Indeed, methinks you might know him better than most."

All eyes fell on Stephanie. She had the sneaking feeling that her family suspected her of being a patriotic activist, if not the dark rider himself! Let them think what they wished, Stephanie thought recklessly. It would do her little good to deny their darkest suspicions, even if she could. Her family had always been quick to link her name with unconventional activity.

"Aye, perhaps I do, Mr. Hollister," she sighed,

unabashed. Nonchalantly, she set her glass aside and spared Cole a momentary glance. "I think the colonies are coming of age. Before much longer, citizens who support the English throne will be the ones ostracized. Patrick Henry, the orator from Virginia, maintains that we are no longer citizens of separate colonies, but Americans, one and all. I happen to agree with his opinions on colonial rights and liberty."

"And you have always been a rebel looking for a cause, haven't you, Stephie?" Dyer questioned with narrowed blue eyes.

Like a butterfly floating over a meadow, Stephanie fluttered across the room to place a fleeting kiss to her father's cheek. "Aye, I suppose I have. And do not be surprised when you find dozens of us rebels appearing from the cracks in the wall to take our place beside other patriot Whigs. 'Tis my opinion that an occasional riot would do wonders for some of our apathetic citizens."

After Stephanie swept superbly out of the parlor on the wings of her bold prediction, Eileen smiled apologetically at Cole. "You were forewarned, Cole. I only hope you will be forbearing of our youngest daughter. She is a mite outspoken and prone to orneriness. In fact, she thrives on shocking those around her."

"I have taken no offense, madam," Cole assured her as he rose to full stature. "Plainspoken though she is, Stephanie speaks the truth. If the patriots have their way, the colonies will be linked by one common cause. Parliament has dared too much with Navigation Acts that restrict our trade with only English ports. I fear the Sugar and Stamp Acts are only the beginning of tyranny. We have been taxed without representation in Parliament. The English are the cause of our depressed economy and they are striving to keep us dependent on

162

them with these new laws. If we do not stand together to defend ourselves, England will see that we pay every debt incurred by their war with France and that we will never have a voice in government."

"Aye, the time is coming," Dyer quietly agreed. "I only hope England will take note of the protests and change their policies. I have no wish to see our conflicts evolve into a full fledged war."

Cole nodded grimly, but he made no reply. Bidding the Wakefield's good night, Cole climbed the stairs to his suite. Although his thoughts were full of political issues, there was a face emerging from his troubled musings. It was a lively, expressive face, dominated by twinkling emerald eyes and long, thick lashes.

The moment Cole strolled into his room, his gaze landed on the alcove bed. A tidal wave of memories splashed over him. He could see that pixie with the red-gold hair floating toward him. She was unaware that he was there waiting for her, that he was on fire for her. And if that feisty leprechaun would grant him three wishes, he knew exactly what he would want . . . thrice. But he had the odd premonition that *three times three* wouldn't be enough. Every memory of Stephanie made the hunger more intense. Cole couldn't help but wonder if he could ever satisfy the monstrous craving Stephanie had aroused in him.

Cole laughed mirthlessly as he ambled to the terrace doors to see Stephanie's caped silhouette drifting in and out of the shadows. Oh, how he wished the next week would fly past and he could put a world between him and that spell-casting witch. He was anxious to attend his business in Boston and return to Maryland to begin hating Rachel. It was far more productive than lollygagging about, reliving fantasies that would never again collide with reality.

Stephanie wanted nothing more to do with him. She

163

had remained cold and unapproachable each time she darted through his suite to escape the mansion at midnight. And tonight she had spirited away before he had returned to his room. He had no opportunity to speak privately with her.

Nervous energy hounded Cole as he wore a path on the balcony. He, too, felt the urge to roam the darkness like a restless specter. Remaining in the confines of a room that still lingered with the enticing scent of jasmine was unholy torment. He refused to crawl into bed and close his eyes, knowing Stephanie's bedeviling image would come to haunt him as it did each night. Her mere presence in the mansion kindled a flame of wanting. He had but to stare at her exquisite profile and desire flooded over him. He gazed into those sparkling pools of emerald and he saw in Stephanie everything he had once been—the free-spirited rebel that even his domineering father couldn't control, the adventurer who defied death, just to confront challenges that tested his capabilities.

Determined to outrun the conflicting emotions that pursued each other through his mind, Cole took the balcony steps two at a time. He longed to escape the prison of memories of that emerald-eyed leprechaun. He would venture to the smoke-filled taverns of Mystic to find companionship and drink Connecticut rum until his eyes blurred and his mind was numb.

But even as he swung onto one of Dyer's mounts and reined toward the village, Cole could feel Stephanie's ever-lingering presence riding in his shadow. He could still see her exquisite figure outlined in the spotlight of the moonbeams that had sprinkled into his room that mystical night an eternity ago. He could feel her satiny skin beneath his exploring caresses, taste those dewy lips that had become his maddening addiction.

He was never going to warm to timid, bashful

Natalie Wakefield or the beautifully poised Adeline, he thought dispiritedly. Neither of them held the lure Stephanie did. Neither of them could touch as many of his emotions in a lifetime as Stephanie could touch in the course of an evening.

Cole nudged the steed in the flanks, sending him off in a lunging gallop. If it was possible to outrun a haunting apparition, Cole intended to do just that. He resented Stephanie's illogical hold on him and yet he was helplessly drawn to her. She was everything he could never be again and he was fighting like hell to keep the specter of his past buried. But that hard-living, reckless personality had been buried alive and Cole knew that any connection with the high-spirited pixie would cause him to revert to his old ways.

He couldn't allow that to happen. Cole lectured himself sternly. He was a man of responsibility now. He couldn't go off half-cocked, pursuing a feisty sprite who was chasing her own rainbows. He was destined to follow in his father's footsteps. He had promised Coleman Douglas Hollister the Second that he would assume the distinguished position of lord and master of the Maryland plantation. Cole had to uphold that vow, and that was the beginning and end of it!

Chapter 10

Restlessly, Stephanie flounced on her bed, begging for sleep to overtake her. But nothing she had done during the day seemed to curb her anxiety. When the walls of her room began to close in around her, Stephanie had fled the house in her usual manner—through the guest suite. She had not taken the time to note if Cole had been tucked in the alcove bed or if he, too, had been compelled to wander in the darkness.

Stephanie had returned by the same route, certain her wild ride would allow her to settle down to a decent night's sleep. The tactic had failed miserably. Stephanie was still wide awake, still tormented by a perplexing man and a night that had no rightful place in her life.

Obeying Dyer's demand and following her own common sense, Stephanie had religiously avoided Cole. Well, all except for her defiant flights through his suite during the night, she silently amended. He had made no attempt to stop her and for that she was thankful. Stephanie had not wanted to retest her reaction to that dark-eyed devil in elegant clothes. But neither was she going to permit him to think he had frightened her into finding an alternative route!

Thus far, there had been no uncomfortable situations. Stephanie joined in the family's conversational gatherings when she was invited. She took occasional meals in the dining room and watched Eileen and Dyer throw Natalie and Adeline at Cole. And all the while, Cole's penetrating gaze bore into her, making silent demands. How would Dyer react if he knew his prize husband candidate for Natalie had slept with Stephanie? Would he forgive his guest's indiscretion in his eagerness to see Nattie married?

The sacrificial lamb, Stephanie mused in self-pity. She had always been the family's scapegoat. If a social function went sour, it was *her* fault. If one of Natalie's beaux was afflicted with a roving eye and turned his attention on Stephanie, that was *her* fault too. Why, if the colonies declared war on England, Dyer would probably contend that Stephanie had singlehandedly instigated the conflict!

Angrily, Stephanie punched her pillow to relieve her frustration. It didn't help. She should pack her bags and run away, she thought sullenly. Then she wouldn't be burdened with all these frustrating secrets, taxed by her father's accusations, hounded by the rogue who had stolen her innocence.

Run away and leave Wesley, Natalie, and Adeline to resolve their own problems? Stephanie groaned miserably. She couldn't live with her conscience if she turned her back on her family. In their own way they needed her. And it was their dependence on her that formed the walls of *her* prison. It was the closest Stephanie had ever come to feeling wanted and needed in all her twenty years. Maybe she was a glutton for punishment but she couldn't walk out on those who depended on her.

And to make matters worse, she couldn't route Cole Hollister from her thoughts. Each time she let her guard down she could see his craggy features and raven hair materializing in her mind's eye. He was there, hovering only a few breathless inches away. She could almost feel his masculine body forging familiarly against hers, teaching her things she had never known about passion—things he had no right to teach her! Her husband should have been granted that privilege, she thought bitterly.

And why had she surrendered to Cole's practiced seduction? Had she become a slave to passion? Why did she find herself wondering how it would feel to reach out and touch him as intimately as he had touched her? He was not the man who should have aroused her slumbering desires. He had used her to satisfy his lusts while he courted Natalie and Adeline. He had taken *her* into his bed, and God help her, now she was longing for *his* experienced caresses and kisses.

This is madness! Stephanie reprimanded herself with a mental slap. In another week or two Cole would sail away and she would still be here, wrestling with her conscience and the problems at hand. Forget that devil! He wants your soul, just so he can proclaim he has taken possession of it.

The creak of the door caused Stephanie to bolt straight up in bed. Her keen eyes focused on the tall, muscular form who filled the entrance to her boudoir. A startled gasp erupted from her lips when Cole, bare-chested and barefooted, swaggered toward her. Sweet mercy, speak of the devil and he appeared!

Cole was intoxicated and bewitched. The lantern light filtered through Stephanie's transparent gown, providing an enticing wrapper for a lovely package. Even through bloodshot eyes he could see the full swells of her breasts and the narrow indention of her waist beneath the gossamer fabric. The golden light glistened in the waterfall of red-gold curls that spilled over her shoulder like molten lava. Her exquisite features were framed by the shadows and flickering light, giving her a supernatural appearance—like a sweet, tempting angel.

Cole had made it a ritual to strike out for Mystic when darkness cloaked the Connecticut coast. He had attempted to cure his craving for Stephanie by punishing his body with rum. His treatment for this terminal fever had proven ineffective. Each time he ascended the steps of the balcony, he was reminded that Stephanie had followed the same route to meet the man in her life and to perform whatever activities she indulged in when the sun hid its face for the day. A week of wanting had built into a need that no amount of liquor could diminish.

Oh, he had rattled off a hundred excuses as to why he should stumble into the guest suite and collapse on his own bed. Aye, he had lectured himself on the hazards of becoming involved with a firebrand who could destroy his inhibitions and make him react with reckless impulse. Cole had applauded himself for seven days, praising his unpenetrable self-control. But all that silent encouragement hadn't worked worth a tittle. Tonight he had lost his battle of self-conquest. He wanted Stephanie and he didn't care what he had to sacrifice to have her again.

Without a word, Cole moved toward the canopy bed. To Stephanie's amazement he sat down beside her as if he belonged there.

"What is it you want?" she hissed, worming as far away as the double bed would allow.

A lopsided smile dangled on the corner of his mouth as he braced himself on his arms, causing columns of muscles to bulge beneath his flesh. "What does a man usually want when he seeks out a woman's bed-chamber?" he drawled, his voice heavy with the effects of liquor and unfulfilled passion.

"You're drunk!" Stephanie snapped in accusation.

"And you are positively enchanting," Cole complimented with a leering smile.

Stephanie folded her arms beneath her breasts and thrust out her chin. "I demand your humble apology for barging into my room and then I expect you to make a hasty retreat."

Cole gave his tousled raven hair a negative shake and grinned outrageously.

"I'll scream the walls down," she threatened.

With a sloppy gesture of his arm, Cole's painted an all-encompassing circle in the air. "Send them crashing down," he insisted slurrishly. "And when Dyer charges in to see what has caused all the commotion, I will tell him how you sneak out of my room each night to meet your mysterious lover or to do whatever else you do while the rest of your family thinks you are sleeping."

So he intended to blackmail her, did he? That lowdown, miserable rat! "And I suppose if I beg and plead for your silence in this matter you will hold your tongue . . . provided I allow you to make love to me again," she sniffed distastefully.

Since Stephanie had minced with no words, Cole saw no reason to pretend he hadn't contemplated that strategy. It was sinful and wicked of him to back her into a corner and he hated himself for resorting to such tactics . . . but not enough to deny himself the pleasure he knew Stephanie could provide.

"That is precisely the price I demand for my silence," he admitted unrepentantly.

Stephanie waited, hoping he would roughly grab her and she could pound him flat. Then she would have every reason to inflict punishing blows on this wily rake. But he allowed her no excuses for retaliating with violence. His masculine body loomed beside hers as he stretched out on her bed. His rum-laced breath whispered softly against her cheek. His hand glided over her belly, drawing lazy designs around the silk fabric that covered her breasts. Stephanie felt a fire spreading across every inch of flesh he touched.

"Is it a crime for a man to want a woman in his arms?" Cole murmured as his lips traced the swanlike column of her throat. "Do you preceive me as some hideous monster who wants to gobble you up for the mere challenge of it?" Soft laughter rumbled in his chest as his kisses followed her collarbone, spreading waves of pulsating fire in their wake. "I am only a man, with a man's needs. I cannot say for certain what spell you have cast over me, my green-eyed leprechaun. But there is no antidote . . ."

His sensuous mouth languidly lifted to brush across her quivering lips. "I crave your kisses," he confessed huskily and then helped himself to a taste of her tempting mouth. "The night we made wild, sweet love burns in my thoughts. I stare at you from a safe distance, knowing you are forbidden fruit. But it hasn't stopped me from wanting you . . ." His fingertips delved beneath the hem of her negligee to make stimulating contact with her ultrasensitive flesh. "Tell me you don't want to recapture those delicious memories and I will go away."

Stephanie couldn't have recited her name at that moment, much less order him out of her room. Her heart had catapulted to her throat to strangle her. She wanted to send him away, to ignore the masculine fragrance that warped her senses. But instead of pushing him back, her betraying arms slid over his broad shoulders, marveling at the strength that lay in repose. Cole Hollister was all man and he could make a woman feel every inch a woman.

His rough sensuality came pouring out when he took her lips under his, savoring and devouring her in the same moment. And there, beneath the face that had been trained in impassiveness, beneath the refined manners, emerged the wildly exciting rogue who could touch Stephanie's wild heart. She was attracted by his rugged vitality, by the duel personality of this man. Even if she grew a shell, she doubted it would protect her from the magnetism that compelled her closer. When Cole shed that staunch demeanor of propriety and elegance, Stephanie was awed by the dramatic transformation. Cole could breathe the fire of desire into her and make her a wanton woman, a woman who was left wanting a man she could never have.

As his skillful caresses demolished each barrier of defense, Stephanie's breath came in short, erratic spurts. No words would form on her lips—words that should have been voicing her protests. Stephanie struggled in her battle of self-conquest, but she knew she was a lost cause when her lashes fluttered up. Suddenly, she was engulfed by intriguing black flames. His dark eyes were burning into her, relaying messages that required no verbal explanation. There, in those pools of liquid ebony lay raw, naked emotions, emotions Cole concealed for the rest of the world. But the potent feelings he expressed in the look he gave her made Stephanie shudder involuntarily. She knew Cole was totally aware of her and she was vividly aware of him.

Where were defiance and willpower when she needed them most? How could she deny him when she ached to set her hands upon his muscular flesh and seek out the hard planes of his body. God help her for admitting it, but she wanted to caress him, to know him as she knew no other man.

Was there a special fire in hell to eternally roast women who shamelessly gave themselves up to physical pleasure? Was she to be forever damned for this insane need that defied rhyme and reason? Stephanie swore this would never happen again. She assured herself that her attraction to Cole could be contained and controlled. But as his warm lips melted on hers, making intimate promises of pleasures to come, Stephanie broke every vow she had made. His protective arms were like a blanket she cuddled into. His hair-matted body was merely an extension of hers—flesh belonging to flesh, heart beating in perfect rhythm with heart.

While she gave herself up to his passionate kiss, her hands began to wander across the taut muscles of his back. Brazenly, she discovered the curve of his hip and the corded tendons of his thighs. And when he returned her touch, caress for caress, Stephanie knew there was no turning back, no denying the flames that bridged the small gap between them.

Their first night together, she realized, had been only the initiation of passion. Now Stephanie knew what awaited her when she took flight to explore the far horizons. Her body reveled in his tender fondling, ached to become his possession.

A muffled sigh escaped her lips as his kisses spread a sea of pleasure over her, leaving her bobbing in a reckless kind of splendor. He touched her everywhere, practicing exquisite torture, making her writhe in the sweet agony of his lovemaking.

The years of self-imposed reserve fell away as Cole worshipped Stephanie's exquisite flesh. Like a lion rousing from a long nap, Cole felt his dormant emotions bubbling toward the surface. Caressing her excited him. Kissing her unleashed the floodwaters of mindless passion. His gentleness transformed into hungry impatience. His kisses devoured. His arms encircled her, crushing her inexperienced body against his.

Cole could not seem to get close enough, could not satisfy the craving that tore at his body and soul. This high-spirited elf had freed the prisoner of his living past. She made him feel whole and alive again.

One wild, breathless sensation after another shot through his soul. Cole groaned in unholy torment, knowing he was about to lose complete control and uncaring if he did. And when he came to her, whispering how she pleased and excited him, he felt as if he were coming home from a long voyage. Although he had known this dazzling nymph less than two weeks, it was as if she had always been a part of him, as if she somehow belonged to him.

A tiny gasp of pleasure burst free from Stephanie's lips when Cole became the warm, compelling flame within her. He was feeding the fire that was already blazing out of control. Stephanie dug her nails into the taut muscles of his shoulders and held on for dear life while rapturous sensations assaulted her from all directions. As he thrust deeply within her, setting the sweet cadence of passion, the world spun furiously out of orbit. Stephanie could see nothing. She could only feel Cole's massive body forging into hers, bringing ineffable pleasure. It was folly . . . madness . . . Stephanie was helpless to understand why this ebony-eyed devil could take hold of her soul and send her skyrocketing beyond the stars.

And then the dark world exploded and the myriad of sensations that had crowded in upon her diverged like a shooting star shattering into a million pieces. Flecks of piercing white-hot lights sprinkled across her body and soul and she cried out in the rapture of it all.

It was the sublime paradox of passion. Although Stephanie was chained so tightly in Cole's arms she could barely draw a breath, she had never felt so wild and free. She was revolving inside a never-ending circle, exploring that dimension of time and space that transcended all she had ever experienced. Her untutored body arched toward his, striving for delirious depths of intimacy, wanting more of this ecstatic pleasure, yet unsure she could survive it.

When his massive body shuddered upon hers, Stephanie bit her lip to keep from crying out. She was tumbling pell-mell through space, engulfed by a splendor that defied all previous sensations. And for what seemed forever she was suspended in that dark, sensual universe that only lovers could explore.

It was a long moment before Stephanie saw the perimeters of reality drifting slowly toward her. And it was even longer before her paralyzed mind began to function. Stephanie snuggled against Cole's sinewy length, amazed that all the perplexing problems that had hounded her thoughts did not seem so insurmountable. Deep down inside she knew this unexplainable attraction she felt for Cole would only complicate her life. But it suddenly didn't matter. He had chased the world away and she had soared like an eagle in a cloudless sky.

Stephanie was stung by the odd sensation that if she remained in Cole's protective embrace, no harm would come to her. It was a relief to turn to someone else for once in her life, instead of being the rock everyone else leaned on.

Her opinion of Cole Hollister was beginning to change. Learning that he defied the British by transporting Spanish and French goods to the colonies made her realize that Cole, who fit the image of a wealthy aristocrat, was a patriot at heart. She could never picture herself caring for a man who was devoted to the Crown.

Caring? Stephanie landed on that word and blinked bewilderedly. She *did* care about this complicated man, insane as it may seem. She hadn't meant to, but somehow he had burrowed his way into her heart and into her thoughts when she would have preferred not to have him there at all.

The startled expression on Stephanie's impish features provoked Cole to smile curiously. "What is it, little leprechaun?" he pried as he traced her delicately carved features. "Share the thought."

Stephanie reached out to brush her hand over the thick muscles of his chest and shoulders. "Don't ask me to explain why, since I cannot explain it to myself, but I think I like you, Coleman Douglas Hollister the Third . . . stuffy name and all."

Cole chuckled at her delightful honesty. "And I like you, my lovely elf. Why else would I overstep my host's hospitality and risk placing my head on the chopping block? When your father insisted that I make myself at home, I seriously doubt that he implied I could help myself to his bewitching daughter."

"I would conclude that 'tis because you are a lusty dragon with a voracious appetite for women," Stephanie said candidly. "You needn't pretend you feel something special for me. I am not so naive to think men never seduce women unless they are helplessly and hopelessly in love. Passion for passion's sake is a common flaw of the male species."

A wry smile pursed Cole's lips. Like a graceful jungle cat, he rolled sideways, pinning Stephanie against him, causing her glorious mane of red-gold hair to spill over the pillow like an erupting volcano. "You fail to give yourself credit, Steph," he contradicted. "You stir my emotions like a witch concocting black magic in her caldron. *You* are the one ingredient that creates a unique brand of passion."

Her gaze searched the smoldering depths of ebony. "Are you saying lovemaking isn't always like this?" she

176

questioned innocently.

The playfulness evaporated. Cole stared down into her enchanting face, fully aware that lovemaking had never been quite like this. Sensations and emotions were blown out of proportion when he was in Stephanie's silky arms. The feelings that engulfed him left his past experiences drowning in a murky haze.

"Nay," he informed her, his voice heavy with mounting desire. "With you, 'tis something rare and special."

His head came deliberately toward hers. Gently, he savored the honeyed softness of her lips. He could feel her satiny flesh beneath his stroking caress. He had hoped he had satisfied his unreasonable need for this curvaceous pixie, but the craving was like an eternal spring. It was the hot, bubbling river of passion that he had discovered, Cole mused as he gathered Stephanie closer. When he touched her, sensations gushed through him like a boiling potion that seared him from inside out.

Stephanie felt herself sinking into dark, sensual depths all over again. Cole could make her feel special, even when she knew better. But when he whispered compliments in that low, sexy voice of his, Stephanie believed and she reponded.

The sound of a pebble rattling against the window-pane caused Stephanie to freeze. "Wes . . ." The name burst from her lips before she could think to bite it back.

Cursing, Cole glared at the window, only to see another pebble collide with the glass. The magical spell was broken and Stephanie squirmed away to retrieve her gown. When she attempted to bound from bed to answer Wesley's call, Cole's hand clamped around her wrist.

"Who is he? What does he mean to you?" Cole

demanded to know.

Another pebble clattered against the window, dragging Stephanie's eyes away from Cole's probing stare. "I have to go to him," she murmured, refusing to answer his questions.

"Damnit, tell me!" Cole hissed in frustration. For the life of him he didn't know why he was being so all-fired possessive. But the thought of Stephanie spiriting off into another man's arms stoked the flames of his usually well-controlled temper.

Stephanie wormed her arm from his grasp and wiggled into her gown on the run. Growling under his breath, Cole watched her hasty flight through the door. Who the devil was Wes? And why did Stephanie race off to meet him each time he tossed a pebble or flickered a lantern in the darkness? What hold did this man have on her? And why did Cole care so damned much?

For a split second Cole found himself comparing Stephanie to Rachel. But his common sense quickly denied any comparisons. Stephanie had not invited Cole to *her* bed. The situation was completely different. This time *Cole* was the other man, the first man to take possession of Stephanie's body. Wes whoever-he-was may have her heart . . .

The thought had Cole cursing a blue streak. Why was this witch's heart so blasted important to him? Cole had told himself a hundred times that this affair would be over and done when he cruised out of Mystic. He needed a woman like Natalie or Adeline if he meant to take a wife. They were calm, gentle, and dependable and Stephanie would never be any of those things. Indeed, she would scoff at the very idea of behaving in a conventional manner.

Even while Cole was padding down the hall to the guest suite, telling himself it made no difference that

Stephanie was tied to the man who came to her only in the dark of night, he couldn't quite convince himself. For some unexplainable reason it wasn't enough to take possession of Stephanie's luscious body in stolen moments of passion. He also wanted her heart and soul—that which her mysterious beau obviously had.

Leaning negligently against the balcony doors, Cole watched Stephanie fly into another man's arms. Irritation welled up inside him. With his teeth set in grim determination, Cole marched across the balcony and placed one foot on the step before he regained his self-control. What did he think he was going to do? Prance up to the chummy couple and drag Stephanie back to his room?

Heaving an exasperated sigh, Cole reversed direction and resettled himself against the doorfacing. For several minutes he stood as a posted lookout while Stephanie and Wes strolled through the swaying shadows, hand in hand. He knew he had no right to be furious with Stephanie. After all, Cole was courting Natalie and Adeline, trying to decide which one of them would better suit as his wife. He couldn't condemn Stephanie for running off to meet Wes. Yet now that the boot was on the other foot, Cole sorely felt the pinch. He was *jealous,* for God's sake! He was green-eyed-monster jealous!

When Stephanie bounded up the steps and swerved around the corner to reenter the guest suite, Cole was there to roughly yank her to him. She found herself staring up into a chiseled face that looked as if it might crack at any second.

"Now you are going to tell me who Wes is and why you only meet him at midnight," Cole growled at her.

There was no circulation in Stephanie's arms. Cole had gripped them so fiercely that they were numb. "You are hurting me," she snapped. "And you have no

179

right to pry. Do you expect me to tell Wes why you were in my room with me when he rapped at the window? Are you going to explain why you seek me out after you court my sisters during the day?"

If Cole could have answered those questions, he would have known why he was aggravated with this sassy minx. But there was no time to sit down and analyze his thoughts and actions.

Stephanie took advantage of his silence. "Isn't it enough that you have made me a hypocrite? Isn't it enough that you are carving my conscience into shameless pieces?" When Cole loosened his grasp, Stephanie shook herself free and drew herself up to proud stature. "I detest repeating myself, but I fear I must. Tonight didn't happen, and if it happens again, it will only complicate both of our lives. You have deprived me of the gift I would have saved for my husband . . . *if* and *when* I am ever allowed to truly have one! You don't want the emotions and personality that are tangled in a woman's body. You care only to derive physical pleasure at *her* expense."

Her green eyes were spitting fire as she glared into Cole's rugged features, frying them to a burnt crisp. "And if you think either of my sisters will wind up as your wife, you are deluding yourself. As a matter of' fact, you would save yourself a great deal of time if you sashayed over to Reynolds Inn and sought out a trollop to ease your lusts."

As Stephanie spun on her heels and shot toward the door, Cole frowned in confusion. What the hell was she ranting about? Why weren't Natalie and Adeline wife material? And how did she know there were trollops running around loose in Brice Reynolds's Inn?

Muttering to himself, Cole stalked toward his bed and shut himself in it. Women! He should have known better than to go chasing after that fiery minx. Her middle name was trouble. He had known that since the first time he laid eyes on her.

And Stephanie was right. He should pack his bags and take up residence at the inn. He didn't need any of the Wakefield daughters as his wife. There were plenty of women in Maryland who would leap at the chance to become Mrs. Coleman Douglas Hollister the Third.

Chewing on that arrogant thought, Cole yanked the sheet over him and slammed his head against the pillow—or at least that was what he intended. Unfortunately, his head crashed against the inner wall of the alcove bed during his temper tantrum.

"I'll leave you alone," Cole sneered at the bewitching image who rose in the darkness. "As a matter of fact, I'll pretend you don't even exist!"

But spouting resolutions didn't solve the problem, Cole found out as the week dragged on. The following morning he announced his intention to rent a room at the inn and Dyer took offense. Realizing it wasn't wise to anger the man who was building his ship, Cole relented. If Dyer held grudges, Cole might find himself ten minutes at sea and sinking.

And even though Cole vowed never to spare Stephanie so much as a glance when they crossed paths, his eyes kept betraying him. When she dropped into her chair at the dinner table, he found himself taking note of her voluptuous figure and those incredible green eyes. When she spoke, he was uncontrollably stirred by her soft, husky voice. And when she breezed past him, his senses savored and clung to the alluring scent of her perfume.

Each time darkness descended, he watched Stephanie take flight through his room, wondering if he would have to lock himself in the bed in the wall to prevent pursuing her. Again his self-restraint threatened to crack and Cole took to his own nocturnal prowling. It wasn't a cure for what ailed him, but rum did relieve the symptoms . . . temporarily. Cole was absolutely certain by the end of the second week that the only way to forget that high-spirited leprechaun was to put her out of his life. And he intended to do just that the moment his newly purchased schooner was seaworthy. He was going to sail out of port and never look back. And if he ever again entertained the thought of cruising into Mystic, he was going to have his head examined!

Chapter 11

Taking particular care, Cole dressed for the ball the Wakefields were giving in their home. To satisfy Dyer's greatest whim, Cole had consented to escort Natalie to the party. Not that he should complain about being in the company of the sultry brunette, Cole reminded himself. But Natalie had never warmed to him. She was polite but standoffish, just as she had been since the first day they met. Adeline was pleasant company, but she seemed hesitant to overstep the bounds set by her father. And Stephanie . . .

Cole strangled the thought. That firebrand was not the woman he needed in his well-structured life. She made him feel impulsive and reckless. Cole gritted his teeth and silently tacked on the confession that he wasn't sure he could handle a woman like Stephanie. She was too much woman for the average man.

A wry smile trailed across Cole's lips, wondering if even the man of his past would have been able to handle that free-spirited vixen. But if he had met Stephanie three years ago . . .

Dismissing the whimsical thought, Cole tugged at the sleeves of his shirt, leaving the laced cuffs protruding fashionably from the sleeve of his waistcoat. Dressed fit to kill, Cole ambled to the door and mentally braced himself to stand beside Natalie in the receiving line. Once he had met all of Dyer's guests he would aim himself toward the study and a tall glass of wine. He was sure he was going to need a stiff drink after Dyer suggested that there might be an announcement of his eldest daughter's wedding.

Cole had methodically turned the idea over in his mind the past week. But he doubted he could be satisfied with shy Natalie after he had been entranced by the curavceous leprechaun with the bedeviling green eyes. If the Wakefield family ever came to Maryland to visit, Cole would forever be forced to retest his reaction to Stephanie. Nay, it simply wouldn't work, even if Natalie would have made the model wife for a plantation owner.

A bitter laugh erupted from Cole's lips as he strode down the corridor to the opposite wing of the mansion. Why was he fretting about how he was going to get through life with Stephanie as his sister-in-law when he wasn't even sure he could get through this night! How was he going to stand and watch while Stephanie pirouetted around the dance floor in dozens of arms, none of which would belong to him? How was he going to tolerate her carefree laughter, knowing he wasn't the cause of it? Wine, plenty of wine, Cole diagnosed as he paused in front of Natalie's bedroom door. The only way to remain immune to the one woman he couldn't and shouldn't have was to drink himself a thousand miles out of his mind.

With Natalie draped on his arm, Cole retraced his steps down the hall. He froze in his tracks when Stephanie stepped from her room, looking like a royal princess on her way to court. A tierra of jewels crowned her red-blond curls that were piled upon her head. Her shapely figure was enhanced by the emerald green brocade gown that was adorned with frilly lace. The daring neckline displayed the luscious swell of her bosom and Cole felt himself go up in smoke.

Lord, she was breathtaking! Even Natalie with her glorious auburn hair and burgundy gown could not compare to her youngest sister. There was a natural radiance about Stephanie, some undefinable quality that set her apart from other women and made men want to reach out to touch her. Quite simply, Stephanie, in all her dazzling beauty, was the essence of spirit itself. A man felt warm and exhilarated inside, just admiring her from a distance. And when he dared to venture too close ... well, Cole was the walking example of unfulfilled desire.

Stephanie was not immune to Cole's devastating appearance. He looked positively gorgeous in his snug black breeches and tight-fitting waistcoat. Gold embroidery embellished his velvet jacket, giving him a look of regal authority. The gold silk shirt enhanced his tanned features and Stephanie would have swooned if she hadn't been made of sturdy stuff. But she held her composure and allowed herself the visual torment of inspecting him from head to toe.

It was all she could do not to gawk like an awestruck schoolgirl. Cole didn't even have to speak to captivate their guests, Stephanie thought as her eyes drank in his virile physique and elegant clothes. His striking good looks said it all, and Natalie would be the envy of the party. Cole was born to wealth and he handled his distinguished position well. Aye, there was a certain arrogance about him, but not an ounce of it was unjustified. He was everything a normal woman would want and women would flock to him like metal drawn to a magnet. And Cole Hollister was not unaccustomed to being the center of attention. He just seemed to belong there.

Stop this foolishness, Stephanie chided herself gruffly. There was no sense drooling over this man. They could never mean anything to each other. It was too late for that. Had they met in another time, another place . . . Stephanie chopped the wistful thought in two. Their brief but passionate affair was over and it was for the best.

Sporting a deliciously mischievous smile, Stephanie shifted her attention to her sister. "Natalie, please instruct Papa to extinguish all the extra lanterns he lit throughout the house," she insisted.

A muddled frown puckered Natalie's brow. "Whatever for, Stephie?"

Stephanie indicated Natalie's handsome escort. "I do believe Coleman Douglas Hollister's radiant presence in the ballroom will produce enough heat to ignite at least a dozen flames."

A low rumble of laughter echoed in Cole's chest as he watched Stephanie pivot around and float down the hall. It amazed him that this vivacious nymph could set off so many emotions within him so quickly. Desire, frustration, amusement, and admiration were all fighting to gain control. But not one single feeling could emerge from the turmoil to take command of the field. A man was not allowed to feel one emotion at a time when he confronted that complex beauty. They came at him in multiples of four.

"I accept your compliment, Stephanie," he drawled after her, his voice like a lingering caress. "But I don't think I will be allowed to start any fires with the resident arsonist crowding my limelight."

Stephanie paused at the top of the steps, her gaze running from the tip of his freshly polished boots to the top of his shiny raven head. She grinned in spite of herself. Even with Cole's starched and pressed manners, he still had the ability to fling witty rejoinders. She liked that. Cole had possibilities. With a little instruction, she could bring out the reckless rake within him. Cole might prove to be more than the run-of-the-mill aristocrat. It was a pity she didn't have the time to take some of the starch out of him and encourage the wildly exciting rogue to break free of that prison of self-reserve.

Hastily, Stephanie discarded the tantalizing thought of turning this handsome prince into a hellion. Her father had warned her away from Cole for Natalie's benefit and Stephanie had already discovered the folly of allowing herself to care too deeply for Cole Hollister. And if Dyer had known about his seemingly quiet and bashful daughter, he would have been shocked out of his boots. Stephanie wondered how long it would be before Dyer found out about Natalie . . . and Adeline . . . and even herself!

Stephanie opened her mouth to taunt Cole for the mere pleasure of fencing words with him, but Dyer appeared out of nowhere to cast her a disapproving glance. "Stay away from him, Stephie," Dyer warned in a hushed voice as he shepherded her down the steps beside him. "I'm not blind. I have seen the way Cole stares at you when he thinks I'm not looking. And please try to be a little less enchanting for one night." He stared pointedly at his youngest daughter's bewitching profile. "Natalie can use all the help she can get. She is sorely in need of a suitable husband."

Stephanie pasted on a blinding smile. "If you had bothered to consult Natalie on the matter, you might be surprised to find that she disagrees with you, Papa," she told him frankly. "You should get to know Natalie. Even with your years of coddling and pampering, I don't think you really know your eldest daughter."

Dyer glared at Stephanie and clamped a tighter grip on her forearm. "Just do as I ask for one night. I don't want you to make this party—perhaps Natalie's engagement party—a disaster."

"I will try to behave myself," Stephanie told him, her tone lacking sincerity.

"Don't *try*, do it," Dyer demanded. "I don't wish to spend the night wondering if calamity is about to avalanche upon us. Coleman Hollister is off limits and I had better not see you encouraging him."

Encourage him! Stephanie nearly burst into a laugh. If her father knew the real Coleman Douglas Hollister the Third, he would not have made such an outrageous statement. She could not even run to her father, crying that she had been used to satisfy Cole's lusts. Dyer would accuse *her* of seducing Cole. Her own father didn't trust her!

After enduring the introduction and innuendos in the receiving line, Cole made a beeline for the study. When he had downed two glasses of bottled courage, he propelled himself toward the ballroom. It was just as he had predicted. Stephanie was the focal point of the party. Men revolved around her, vying for her attention and the opportunity of holding her in their arms. Her lighthearted laughter rang in his ears like a choir of chanting angels. The sparkle in her sea green eyes was like sunrays spreading across ocean waves. She was where she had always been—just out of reach—compelling him closer when he knew he should turn tail and run before he fell in over his foolish head.

Feeling an obligation to his date and determined to compensate his envy, Cole scanned the crowded room to locate Natalie. She was propped against the wall beside the refreshment table, looking as if she had misplaced her last friend.

The moment Cole drew her trim body against his,

Natalie shrank away as if she had been stung. Cole frowned in annoyance. "What is the matter with you, woman? I am only dancing with you. 'Tis hardly rape I have in mind," he grunted sarcastically. "Your father is pushing for my marriage proposal and you act as if you cannot tolerate the slightest touch!"

Natalie's face whitewashed. Her lack of nerve refused to allow her to retaliate to his intimidating remark. She simply followed his lead, resembling a wounded dog that would have preferred to slink into a dark corner.

The wine and Cole's sour disposition had taken its toll. Cole was in no mood to pretend to enjoy himself in Natalie's company. He wanted Stephanie in his arms and no substitute was going to satisfy the gnawing hunger. Not Natalie, not Adeline, no one but Steph.

When the minuet ended, Cole guided Natalie to her place on the wall and then sought out Stephanie. Although she was surrounded by a throng of admirers, Cole removed bodies from his path to place himself at Stephanie's side. Before she could register a protest, Cole grasped her hand and led her to the dance floor.

"I had no idea you were so rude," Stephanie teased the gallant aristocrat. "I had already promised the dance to someone else and Papa will scold me for going near you. If you wish to remain in his good graces, this will be our first and last dance."

Cole had no intention of being told what he could and couldn't do. And he was not about to let a clump of men keep him from what he wanted. He had enough of playing the proper-mannered gentleman.

Holding Stephanie closer than necessary, Cole leaned down to brush his lips against the trim column of her neck. A grin formed on his mouth when he noticed that Dyer had turned an unbecoming shade of red. "I can always claim that your unconventional behavior finally rubbed off on me," he chuckled softly.

Stephanie also caught her father's fuming stare. "And Papa will believe it," she grumbled, battling the forbidden sensations of being held in Cole's powerful arms.

He pulled her full length against him, allowing her to feel the hard contours of his body while they swayed in rhythm to the music of the orchestra. Cole was certain he had overdressed for the occasion. He was hot and shaky. Touching this lovely sprite ignited fires that refused to be ignored. The memories of their nights of secret splendor closed in around him like a flaming fog. He remembered every divine moment, every glorious sensation, as if it were recurring right in the middle of the dance floor!

Dyer was shocked to see that Stephanie and Cole were about as close as two people could get without overstepping the bounds of common decency! With his jaw clenched in icy disdain, Dyer stalked over to grab Natalie's hand. With his eldest daughter in tow, he cut his way through the crowd to substitute Natalie for Stephanie.

Taking Stephanie by the arm, Dyer sped her toward a secluded corner. "If you cannot behave yourself, I will have you locked in your room," Dyer hissed angrily. "*Natalie* is to be Cole's wife and I will not have you throwing yourself at him just to spite me!"

Stephanie inhaled an indignant breath, prepared to fling a suitably nasty reply, but for once she held her tongue. She could talk until she was blue in the face and still Dyer would think her guilty of whatever crime he decided she had committed.

When Dyer stomped off in a huff, Stephanie muttered under her breath. As she glanced about her, she found herself the recipient of several disapproving stares—mostly from women who envied the fact that

190

she had been enveloped in Cole's powerful arms. Well, they were all welcome to him, she thought resentfully. The man was trouble—more than two hundred pounds of it. But it would take a courageous woman to handle a man like Cole Hollister. He was not at all what he seemed. Indeed, the man was *double* trouble. A woman was never certain which contrasting personality she would encounter until the moment was upon her.

Feeling the need for a breath of fresh air, Stephanie aimed herself toward the terrace doors and slipped outside. Her frustration dissolved when she spied Wesley Beacham clinging to the shadows, staring through the window at the crowded ballroom.

Impulsively, she sailed toward him, her arms outstretched. But she had no idea that Cole had relinquished all pretense and had followed in her wake to see her fly at Wesley as if he were her long lost lover.

"My, but you look bewitching, little imp," Wes complimented as he pressed a light kiss to her forehead. "I don't know which attire fascinates me most—your caped bandit garb or this elegant array of ruffles and lace."

"Flatterer," Stephanie mocked. A bright smile pursed her lips as she brushed her fingers through Wesley's thick brown hair. "You always did know the way to my heart."

Wesley breathed a frustrated sigh. "And you know what weighs heavily on *my* heart and soul, Steph. This cussed waiting is driving me mad! I want to announce my marriage to the world instead of hiding it."

Stephanie curled her arm around his waist and laid her head against his shoulder. "It doesn't seem fair, does it? When two people care deeply for each other, they should be together, living as man and wife. Loving transcends the rigid cast system of society and I detest the fact that British law prohibits you from claiming your rights." She tilted her head back to grace him with an encouraging smile. "Hopefully, you will soon be free of your indentureship and . . ."

While Stephanie and Wesley were lost in conversation, Cole was scraping himself up off the terrace. Stephanie was married to this servant, the man Cole met when he signed the register at Reynolds Inn? Damnit, that was illegal! Cole laughed bitterly at the thought. Since when had this misfit concerned herself with legality? Why should he be surprised that Stephanie had defied British regulations by secretly marrying a man who had sacrificed his personal rights for the years of his indentureship? Indeed, why should anything about Stephanie surprise him?

Obviously this was the man Stephanie sneaked off to meet most every night. How else would Wes have known she garbed herself in a black cape and breeches unless he was the one who was lurking in the shadows with his confounded pebbles and lanterns? This was Stephanie's husband? Cole recalled what Stephanie had said about how he had deprived her of the gift of innocence that was meant for her husband. Now he understood all too well! Stephanie allowed herself to be seen about Mystic on the arm of various gentlemen. But it was all a charade. She passed herself off as an eligible heiress because her father wanted his daughters married off in chronological order.

This minx was biding her time until Natalie and Adeline wed, waiting until she could announce her *illegal* wedding to this redemptioner. Cole scowled to himself. No doubt, Wesley thought his bride was pure and innocent and expected just that when he was finally permitted to have her as his wife in every sense of the word.

A strange brand of anger sizzled through his bloodstream. He knew he had no right to be jealous and that he should turn and walk away. But damnit, marriage or no marriage, *he* was the only man who had possessed Stephanie's luscious body. And by law, she really didn't have a husband, he rationalized as his irritation swelled out of proportion.

Inspired by his unreasonable jealousy, Cole did something he had never done before in his life. He stalked toward Stephanie before he was forced to watch her melt all over her secret love. Cole didn't have the faintest notion what he intended to say. All he knew was that he was mad as hell and he wanted to punch Wesley what's-his-name right in the jaw for capturing this wild firebrand's heart.

A startled gasp erupted from Stephanie's lips when Cole Hollister appeared from the shadows. "What are you doing out here?" she snapped in annoyance.

"What are *you* doing out here?" Cole threw back at her, his voice carrying a biting edge. "You are supposed to be entertaining your houseful of guests, not dallying with the uninvited pests and insects that are attracted by the bright lights." His scorching glare fried Wesley to a burnt crisp.

The insulting sermon caused Stephanie to stiffen like an arched-backed cat. "If you are practicing making a nuisance of yourself, go bother someone else. You are not my father and I do not have to answer to you," she hissed poisonously. "What I do is my own business and I will not have you degrading Wesley! For all your polish and finery, you are not half the man he is!"

"Someone needs to keep close tabs on you," Cole ground out between clenched teeth. "You have run wild so long that you are practically unmanageable. If your father knew you were out here, mingling with the servants, he would be hopping up and down with fury."

The thought struck home, making Wesley all too aware of his hopeless predicament. "The gentleman is right, Steph," he breathed deflatedly. "If I owned a gun, I would wander off and kill myself."

A wicked smile dangled from the corner of Cole's lips. He reached into his waistcoat to produce his flintlock. "Would you care to borrow mine?" he questioned flippantly.

Stephanie could have stepped on Cole and squashed him flat for making such a sarcastic remark. Cole was the one who needed to be removed to a higher sphere. Couldn't he see that Wesley's spirits had already shriveled up into nothing?

"I suppose you are one of those arrogant asses who thinks a man is less a man because misfortune keeps him in bondage," Stephanie hurled nastily. "Well, let me tell you something. Mr. High and Mighty Hollister! Wesley was educated in one of the finest colleges in Dublin. He would have more degrees than a thermometer if family hardship had not forced him to sell himself for the price of passage to America!"

Stephanie inhaled an irritated breath and blazed on. "Just because you were born with a silver spoon in your mouth doesn't make you a better man than Wesley. As a matter of fact, he seems more the gentleman than you are!"

One heavy brow elevated to a taunting angle as Cole raked Stephanie up and down. "Oh, is that so?" His tone was warped with sarcasm. "If that is true, why are *you* guarding him like a dragon? If Wesley whoever-he-is deems his integrity has been insulted, he should defend himself."

Wesley moved Stephanie aside to confront the elegantly dressed rogue who stood at least six inches taller and fifty pounds heavier. In his diplomatic tone he responded to Cole's taunting comments. "I do not wish to cause a scene, sir. And I do not want to make trouble for Steph. I beg your silence in this matter."

"I will pretend I saw and heard nothing if you promise to make no more attempts to see *Miss* Wakefield," Cole bartered.

Wesley's gaze dropped to Stephanie's agitated expression. "You have my word, Mr. Hollister." When Stephanie opened her mouth to protest, Wesley pressed his index finger to her lips to stifle her. "He is right, love. Our association will only get you into more trouble. That is the last thing I want."

Damn that Cole Hollister, Stephanie silently cursed. He had his nerve, pasting stipulations on whom she could and couldn't see! Who did he think he was anyway? Her guardian angel?

When Wesley reached into his vest pocket to fish out a folded paper and handed it to Stephanie, Cole growled under his breath. "A love letter, Wesley? There will be no more of those either!"

Stephanie's fingers clenched around the parchment, wishing it was Cole's neck that was clutched in her fist. "I thought Papa dragged you home to court my sister. I had no idea your ultimate purpose was to spy and tattle on me if I misbehaved."

The cogs of Cole's brain were cranking, searching for an appropriately sarcastic rejoinder to fling at her. He landed on one and quickly put it to tongue. "When a woman manages to botch up her life as clumsily as you have, someone needs to take her under wing and iron out the unbecoming wrinkles in her soul. You, my dear Stephanie, are a misfit."

"And you are a miserable son of—"

Before Stephanie lost what was left of her highly explosive temper, Wesley clamped his hand over her mouth and hooked his free arm around her waist. Stephanie had bared her claws and Wes was not about to let her sink her nails in Cole's flesh, though he agreed the rogue deserved it.

"Which sister are you courting?" Wesley questioned Cole, immediately changing the subject.

Cole frowned at the abrupt inquiry. "Natalie."

Quiet laughter bubbled from Wesley's lips. He grinned conspiratorily at Stephanie, who had finally relaxed in his arms. "Haven't you told your friend that Natalie isn't interested in courting men?" he snickered.

Wesley's wry grin flooded over Stephanie, dissolving the last of her irritation. "Nay, I have neglected to mention the fact to Mr. Hollister. Indeed, I would have preferred to let him fumble along, wondering why she had not melted beneath his charm . . . what little there is of it," she tacked on tauntingly.

Cole glanced back and forth between the two smiling faces. "And just what is wrong with Natalie that makes her immune to the men Dyer steers in her direction?" He thought he already knew the answer, but he would have appreciated hearing his speculations confirmed, rather than drifting in a sea of conjecture.

Stephanie shrugged a partially bared shoulder and tossed Wesley a secretive smile. "My dear sister displayed her preferences more than a year ago. 'Tis a pity you don't understand, Mr. Hollister. But if you have been harboring the delusion that you can somehow sway Natalie and persuade her to accept a marriage contract, you are sorely mistaken. Nattie will not agree to wed you, nor any other man Papa selects for her."

Cole knew what Stephanie was trying *not* to say, but she had just confirmed his darkest suspicions. It was just as he thought. Natalie preferred women. Poor Dyer. He was wasting his time trying to marry off his eldest daughter.

Tossing the thought aside, Cole clamped his arm around Stephanie's waist and hauled her up beside him. "I will accompany Stephanie back to the ball before she is missed," he said stiffly. It was killing him to think of feisty Stephanie married to this soft-spoken redemptioner. She was too much woman for Wes! "If you do not keep your vow of steering clear of Stephanie, life will become very difficult for you."

"It already is," Wesley grumbled bitterly.

As Cole shuffled Stephanie along beside him, she struggled to escape his vise grip. My, but he had strong hands and arms, she mused acrimoniously. His fingertips bit into her ribs, very nearly cracking them in two.

"You are hurting me," she growled, glaring holes in his expensive waistcoat.

"Not as much as I would like to," Cole muttered spitefully. "And if you don't start behaving like a lady, I'm going to turn you over my knee and give you the thrashing your father neglected."

"You wouldn't dare," she challenged, her voice carrying a most unpleasant edge.

A satanic smile settled in his craggy features and his teeth gleamed like polished pearls. "My dearest Stephanie, I would do it in a minute. And what's more, I would derive immense pleasure in tanning your backside until you couldn't bear to sit down!"

"It seems I made the blundering mistake of thinking you were a gentleman." Stephanie wrapped the words around her tongue and flung them at him. "But the truth is, you are a conniving wolf in sheep's wool. Beneath your tailored coat is a man who directly contrasts the impression you wish to convey to the public. You are walking proof that clothes do not make the gentleman. Indeed, you are an elegantly dressed rapscallion!"

"Tsk, tsk. Sticks and stones . . ." Cole clucked, undaunted by her tirade of insults.

"Ah, what I wouldn't give for a barrel of sticks and

stones . . . to hurl at your monumental arrogance," she sniped.

The moment Cole opened the terrace door, his expression changed and so did Stephanie's. Any onlooker would have thought they were involved in a pleasant conversation. But nothing could have been farther from the truth. And if a man could be sentenced and hanged for crimes he was *contemplating* committing, both Cole and Stephanie would have been climbing the steps to the gallows.

The fact was, they could have strangled each other without batting an eyelash. Cole was furious that Stephanie had embroiled herself into an illegal marriage with an indentured servant. Stephanie was outraged that Cole had sneaked up on her and begun spouting commands as if he were her personal guardian. Damn the man. Wasn't he satisfied with using her as his private whore? Did he think he could rule her life as well? If he thought she would submit to his tyranny, he had another think coming. Hell would sooner drip icicles!

Chomping on that bitter thought, Stephanie accepted the glass of punch Cole had retrieved for her. Oh, how she would have loved to pour the cool drink on his head. The arrogant lout.

Cole could have read the spiteful thoughts as if they were printed on Stephanie's forehead. A wry smile brimmed his lips as he gestured his raven head toward the drink she was contemplating throwing on him. "I wouldn't if I were you, my dear," he purred in sticky sweetness, "lest you wish this entire crowd to witness your well-deserved throttling."

Stephanie was growing more agitated by the second. Never had a man talked to her the way Cole had in the last quarter of an hour—issuing threats, making unreasonable demands. Cole Hollister had sashayed into Mystic, appointed himself king, and attempted to make her his devoted servant. He seemed to think she should be grateful for the crumbs of attention he threw at her, for the *honor* of sharing his lusty brand of passion in stolen moments of the night. There was no reason for his misplaced feelings of possessiveness toward her. For the life of her, Stephanie could not fathom why Cole would even want to take her under his wing. And, by damned, she was not about to be browbeaten by this overbearing rake! The next time she got him alone she was going to land another blow to his conceited jaw! But it would be no accidental punch. She was going to club him on purpose, to repay him for meddling in her life!

Chapter 12

While Stephanie and Cole were practicing civilized warfare, Brice Reynolds was lounging against the door of the ballroom. Although he had not been invited to the grand affair, he was there just the same. It was his intent to prove to his friends and neighbors that he had no fear of the threats made against him by the patriot mob that had been heckling him the past week. And he wanted it known that Stephanie Wakefield held no threat either.

Brice had the sneaking suspicion that Stephanie was behind the protests and the threats that were designed to force him into resigning his position as stamp agent. But he had no proof that the mischievous misfit had plotted against him. Brice hoped his appearance would set fuse to Stephanie's volatile temper and she would blurt out a confession that he could tattle to the British magistrate. Nothing would have made Brice happier than to see Stephanie Wakefield whipped for defying the Crown. She would serve as an example to all those rebels who had stormed his inn, threatened to destroy his property, and had him tarred and feathered.

When Stephanie glanced around the crowded room, looking for an excuse to leave the infuriating Cole

Hollister standing all by himself in the corner, she spotted Brice Reynolds. Cole's intimidating commands had already caused her temper to boil. But the sight of Brice was like setting a flaming torch to a sea of kerosene.

Brice had the incredible audacity to show his face in her home after he had publicly humiliated her. How dare he invade this party! The spiteful thoughts that had been buzzing through her mind were suddenly directed toward the devious Brice Reynolds. First she could make Brice the target of her irritation. And when she finished pounding that varmint flat and mailing him to King George, she would stuff Cole Hollister in an envelope and have him sent to the edge of the earth, never to be seen or heard from again.

Cole's face turned as hard as granite when he noticed who had captured Stephanie's attention. He could see her petite body going rigid in preparation for battle. The expression on her face spelled trouble. What this spitfire was contemplating was anybody's guess. Cole didn't have the slightest idea what she was planning, but he swore there were at least a score of vengeful plots hatching in her mind. She was one of those women who delighted in the challenge of rattling the lion's cage. If Stephanie was allowed to have her way, Brice Reynolds would be choking on his just desserts in a matter of minutes, with her father's guests as witnesses!

"Steph . . ." Cole's voice held a quiet warning. "Sometimes 'tis wise to consider the repercussions before plunging headlong into a fight. Decide how and where you intend to retreat after you finish the skirmish. If you give Brice the flimsiest excuse, he will have you dragged back to court . . ."

Stephanie didn't want a lecture on war tactics. She wanted revenge and she hated when Cole was right. Her breath came out in a rush. She couldn't very well march up to that weasel who was beaming in smug satisfaction and dump the punch bowl on his head. If she employed that technique, *she* would look the culprit.

Nay, she would have to devise a way to place the blame on Brice. Her eyes fell to the parchment Wesley had given her, and a wry smile replaced her spiteful frown.

"Are you a coward, Cole?" she questioned point-blank.

Cole studied her speculatively, wondering what she had in mind. "I like to think not."

"If you suspect you might possess any fainthearted tendencies, I suggest you take this opportunity to fade into the woodwork," she murmured, her gaze glued to the strutting peacock—Brice Reynolds.

"What are you planning, minx?" Cole queried cautiously.

An impish grin set her jewel-like eyes to sparkling with devilish glee. "'Tis referred to as *the direct approach,*" she informed him. "If one wishes to ignite a quick fire, one grasps a torch instead of rubbing two sticks together."

"Steph . . ." Cole growled softly. "You are asking for trouble, perhaps more than even *you* can handle."

Her red-blond curls fluttered about her lovely face as she gave her head a denying shake. "Nay, Brice is the one asking for trouble by showing his face here tonight. I intend to indulge him."

Before Cole could utter another word of caution (and he had dozens of arguments against the folly of direct confrontation), Stephanie wedged her way through the crowd toward Brice. Grumbling, Cole thrust his drink into a guest's empty hand and followed in Stephanie's wake. Since he had dedicated himself to keeping Stephanie out of trouble, he was obliged to keep a close eye on her. He was a fool to think he could control the likes of hurricane Stephanie, he told himself sourly. Stephanie was a disaster waiting to happen!

"Ah, Brice, how wonderful to see you again." Sticky sarcasm dripped off her lips. Stephanie raked Brice's stout physique. He reminded her of a gigantic beetle in his black waistcoat and red silk vest and Stephanie was sorely wishing she could step on this oversized insect and mash him into the floor.

Brice's thick brows elevated in response to Stephanie's remark. "I thought my presence here would infuriate you, dear Stephanie," he taunted with a froglike smile. "Indeed, I was counting upon it." His gaze lifted to see Cole's massive frame standing behind Stephanie as reinforcement. "Did you bring along your guard dog to rescue you in case you misplaced your manners again?"

Stephanie countered with another pretentious smile. "I am in the habit of fighting my own enemies, Brice. The fact is, Mr. Hollister came along for the amusement of watching you stick your foot in your mouth. And I, for one, hope you choke on your sole."

Her gaze drifted to Natalie, who was watching with wide, apprehensive eyes. With a slight inclination of her head, Stephanie silently suggested that Natalie make a hasty exit through the terrace door. Once Natalie was safely out of the way, Stephanie refocused her attention on Brice. And by that time, Brice's puckered face was a putrid shade of purple.

"If you dare insult me in front of these good people a second time, I'll have you whipped instead of ducked," he threatened with a venomous hiss. "And if you sic your patriot friends on me again, I will have you swinging from a rope, woman."

"Will you run and rattle to the British magistrate like you did last time?" Stephanie parried mockingly.

203

"Surely you don't think the magistrate is going to hold an innocent woman personally responsible for having you tarred and feathered, even if you offer him a bribe."

"I do not have to bribe the man," Brice crowed like an indignant rooster.

"But you could most certainly afford to if it came to that, couldn't you, Brice?" Stephanie's delicately arched brow climbed to an intimidating angle. "With all the underhanded profits you are making from your female indentured servants, you will soon be as wealthy as my father." Her green eyes flooded over Brice's elegant clothes. "Do you suppose the patriots will become more violent when they learn what has been going on in Reynolds Inn?" Stephanie nodded thoughtfully. "Aye, 'tis my prediction that you will be carried out of town on a rail . . . after you have been justly punished for your crimes."

The subtle remarks made Brice swallow his tongue. She knew! How could she have found out? A wordless growl erupted from his lips. Wesley Beacham had broken the confidence. Damn that bastard. Brice swore he would never let that backstabbing accountant get free of bondage. He knew too much!

"What did you do to make Wes loose his tongue?" Brice snarled in question. "Give him that luscious body of yours? No doubt you tried to pay for his freedom so you could keep him as one of your many studs. A woman with your *low* morals . . ."

"*My* low morals?" Stephanie scoffed incredulously. "You are the most unprincipled man I have ever met, Brice Reynolds. First you bribed the magistrate to ensure you received the position as stamp collector. You bought yourself a capable, intelligent servant to do your bookkeeping. You are forcing Wes to keep your dastardly secrets because he has no civil rights that permit him to speak out against you. Now you are trying to work around the law and keep him in servitude by forcing him to marry one of your bondswomen. Wes would only be *half* free, wouldn't he? You would make certain that you held Elizabeth Marrow's indentured contract over him forevermore.

"And if those were not crimes enough, you have taken defenseless women who have sold themselves into your service and ordered them to accommodate your guests at the inn—all sea captains and sailors who sail away, never to divulge your disgusting secret." Stephanie inhaled a deep breath and raked the miserable scoundrel with scorn. "You? Respectable? Mr. Reynolds, 'tis a contradiction in terms."

"You have no proof of what you are saying," Brice snorted, his eyes darting frantically about him. It infuriated him to note the condemnation that spread across the faces in the crowd. "Your false accusations will never stand up in a court of law. You are only trying to turn public opinion against me and incite your Whig friends into another riot."

"I have all the proof I need," Stephanie contradicted. A spiteful grin tugged at her lips as she unfolded the parchment Wesley had given her. "I don't think the sheriff or magistrate will have difficulty believing me when the evidence is here in black and white."

Cole was hanging on their every word, as was every other eavesdropper in the ballroom. The orchestra had set their instruments aside when the guests migrated toward the corner where Stephanie and Brice were standing. Cole didn't know exactly what was going on, but Stephanie's comments had untangled a few puzzles he had been unable to solve.

It was obvious that Stephanie had attempted to buy Wesley's freedom so they could be properly married. Brice had rejected the offer because the servant could voice incriminating evidence against his master. And it seemed the proprietor of Reynolds Inn was forcing young bondswomen to whore for the guests at the inn. So that was why the young serving maid had approached him the first day he arrived in Mystic, Cole thought as he glared at Brice. The girl hadn't really wanted to offer her body to him, but Brice had demanded it. Brice was taking the payment the women received for doling out favors, none of which counted toward paying off the debt of indentureship. There was no telling what punishment the women were to receive if they did not comply with Brice's wishes. A beating? Slavery, or perhaps a longer indentureship?

Brice's face blanched chalk-white to match his powdered wig, and Stephanie snickered victoriously. She knew she had Brice backed against the wall. The other guests were watching and listening, doubting the man had even a smidgeon of respectability. Now all Stephanie had to do was fray Brice's taut nerves and his temper would snap.

A thoughtful frown creased Stephanie's brow as she looked Brice up and down. She gestured a slim finger toward the wig that capped his prematurely bald head. "It seems your barber missed a spot when he powdered your wig." She indicated the left side of his head, just above his elephant-sized ears. "This side of your hairpiece is not the same color, Brice," she informed him. "But luckily for you, I will help you remedy the problem."

As casually as if she were arranging silverware on a table, Stephanie removed the wig in question. The crowd parted as she walked purposefully toward the refreshment table. Grinning in spiteful satisfaction, Stephanie dowsed the hairpiece in the frothy red punch. A shocked gasp rippled through the crowd of observers when Stephanie scooped up the wig and marched back toward Brice.

Cole knew exactly what was coming next. He could see the mischievous glint in Stephanie's lively green eyes. It was difficult to keep a sober face when he knew Stephanie had devised a way to repay Brice for her humiliating ducking.

Smiling as proudly as if she accomplished the greatest favor one person could do for another, Stephanie strode up in front of Brice. With one graceful move she replaced the red mop of hair on Brice's shiny head. If a pin had dropped on the floor, it would have resembled the sound of a chisel colliding with bedrock.

"There," Stephanie cooed sweetly. "Now your wig is uniform in color."

Red punch dripped from the top of Brice's head onto his white silk shirt. The crowd waited, wondering if Brice would retaliate or slink away with his tail tucked between his legs. Brice had been exposed for his skulduggery. Assuming the position of tax collector had made him unpopular with his neighbors, but Stephanie's accusations had completely turned the town against him. Brice could see the condemnation written in every face that was glaring at him.

Being bested by this sassy firebrand was simply too much! Brice chanced to lose everything he had worked so hard to acquire. And all because of this green-eyed witch, Brice thought murderously.

His fingers curled and his mouth tightened in a malicious sneer. "You little bitch!"

He lunged at Stephanie like an enraged panther. His hands closed around her throat, cutting off her breath. Stephanie clawed at him, leaving bloody gashes on his face, but Brice was relentless. He meant to kill her where she stood, oblivious to the eyewitnesses who were frozen in shock . . . all except one, that is.

Suddenly, Brice was snatched away and Stephanie could not believe what she saw next. She had pegged Cole as an outwardly calm, nonviolent man who sought to hide his wild savagery. In most incidences, Cole employed diplomacy and used brutality only as a last resort. But from the looks of things, Stephanie had totally misjudged this seemingly sophisticated aristocrat. The killer instinct was gathering like thunderclouds in those stormy black eyes. The shell of refinement cracked wide open and the rugged rogue who loomed beneath the surface poured forth like an erupting volcano.

To her bewilderment, Cole snarled like a disturbed grizzly bear. With lightning grace, he sprang on Brice. Cole's fingers clenched into the ruffles on the front of Brice's shirt. Brice found himself hoisted off the floor, his legs dangling in midair. He squawked in fearful anticipation when he was catapulted across the room like a blunt-end spear. A pained grunt erupted when his body collided with the solid wall. Amid the stars that encircled his head, Brice saw Cole charge at him like a bull attacking a matador's cape. Brice's breath came out in a pitiful groan as he doubled over to protect himself from another punishing attack. But Cole clamped his hand around Brice's chin, bringing him back to an upright position. Then, a doubled fist swished through the air to connect with Brice's already stinging jaw.

The sound of flesh cracking against flesh made Stephanie wince uncomfortably. She had seen one or two brawls on the wharf, but she had never seen one man pulverize another. And that was exactly what this *seemingly* civilized gentleman was doing to Brice! Somewhere in Cole's past, he had learned to fight and fight exceptionally well. Cole was ferocious, quick, and unbelievably powerful.

Brice couldn't return the blows or protect himself from injury. Cole was so agile that he danced circles around the staggering Brice. Like a bear rearing on hind legs to swat his prey with his deadly paws, Cole pelleted Brice from one direction and then another. Each time Brice's knees threatened to buckle beneath him, Cole grabbed hold of his shirt and drew him up to full stature to land another well-aimed blow.

Stephanie stood back, her mouth gaping. Where in the world had this supposed gentleman learned to fight like that? His entire body was a lethal weapon! It was apparent that Cole had a high threshold on his temper. But once it snapped he literally came unglued. Stephanie was eternally thankful she had never pushed Cole to this frenzied point. She would hate to be on the receiving end of those flying legs and fists!

"Hollister!"

Dyer's voice cracked like thunder, jolting Cole back to his senses. But the instant Cole glared at Brice, who had wilted to his knees, murderous fury sizzled through him again. The moment Brice had wrapped his stubby fingers around Stephanie's neck, Cole had reverted to his old ways. The repressed savage in him bubbled in his veins and he began to react instinctively.

Even now, when he had beaten Brice to a pulp, Cole felt the uncontrollable urge to hit him again. Dragging in a steadying breath, Cole clamped an iron grip on himself and resisted the temptation.

"If you ever dare to lay a hand on her again, so help me God, I will see you roast in hell!" Cole's voice was as hard as a headstone.

Brice stared, blurry-eyed, at Cole's polished boots. The man was looming over him like an avenging god. This last bit of humiliation was too much for Brice to endure. Hatred boiled within him, poisoning logic. Twice Cole Hollister had stepped between him and

Stephanie, preventing Brice from satisfying his thirst for revenge. That thought provoked a maddening need for spiteful satisfaction—the kind that knew no fear. As Brice's eyes lifted to meet Cole's dark, chisled features, he reached inside his jacket to grasp his pistol.

Cole reacted in a split-second. Intent on stomping this disgusting bastard into the floor, Cole spun sideways to thrust out a leg. But Brice's finger frantically clutched at the trigger. He was determined to put a bullet through Cole's heart.

Stephanie had been standing in the wings, content to let Cole do what she wished she could have done. But the instant she realized what Brice intended, she sprang into action. Panic spurred her to thrust herself between the men. Instead of running like a frightened rabbit or diving for cover like most of the guests, Stephanie threw herself into harm's way to redirect the pistol toward the ceiling. Her attempt to save Cole from being shot through the heart was successful, but the sound kick Cole had meant for Brice collided with her hip. Before she could groan in pain the pistol discharged, catching her in the shoulder.

A piercing cry erupted from her lips as fire streaked down her arm. Blood instantly stained her gown. Stephanie wasn't certain which hurt worst—Cole's devastating mule-kick or the gunshot wound. It was difficult to tell when both her right arm and leg were pulsating with agony.

Another vicious growl exploded from Cole's lips when he saw what the maniac had done. With a fist of steel poised in midair, Cole recoiled and struck. Two hundred and twenty pounds of solid strength delivered a blow that put Brice Reynolds out of everyone's misery. And it was that brain-scrambling assault that convinced Stephanie that Cole had been holding back. If she had not seen Brice launched through air to slam

210

against the wall, she would have sworn a man was incapable of hitting any harder than Cole already had! Cole Hollister had just demonstrated how dangerous he could be when he was provoked to killing fury. Beneath that sophisticated veneer of clothing was a man who could fight like the most fearless lion ever to stalk the jungle. Stephanie decided, then and there, that Cole Hollister was the essence of savage civility. Cole may have dressed like an affluent aristocrat but when he was furious, he certainly didn't fight like any gentleman she had ever seen!

With no concern as to whether Brice was dead or alive, Cole scooped up Stephanie and held her close. His mouth brushed tenderly over her ashen lips, apologizing over and over again for kicking *her* instead of Brice. With Stephanie clutched tightly against his heaving chest, Cole stepped over Brice's crumpled body without breaking stride and aimed himself toward the steps.

"Call the sheriff! Fetch the doctor!" Dyer ordered his guests.

The ballroom was evacuated like a swarm of ants abandoning a contaminated den. Guests were dashing toward their carriages, gossiping as fast as their tongues would wag. The Wakefields' ball had begun as one of Connecticut's most envied social events of the season and had prematurely ended in catastrophe.

"You can put me down," Stephanie insisted. Cole was holding her so close that she feared her father would scold her, even when she was wounded. She wouldn't have put it past him. "I was not injured in the foot."

"But you sustained a hard kick in the thigh," Cole reminded her softly. "God, I'm sorry. I would give most anything to turn back the clock and relive that moment."

211

Stephanie was becoming more uncomfortable by the minute. The entire family had fallen into step behind Cole and she feared they would suspect something was going on! "Cole, please," Stephanie grumbled, squirming in his arms.

"I will not risk having you faint at the sight of your own blood," Cole countered, his voice wavering between frustration and concern. "You have buckshot lodged in your shoulder and, no doubt, a welt the size of my boot heel on your hip." His dark eyes sketched Stephanie's waxen features, grimacing at her lack of color. "If I set you to your feet you might keel over and tumble down the stairs. The last thing you need in your condition is to break your lovely neck!"

Dyer leaped up the steps two at a time. "Is she all right?" he questioned breathlessly. When he spied Stephanie's ashen face, he gasped in shock. Swiveling around he barked orders to the rest of the family. "Addie, fetch the smelling salts in case your sister faints. Eileen, boil some water to cleanse the wound. Nattie, get some bandages." A puzzled expression clung to his wrinkled features. "Nattie?" His gaze searched the procession of family members and guests who were scurrying around at the bottom of the steps. "Where the devil is Nattie?"

"Forget Natalie," Cole growled bitterly. "Stephanie is the one carrying the bullet that was meant for me."

"Nattie should be here to share this family crisis," Dyer argued and then threw up his hands in exasperation. "Lord, I hope she isn't lying somewhere in a dead faint! The girl has a weak stomach."

"Nattie has her own crisis to consider," Stephanie declared as she watched her mother and Adeline clamber up the steps, prepared to attend to their nursing duties.

"What are you ranting about, girl?" Dyer muttered

and then shot Cole a quizzical glance. "Do you know what she is talking about? Does *anyone* know what Stephie is talking about? Every accusation she made against Brice was a surprise to me!" he burst out. "I never know what is going on around here!"

Cole knew exactly what was going on but he wasn't about to divulge any information concerning Dyer's favorite offspring or the secret marriage of his youngest daughter. If Dyer were assaulted with that barrage of shocking knowledge, *he* would crumble into an unconscious heap and he would be no help at all!

"Put me down, Cole," Stephanie demanded, jostling him from his pensive musings. "'Tis time I straightened this mess out."

Reluctantly, Cole obeyed the command. He wasn't sure Stephanie should be walking on her own accord, but as always, she seemed determined to have her way.

Bracing herself on Cole's sturdy arm, Stephanie inhaled a shuddering breath and recomposed herself as best she could. It had taken a shot in the arm to make her realize enough was enough. It was time to air the sheets and Stephanie decided to grasp each corner and give them a good shaking. She had been harboring too many secrets and she was tired of bearing everyone else's problems.

The fiasco at the party had set off a chain of events that bumfuzzled everyone in her family, and Stephanie thought it was time her father knew what was going on. Enough pretense. Tonight seemed to be right for exposing little-known truths and Stephanie had taken it upon herself to clear up every question and speculation that was buzzing through her family's minds . . . not to mention a few well-hidden secrets that had never even entered her father's head!

Indicating the second door in the north wing, the room which was surrounded by another convenient balcony that had seen its share of traffic, Stephanie directed Cole to lead her forward.

"That isn't your room," Dyer reminded his youngest daughter, certain her terrifying experience had rattled her brain.

Stephanie flung Dyer a withering glance. The poor man had been wearing blinders for the past year and a half. He didn't have a clue about Natalie. But within a few minutes he was going to know his eldest daughter extremely well!

"Believe it or not, Papa, I know exactly what I'm doing and where I am going. Please bear with me," she requested as she limped down the hall.

In silence, the entourage followed Stephanie. Not a soul knew what was about to take place except Stephanie. She knew perfectly well what must be done for the good of all concerned. And before the night was out, Stephanie intended to burn every bridge in front *and* behind her!

Chapter 13

Without bothering to announce herself, Stephanie grasped the knob and flung open Natalie's bedroom door. The portal crashed against the wall, causing dribbles of dust to sift from the woodwork. She could not say for certain who looked the most surprised by what they saw—Cole, Dyer, Eileen, Addie, Nattie, or Wesley. It was a close contest. When mouths fell open, wooden teeth would have clatterd to the floor . . . in the event that anyone had been wearing them.

"For God's sake, Natalie!" Dyer croaked aghast and then clutched his arm around his wife when she sucked in her breath and swayed toward him.

Natalie and Wesley Beacham were cozily tucked in bed with the sheet clutched beneath their chins. Their eyes were bulging from their sockets and their faces were void of color. Frantically, they looked to Stephanie, who was pressing Cole's handkerchief over her shoulder wound.

Cole could have been knocked down by the slightest breath of wind. He couldn't believe what he was seeing! What the devil was Natalie doing in bed with *Stephanie's* illegal husband, the one Stephanie had so fiercely defended the previous hour? And for that matter, what was Natalie doing in bed with anyone of the male persuasion? Cole had concluded that Nattie wanted nothing to do with men. She had certainly behaved as if she detested *his* touch each time he went near her!

Anger simmered inside Cole as he glared daggers at Wesley Beacham. What was there about this meek, mild-mannered man that drew women like flies?

Cole had been furious to learn that Stephanie and this sneaky varmint were secretively married. But the thought of Wesley slipping around with Natalie while Stephanie was standing there, wounded and bleeding, was simply too much!

After Cole had deposited Stephanie in a chair, he stalked toward the bed. He looked every bit as ominous as he had been when he pounded Brice into the ballroom floor.

"Cole, what are you going to do?" Stephanie squeaked, struggling to gain her feet and stop him before he did something crazy.

Cole didn't bother to respond. He merely doubled his fist and buried it in Wesley's sagging jaw. When he had satisfied his craving for revenge he wheeled back around to stare at Stephanie. "Since you are in no condition to repay your husband's infidelity, I decided to do it for you."

"Her husband?" Dyer howled incredulously. When Eileen gasped for breath, Dyer clutched her to him. "Steady, Mother."

But Eileen couldn't get a firm grip on herself. Seeing Natalie in bed with a man that Cole identified as Stephanie's husband caused Eileen's composure to unravel like a ball of twine tumbling downhill.

The shocked look on her parents' faces provoked Natalie to wail like a banshee. Her wild gaze swung back to Wesley and she pressed trembling fingers to his chin. After she inspected his bruised jaw, her tormented eyes flew to her youngest sister. "Stephie, I depended on you. I trusted you . . ." She sobbed hysterically. "You promised to protect the secrets . . ."

Cole was completely confused. A muddled frown sank into his craggy features. "What the sweet loving hell *is* going on around here?" he growled in question. "I thought—why is she?—you said . . ."

Stephanie waved Cole to silence and bit back a mischievous grin. It was obvious that Cole had overheard the entire conversation on the terrace. But it was even more apparent that Cole had dashed to a cliff and jumped to the wrong conclusion. He had misconstrued what she and Wesley had said to each other. Before Stephanie could direct a reply to Cole's jumbled questions, Natalie began to shed a sea of tears.

"Stephie, you gave me your promise. Why did you betray me?" Nattie choked out as she clutched her arms around Wesley's neck, very nearly strangling him.

"Because I can no longer carry the burden of everyone else's secrets," she announced as she massaged her aching arm. "I have been caught in the middle once too often."

"I see what you mean," Wesley murmured, taking note of the blood stains that soiled Stephanie's elegant gown. "Perhaps 'tis time to drag all the skeletons from the closet and face the dreaded consequences."

"Skeletons?" Eileen groaned before she wilted into a faint.

After Dyer wrapped a supporting arm around his limp wife to prop her against him, he glowered at Natalie and Wesley. "Damnit, Nattie, you had better start talking," he roared in outrage.

Natalie had misplaced her tongue. She had swallowed it, in fact. Her horrified gaze slid to Stephanie, silently imploring her youngest sister to explain everything before Dyer sought out his pistol and shot the both of them.

Sighing heavily, Stephanie leaned back against the chair. It was obvious that Natalie could not even be shocked into spilling her confession. Again, Stephanie was forced to portray the liaison. Carefully, she formulated the words and spit them out in perfect precision.

"The reason Nattie has never warmed to any of the men Papa hauled to our doorstep is because she fell in love with Wesley Beacham more than two years ago. They have been meeting secretively. Nattie was afraid Papa would never give permission for her to be courted by a man who was bound by debt."

The look on Dyer's face confirmed Nattie's speculations. He would have protested courtship and he was irate to see how far along this secret romance had progressed!

"Because Nattie and Wes cared so deeply for each other, they decided to marry, even if the contract would not be recognized in a British court of law. Eight months ago Nattie sneaked down the balcony, tiptoed across the roof of the kitchen to the oak tree, and spirited off to meet Wes. They traveled to the justice of the peace in Stonington."

"But 'tis illegal to wed an indentured servant!" Dyer sputtered as he sliced Nattie a condemning glare. "Even the colony of Connecticut won't recognize the contract."

"'Tis exactly why they spirited off to another village where no one knew them," Stephanie informed her father. "And since the marriage cannot be publicly announced, Wesley follows the unconventional route to Nattie's bedroom during the night to join his wife."

Dyer rearranged his wife in his arms when she began to rouse. But his full attention was on his new son-in-law. The glower Dyer hurled at Wesley was meant

218

to maim.

Stephanie hurried on with her explanation before Dyer was provoked to violence. "Nattie and Wesley hoped to keep their marriage in confidence until Wesley completed his indentureship to Brice Reynolds in six more months. But certain circumstances required them to marry legally . . . posthaste." Her voice was heavy with pain and exhaustion, but she struggled to clarify the complications and resolve the dilemma.

When Eileen came to her senses and blinked, Stephanie smiled impishly. "Mother, you will be pleased to know you will become a grandmother by spring."

The news was too overwhelming for Eileen, who had been unconscious when Stephanie explained that it was *Nattie* who was married to Wesley. The thought of Nattie bearing the child who belonged to Stephanie's husband was devastating. Again, Eileen fainted dead away.

Dyer muttered under his breath and nodded for Stephanie to continue while he maneuvered Eileen's drooping body into his other arm.

"Once Wesley was a free man, Nattie intended to tell you of her preference, Papa. You would not have complained quite so much if Wesley were a legal citizen of the colonies. But with the baby coming, they needed to repeat the second set of vows and quickly," Stephanie declared emphatically.

"I tried to offer Brice Reynolds money to compensate for the last six months of Wesley's indentureship. He refused and Nattie and Wesley became frantic. Matters went from bad to worse when Brice attempted to strong-arm Wesley into marrying Elizabeth Marrow. He was going to give Wes the freedom he craved by releasing Elizabeth, who had not taken to the immoral, degrading services Brice expected of her at the inn. But

Wesley would not truly have had his freedom and Brice would still have had an indentured office manager chained to him. If Wesley ever tried to speak out against Brice, the proprietor of Reynolds Inn intended to claim that Wesley had married a woman who was still indentured. In short, Brice's plans were to include a form of blackmail."

Stephanie expelled a tired sigh. "Things were becoming an incredibly tangled mess. Wesley couldn't marry Elizabeth when he was secretively married to Nattie, who is carrying his child. Since Brice refused to cooperate, Wesley and I had to expose him for the scoundrel he was. Brice has been buying indentureships of attractive women and forcing them to accommodate his male patrons. Wesley made a copy of the ledger that indicated how much money each woman had handed over to Brice—none of which counted toward the debt of indentureship. Reynolds was forcing prostitution on every female servant who was bound to him. The secret was safe because the sailors left port without informing the citizens of Mystic that Brice was also running a bordello, an establishment which has long been considered unlawful in our community."

Cole stared bewilderedly at Stephanie. Lord, he had leaped from one ill-conceived conclusion to another. Stephanie's rowdy reputation had led him to believe that she had brought catastrophe upon herself. But when the truth was known, Stephanie had only been protecting her oldest sister and her brother-in-law, one she obviously cared a great deal about.

Stephanie had sacrificed herself and her reputation to ensure Nattie's happiness. Why, the little leprechaun deserved a medal for service above and beyond the call of duty to her family. All her sneaking around in the darkness was to make the necessary arrangements. Stephanie had conversed with Wesley each time he came and went from Nattie's boudoir!

While Cole was lost in contemplative deliberation, Stephanie was surveying her father's distraught expression. A sympathetic smile trailed across her lips. All Dyer's aspirations for Natalie had caused the family undue stress. But he had never known of all the scrambling that was going on behind his back. And Stephanie was nowhere near finished. There were still volumes of information to dole out before each well-kept secret was divulged.

"Because Papa decided that his daughter had to marry in chronological order Adeline was also placed between a rock and a hard place. Adeline could not announce her secret engagement to Richard Stover until Natalie was finally married."

Her eyes swung to Addie, who was beginning to fidget under Dyer's narrowed gaze. "The secret engagement between Addie and Richard was the reason I was racing your prize stallion, Papa," Stephanie elaborated. "Richard was bound and determined to speak to you in regard to your rule of marriage. He wanted to come on bended knee and beg for Addie's hand. I told him that his proposal would place undue pressure on Nattie. But I couldn't tell Richard that Nattie was already married and that his request would stress Nattie when she was in the first fragile months of pregnancy."

Stephanie drew in a weary breath, determined to lay the truth out in the open before she collapsed from loss of blood. "I challenged Richard to a race. If I won, Richard promised to hold his tongue for another six months and to keep the engagement to Addie a secret. If Richard won, he would ask for Addie's hand, thus stirring up more trouble than he ever imagined." A faint smile tripped across her lips as Dyer stared dazedly at her. "You see, Papa, Richard wasn't humiliated that he was bested by a woman. He was annoyed that he couldn't proclaim his love for Addie and begin making arrangements for his own wedding."

"Engaged? Adeline . . . engaged?" Eileen roused in time to learn that her pride and joy was betrothed and that the citizens of Mystic were unaware of the delightful event. But that news, piled on top of the bits and pieces of information she had caught between her lapses, was far too devastating for Eileen to handle. She folded up like a dainty flower scorched by the hot summer sun.

Dyer scowled and dragged his wife into a vacant chair. Unceremoniously, he dumped Eileen into it. "Are there any more surprises you wish to spring on us, Stephie?" he questioned irritably. "If there are, be quick about revealing them. I don't think your mother will survive another fainting spell!"

Stephanie pushed herself up on legs as sturdy as wet noodles. She slapped Cole's hand away when he offered a supporting arm. "You need not play the chivalrous knight, Coleman Douglas Hollister the Third. If it weren't for you, I would still be—" Stephanie slammed her mouth shut and silently glared at Cole before returning her attention to her frustrated father.

"Aye, there are one or two matters I wish to clarify," Stephanie told her father. "You condemned me for shoving one of my beaux in the mud, but if you had heard all the terrible things he said, you would have assisted me in rubbing his face in the street! He thought Nattie to be the kind who preferred women to men. He suggested that I sleep with him to prove that I did not share my older sister's policy of steering clear of men."

Dyer's face flushed beet red. "He thought Nattie was a—" A low growl erupted from his chest. "Why that miserable, low-down . . ."

Exhaustion and loss of blood were quickly catching up with Stephanie. She knew it was a matter of time before she collapsed like her mother. Before that happened, Stephanie gestured a droopy hand toward the bed and then stared pointedly at Dyer.

"Nattie and Wes are man and wife, whether or not the colony of Connecticut or the British recognize the marriage. They deserve a chance at happiness, even if misfortune caused Wesley to sell himself for the price of passage from Ireland."

Stephanie hobbled around to indicate her other sister. "Adeline and Richard have every right to announce their engagement and make preparations for their wedding. If you deny them, Papa, you will force them into a secret marriage. They may also find themselves in the same predicament as Nattie and Wes."

Next, Stephanie gestured to both her mother and father. "The two of you must allow your daughters the freedom of which they have been deprived. If you don't stop smothering Nattie and Addie, you are going to choke the life out of them. They both harbor guilt for deceiving you, but your strict rules have brought them to this."

Darkness began to close in around her like a circling vulture waiting to swallow her up. Stephanie fought the dizziness and staggered to maintain her balance. She glanced up at Cole with dull eyes, uncertain if she were still annoyed with him for trying to meddle into her life or thankful he was close enough to latch on to when she felt herself folding up like an accordion.

"If there is anything I left out, perhaps Cole can explain." Her words were forced and her voice sounded very unlike her own. Stephanie imagined she was standing at the end of a long, dark tunnel where sound continually echoed around her. "I am not feeling very well . . ."

As quick as a pouncing cat, Cole slid an arm beneath Stephanie's knees and lifted her into his arms. Red-gold curls came uncoiled as Stephanie's head dangled off Cole's forearm.

A quiet smile pursed Cole's lips. He stared at Stephanie's soft, bewitching features. Here lay the pulse of the Wakefield family—their champion, their defense, their misfit. Cole felt as if he had been riding on an emotional carousel the past hour. He had been stung by envy, irritation, amusement, murdering fury, disbelief, and now concern. Stephanie was directly and indirectly responsible for every emotion with which he had been forced to deal.

My God, he thought as he cuddled Stephanie's unconscious body in his protective embrace. How could such a petite bundle of spirit stir so many potent sensations in him? He had prided himself in self-control. He was a man who recognized the problems he faced. He studied them, analyzed them, and then he methodically proceeded to solve them. But he had been behaving like an impulsive lunatic since early morning! And all because of and in spite of this delightful green-eyed leprechaun.

What was his life going to be like when he sailed away from Mystic? He should have known better than to drop anchor in a harbor that held such a bewitching name. Indeed, that was his first foolish mistake. His second blunder was becoming preoccupied with a feisty little imp who could turn him every which way except right side up.

How was he going to cruise back to Maryland and forget this rambunctious romp Stephanie had taken him on? And worse, how was he going to tuck away the man and the emotions he had spent the last few years repressing after Stephanie had forced them all out? Before he met this spell-casting pixie, Cole had been able to keep his feelings bottled up, showing no visible signs of frustration. His face had become a well-schooled mask that displayed nothing but impassiveness unless he considered it to his advantage. Ah, it had been such a long time since he had lived so recklessly, with such emotion. It felt good to express his true feelings, to let them explode . . .

"Cole?"

Cole lifted dark, pensive eyes to note that Dyer was appraising him with a speculative smile. "It seems I have been blind," Dyer confessed. His gaze shifted to Nattie, who was still blushing profusely. "I have a new son-in-law and a grandchild on the way." His eyes darted to Adeline, who was nervously tying knots in the bandages she had been ordered to fetch. "My second daughter is engaged and I have yet to congratulate her fiancé." His attention circled back to Cole, who was impatiently standing on one foot and then the other. "Blind though I have been, I have noticed that there is something going on between you and Stephie, as much as I tried to prevent it. Indeed, you both risked life and limb to defend each other against Brice. She took the bullet with *your* name on it."

Dyer elevated a bushy brow and his smile broadened into a sly grin. "From the looks of things, you and Stephie have become . . ." He allowed the insinuation to dangle in midair. "Do you also have a secret marriage or betrothal you wish to confess to me, Cole? If so, now is the time to expose any lingering secrets."

Cole didn't know what devil possessed him to do what he did next. But he was striding toward Dyer with Stephanie still draped in his arms. After maneuvering Stephanie's limp body, Cole extended his arm to shake

Dyer's hand.

"Hello, Father," he greeted cheerfully.

Lord, had he really said that? Cole yelled at himself. Aye, it was what Dyer anticipated, what he wanted to hear. Dyer was demanding confirmation of his suspicions. An eagerness to include Cole as part of the family was written all over Dyer's face. But why had he accommodated Dyer, Cole quizzed himself. It was pure insanity! He wasn't even sure Stephanie liked him. After their trenchant argument on the terrace, she resented his intrusion and his tyrannical remarks. Sweet mercy, she would crucify him when she found out what he had implied to her father!

A pleased smile blossomed on Dyer's lips. "I thought you would make a fine addition to our family . . . although I had selected you for Natalie." He sighed heavily. "Now I suppose I should begin making preparations for a triple wedding." Dyer chuckled as he winked at Natalie and Adeline. "We may as well make the public announcement and save Eileen weeks of stewing, not to mention buckets of tears. She can get her crying over with all at once."

After Dyer hoisted Eileen onto his shoulder, he indicated the door. When Wesley and Natalie were finally granted privacy and the entourage was filing down the hall, Dyer shot Cole a wry glance. "You had better enjoy these quiet moments, son. Stephanie will only allow you peace while she sleeps. You witnessed the turmoil she caused during the course of the evening." Dyer chuckled heartily as he carried his wife toward their room. "If you are deluding yourself by thinking this was a rare incident, you are greatly mistaken. Stephanie can transform the mundane into mayhem. She doesn't have a rebellious streak. She is rebellious from the top of her head, to her toes, and all parts in between. My youngest daughter pours more

226

living into a week than most of us manage in a month. I hope you are fully aware of what you are getting yourself into."

The words were on the tip of Cole's tongue to confess that he had only been teasing Dyer. But he quickly swallowed them when the physician scurried up the steps to attend his unconscious patient.

For the next few hours Cole was distracted by lending the doctor assistance in extracting the bullet lodged in Stephanie's shoulder. Later he would have a heart-to-heart talk with Dyer, Cole promised himself. Later he would explain there was no secret marriage or betrothal between them . . . as soon as he made certain Stephanie was resting comfortably.

But later never came and Eileen was buzzing about making preparations for a hasty triple wedding that had all the elegant trimmings known to society. And by that time, Cole didn't have the heart to admit that he and Stephenie had never discussed anything remotely close to marriage! Besides, Dyer wouldn't have believed him for a minute, wouldn't *want* to believe him.

Cole groaned as he fell into his bed. He still could not believe what he had done. God help him when Stephanie discovered what he had blurted out in a momentary lapse of sanity. The apprehension of breaking the news to her was nine kinds of hell. It was the evening of the second day after the shooting and Stephanie was still drifting in and out of consciousness, drowsy from the effects of the laudanum the doctor had prescribed. She had not roused enough for him to explain what had happened. The longer Cole procrastinated in telling her, the more difficult it would be to confess what he had implied to Dyer.

Perhaps Stephanie would find it amusing, Cole consoled himself as he flounced on the cot Dyer had toted up to Stephanie's room. After all, Steph had been blessed with a delightful sense of humor. But the sensible side of his brain doubted that Stephanie would take the news so lightly. Nay, Cole had the feeling Stephanie would be fit to be tied when she knew. She had already raked him over the coals for interfering in her life. Hell, she would take offense knowing that he had even *pretended* they were married . . . or about to be married!

A doleful groan erupted from Cole's chest. Why had he given way to such a ridiculous impulse? There was only one answer, Cole told himself tiredly. He had, quite simply, misplaced the good sense he had been collecting these past three decades. When he had stared down into Stephanie's pale features, seeing her wounded and vulnerable, he had forgotten himself.

And now here he was, sleeping on a cot in Stephanie's boudoir, as if he belonged here! Dyer had taken for granted that they were man and wife when Cole referred to him as *father!* And when Stephanie woke to find that he had pitched his tent in her bedroom, she would go right through the ceiling.

But one thing was for certain, Cole reminded himself grimly. He couldn't pack his bags and slink away. If Stephanie threw a tantrum and called him unrepeatable names, he had to endure her verbal abuse. After all, he had asked for it. And knowing Stephanie (and he had come to know her quite well), she would read him the riot act, just as soon as she regained her strength.

228

Chapter 14

A groggy moan tumbled from Stephanie's lips as she fought her way through a haze of darkness. She ached all over but her arm and leg hurt like hell. Stephanie felt as if a butcher had made mincemeat of her flesh.

Heavily lidded eyes lifted to perceive the shadows flickering in the lantern light. Her gaze slowly inspected the room and then landed on Cole's massive frame. He was stretched out on a cot in *her* room. Stephanie gasped at the audacity of his occupying *her* space. What in heaven's name did he think he was doing in her boudoir? Did he still think he had been appointed as her guardian angel?

Her attempt to roll to her side caused her to groan in pain. Every muscle complained as she eased up on one elbow. The glass of water that sat upon the nightstand seemed miles away, especially with her arm bound against her chest. Inching toward the edge of the bed, Stephanie stretched out her good arm to clasp the glass.

The creaking of the bed brought Cole awake with a start. When he saw what Stephanie was about, he leaped from his cot to assist her. Stephanie's eyes widened in shock when Cole loomed over her, as naked as the day he was born.

Stephanie flushed in embarrassment and scolded herself for staring at his virile physique. Never had she been allowed the unhindered view she was receiving and it rattled her. She had been in the process of reaching for a drink of water. But when she became preoccupied with *drinking* in the sight of Cole Hollister in all his splendor, the glass clanked to the floor.

"You could have put on your breeches," Stephanie snapped grouchily. Summoning her will, she dragged her eyes off his hair-roughened body and focused on his stubbled face.

Cole glanced down his torso as calmly as you please. A wry smile quirked his lips, knowing exactly what had caused Stephanie to lose her grip on the glass. "I was in a hurry to assist you," he defended, his voice crackling with amusement. "Forgive me for not taking the time to cover myself. But after all, we know practically all there is to know about each other. 'Tis a little late for modesty."

Damn, but it was hard not to stare, Stephanie thought to herself. Cole was a mass of brawn and muscle. His well-proportioned body drew her eyes like a magnet and she marveled at his arresting physique.

"I was managing quite well by myself until you lunged at me, stark naked!" she muttered crabbily. "And why have you set up camp in *my* bedroom? Don't you think my family will notice your cot planted in the middle of the room? You shouldn't be here." A muddled frown furrowed her brow as she forced her straying eyes back to his handsome face. "And why are you *still* here? I thought you would take up residence elsewhere when you learned that my sisters were unavailable for marriage."

Cole parked himself beside her on the bed, making her more uncomfortable than she already was. "Did you truly expect me to leave when you were hovering between life and death? After you threw yourself in front of a bullet that was meant for me?" Quiet laughter rumbled around his chest. "What kind of man do you think I am, love?"

Stephanie cast him the evil eye. "The kind who has never possessed an ounce of modesty. Will you *please* don your breeches! I am not accustomed to keeping company with naked men."

Cole lifted a teasing brow. "Am I embarrassing you, Steph? You? The woman who delights in dropping cannonballs in everyone else's lap? The woman who led her entire family to her sister's boudoir while she was abed with the husband no one knew she had? A woman who—"

"You have made your point," Stephanie growled sourly.

Leaning closer, Cole tenderly tugged at the edge of the bandage. "We had better see how our patient is coming along. With all your flouncing about, you may have torn open the wound the doctor so meticulously stitched back together." Genuine concern etched his craggy features as his attention returned to her ashen face. "Are you feeling any better, Steph?"

"If you must know, my arm feels like it was put through a meat grinder and my hip feels as if it were on the receiving end of a mule's kick," she replied wearily.

"Shall I kiss them and make them better?" His dark head came toward hers, his cocoa brown eyes fixed on the sensuous curve of her lips.

His kiss was like a gentle breeze caressing her mouth. Stephanie surrendered without giving her response a second thought. But once the fog of pleasure cleared, she frowned puzzledly.

"Why are you being so nice to me?" she wanted to know. "We have servants aplenty. Any one of them

231

could have attended to me during my recuperation."

A devilish grin bordered his lips as he traced his index finger over her exquisite features. If wishing could make it so, he would supplant the color of roses in her cheeks and replace the lively sparkle that had dwindled during her illness. "I'm being nice to you because your father told me to," he replied on a chuckle.

Stephanie pulled a face at him and then smiled despite herself. "I had you pegged as a somber, straitlaced aristocrat who resented his savage tendencies," she admitted. "But after the fracus at the ball I realized that I still haven't quite figured you out. It appears that sometime during your questionable upbringing you shed the refinement of civilization and adopted the life style of heathens."

Stephanie didn't know how close she had come to the truth and Cole wasn't about to tell her. The memories of the past were laced with pain and Cole had spent three years attempting to forget the kind of man he had become and what had happened because of it.

Cole shrugged a broad shoulder. "'Tis just that your orneriness is contagious," he countered evasively. "Suddenly, I cannot explain why I do the crazy things I do."

"You are beginning to sound a great deal like my father," Stephanie murmured, strangely content to have Cole lounging beside her. "He swears I am a bad influence. He refers to my affliction as the reverse effect of the Midas Touch. King Midas turned objects into gold and Papa thinks I transform them into disaster."

Low laughter filled the small space between them. Cole flicked the tip of her upturned nose. "Little leprechaun, you *are* a bad influence on me. Once I was the epitome of calculated decision and thoughtful analysis. Now, when tempted by careless impulse, I yield to it . . ."

Again his mouth slanted over hers, sharing a breath that caused her heart to drip all over her ribs. The tantalizing aroma of masculinity swamped her senses. But when his adventurous hand dived beneath the sheet to make titillating contact with her bare flesh, Stephanie flinched.

What devil possessed Cole? Was he utterly mad? What if a member of her family barged in and saw them?

"Stop that," she ordered, her voice cracking with the side effects of aroused desire. "I am a sick woman. Have you so quickly forgotten?"

Cole would have preferred to continue his leisurely caresses, but he decided he had better get his confession over with. What he had to say would spoil the mood of the moment. But procrastinating would only make matters worse.

"You are not half as sick as you are going to be when you learn what transpired after you lost consciousness," he said, and sighed.

Concern swallowed her waxen features. Willfully, Stephanie pushed up to look him squarely in the eye. "Papa didn't kick Wesley out of the house or disown Nattie, did he?"

Cole gave his raven head a quick shake. "Nay, Dyer has graciously accepted Wes as his son-in-law. Now that the sheriff has given Wes his freedom and full control of Reynolds Inn, your brother-in-law is a man of property. Wes's first order of business was to release the bondswomen Brice had forced to pleasure his guests. The citizens of Mystic demanded Brice's hasty trial. He has been sentenced to Connecticut's state prison at Newgate." A proud smile curved his sensuous lips. "Thanks to you and your tireless efforts, Brice is behind bars, your sisters will both be married in

233

church, and Wes is free from bondage. You accomplished all your purposes, my little leprechaun."

Stephanie breathed a thankful sigh. "I'm relieved that Papa is being reasonable." A muddled frown creased her features. If everything was coming up roses, why was she going to be twice as sick as she was? Cole wasn't making sense.

Her befuddled gaze slid to her injured shoulder. Had she lost the use of her arm? Was that why her elbow was braced securely against her ribs? Was she to be crippled for life? Was that what Cole was referring to?

Stephanie gulped apprehensively and then mustered her courage. "What haven't you told me, Cole? I have to know. Will my arm always lay uselessly against my ribs?"

Cole inhaled a deep breath and blurted out the truth. "Nay, your arm will be as good as new in a few weeks. But your father is under the impression that there is something intimate between us. Eileen is making preparations for a triple wedding, which will be held as soon as you can stand on your own two feet."

There, he had said it. Now there was naught else to do but wait for Stephanie to explode. Sure enough, she did.

"What!" Stephanie bolted straight up in bed, but Cole gently pushed her to her pillow. "Where did he get such a crazed notion? We aren't getting married!"

"Lower your voice before you wake the whole house," Cole whispered, glancing expectantly toward the door.

"That is the most preposterous thing I have ever heard." Stephanie tried to keep her voice down, but she was frantic. "Why didn't you tell Papa he had leaped to an erroneous conclusion? We can't have my parents sending out invitations for a marriage that won't be taking place!"

234

Cole stretched out beside her and propped his head on his hand. "I had a sick patient to attend," he defended. "Your family has been drifting about on a cloud, delighted with the novelty of arranging a *triple* wedding. I didn't have the heart to march up and burst the bubble they have been floating around on."

Stephanie glowered at his unconcerned smile. "Am *I* to be the one to spoil the mood of the moment? Must I always be the one left with the difficult tasks?" Stephanie expelled an exasperated breath. "First it was Nattie who begged and pleaded with me to help her free Wesley. Then Addie requested that I persuade Richard to keep the silence instead of rushing to Papa with a marriage proposal." Stephanie threw up her good arm and let it drop loosely at her side. "I thought you had backbone, Cole Hollister. Again I find I have made a gross error in judgment!"

His ebony eyes drilled into her puckered face. For a long, moment he continued to stare at her, quiet and watchful. "Would marriage to me be so distasteful, little nymph? I can give you anything you desire—silks, furs, jewels. We both represent respectable families. A marriage between us would benefit both of us. My family produces exports and your family builds ships to carry them to foreign ports."

Perhaps Stephanie was a hopeless romantic, but it rankled her pride to be on the receiving end of such a bland proposal. Why, he was explaining the advantages of marriage as if he were describing how to hitch a team of mules to a wagon! Marrying Coleman Douglas Hollister the Third would become a repetition of her past. She would have everything to make her comfortable—luxury and wealth—just as she had had during her empty childhood. That was not what Stephanie anticipated from marriage. It had to be more than the merger of wealth to wealth. Damnit, she wanted to be loved and cherished for the first time in her life! Cole couldn't give her what she needed most—devotion, respect, and love. All he wanted was physical pleasure from a woman's body. The rest of the time he wouldn't give a whit what she was doing, as long as she did it somewhere out of his way!

"It would never work between us," Stephanie declared, thrusting out a stubborn chin.

She didn't want to consider wedding Cole. Besides the absence of love, she would never fit into his well-organized, methodic life. He was like a map leading from one location to another and she thrived on spreading her wings and flying off in any direction the wind took her.

Cole required a refined, dignified hostess who would stand dutifully beside him and manage his home. Stephanie could never be what he expected of her, even if she tried. A dull, mundane life of planning meals and dinner parties, never bolting off astride some high-spirited stallion for the mere challenge of it, would drain her spirit and squelch her zest for living.

Giving the matter further deliberation, Stephanie could not help but wonder why Cole would even consider allowing her family to labor under the false impression that they were to marry. What could he possibly hope to gain? He could do business with her father without signing a marriage contract. Dyer already liked Cole. That had been obvious since the moment Cole set foot in Mystic.

"Just why are you considering marrying me?" Stephanie questioned pointedly. "Surely 'tis not because you had your heart set on joining the Wakefield name with Hollister. Just because my other two sisters are spoken for is no reason for you to feel obligated to tie yourself to the family misfit merely to obtain my father's services, should you find yourself in need of them again." She heaved a perplexed sigh and studied him musingly. "For a man who appears, for the most part, logical and practical, I cannot fathom your reasons for continuing with this ridiculous charade."

His attention was fixed on the incredibly tempting curve of her lips and those spellbinding emerald eyes. "Because you amuse me, Steph," he answered absently.

An impish grin quivered on her mouth. "If 'tis amusement you wish, hire yourself a clown," she suggested flippantly.

"I couldn't make love to a clown," he parried.

Distracted by her inviting lips that twitched in a smile, Cole bent close. He hungered for the sweet taste of her. He was being riveted by the undefinable sensations that trickled through him each time he stared too long and then dared to touch this high-spirited minx. She had always been his downfall.

His lips played softly on hers, holding intimate suggestions, stirring tantalizing memories of the past. When he finally withdrew, Stephanie fought to regain control. She could not deny that this dark-eyed rake aroused her. But it was merely physical attraction that made her heart slam against her ribs when he touched her. Marriage was a serious matter that would affect the rest of her life. She would never be a man's plaything, the social director for his plantation. She wanted a man who would love her for what she was, not a man who would dominate her and use her.

Stephanie looked into those shimmering chocolate brown eyes. Why had she allowed herself to get mixed up with this dashing rogue in the first place? Why was it so important to her that he see her not only as a woman but as his equal? Why did she want something from him that she doubted he could give? Was there some hidden reason why Cole wanted to marry her? Was he truly beginning to care about her?

"Are you falling in love with me, Cole?" she asked him outright instead of wrestling with the hopeful speculation.

Cole stared at her for a full minute. He had been caught off guard by her pointed inquiry. My, this firebrand certainly believed in laying the cards out on the table. She asked direct questions of him, but she was the mistress of keeping secrets. Indeed, Stephanie was a walking contradiction. Even when she insisted that she never again wanted to fall into his arms, she had responded in reckless abandon. She was complex and unpredictable and Cole was involuntarily attracted to her. Those green eyes challenged and stirred him. Those petal-soft lips tempted and tormented him. Stephanie made him feel emotions that he had once been able to control. . . .

"I haven't quite puzzled that out yet," he chuckled lightly.

"Another diplomatic answer," Stephanie smirked. "You have neither insulted nor complimented me. Indeed, you voiced words without saying anything at all."

"We complement each other," Cole clarified. "You are wild and free and you have often called me starched and pressed. Perhaps if we marry, we can neutralize each other."

Silence stretched between them, each one contemplating what it would be like to share the same life, the same house . . . the same bed.

"Do you think you have fallen in love with me, Steph?" Cole blurted out, finding that her straightforwardness was also contagious.

An impish grin claimed her exquisite features, and she countered his question with a question. "Would it wound your male pride if I said I haven't?"

Cole thought it over for a moment. "Nay, I have

given you no reason to love me." A roguish smile dangled on the corner of his mouth. "But you do care for me, whether you realize it or not."

Stephanie burst out laughing. "My, aren't you the arrogant one, Cole Hollister. What have I done to give you the slightest indication that there is something special about you?"

"You threw yourself into harm's way to protect me," he reminded her. "The incident occurred only minutes after you told me I was annoying, overbearing, and tyrannical. If you truly wanted me out of your life, all you would have had to do was stand aside and pray that Brice's bullet found its target."

Stephanie grinned wryly. Her hand lifted to rearrange the curly raven hair that spilled down his forehead. "I'm afraid you misunderstood my actions. My reasons for stepping between you and Brice were purely selfish. If Brice had killed you, I feared it would take me five years to locate all your lovers in various seaports and inform them of your untimely demise."

Cole was as sober as a judge, intent on convincing her to accept his proposal, even if he didn't know why the hell he was even considering it. "You need me, Steph," he had the unmitigated gall to say.

"Whatever for?" she scoffed at him.

Damn this man. There wasn't a boulder big enough to crack his monumental arrogance. Just because he was handsome, charismatic, intelligent, and wealthy didn't mean she couldn't resist him! Stephanie had been propositioned and courted by some of the wiliest rakes in England and the colonies. Aye, he had compromised her in moments of weakness, but she could resist Cole Hollister the Third if she truly wanted to, Stephanie told herself proudly.

Her chin tilted to a defiant angle as she assessed his swarthy physique, wishing she could find at least one flaw to criticize. There were none. Stephanie had already tried that tactic and had come up empty-handed. "I have managed all my life without my parents' guidance or concern. I hardly think I *need* you. I rather suspect you to be the kind of man who would make unreasonable demands on his wife. In a matter of weeks I would resent your commands. And in a few months we would begin despising each other because we are both strong, willful individuals. To spite me, you would seek out female companionship. And to retaliate I would search out a man to satisfy my feminine cravings."

Stephanie squirmed to find a more comfortable position and then purposely glanced the other way. "I have money enough to provide for servants to see that there is food on my table and clothing in my wardrobe. And if I want a man, I can have one without marrying him. I do not need you, Cole, and you don't need me. You are wealthy enough to purchase any services that will make your life satisfying. There will be no marriage between us. We have nothing in common."

Cole's dark eyes narrowed in annoyance. He had been listening intently until Stephanie made the remark about finding pleasure in other beds. The thought struck a sensitive nerve.

Cole loomed over her with that intimidating skill that infuriated Stephanie. Damn, but he could do it well.

"If we were to marry, there would be no bed-hopping. I want you in my bed and that is exactly where you would stay," he growled down at her.

Stephanie winced at his harsh, demanding tone. He needn't be so blunt about what he expected from this obvious mismatch! She already knew lust motivated Cole when it came to women. She had known that since the night he drew her into his lair without even knowing who she was! All he wanted from a woman was what she could give him between dusk and dawn.

Confound this staunch aristocrat with his haughty airs and rigid rules! She ought to marry him just to spite him. She would teach him a few lessons about women that he would never forget!

Stephanie glared at the broad mass of brawn and muscle that towered over her. "Very well, since the wheels have already been set in motion, I will marry you, Cole Hollister," she consented, her tone more resentful than jubilant. "But there will be no chains." Although Cole opened his mouth to comment on her stipulation, Stephanie rushed on, "I expect to come and go whenever I please. I also refuse to be dictated to or restrained in any manner."

"But you will not wander in and out of other men's beds," Cole scowled down at her. "I will not stand for it!"

"Fine. Then you can take it *lying* down," she mocked breezily. "But I will not become a slave to any man, even if he is my husband."

Cole gritted his teeth and resisted the urge to shake Stephanie until her teeth rattled. If she had not been injured, he might not have been so lenient with her.

Somewhere along the way this conversation had run amuck. Cole had intended to proceed calmly and rationally. But Stephanie was not a reasonable individual. She was defiant by habit. In fact, she would argue with the wall for the mere challenge of it. But if she thought for one minute that he would allow her to climb into her black breeches and cape and prowl the darkness, she thought wrong! No wife of his was going to be the subject of vicious gossip. He had a reputation to uphold and she could damned well conform to it!

While Cole sat there, matching her glare for glare, he began to wonder if perhaps Stephanie needed a man like the dark vigilante who stirred up patriot tempers and spread rebel pride throughout the colonies. Aye, that was exactly what she needed, he assured himself. Once she had traipsed around with *that* breed of man, she would realize she was not in his league. Then perhaps she would be content to be Cole Hollister's docile wife and plantation mistress.

When Stephanie had had a full helping of the men who lived dangerously, she would come racing back to his arms for protection. A wry smile flitted across his lips when he landed on that thought. Perhaps he could arrange for this feisty misfit to meet a few of the rowdy individuals who incited riots. They would scare the wits out of her and she would decide her future husband wasn't a bad match after all.

"'Tis agreed, Stephanie," Cole said stiffly. "I will not question your comings and goings and you will make no complaint when I am gone for weeks on end. And you will not interrogate me about what I have been doing with *whom*."

A strange brand of jealousy shot through her, but she puffed up defensively to compensate for that irrational emotion. "Why should I care how you spend your time as long as you are supporting me in the manner to which I have grown accustomed?" she sniped sarcastically. "Not a day has dawned that I have not been able to find something to preoccupy me. I seriously doubt that I will miss you when you're gone. Indeed, I might find that I prefer your absence to your presence."

Cole didn't know exactly why he was so agitated, but he was. By God, he wasn't annoyed. He was furious! That stubborn little minx had her heart set on disliking him from here on out. Well, that was fine and dandy. She didn't have to like him; she only had to marry him.

Marry him? Hell, why had he even offered? He and

242

Stephanie would kill each other! She was obstinate and he was headstrong. They were already crossways of each other and they hadn't even taken the vows. Just wait until she repeated the promise to love, cherish, honor, and obey, he thought spitefully. Once she had said them, he would hold them over her for the rest of her life!

"Perfect," Cole snapped back. "We will be wed and we will share the same space. We will make certain we don't get in each other's way. Your father will be delighted to have you off his hands and I will no longer be hounded by women who think to marry me for my money."

"I can think of no other reason why a woman would consent to wedding you," Stephanie piped caustically.

"Can't you?" his eyes raked over her, looking straight through the sheet to visualize her shapely flesh. "You may be begging to share my bed when I leave you all to yourself, all too often . . ."

"The Sahara would sooner be soaked with flood water!" Stephanie flung at him. "I can think of nothing that would make me happier than avoiding your bed, now and forevermore."

Impossible man! He was so damned sure of himself that it stoked the fires of her temper. Oh, how she would like to prove him wrong! She had *yet* to plead for his touch and she wasn't about to start now.

The smile that thinned his lips was so tight Stephanie feared they would snap under the pressure. His glare spoke volumes, none of which Stephanie dared to ask him to translate into words.

"One day, my rebellious bride-to-be, I will not only see you waiting in my bed, but I will hear you say you love me," he prophesied haughtily.

Stephanie exploded in incredulous laughter. "That will surely be the day that hell is besieged by a blizzard!" she sniffed just as haughtily. "And if that day should ever come, I would cut out my tongue before I made such a humiliating confession."

Cole felt his nerves of steel melting. If he didn't find something to punch to ease his frustration, he feared he would resort to taking out his anger on the true source of his irritation—this sharp-tongued, quick-witted, hellion with snapping green eyes and red-gold hair. Swearing under his breath, Cole launched himself out of bed and stormed toward the door.

"Where are you going?" Stephanie called after him.

"You have no right to ask, remember?" Cole threw over his shoulder. "Not now or *after* we are married."

Stephanie pushed up in bed, stifling an amused grin. "I was not asking for myself," she clarified. "But if you intend to stalk down the hall, the rest of the family would probably appreciate it if you took the time to step into your breeches first."

With all the dignity he could collect while Stephanie was grinning smugly, Cole marched back to the cot and snatched up his trousers. After he had thrust his legs into them, he breezed out the door, destination unknown.

Exasperated, Stephanie eased onto her back and glared holes in her canopy bed. Why was she allowing Cole Hollister to upset her? And more importantly, why had she accepted a marriage proposal from a man who didn't love her and probably never would? Aye, she felt something for Cole that she had never experienced with another man, but was it love?

Of course it wasn't, Stephanie told herself sensibly. It was passion, pure and simple. Cole had made her vulnerable to his skillful lovemaking. But Cole was the kind of man who took possession of a woman, a ship, or land, just because he could. And if he thought he could mold her into the type of woman he thought he needed—subservient, devoted . . . well, he was in for the surprise of his life! He promised her freedom and by damned she would hold him to that vow. They would see who was stronger and who buckled under first. And it was *not* going to be Stephanie Wakefield!

While Stephanie was plotting Cole's ruin, Cole was silently planning Stephanie's downfall. He was frustrated and angry and (God forbid) vindictive. But damnit, Stephanie had asked for trouble. She may have been able to wear other men down with her relentless persistence or obtain her way by wrapping them around her little finger. But she was not going to browbeat Coleman Douglas Hollister the Third. He would not cater to that ornery sprite. He was going to give her the same medicine she dished out. And one day she was going to want him in every conceivable way . . . just see if she didn't!

Cole decided to dedicate his spare time to devising a way to melt Stephanie's rebellious heart. He would hear her admit that she wanted a true marriage, that he meant something special to her.

While he was making his way through the darkness in search of Mystic, Cole expelled a troubled sigh. As stubborn and willful as Stephanie was, he might not live long enough to see the day she confessed to care for him. Lord, he should have started this crusade a decade earlier. There might not be enough years in a man's lifetime to whittle away the stubborn callus that encased Stephanie's wild heart!

Part II

When the heart is a-fire, some sparks will fly out of the mouth.

Chapter 15

A dismal sigh escaped Stephanie's lips. Absently, she stared across the rolling waves as the schooner sailed toward Boston. Seagulls dipped and dived above her, flapping and screaming as if they resented the intrusion of the ship that cut through their domain. Stephanie saw the circling gulls and heard the incessant popping of the sails that loomed over her like a thick white cloud. But her thoughts were on the hectic week she had endured.

She and Cole had played a charade for her family's benefit. Although they were annoyed with each other, they pretended to be anxious to take their wedding vows. While Nattie and Addie were grinning from ear to ear, bubbling in anticipation, Stephanie found it necessary to force her smiles. She was happy her sisters were marrying for love but she could not help feeling a little sorry for herself. Like idiotic fools, she and Cole were marrying to challenge and defy each other. It was insane and Stephanie sorely wished she hadn't been so hasty in her decision.

During the time she was mending from her injuries, Cole had portrayed the dutiful fiancé. He had pampered her in front of her parents, assuring them that he truly cared about her. But Stephanie knew it was only a ruse. He had proved that by doing an about-face the moment they walked across the gang plank of this magnificent schooner. All of her belongings were carried on board and unceremoniously dumped in the small niche beside Captain Hollister's great cabin. Cole had barely given her the time of day since he opened sail and left Mystic on the far horizon.

Cole had popped in and out of ports along the coast, toting boxes of unidentified goods. He would return to the ship, cast Stephanie that smug smile he wore so well, and then refuse to tell her what the devil he was doing. The few meals they had shared offered no privacy. Cole invited the officers of his crew to join them and pay their respects to his new lady. They had said nothing relevant to each other in days. Even a good argument would be better than this civilized warfare of matching iron will against stone will.

Oh, he had pretended to be pleasant enough, Stephanie mused in bitter retrospect . . . as pleasant as a coiled cobra one wouldn't dare disturb, she added resentfully. Cole addressed her in clipped, precise sentences. He inquired if she found her accommodations satisfactory and she replied with a stiff affirmation. He asked if the meals met with her approval and she smiled graciously.

But on the inside, behind the mask of her smile, Stephanie was hurting. Cole's cold-shoulder treatment reminded her of those years of neglect at home. Her family fussed over her sisters and barely acknowledged her presence. Now Cole was following the same frustrating technique. History was repeating itself and Stephanie found herself becoming more rebellious and resentful by the second. Cole paid more attention to his crew and his new ship than he did to his newly acquired wife!

Some honeymoon this was turning out to be, Stephanie muttered as she glanced toward the quarterdeck to see Cole manning the wheel. She could climb upon the taffrail and leap overboard and Cole probably wouldn't give a whit!

Stop pitying yourself, Stephanie scolded. Cole is deliberately trying to irritate you. *And you should respond accordingly,* replied the devil that was perched on her shoulder. Two can play his game.

A mischievous smile pursed her lips. Stephanie wheeled toward the steps that led to her cramped quarters. As soon as she had peeled off her silk gown, she rummaged through her trunk to locate her black breeches and shirt. If she were to be caged on board this schooner, she may as well learn all there was to know about it. She had always wondered how it would feel to stand behind the wheel, commanding one of the ships her father had built.

The moment Cole stepped down from his wooden throne and returned to his cabin, Stephanie fully intended to approach the helmsman, requesting that he teach her the ropes. She had never been a bystander when she could participate, she reminded herself. And by damned, she was going to be a part of the workings of this ship!

With that determined thought buzzing through her head, Stephanie tied her lustrous mane of hair into a long tail that cascaded over one shoulder. She checked her appearance in the mirror, satisfied that her garb was daring yet decent. If Cole was offended when he saw her traipsing about in breeches, that was his problem. After all, he had left her to her own devices. He couldn't very well complain about what she chose to wear after he had given her free rein in this mock marriage.

Stephanie was delighted to see that Cole had gone

below deck while she was changing clothes. Her gaze lifted to see the helmsman, Robert Forrister, behind the wheel. With a bouncy spring in her walk, Stephanie aimed herself toward the quarterdeck.

The moment Robert saw the vision in black floating toward him, his knees threatened to buckle. He had had the pleasure of being introduced to Captain Hollister's wife the first evening they sailed and it had been love at first sight. Never had he laid eyes on such a lovely angel. When Stephanie smiled, the sun burned brighter. And when the light reflected off those dazzling green eyes, Robert swore he had been granted a glimpse of paradise.

"Hello, Robert," Stephanie greeted cheerfully.

Robert melted like lard in a frying pan. "Good evening, Mrs. Hollister," he murmured, his gaze sliding the full length of her curvaceous figure. Lord, she was every bit as gorgeous in trim-fitting breeches as she was in her elegant gowns, he mused dizzily.

Stephanie grinned beneath his poignant stare. At least Robert liked what he saw, even if Cole didn't. "I have been told that I lean toward the unconventional," she declared saucily. "I realize my garments would not be proper on land. But it seems infinitely easier to maneuver about a ship when one is wearing breeches."

"You will hear no complaint from me, no matter what you wear," Robert assured her huskily. "You look breathtaking."

Stephanie flashed him a blinding smile and sashayed forward to peer out over the white caps. "Will you show me the technique of manning the wheel, Robert? I am fascinated with the possibility of steering this magnificent ship my father constructed for my husband."

Robert might have protested that Cole never permitted anyone but Ben Hogan, Robert, or the

252

captain himself to command the ship. But since Dyer Wakefield had designed this vessel and Stephanie's husband had purchased it, it only seemed natural that this shapely beauty could do what she wished since it was all in the family.

"My pleasure, Mrs. Hollister," Robert mumbled, still distracted by the bewitching sprite whose tantalizing fragrance had begun to warp his senses.

"Stephie," she corrected as she eased up beside Robert. Stephanie resented carrying around Cole's name. It made her feel as if she were one of his worldly possessions. And she would never be that! "Now tell me everything there is to know about this great sea lady."

As Robert wrapped his arms around her to properly place her hands on the wheel, Stephanie concentrated on his every word. Ah, this was far better than moping about feeling sorry for herself. To hell with Cole, Stephanie thought defiantly. He had made certain she had nothing to do and all day to do it. He was purposely ignoring her, waiting for her to become so bored and restless that she crawled to him for companionship. Now that she was in *his* domain, he expected her to become totally dependent on him. Stephanie was not about to let that happen. She had never depended on anyone and she was not about to start now.

A knowing smile brimmed her lips when Robert pressed closer than necessary to instruct her. The clever, calculating Coleman Douglas Hollister the Third had overlooked one minute detail, she mused spitefully. This ship was swarming with men. If she longed for male companionship, she would not have far to walk to find it. As a matter of fact, Robert seemed eager enough to offer himself as a companion and he was easy on the eye. Let Cole see how he liked it when his wife sought out other men to while away the hours!

It was while Stephanie was grinning in impish satisfaction and while Robert was taking full advantage of the situation that Cole stepped upon the main deck. He had been in deep conversation with his first mate until he spied the cozy scene at the helm. The sight of Stephanie garbed in seductive black and encircled in Robert's arms turned Cole's disposition as sour as green apples.

Cole's features turned to chisled granite. He coiled as if he were preparing to spring into action and his blood was at a rolling boil. All his meticulous planning had gone awry. He had anticipated that this restless she-cat would turn to him when she grew tired of ambling aimlessly around the decks. He had expected that her confinement on the ship would be to his advantage. Obviously, he had miscalculated. Stephanie looked happier than he had seen her in more than a week and he had wasted his time plotting to lure her to him.

Damn that minx! She had turned her charm on the tall blond sailor and Robert had turned into mush. Cole envied Robert. *Cole* should have had his arms around his comely wife. *He* should have been the one lost to the enticing scent of jasmine. *He* should have been the one standing so close that he could see the sunlight sparkling in those lively green eyes!

When impulse bade him to protect what was rightfully his, Cole braced his neck like a ram about to butt heads with his foe. But before he could charge toward the helm, the first mate grabbed his arm, holding him at bay.

"You told me to stop you any time you looked as if you were about to fly off the handle," Benjamin Hogan reminded Cole. "You better get a grip on yourself, C.D."

Cole willfully concentrated on Ben's words, knowing he had come dangerously close to darting off, half-cocked. Inhaling a deep breath, Cole suppressed his jealousy. But it was damned difficult when Robert was enjoying what Cole had been deprived of.

A curious frown plowed Ben's bushy brow. "I wish the hell you would explain what's going on, C.D.," he grumbled. "First we sailed out of Annapolis and you swore you hated Rachel Garret and that you wouldn't marry her if she was the last female on the planet. Then we dropped anchor in New York and you decided you hated women, just on general principle." Ben heaved a perplexed sigh. "You sailed all the way to the Indies and back on that resolution. But when you came aboard from Mystic, you had a pretty young wife in tow. Now you're acting like a jealous monster just because Rob is hovering over the girl. I don't know what the devil you expect. Stephie is so pretty she just naturally draws men like flies. You've been ignoring her as if she weren't even here, and yet you don't want anyone else around her!"

The irritation flooded out of Cole's rigid body. Ben was right. Cole had contradicted himself so many times the past few months he didn't know what he believed these days. And he certainly hadn't been himself since he herded that muddy little leprechaun to his room in Mystic.

Ben looked Cole up and down and then grinned tauntingly. "If it isn't too much trouble, would you mind telling me why you're playing this cat-and-mouse game with your lovely bride? I'd like to know why you dumped her belongings in *my* quarters and shuffled me off to room with Robert. A man and wife usually share the same bed, at least that was my understanding," he added on a snicker. "And when you finish explaining all that, you can tell me why you told me to keep a close watch to make sure you don't do something crazy where you new lady is concerned."

Cole didn't say a word. He just stood there glaring poison arrows at Robert and Stephanie.

Ben thrust his fingers through his wiry mop of red hair and then sadly shook his head. "I tried to teach you everything there was to know about the sea, but it seems to me I should have given you a few pointers about women. If you want your wife to like you, you are going about it backwards."

Cole's eyes swung around to fling Ben a silencing frown. He was in no mood for another lecture. "You don't know Steph the way I do," he defended gruffly. "If I treated her the way you think a man should behave around a normal woman, she would have her footprints all over my back."

Ben's gaze lifted to study the enchantress whose fascinating curves and swells were well displayed in her form-fitting garb. "She looks normal to me. Seems she's got nice curves in all the right places and there are no missing parts, as near as I can tell," he contradicted on a chuckle.

For Christ's sake, now it was *Ben* who was ogling Stephanie, Cole thought resentfully. The moment Cole called attention to that high-spirited pixie, Ben was lost in his own private fantasy. Muttering, Cole spun on his heels and stalked back to his cabin. He was not going to torture himself by watching Stephanie wrap Robert around her finger. And he was not about to hang around to see Ben buckle beneath Steph's irresistible charms either!

When Cole stomped into his cabin, he let out his breath in a frustrated growl. Nothing had gone according to plan. For more than a week he had treated Stephanie with cool nonchalance, except when they had been under Dyer's watchful gaze. When they came aboard the schooner he had purposely spent more time with his crew than with his wife. But still Stephanie had not come to him, begging for even a smidgeon of his attention.

Damnit, why couldn't she depend on him the way she had when she was recuperating from her wounds? At least then Cole had had reason to wrap a supporting arm around her. Now he had not one flimsy excuse. They had made a pact, a daring challenge. If he went to her, Stephanie would mock his lack of willpower. How could he salvage his pride if he crawled back to her after he had loudly announced that *she* would be the one who came to him?

"Damned woman," Cole grunted as he latched onto a bottle of Connecticut rum. Frustrated, he dropped into a chair and tipped up the bottle. Cole had employed this technique of forgetting when he didn't want to remember on a number of occasions. But he had not drunk himself insane in years. Yet, he was contemplating it now. He and Stephanie had yet to share the marriage bed and the memories of those nights they had spent together kept him burning on a slow flame.

He knew it was only a matter of time before Stephanie weaved her spell over the entire crew. Cole was already jealous of the attention Steph was bestowing on Robert. He hated to think how he would react when the whole lot of sailors were following behind her like a litter of lovesick puppies.

Before that troubled thought got the best of him, Cole emptied his glass in one swallow and glared at his empty bed. As the liquor took effect, smoothing the frayed edges of his nerves, Cole broke into a silly smile. He was going about this all wrong, he concluded. He was taking the challenge of winning his wife's affection much too seriously. Stephanie had always teased him

257

about being a stuffed shirt with overly polished manners. Perhaps she would prefer a rowdy rogue who behaved the way she did. If she wanted *rough* and *rambunctious,* he would give her an ample taste of it.

Toying with that idea, Cole guzzled more rum. Aye, while he was aboard this schooner he could do whatever met his whim. His men wouldn't question him. They had seen him at his best and worst. They understood him as well as he understood himself.

After an hour of thinking and drinking, his civilized veneer began to warp. Cole was feeling no pain. And in two hours Cole couldn't remember what had put him and his wife at odds. He felt reckless, as if he could take on the world and conquer it.

Ah, it felt good to shed the confining armor of self-reserve. He no longer had to conform to the sophisticated rules that shackled a man of his station in life. Cole swore that if he spread his wings, he could fly. Indeed, there was nothing he couldn't do if he had a mind to!

Nursing that deluded thought, Cole gathered his feet beneath him and weaved toward the door. By damned, Stephanie Hollister would not best him. If she thought she was the mistress of misfits, the darling of unconventionality, she had met her match! Cole was going to teach that sprite a few things about *daring* and *reckless* that would scare the wits out of her. She lived for thrills and Cole intended to see that she experienced a few.

Entrancing laughter bubbled from Stephanie's lips as she listened to the rollicking stories of the crew. They were whiling away the hours after their tasks were completed and they had graciously invited Stephanie to join them. Ben had related the tales of his life on land

and sea. Some of the stories were brimming with adventure and others were filled with danger. A few were amusing boasts, ones Stephanie would not allow herself to believe. But she enjoyed the camaraderie. It prevented her from dwelling on the impossible man she had married on impulse.

And then, when all crew grew quiet and darkness settled over the ocean like a cloak, Ben began spinning a tall tale of a man he had known during the French and Indian wars. He had been a daredevil who had taken his younger brother on some of the most fantastic adventures Stephanie had ever heard. At first Stephanie wondered if Ben was referring to himself. She knew he couldn't have been talking of Cole since his family included only his father. But whoever the man was, Stephanie was captivated, especially when Ben divulged that the renegade had become one of the colonies' most devoted and daring patriots.

When she quizzed Ben about the man's identity and his whereabouts, the first mate only smiled. "He can be found thundering about the countryside on a slapping black stallion," Ben informed her. "He's one of the men who assumes the role of the legendary Joyce Jr. He's the spirit that seeks to unite all rebels in a single cause." He winked at Stephanie and then leaned back to puff on his corncob pipe. "You might have the pleasure of seeing him in action when we arrive in Boston. Cole is acquainted with him. Indeed, 'tis one of the main reasons we're sailing to Massachusetts. But I'm not sure Cole would want his pretty wife gallivanting about with the likes of that rascal. He usually brews trouble wherever he goes."

Stephanie flashed Ben a mischievous grin. "My husband has said the same about me. Perhaps I *should* become acquainted with this renegade. We might have a great deal in common."

Ben returned her contagious smile. Aye, he was beginning to see what Cole meant about this minx being different from most women. There was a living fire dancing in those intelligent green eyes. There was a hint of deviltry in her grin. Cole constantly referred to Stephanie as an ornery leprechaun and Ben was becoming aware that the captain had selected an accurate term for this feisty little pixie.

"All the same, Stephie, I don't think C.D. would want you within ten feet of this man . . ." Ben's voice trailed off when he heard the click of boots upon the deck.

To Stephanie's amazement, she saw Cole strutting forward like a rooster high-stepping in mud. A bottle of rum dangled from his fingertips and a devil-may-care smile hung on one corner of his mouth. The lantern light flooded over his swarthy physique, capturing his bronzed features. His raven hair lay in disarray. His white linen shirt gaped, exposing the thick matting of hair on his chest. His breeches were tucked in the tops of his boots, calling attention to the long muscular columns of his legs. Cole resembled a prowling pirate in search of a buried treasure, and Stephanie was baffled by the abrupt change in his appearance. This was *not* the sophisticated aristocrat who had taken up residence in her father's mansion. If Stephanie hadn't known better, she would have thought Cole was the dark demon Ben had just described. There was a faintly dangerous expression on his craggy features, a wild recklessness about the way he ambulated across the deck.

"Looks like the captain has been sampling the Connecticut rum," Ben tittered. "And it must be potent. It brought out the devil in him."

Cole's careless gait brought a hushed silence over the crew. They all glanced up from their improvised chairs—wooden kegs that had been dragged into a circle.

"The lady belongs to me," Cole snorted, casting each man the evil eye. "You've been told . . . I won't repeat myself."

Ben came to his feet to warn Cole that he was about to make a fool of himself and then thought better of it. Cole didn't look as if he wanted to be reminded. Indeed, crossing Cole in his present frame of mind could be hazardous. Ben decided this was one time he wouldn't portray Cole's guardian angel. The jealous green dragon had taken up residence in Cole's brain and he was breathing fire.

With a quick nod to the rest of the men, Ben ambled away. Stephanie found herself abandoned in a matter of seconds. No one had dared to confront the surly Captain Hollister in his present mood. Stephanie had seen Cole under the influence of liquor only once. But there was no comparison. Cole looked positively threatening with that challenging smile tugging at the side of his mouth. For the first time ever, Stephanie felt a snake of apprehension coiling on her spine. If she defied him, she wondered if he would tear her limb from limb.

He wouldn't dare, Stephanie consoled herself. The crew would surely come to her rescue.

For several minutes Stephanie employed the tactic of ignoring Cole, hoping he would crawl back under his rock. But he just stood there, staring at her and *through* her until she could endure no more of the tense silence.

Her eyes lifted to meet those dark shimmering eyes that were streaked with red. "You certainly have an uncanny knack of breaking up a pleasant conversation," she mocked with more bravado than she actually felt.

Cole kicked aside one of the kegs, sending it rolling

261

across the deck to crash against the bulwark. His hand shot out to snare Stephanie's wrist. Before she could protest, he yanked her to her feet and captured her in one steel-hard arm. "Come along, vixen," he drawled. "You thrive on adventure. 'Tis time you had a true taste of it."

Although Stephanie set her feet to prevent going anywhere with Cole, she found herself swiftly uprooted. He dragged her toward the mainmast and swung her up in front of him.

"You'll delight in the view from the crow's nest," he insisted with a wicked chuckle.

"I like it just fine from the deck," Stephanie mumbled as Cole swatted her backside, demanding that she shinny up the timber.

"Where's your adventurous spirit?" Cole taunted as he grabbed a nearby rope and pulled himself upward.

Before Stephanie reached the steadying beam of the lower mainsail, Cole had hopped upon it. Grasping Stephanie's arm, he hauled her up beside him. She was coming close to losing her temper. Cole was manhandling her and she didn't appreciate it one iota.

"You are behaving like an ass," she hissed as she wormed to be free of his suffocating arms.

Cole didn't ease his grasp; he tightened it. A roar of laughter exploded from his lips. "What do you expect of a man who married a muleheaded woman?" Clutching the rope that hung directly in front of him, Cole flashed her a daring grin. "Hold on tight if you value your life. I'm going to give you a tour of this ship that few women have ever seen. If you survive it, you will have your own tall tales to relate to your grandchildren."

Stephanie felt herself tense. She didn't like the sound of that. "*If* I live to have any," she finished for him in a resentful tone.

What in heaven's name was Cole trying to prove? And why was Ben standing below them, grinning instead of rushing to her rescue? Lord, if she lived through this madcap prank of Cole's, she was going to strangle him. Nay, that wasn't punishment enough, Stephanie amended. She would poison him, stab him, shoot him, and *then* strangle him for behaving like a maniac!

"I would have expected—" Stephanie words became a startled squawk when Cole sprung off the beam and sent them flying through the air like trapeze artists. The wind came rushing past her face and the deck of the schooner sailed beneath them at incredible speed.

Sweet mercy, this was suicide, Stephanie thought sickly. Cole had drunk himself insane and she was about to be punished for every sin she had committed . . . as well as a few she hadn't!

Chapter 16

Stephanie had never been so terrified in her life. She wasn't afraid of heights, but then, she had never attempted death-defying aerial maneuvers thirty feet above the deck of a ship! Like a cat clawing its way out of water, Stephanie sank her nails into Cole's neck and held on for dear life.

When they finally collided against the foresail, Stephanie swore they would bounce backward and plunge to the deck. How Cole managed to clutch another dangling rope in the nick of time baffled her. In his drunken state it was a wonder he hadn't grabbed a handful of air and sent them toppling from this precarious perch.

"You're going to kill us!" Stephanie choked out. She clung to him like a vine and she didn't dare look down.

Cole shrugged carelessly. "Since we can't seem to live together, we can die together," he snickered. "Are you having fun, my lovely spitfire?"

"Nay!" Stephanie snapped furiously. "If I am going to get myself killed, *I* would like to be the one to decide when and where."

He stretched upward to clutch the beam above them. His free hand folded around Stephanie, forcing her to overextend herself and climb to the next perch. When she had safely fastened herself to the higher timber, refusing to budge, Cole unclamped her hands and hooked his arm around her waist.

"Oh, my God . . ." Stephanie squeaked as her heart catapulted to her throat. The distance between the fore-topsail and the upper main-topsail of the mainmast seemed a thousand miles. Stephanie knew Cole intended to soar through space to reach the next lofty perch, but she wasn't sure the rope he clung to would span such a great distance.

And if the rope wouldn't stretch, where would that leave them? They were already hanging over the bow of the ship with an entire ocean beneath them. If Cole missed his mark, they would swing backward, collide with the jib sail, and be flung into the sea, never to be seen or heard from again.

Cole looked as graceful as a swan as he glided through the air, but Stephanie spoiled his daring performance by screaming at the top of her lungs. Praying nonstop, Stephanie squeezed her eyes shut, awaiting the inevitable. . . .

Robert sucked in his breath as the two oversized birds sailed between the foremast and the mainmast. His fists were clenched around the wheel, ensuring the ship made no sudden lurches while Cole was practicing his life-threatening feats.

"Gawd, he's going to kill her for sure," he gasped as he listened to Stephanie mutter "Oh, my God" at regular intervals.

Ben leaned back against the rail, his bushy red head tilted backward to view Cole's wild shenanigan. "Nay, he isn't. C.D. is as agile as a cat," he assured Robert.

"And he's also soused," Robert grumbled. His

shoulders slumped in relief when Cole clutched another dangling rope to steady himself against the topsail. His eyes rolled in disbelief when Cole pulled Stephanie up to the main topgallant sail. "If they fall, there will be naught else to do but mop the deck and toss their splattered remains into the sea."

Ben snickered, not the least bit concerned by Cole's tomfoolery. "You haven't known the captain as long as I have, Rob. He came to sea with me when he was just a lad. Why, I've had him climbing all over the riggings. I've seen Cole fly back and forth between the foremast, mainmast, and mizzenmast a hundred times." A sly smile sank into his weather-beaten features. "I can't say for sure what he's trying to prove with this stunt. But drunk or sober, Cole could trip along those sails and ropes without missing a step. Hell, he could probably even do it in his sleep."

Robert clamped his mouth shut. It would do no good to debate the issue with Ben. The old man thought Cole to be a flawless saint. But Robert would have felt less uneasy if Cole had sprouted a set of wings.

When Cole reached the moonraker sail, he gestured toward the myraid of stars that sparkled in the black velvet sky. "Take a good look, little witch," he chuckled recklessly. "This may be as close as you ever come to heaven."

Stephanie felt a bit more secure now that Cole had wrapped himself around her and pinned her against the top of the mast. She could feel the rough timber at her back and Cole's sinewy length meshing against her front side. She looked past the daring grin that twitched his lips and stared at the sea of brilliant stars.

She had very nearly met her demise in the process of reaching this lofty perch, but the view was indeed spectacular. There was a strange exhilarating feeling that came with standing so high above the rolling ocean. It was as close to flying as Stephanie would ever come. The breeze was caressing her face, causing the unruly strands of red-gold to trail wildly behind her.

"Do you do this often?" Stephanie inquired, returning her eyes to his craggy features. "Try to kill yourself, I mean."

Stephanie felt his deep skirl of laughter vibrating against her chest and she became vividly aware of the man who was molded familiarly against her. She could feel his hard strength and she shared each leisurely breath he inhaled. She remembered other times and other places when they had been as close as two people could get. . . .

But this was not the time or place to recall all those ineffable sensations, Stephanie chided herself sternly. Yet when his dark head inched toward hers, Stephanie forgot her lecture on sensibility. Cole had literally taken her higher than she had ever been. Her heart was pumping furiously. Her senses had been sharpened by the hair-raising experience and she was feeling as alive and reckless as Cole had been behaving.

His lips were cool and moist like the ocean breeze, but the warmth generated by his body absorbed into hers, warding off the evening chill. Her pulse pounded like hailstones thumping on a tin roof. The taste of him evoked those forbidden sensations of pleasure and sent them spreading through every part of her being, further intensifying her awareness of him.

As his mouth drifted along her throat, Stephanie felt herself crumble like a pillar of sand pelted by a windstorm. "We shouldn't be doing this," she said breathlessly.

"Nay, and we probably shouldn't be here either," Cole concurred as he nuzzled against her gaping blouse to feel the tempting bare flesh of her breasts against his lips. "But then, we are living dangerously, Steph. Every moment becomes more precious when one knows it could be the last. . . . And we are going to make every second count. We are going to enjoy life to the fullest."

Stephanie felt her knees turn to jelly as his lips whispered across her breasts to bare the taut peaks to his all-consuming gaze. They were both mad, Stephanie decided. He was going to make love to her, here and now, and she was going to let him! She was going to break every vow she had made and she didn't care!

Cole was on fire and his inhibitions were smothered with rum. He had intended to introduce Stephanie to the daring, reckless personality that he usually kept tucked deep inside him. But he had not intended to break *his* vows either. He had spent a week and three days wanting this woman. He had survived ten days and ten kinds of hell, telling himself that he would hear this high-strung hellion beg for his caresses. But his pride didn't seem so important now, not when Stephanie was responding to his touch in reckless abandon, clinging to him, not because of the towering heights but because she wanted him close.

"Take me even higher," Cole rasped before his lips returned to claim her sweet mouth. He pressed intimately nearer, wanting things he couldn't have, considering their location and the curious audience below them.

Like a puppet moving upon command, Stephanie unclenched her hands from the beam behind her and curled her arms around his neck. She was lost to those ebony depths. She was living part of their darkness. Her body brushed provocatively against him as she stretched up on tiptoe to return his sizzling kiss.

Cole felt as if the mainmast had become a lightning rod and he were fried to it. Stephanie had never kissed him with such unleashed passion. Lord, how he ached to shed these hindering garments that separated them. How he longed to love her the way a woman like Stephanie deserved and needed to be loved.

A groan of unholy torment bubbled in his throat. He savored and devoured her as he crushed her to him with the one hand that wasn't wrapped around the mast. He could feel every divine inch of her. The imprint of her soft, supple body was a direct contrast to his muscular hardness. It left him hot and aching. He wanted to possess her, to give of his strength, to capture an ounce of her undaunted spirit.

Damn, why couldn't he have dragged this wildcat to his cabin instead of hauling her to the tip-top of the ship? He must have been out of his mind! There was only so much a man could do when he had to cling to the mast to avoid falling.

"Now what are they doing?" Robert questioned impatiently.

Ben crossed his arms over his bulky chest and grinned. "You've got the same view I have, Forrister. It looks to me like Cole is kissing his wife. And it's about time he paid a little attention to her. But I think Cole climbed in the wrong direction if he wanted privacy," he tittered.

Robert grumbled under his breath. He knew he had no right to be jealous of Cole. But blast it, Rob had stood all too close to that shapely nymph and he knew the devastating effect she had on a man. Several minutes earlier Robert was questioning Cole's sanity. But at the moment, Rob would have eagerly exchanged places with the captain.

When Cole finally saw the futility of where he was and what he was doing, he led Stephanie along the same dangerous path across the pulleys, ropes, and sails. Stephanie was far too distracted with the man who held her protectively to him to notice that the crew was milling about the deck. And when Cole finally set her to her feet, her gaze remained fixed on him, studying him as if it were the first time she had laid eyes on him.

The Cole Hollister she had met tonight was an entirely different man. She saw in him a recklessness that he had never displayed. For days she had gone through the paces of living while she recovered from her wounds and while they cruised the seas. But Cole had erased those mundane hours in a matter of minutes. He had made her totally aware of him, cognizant of his powerful strength and unerring abilities.

As Cole grasped her hand and weaved his way through the silent crowd, Stephanie frowned curiously. Did the dark, daring side of Cole's personality emerge only when he heavily indulged in liquor? She had seen the half-savage side of his personality the night Brice Reynolds attacked her. She already knew there was more depth to this handsome aristocrat than met the eye. But tonight he had flung the doors wide open, allowing even more of his complex personality to seek the light.

Stephanie was so immersed in thought that she didn't realize where Cole was leading her until he pushed open the door to the great cabin. Reality came rushing back and Stephanie wormed free of his grasp. "I think 'tis best that I return to my own room," she murmured, refusing to meet his pointed stare.

Cole chuckled devilishly as he moved her aside to close and lock the door. Leisurely, he swaggered over to grab another bottle of rum and guzzled several swallows. One thick brow lifted in amusement as he raked her shapely figure, making no attempt to disguise the male appreciation of what he saw.

"When did you develop this practical streak, minx?" he questioned. After pouring down another drink, straight from the bottle, Cole approached her like an invading army offering no direction for retreat. He braced his arms on either side of her, pinning her back to the wall. His knee insinuated itself between her legs, preventing the possibility of escape. "I thought you thrived on adventure, spontaneity, and impulsiveness."

"Ordinarily I do, but I doubt you will even remember what happend when you wake tomorrow," Stephanie replied, helplessly drawn to the rock-hard warmth that enveloped her. "I don't wish to be a man's forgotten memory."

"I'll remember every moment," Cole guaranteed in a low, husky voice that sent a team of goose bumps flying across her flesh. "There are some things a man never forgets, no matter how much rum he consumes. You, my little green-eyed witch, are the stronger potion."

Cole grabbed a handful of red-gold curls and tilted her head to his demanding kiss. His free hand splayed across her derriere, pulling her closer, letting her feel his fierce need for her.

"We're going to make love as if there were no tomorrow," he growled provocatively. Swinging her into his arms, Cole navigated his way across the cabin. "And neither one of us is going to forget what we are going to do to each other."

Stephanie had never been handled so roughly in her life. Cole was domineering and physical and Stephanie found that she liked his rough edges. His forceful ways reminded her of a damsel being swept away by a dark, fearless knight. His devil-may-care charm stirred her far more than the polite, impeccable manners displayed by the arrogant aristocrat Cole usually portrayed.

The truth of the matter was she had quickly lost interest in men who catered to her, ones she could dominate. But Cole was a constant challenge. He was his own man, even when he was all polish and shine. And now that he *wasn't,* he thoroughly intrigued her.

Her thoughts scattered when Cole recklessly tossed her on his bed. A roguish grin quirked his lips as he stood with feet askance, raking her with those dark, penetrating eyes. He peeled off his shirt, popping buttons that scattered here and yonder. Carelessly, he tossed the garment aside—a gesture that was so unlike the sensible, methodic man she had married.

Stephanie decided it was indeed liquor and anger that brought out the renegade in Cole Hollister. He was wild and reckless and she wanted to recapture those same carefree sensations she had experienced while they were perched high above the deck.

His mood brought out the deviltry in her. With her eyes glued to the massive expanse of his chest, Stephanie slowly unbuttoned her shirt and watched those cocoa brown pools flood over her bare flesh. She felt the heat of his gaze as it traveled across her skin, arousing her just as surely as if he had reached out to touch her.

"Temptress," he chuckled, delighted by her boldness.

"Devil," she flung at him. A seductive smile brimmed her lips as she propped up on her forearm and shook out her hair, sending it into a glorious waterfall that tumbled over her breasts. "I doubt my stuffy, properly mannered husband will believe me when I confess I was seduced by the likes of you."

One dark brow arched to a teasing angle. Cole bent upon one knee to loom over her. He made no attempt to disguise the hunger or his admiration of her beauty. "Tell him the truth," Cole insisted, his voice husky with barely contained desire. "It was the witch in provocative black breeches who roused this dragon and set him on fire with desire."

His tanned finger circled the rigid peak of her breast, causing Stephanie's heart to skip several vital beats. His mouth curled into a rakish grin when he noted her reaction to his caress.

"You like my touch, don't you, witch?" he whispered hoarsely. "And you crave my kiss." His warm lips feathered over each roseate bud, making Stephanie ache to the very core of her being. "Admit it, you want me in the same wild ways I want you."

This Cole Hollister seemed to have twice the normal number of hands and they were doing impossible things to her naive body. His candid, earthy comment forced her to face her desires rather than deny them.

"Aye, I do," Stephanie heard herself say without a moment's hesitation.

His hands and lips swirled across her belly and then ascended to trail from one taut peak to the other. "How much, minx? With all your heart and soul?" She felt his words echoing across her sensitive flesh, felt his bold caresses setting white-hot fire to her nerves. "If there is no tomorrow, will you grieve and say that you have been cheated out of a lifetime? Or will tonight be the only *forever* you desire?"

Stephanie swore she had sunk through the mattress. A tiny moan tripped from her lips as his kisses and caresses blazed a searing path across her abdomen. The world was turning a darker shade of black and Stephanie was being swallowed alive. Tantalizing sensations were riveting through her, creating gigantic cravings that she wondered if anything could satisfy.

His skillful caresses glided beneath the gaping band of her breeches to ease them from her hips. Reverently, his gaze ran the length of her delicate body, marveling at her unrivaled beauty.

"Will loving me be enough?" Cole persisted as his hands and lips continued to set new fires.

When he settled down to the serious business of kissing her senseless, Stephanie felt the world slide out from under her. He knew just how to please a woman, to make her ache with the want of him. Aye, his brand of passion satisfied her, she thought as he roused her to dizzying heights of pleasure. And God help her for admitting it to herself, but she wanted them to share a true marriage. She wanted to be needed, to be loved just the way Cole was loving her now, as if she alone was his precious treasure.

Cole was driven by a strange, compelling need. He wanted answers to his probing questions. He wanted this sweet witch to cherish what he had to offer. He longed to be the fire that inflamed her dreams. It was vain and selfish and demanding, but Cole couldn't help himself. Just once he wanted her heart and soul within his grasp. He yearned for the chance to arouse something deep within her, something that couldn't fade when the loving was over.

"Tell me, Steph," he commanded as he mapped the curvaceous terrain of her body, worshipping flesh that was as soft and exquisite as satin.

"Aye," Stephanie murmured, her voice wavering with unrestrained passion. Her hands folded around his face to bring his lips back to hers. "Love me all night . . . forever . . ."

Cole melted into liquid fire and her kiss was the gentle rain that contained the flames. He was burning up on the inside. But when her hands slid over his laboring chest to work the buttons of his breeches, Cole found his flesh inflamed as well. The two blazes were burning back on top of each other like a holocaust that engulfed all within its path.

As Stephanie divested him of his breeches, her

caresses investigated every inch of hair-roughened flesh, learning him by touch. The feel of her gentle hands upon his skin was sweet, maddening torment. Her innocence made her inquisitive. He watched those emerald green eyes follow the tantalizing flight of her hands across his flesh. He felt the pleasure she gave and he watched it recoil upon her when she came to know his body even better than she understood her own. Naive though she was, she had quickly learned how to take a man to the edge of sanity with her light, exploring caresses.

Stephanie relished the power she seemed to hold over him. It made her even bolder. Cole was permitting her to have her way with him, to possess him with her kisses and caresses. And she was caught up in the experience of truly knowing a man, knowing him in ways that were too precious and tender to ever forget.

When Cole's hands folded over hers and led them to the hard flesh that covered his heart, Stephanie became totally aware of the disturbing effect she had on him. His pulse was running wild and his eyes were dark like a brewing storm.

"Do you want to hear the words?" Cole murmured as he came upon his knees. His arms slid around her waist, his hands gliding up her back to tip her head to his. "Do you want me to confess what you do to me?"

That impish smile that haunted his dreams blossomed on her features. "Show me," she requested. Her lips parted invitingly. "Deeds are far more convincing than the most eloquent words."

Laughter rumbled in his chest as he sent her tumbling with him into the sheets. But the playfulness dissipated when passion exploded. It was a wild coming together, like the crash of thunder and the piercing flash of lightning. Passion's storm unleashed upon them and they clung fiercely together, riding out the swirling wind that devastated all within its path.

Stephanie wasn't certain she could survive the wild, turbulent sensations that buffeted her. She was reminded of wind-tossed waves beating against the boulders that lined the seashore. And before she could catch her breath from the first gigantic waves, another wall of ecstasy plummeted upon her.

Cole was crushing her to him, driving into her with a savage brand of passion. But she welcomed his hard thrusts, pleading with him to satisfy the craving that consumed her, body and soul. It bewildered her that pleasure could be so satiating and yet so incredibly maddening all in the same moment.

And then suddenly Stephanie found herself in the grip of sensations that defied all that had come before. No words could be linked to what she was feeling. It was the quintessence of all emotion, so pure and unique that it transcended the universe of human understanding. She was no longer an entity unto herself. It was as if Cole were truly a living part of her and she of him. She felt his power and strength as if it were hers to command, as if their bodies and souls were two integral parts that could not exist without the other.

The dawn of understanding came as the windblown fires of passion burned themselves out. Stephanie knew what Cole had asked of her. His loving was indeed enough to last until eternity. If the world were to collapse about her, she could chart her journey through the universe that lay beyond. She had stood at the gate. She had transcended the experiences that were limited to a world of seeing, tasting, and hearing. And that road was paved with love.

Stephanie blinked, baffled at the direction her deep thoughts had taken her. Her wide, astounded eyes focused on Cole's face. Was she truly in love? What she felt for this complex and sometimes infuriating man *was* love in its sweetest form. That was why he had the power to hurt her when he ignored her. That was why she wanted his respect and his affection.

Would these warm, tender feelings ever really go away? Were the sensations she was experiencing the kind that would endure eternity? They seemed so potent just now. But would time cause them to fade?

Stephanie propped herself upon an elbow and stared down at Cole. The look on her face startled him. He lay stock-still, afraid to move for fear of shattering whatever thought had provoked that incredibly lovely expression. It bordered somewhere between wide-eyed innocence and perceptive understanding. Understanding of *what* he couldn't say for certain.

Her index finger sketched his high cheekbones and then descended to trace his jaw. Like a blind woman granted her first vision, Stephanie saw and felt the chisled lines of his face, mapping each one as she committed them perfectly to memory.

Finally, Cole could endure no more. He longed to know what pensive thought was responsible for the expression that claimed her features. Never had he witnessed a look that carried such depth and emotion. "Steph, what's wrong?"

The faintest hint of a smile drifted across her lips as she pressed her fingertip to his mouth to shush him. The sparkle in her eyes grew brighter. "I cannot know for certain until you make love to me again," she told him truthfully.

"Now?" he croaked. Sweet mercy, he wasn't even sure he could move, much less . . . He was not allowed to complete the thought before Stephanie giggled mischievously.

"Am I asking the impossible?" Her twinkling gaze dropped to follow her hand as it breezed across his shoulder to caress the bronzed flesh that wrapped around his ribs. "Impossible for you? I think not," she murmured thoughtfully. Her hand swam across his hip and then swirled over his thigh. "I believe you possess a strength that has yet to be tapped, one that perhaps even you are not aware of."

As her caresses descended and then ascended, Cole found his spent body coming back to life. He could have sworn he had expended every ounce of energy, but desire created strength where there had been none the instant before.

She was a magician and her caresses were silent incantations. She was weaving a spell that no man could resist. It was tender and compelling and built gradually upon him, reviving him until her will was his own.

Cole closed his eyes as her lips melted upon his, spreading a river of pleasure through his blood. The air about them was becoming charged with electricity. Like lightning leaping from one cloud to another, Cole found his nerves tingling with aftershocks. He was back to wanting this spell-casting temptress as much as he had the previous hour. But this time she was setting the cadence of their lovemaking. It was gentle and unrushed. Passion spread over him like a fog rolling in from the sea.

The fierce ardor of desire that had swamped them earlier was in direct contrast to what Cole was feeling now. But the sensations were no less potent. It was just that they had sneaked up on him and consumed him before he realized what had happened. There was something in the way she touched him that stirred him as no other woman had been able to do. Her caresses and kisses were unhurried and she seemed to possess incredible patience. She was cherishing each wandering caress, touching him as if he were her prized possession.

Cole caught his breath when her silken body moved upon his, promising intimate pleasures. As she took him into her soft warmth, her lips slanted across his, stealing his last breath. Cole swore he had died in that splendorous moment when they became one. He was soaring without leaving the glorious circle of her arms.

And then suddenly, each of those remarkably tender sensations burst and passion was as fierce and stormy as it had been before. Cole became starkly aware that there were two distinctly different paths that led to the pinnacle of desire. One was swift and turbulent, the other like a gentle, flowing river. But in the end, it was all the same and his need for Stephanie was as fierce and uncontrollable as it had ever been.

All thought escaped him. Quaking sensations rippled through him, demanding sweet release. Cole clutched her to him as if the world was about to come to an end. Indescribable pleasure surged through his body, satisfying each monstrous craving that called out to him.

"Steph, I love you," Cole rasped against the pulsating column of her neck. "Love you . . ."

The journey back to reality was every bit as slow and languid as the one that had taken him into the soul-shattering dimensions of passion. Between the excessive amount of rum he had consumed and the dizzying pleasure he had experienced, Cole couldn't quite navigate his way home. Dreams overtook him, leaving him hovering just beyond reality's shores.

A quiet smile hovered on Stephanie's lips as she studied Cole's sleep-drugged features. The chiseled lines of his face were soft in repose. Impulsively, she reached over to press one last kiss to his lips.

"And I love you, Coleman Douglas Hollister the Third," she confessed, though her admission fell of deaf ears.

A curious frown knitted her brow as her eyes fell to

the gold medallion that hung about Cole's neck. She had paid little attention to it in the past, but it suddenly occurred to her that she had seen a similar necklace dangling around her father's neck.

Taking care not to disturb Cole, Stephanie lifted the chain to study the medal. On one side was a sketch of the Liberty Tree. On the reverse side was the etching of an arm grasping a pole. On top of the pole was the liberty cap and the words "Sons of Liberty."

Stephanie's mouth dropped open as she brushed her thumb over the medallion. She would have bet her fortune that it was Cole who had given her father a matching necklace. All the time Cole was passing himself off as an apathetic aristocratic he was actually . . . A wry smile pursed her lips as she laid the medallion back to Cole's broad chest. Well, that certainly explained a lot of things. And now that she knew what secrets Cole was protecting, things were going to be different.

Humming that optimistic tune, Stephanie cuddled against his sturdy frame. Tomorrow would be the first day of her new life with Cole. They would no longer be at each other's throats, challenging each other, spiting each other at ever turn. She loved him, he loved her, and she knew they were fighting for the same cause. Aye, tomorrow was going to be a bright new day and Stephanie was anxious to begin it! Now that she had Cole's love, now that she realized his true purpose, they would no longer be crosswise of each other . . . or so she thought! Well, at least Stephanie was granted one peaceful night's sleep, though by dawn, she would see it only as hollow consolation.

Chapter 17

Cole dragged himself up from the groggy depths of sleep, groaning from the aftereffects of his bout with rum. God, he felt horrible. His stomach was pitching and rolling with the waves and his head felt as if it were being used as a drum.

His tangled lashes swept up and he flinched when he felt a warm presence beside him. Warily, his gaze shifted to settle on the flowing mass of red-gold and he went rigid. Stephanie? He had dreamt of the night when she would finally return to his bed to share a splendorous moment of . . .

A muddled frown knitted his brow. Had he invited her to join him or had she willingly come to him? Cole mentally strained to think past the gray haze that clouded his brain. Fragments of memories erupted, falling helter-skelter through his thoughts. He could hear Stephanie's piercing scream splintering through the aching cavity of his head. Had he done something to elicit her cry or was it the product of something one of his crew members had done . . . was about to do?

Cole expelled an agonized groan. Damnit, he couldn't seem to remember. The previous night was a cloudy blur. He did recall feeling as if he were flying.

And there was another odd sensation that tapped at his consciousness. He had felt warm and satiated and . . .

A cheerful whistle vibrated against the cabin door immediately before Benjamin Hogan came bursting in unannounced. His stubby fingers were wrapped around a breakfast tray and his weather-beaten features were brimming with a greeting smile.

"Morning, Captain—" Ben came to a skidding halt when he realized Cole wasn't sleeping alone for the first time since he had returned with his bewitching bride. "Oops."

Stephanie was startled from sleep when Ben's voice resounded around the cabin. Hastily, she rolled to her back to clutch the sheet around her. A self-conscious smile quivered on her lips as she murmured a response to Ben's greeting.

The first mate set the tray on the desk, poured Cole a strong cup of coffee, and offered it to the frazzled-looking captain. "I thought you might be needing this after last night." A merry twinkle glistened in his eyes. "How's your head? A mite tender, I suspect."

"It hurts like hell," Cole replied hoarsely. Cautiously, he tested the steaming coffee, wondering how his sensitive stomach would react to it. The brew scalded his throat and landed with a thud on his churning stomach, evoking another miserable moan.

Ben gauged Cole's reaction and grinned amusedly. "I was afraid of that." Snickering, his gaze swung to Stephanie. "Care for a cup, Stephie?"

She gave her head a negative shake and clung fiercely to the sheet that happened to be all she was wearing.

Sensing her uneasiness, Ben retreated to a far corner and propped himself against the wall. "I came to tell you we docked at first light. But after the night you had, I figured you could use a little extra sleep." A low peal of laughter ran through the air. "I haven't seen you

282

pull such an outrageous stunt since . . ." His voice trailed off as he shot Cole a discreet glance. ". . . well, not for a long time, C.D."

Cole's bloodshot eyes strayed to Stephanie and then he frowned bemusedly. "What stunt?" He hated to ask but he had to know.

Stephanie's and Ben's mouths simultaneously dropped open. "You don't remember?" they questioned in unison.

"Not so loud," Cole howled, and then clutched his throbbing head, wishing he had had enough sense to whisper the command.

Hurt and humiliation registered in Stephanie's eyes. Cole didn't remember anything! Damn him. She had hoped today would be a new beginning for them. But it would only be a continuation of the past. How could he have meant one word he had spoken to her the previous night if he didn't recall doing or saying any of it? All those sweet confessions of how she had pleased him, how he wanted her more than any other woman, how he adored her. . . . They had been empty phrases, she thought deflatedly. He had probably uttered those confessions so many times in order to flatter the women he had taken to bed that they just naturally popped out of his mouth in moments of passion. Double damn him! He felt nothing special and the love she felt for him was still as one-sided as it had always been.

Ben watched the frustrated thoughts pursue each other across Stephanie's entrancing features. From the look of things, he decided it would be wise to offer his rendition of what had happened before Cole found himself in more hot water than he was in already. With any luck at all, his account of the events would prompt Cole's foggy memory.

"After you took to drinking rum, you hauled Stephie

up the mast and sent her on the ride of her life. The two of you were sailing through the air like trapeze artists in a circus."

Cole rolled his eyes in agonized disbelief. He must have been the one who had provoked her bloodcurdling scream. Had she fainted in fright? Had he dragged her to his cabin, disrobed her, and . . . Cole felt sick inside. His gaze lifted, silently pleading with Ben to continue with the rest of the story—and all its grizzly details. Lord, Cole had the sinking feeling he was going to hate himself after Ben finished explaining what had transpired the previous night.

"Rob swore you were going to kill the *both* of you, but you only scared Stephie *half* to death." His admiring gaze drifted back to the comely lass whose red-gold hair was strewn about her bare shoulders. "The lady must be made of sturdy stuff or she would have fainted each time you swung out on a rope and left her dangling in midair."

Cole slumped back against the wall and closed his blurred eyes, grimacing in frustration. Stephanie surely thought him to be a madman. He didn't dare look in her direction. She was probably a mass of bumps and bruises and most likely she was glaring mutinously at him . . . and with good reason.

"After you finally came back to deck, you swaggered down the steps. I don't know what happened next," Ben confessed with a wry grin. "But since the two of you are . . ." His grin grew even broader. "Does this mean I can have my cabin back?"

"Nay, I'm not staying," Stephanie snapped, glowering at Cole, who had sense enough not to glance at her. If he had, he would have been put out of his misery. Her glare was aimed to maim and kill.

Feeling awkward, Ben pushed away from the wall and ambled toward the door. "I took the liberty of sending messages to all your, er, associates in Boston. They should be arriving after lunch to confer with us." Ben grasped the doorknob and flung Cole a parting glance. "Excuse me for barging in on you. I'll leave you to your privacy . . . like I should have done in the first place."

When Ben had disappeared into the companionway, silence fell like an invisible partition between them. For a moment Cole remained propped against the wall, staring meditatively into his coffee cup, wishing he could remember what the hell he had done. Aware of their state of undress, he had a pretty good idea what had transpired after he had dragged Stephanie into his lair. But had she been a willing participant or had he . . . ?

The dismal thought caused Cole to wince as if he had been stabbed from behind. Setting his coffee aside, he retrieved his breeches and stumbled into them. Bracing his bravado, Cole drew himself up at the foot of the bed and forced himself to meet Stephanie's contemptuous glare.

"Before you bombard me with the barrage of insults I so richly deserve, I want to apologize for everything I said and did last night. I'm sure my conduct was inexcusable." Cole exhaled a harsh breath. "If I could remember exactly what I *did* do, I would beg forgiveness for each and every asinine stunt I performed!"

"You wish to apologize for *everything?*" Stephanie prodded, eyeing him somberly. "Every word, every deed, all of it?"

Cole muttered under his breath. She was making this more difficult than it already was. What did she want him to do, get down on his knees and beg a thousand pardons? He had said he was sorry. Didn't that just about cover it all?

285

"Well of course for everything," he snapped irritably.

To his amazement, Stephanie puffed up with indignation. Now what had he said wrong? "Damnation, I said I was sorry. I retract every word I uttered in my drunken stupor!"

Stephanie wanted to hit him. "Fine," she grumbled, her tone carrying a biting edge. Without removing the sheet, she grabbed her discarded clothes and dressed under cover. "I forgive you for being an ass last night. Shall I also forgive you for being an ass every day of your life?"

Cole was completely bumfuzzled. Stephanie was behaving as if she had a bee hive in her bonnet. But for the life of him he couldn't imagine what had put it there. "Would you mind telling me why you are more furious with me than you were before I offered a blanket apology? My intent was to soothe your indignation, not set the battleground for a war!"

After she had fastened herself into her shirt, she stared into his bloodshot eyes. "I think I shall get roaring drunk, make a fool of myself, and then shrug off each and every moment the same way you are trying to do," she growled in annoyance. "'Tis the perfect excuse, isn't it, Cole? 'Tis most convenient for a man to do as one pleases and then blame his shenanigans on an overindulgence of liquor."

As Stephanie buzzed toward the door, madder than a disturbed hornet, Cole snagged her arm. "Will you at least tell me what I said or did to put you in such a snit?"

Stephanie glowered at the hand that held her captive. "Remove it or lose it, Coleman Douglas Hollister," she hissed poisonously. "Obviously what you said and did meant nothing to you. If they had, you would most surely remember. Indeed, you swore to me last night that you would *never* forget, no matter how much rum you had devoured!"

Wisely, Cole loosed his grasp on her forearm. At the moment Stephanie reminded him of a wildcat that was crouched to strike. In her present mood it would take only the slightest provocation to send her flying at him with claws bared.

Stephanie brushed away the handprint, as if his touch were dusted with poison and she feared contamination. Flinging her nose high in the air, she whipped open the door to make her dramatic exit.

Ben, who had pressed his ear to the portal to eavesdrop, stumbled against Stephanie. His face turned the same shade of red as the mop of unruly hair that capped his head.

"Men!" Stephanie fumed as she stalked off to her room.

Giving his head a rueful shake, Ben stared disappointedly at Cole. "You've really done it this time."

"Done what, for God's sake?" Cole bellowed in frustration. The sound of his own voice resounded in his sensitive head and Cole staggered backward, attempting to hold his head in a position that didn't hurt. But there was none. Miserably, he wilted onto the bed. "What time did you say our guests are scheduled to arrive?" he questioned in a softer tone.

"I told them to meet us at one-thirty and to bring the pamphlets with them," Ben replied. "We've already unloaded the goods from the secret compartments in the hull. I thought it best to distribute them before the tax collectors could beat a path to Hancock Wharf to demand that we pay the tariff on the imports."

Cole nodded appreciatively. "My thanks, Ben. I would sorely hate to pay a fine for importing sugar and molasses from the French Indies. I resent every shilling we are forced to *donate* to the Crown."

"Uh . . . Captain?" Ben questioned hesitantly. "Are you planning on telling Stephie what is going on in Boston?"

There had been a time when Cole spitefully vowed to initiate Stephanie into the patriot underground activities and allow her to rub shoulders with some of the unruly rapscallions he dealt with. But Cole changed his mind after the way his crew fawned over that feisty minx. The last thing he wanted was to square off with some of the rowdy mob leaders because they had taken *liberty* at its literal definition. It would be best if Steph was not permitted to meet the dignified *Loyal Nine* or the surly men who ran with the mobs of Boston.

"Nay," Cole grumbled. "She is better off not knowing. The success of our plans depends on strict confidence. Stephanie is the kind of woman who attracts trouble. And to make matters worse, Stephanie *attracts* people who *attract* trouble. I have no intention of throwing her in harm's way since she flies into it all by herself. I can go about my business without having to stew over her."

"She's bound to start asking questions when Adams, Hancock, Revere, and the others come strolling across the deck," Ben argued. "What are you going to do, lie to her?"

"I won't have to. She doesn't know any of them," Cole reminded Ben. "Besides, I intend to send her into town before they are due to arrive."

Ben gave his bulky shoulders a shrug. "Whatever you say. She is your wife, but—"

"You needn't remind me," Cole scowled grouchily. "I shouldn't have married that spitfire. She is giving me fits!"

A quiet rumble of laughter rattled in Ben's chest. "You may have married her on the rebound but Rachel isn't half the woman Stephie is, fits or no fits," Ben declared. "And if you ask me, you should tell Stephie what's going on. She's liable to get herself in more

ACCEPT YOUR **FREE GIFT** AND EXPERIENCE MORE OF THE PASSION AND ADVENTURE YOU LIKE IN A HISTORICAL ROMANCE

Zebra Romances are the finest novels of their kind and are written with the adult woman in mind. All of our books are written by authors who really know how to weave tales of romantic adventure in the historical settings you love.

Because our readers tell us these books sell out very fast in the stores, Zebra has made arrangements for you to receive at home the four newest titles published each month. You'll never miss a title and home delivery is so convenient. With your first shipment we'll even send you a **FREE** Zebra Historical Romance as our gift just for trying our home subscription service. No obligation.

BIG SAVINGS AND **FREE** HOME DELIVERY

Each month, the Zebra Home Subscription Service will send you the four newest titles as soon as they are published. (We ship these books to our subscribers even before we send them to the stores.) You may preview them *Free* for 10 days. If you like them as much as we think you will, you'll pay just $3.50 each and *save $1.80 each month* off the cover price. *AND you'll also get FREE HOME DELIVERY.* There is never a charge for shipping, handling or postage and there is no minimum you must buy. If you decide not to keep any shipment, simply return it within 10 days, no questions asked, and owe nothing.

Get a Free
Zebra
Historical
Romance

*a $3.95
value*

trouble if she doesn't know why you're here and why you're making connections with Adams and Hancock."

"I don't recall asking your opinion," Cole muttered crabbily. "And now, if you'll see that my tub is filled, I'll attempt to revive myself before our illustrious guests arrive."

Deciding it best not to ruffle Cole's feathers while he was nursing a severe hangover, Ben nodded mutely and exited the cabin. When Cole was alone, he collapsed on the bed, groaning in anguish. He could kick himself for not remembering what had transpired the previous night. What had he said that he promised Stephanie he would never forget? Damn, if only he could remember!

Cole swore up and down he would never touch another bottle of Connecticut rum. It had a way of pickling a man's brain. It was for certain he needed to keep his wits about him if he were to deal with Stephanie. She was not the kind of woman a man could arrogantly dismiss. She was as intelligent as he was and a man had to stay on his toes to outguess that firebrand. Now she was furious with him and he didn't have the faintest idea why. That put him at a disadvantage and that was no place to be when dealing with a feisty hellion like Stephanie.

Releasing an exasperated sigh, Cole dragged himself into an upright position when several sailors arrived to slosh water into his tub. While he was soaking his rum-logged body he was going to devise an excuse to cart Stephanie off to Boston. The last thing he needed was for Stephanie to start asking questions about his guests. No matter what Ben said, Cole was not about to involve Stephanie in his plans. She had gotten herself shot because of him. That wasn't going to happen again. Whatever else happened while they were docked in Boston, Stephanie was going to remain safe, Cole vowed himself. She may hate him at the moment and with just cause, but he still intended to protect her. Cole had promised to marry into a respectable family and he was going to deliver Stephanie to his father in one piece!

Chewing on that determined thought, Cole lifted a pitcher of warm water and poured it over his head. He had to regain full command of his wits before his guests arrived. Their council was important. And although this sojourn in Boston would be brief, it must be effective. What was about to transpire in the streets of Boston would become another example for the other twelve colonies.

Stephanie sat at the far end of the table, quietly munching her meal. Her speculative gaze focused on Cole, who was dressed in his elegant garments of silk and velvet. Gone was the reckless rogue of the previous night. Here to stay was the private, pensive man who refused to allow her to share his world or witness his deeply embedded emotions. Stephanie was still on the outside . . . just as she had been when she was living with her family in Mystic. Perhaps he planned to tell her what was going on in his own good time, she allowed. But unfortunately, Stephanie didn't possess that kind of patience.

"Do you intend to tell me what this afternoon's meeting is all about?" she questioned, dragging Cole from his contemplative deliberations.

There was a long pause.

Cole's table manners were impeccable as ever. He carefully chewed his food twenty-five times, swallowed, and then touched his napkin to his lips. His polite manner was driving her up the wall and she felt inclined to throw something at him for placing etiquette before

290

her impatient inquiry.

His well-disciplined countenance gave nothing away. "Business," he told her blandly. "I have merchandise to sell to the citizens of Massachusetts."

Her perfectly arched brows elevated to a mocking angle. "Which merchandise, dear Captain? The *legal* goods procured from British ports or those you have smuggled in from French and Spanish suppliers?"

Cole patronized her with an indulgent smile. "I was not aware that you were overly concerned with the prospect of defying British regulations, my dear wife. Is your concern founded on your apprehension that your cherished husband might be carted off to jail if he is caught with smuggled goods?"

Stephanie countered with a sugar-coated smile. "I doubt I would miss you," she cooed. "How could I miss what I have not had? For the most part, you have ignored me as if I were a mere stick of furniture."

"On the contrary, my sweet," Cole crooned back at her. "I have constantly been aware of you. How could a man overlook such a lovely rose? 'Tis just that I have had a great deal on my mind. And to compensate for what you consider neglect, I insist that we rent you a carriage and send you off on an afternoon shopping spree." Cole paused to drink his coffee, which was laced with his own private remedy for hangovers. "Boston boasts the very latest in fashions. My wedding gift to you will be a wardrobe fit for a queen. When we entertain in Annapolis, I want you to be the envy of all the other ladies in attendance."

Stephanie rolled her eyes at the unaccountable arrogance of the male species in general and Cole's in particular. Didn't he know she could guess his motives, that his evasive tactics only aroused her suspicions? He was trying to buy her off, the rascal, and she damned well knew it!

"How very generous of you, Cole," she purred, her tone dripping with sarcasm. "I do hope you trust my tastes. I should be chagrined if my purchases did not meet your expectations."

Cole eyed her warily. There was a mischievous glint in those emerald pools. "I'm sure your selections will draw no complaint from me. With your gentle breeding you will purchase a few gowns that will compliment your unrivaled beauty and make me ever so proud that I selected you as my wife."

"Your *faith* in me is touching," Stephanie sniffed, her tone contrasting her words. "You have yet to trust me with any of your private thoughts. Indeed, we have barely shared more than the same space for the span of two weeks."

Cole purposefully overlooked her remarks and changed the topic of conversation. "I will see to your transportation as soon as we finish our meal. But I must insist that you return before dark. These are troubled times in Boston. Unemployment and poverty have a way of souring the disposition of many citizens. They are prone to riot and I would be most distressed if you were caught amidst this political and social unrest."

"Your concern overwhelms me," Stephanie purred in mock sincerity. "'Twas only last night that you had me swinging back and forth between the fore- and mainmasts. Is it that you only wish to see me come to harm by *your* hand?"

Cole's taut nerves snapped. His fist slammed against the table, sloshing wine on the linen tablecloth. "How many times do I have to apologize for that?" he grunted crabbily. "Would you prefer that I hurl myself into the sea as proof of my regret, my humiliation?"

Stephanie beamed in sadistic glee. "Indeed, and I would feel ever so much better if you would consent to sail into shark-infested waters before you take the plunge," she stipulated enthusiastically.

Cole managed to regain his composure, but it was a taxing task. His dark eyes bored into her as he quietly replied, "I'm sure what I said and did to you was beneath contempt. But you can rest easier knowing it will never be said or done again." His breath came out in an exasperated rush. "My behavior was inexcusable, Stephanie, but I wasn't myself last night."

"Nay, you weren't," Stephanie murmured with a melancholy smile. "More's the pity. I like the other man better, even if *you* were disgraced by his madcap shenanigans. At least the darker side of Cole Hollister knows how to live life to the fullest. 'Tis a shame *you* cannot take constructive criticism from *him*. At least he knew how to make a woman feel like a woman, not a possession." Her gaze locked with those cloudy pools of ebony. "Do not be so quick to condemn him, Cole. In many ways, he is the better man."

"Stephanie." His commanding voice drew her attention just as she glanced down at her lap, staring ruefully at the soft folds of silk. The indiscernible expression on her face baffled Cole and he swallowed the words that flocked to the tip of his tongue. Easing back in his chair, he granted himself time to reassemble his composure. A controlled smile touched his lips. "Purchase yourself something nice. It will be a peace offering of sorts, not because of what happened but because of the way I . . ." His voice evaporated as he glanced hesitantly at her. "I didn't hurt you, did I? Did I force you to . . ."

Stephanie inflated like an offended bullfrog. Damn him for not remembering how it had been between them! Having the wits scared out of her while they were flying from beam to beam was not half as frustrating as having their night of rapture forgotten. How could she ever have fancied herself in love with this insensitive creature? She was every kind of fool!

"I will indeed compensate for last night by taking advantage of your generous offer," Stephanie assured him tartly, bypassing his questions. "On *that* you can depend, my devoted husband!"

With a flourish, Stephanie catapulted out of her chair. After turning up her dainty nose and presenting Cole with a cold shoulder that dripped icicles, she breezed out the door, proceeded by a tail wind as cold as the polar ice caps.

Cole was going to pay through the nose, Stephanie vowed spitefully. He was trying to buy her forgiveness and shuffle her out of the way with one clever maneuver. Just wait until she returned from her shopping spree! He would regret sending her and he wouldn't dare say one word about the garments she purchased. After all, *he* was the one who had suggested this afternoon distraction and he could damned well pay the full price!

Humming that vengeful tune, Stephanie stalked up the steps to fetch her own carriage. She wasn't helpless, she reminded herself proudly. She was capable of taking care of herself and she didn't need Cole hovering over her like a mother hen. He was trying to keep secrets from her and she knew it. But he was *not* going to keep *her* in the dark and on a short leash! she vowed stormily. His misdirected sense of responsibility for her was downright infuriating. Stephanie didn't want it and she certainlay didn't need it, not unless he was offering it out of affection, which he obviously wasn't.

Cole refused to allow her to be a part of his life. He constantly kept her at arm's length when it came to his business. Well, if that was the way of things, she didn't need *him* summoning a coach to ensure that she traveled in safety. Why, if she was accidentally run down by a speeding phaeton, he probably wouldn't even waste a minute lamenting over the loss of his wife. Damn that man! He was the most frustrating, exasperating creature God had placed on the planet!

Chapter 18

Cole peered at each of his distinguished guests. He had met most of them in New York during a rally against the Stamp Act. The others had become his acquaintances during his last visit to Boston. Each man sitting at the captain's table, defiantly sipping illegally imported wine, was a member of the semi-secret organization known as the Sons of Liberty. In an effort to unite the colonies as one nation to reject Parliament's unjust laws, these staunchly independent men were the soul of the movement that was forming colonial militias and promoting freedom.

To Cole's left sat Samuel Adams. Across the table John Adams, Sam's cousin, thoughtfully studied the contents of his drink. Also occupying seats on the opposite side of the table were John Hancock and Paul Revere. Each man wore the gold medallion that signified his loyalty to the cause of freedom. Although John Hancock provided the major source of funds for the work of the Sons of Liberty, Cole had also given of his time and money to solidify one central organizing force for the colonies. Dyer Wakefield had sent along his contribution to the cause of liberty, matching Cole's generous donation coin for coin.

As Cole dropped the heavy pouches in John Hancock's hand, Sam Adams blessed him with a grateful smile. "I commend you on your work for the cause, Cole," he declared. "Thanks to your efforts, the citizens will soon be joined together to resist Parliament's attempt to force us to pay the brunt of the debts they incurred during the war with France. The pamphlets you and Paul have been distributing by land and sea will serve as a chain of communication between every colony."

"We have received reports from our circuit riders that secret militias have been set up in every town and rural area," John Hancock enthused as he tucked the pouches beneath his waistcoat. "The Sons of Liberty are increasing their numbers daily. If we continue at this same phenomenal rate, we can see to it that every stamp agent and tariff collector in every colony is forced to resign his position before the Stamp Act goes into effect in November."

A wry smile pursed Paul Revere's lips as he shifted his attention to Cole. "After Brice Reynolds was hauled off to prison, the Connecticut patriots in the surrounding areas where you delivered our pamphlets united to protest their tax agents. They even gathered to follow Hartford's stamp distributor into town, jeering and shouting a warning to resign or suffer the consequences." His dark eyes sparkled with pleasure as he gave the report he had received from other patriot circuit riders. "I have yet to hear all the details on how you wrapped Mystic's tax collector into such a neat package, but I'm sure it was gratifying for you to see another Tory bow to the strength of the Sons of Liberty."

Cole broke into a sly smile. "I cannot take full credit for that scoundrel's downfall. 'Twas my wife who was responsible for sending Reynolds to prison. I only provided the fuel to fire tempers against Mystic's stamp distributor."

John Adams chuckled in amusement. "Your wife must be as devout a patriot as you are. Perhaps we should approach her to organize the *Daughters* of *Liberty*."

"I'm sure she would delight in the responsibility," Cole assured his comrades. "But I prefer to keep her safely tucked away. She is only just now recovering from the injuries she sustained during her fiery bout with Brice Reynolds."

"Then I assume you will not allow her to accompany you to tonight's rally on the steps of the old State House," Sam Adams interjected before sipping his wine. "Although I would like to meet one of our female compatriots, I agree that this sort of demonstration is no place for a mending lady. And you will be preoccupied portraying Joyce Jr. during the protest."

"Are you planning a march or merely a meeting of minds?" Cole inquired soberly. He well remembered what happened the last time the crowd became unruly in Boston. The demonstration had come dangerously close to getting out of hand. That was the main reason Cole intended to keep Stephanie clear of this rally. The last thing he wanted was to see her hurt so soon after she had recovered from her wounds. The second reason was because Stephanie invited trouble with her bold daring. If he allowed her to attend, he wouldn't be surprised to see that rebellious minx leading a riot! She thrived on such excitement, even at the expense of her own safety.

"I hope tonight's march does not become as hostile as it did a fortnight ago," Sam continued worriedly. "But I hesitate to make promises. Emotion is running high in Boston. Unemployment has set fuse to short tempers. Taxation without representation—as our

298

comrade Patrick Henry has so appropriately labeled it—has caused bitterness against the loyalists."

"And there are also rowdy rapscallions among us who are itching to fight, even without a cause. If we cannot restrain some of the most boisterous members of the crowd, we might find a few more tax agents enduring more than tarring and feathering before the night is out." Sam paused to stare pointedly at each man. "Bostonians hunger to make their opinions known. Most of their complaints and criticisms have lately been directed toward Lieutenant Governor Thomas Hutchinson. I am not certain how long we can control the crowd. If they degenerate into a mob, we may have our hands full restoring an orderly demonstration for our rights as citizens."

"Our greatest challenge will be learning to control a mob and making each individual aware of the proper way to protest injustice," John Adams commented solemnly. "There is power in numbers and the other colonies look to Massachusetts as their example. We must make the mob work to our advantage. When Parliament realizes we are Americans, not subjects to oppressive tyranny, our demands will have to be met."

"Or else we will be forced to declare war on England," Cole mused aloud. "I pray it will not come to that. I would much prefer that England recognize our rights and retract these unfair acts and restricting laws that hamper our trade and burden our citizens during this sagging economical crisis."

Sam Adams's face was grim. "But if it comes to war, we will be prepared. By that time our colonial militias will be strong and men like Dyer Wakefield will be busy building frigates for our navy. That is why preplanning is essential. We must be organized if we ever hope to rebel against England's strong defenses."

After another hour of discussing the upcoming rally

and arranging plans for future activities, Cole was given a cargo of pamphlets to be delivered in ports along his route to Maryland. He was most thankful Stephanie was still meandering through Boston when his associates filed from the schooner. He hesitated in answering her prying questions. And Stephanie was bound to ask them. She had already given him the third degree before he shuffled her out from underfoot.

Surprise registered on Cole's rugged features when Stephanie appeared on deck. Packages were tucked under each of her arms and two string-bound boxes dangled from each hand. Behind her, virtually un-recognizable because of the heaping stack of packages that hid his face, stood Robert Forrister . . . or at least Cole guessed it to be Rob, judging by his oversized feet.

Cole's wide, disbelieving eyes flooded over the multitude of packages. "I suggested that you purchase a few new dresses, not restock your entire wardrobe," he croaked caustically. "My God, woman, have you forgotten the colonies and its citizens are in a state of depression."

Stephanie tossed him a saucy smile. "I have single-handedly taken it upon myself to remedy the sagging economy," she proclaimed. "Now that your money is circulating through Boston, it should lessen the depression."

Stormy black eyes rolled over Stephanie's sunny smile, leaving a gloomy shadow. "Madam, I am considered a wealthy man, but my orchard is *not* lined with money trees. There is a limit to the amount you can spend on clothes."

"Oh, silly me," Stephanie cooed in mock concern and then batted her big green eyes at him. "You know how we empty-headed women are. Once we traipse off on a shopping spree we simply get carried away."

"Empty-headed, my a—" Cole clamped down on his tongue and glared at his wife's pretentious grin. It suddenly occurred to him that Stephanie was spitefully punishing him for the previous night's shenanigan and whatever else he had done to annoy her during his momentary lapse of sanity.

Cole pasted on a tolerant smile as he ambled over to relieve Robert, who had relied upon memory to navigate his way toward the steps. "Let me take a few of those," he insisted. "I did not intend for Stephanie to employ you as her pack mule."

Leaving one hand free, Cole clamped his fingers around Stephanie's elbow and hustled her toward the stairwell. "Come along, my dear. I am most anxious for you to model my money. I'm sure it will look stunning on you." His tone had a distinctly unpleasant edge, even though Cole was trying to control his temper. That ornery minx, he mused, squeezing her arm harder than necessary. He should shake the stuffing out of her for this retaliatory prank.

"I am sure you will adore all my new clothes," she gushed sarcastically. "I only purchased the ones stitched with silver and gold thread." As proof of her remark, Stephanie waved the bills from several boutiques in front of him.

Cole's eyes popped out when he noticed the tallies for the merchandise. But he refrained from scolding her further for her extravagance until Robert had dropped the packages on the bed and closed the door behind him.

"You delighted in this, didn't you?" he snorted as he tossed the rest of the boxes on the foot of his bed.

"Aye," Stephanie declared unrepentantly. "It would have been cheaper if you had told me who and why you summoned your so-called associates to the ship this

301

afternoon and maneuvered me off to Boston."

A goading smile curved the corners of his mouth upward. "We agreed that my business was my own and yours was yours," he reminded her. "What I was doing and with whom is none of your concern, my dear wife. That *was* the arrangement we agreed upon."

Stephanie gritted her teeth. She might have known he would throw that statement back in her face. But 'twas no matter. Stephanie knew exactly who had come aboard the schooner. She had lingered near the wharf to await Cole's guests. It had been little trouble to question milling sailors about the identity of the nine men who had strode across the gangplank. And it didn't take a genius to deduce what they were up to. Stephanie had harbored doubts about Cole since the beginning. She had known there was much more to Cole Hollister than the prim and proper image he attempted to project. Several of the remarks Robert Forrister and Ben Hogan had made set Stephanie to wondering about Cole. Seeing the gold medallion the previous night confirmed her suspicions. After adding two and two together and coming up with four, Stephanie deduced that Cole was living a double life. Although he tried to keep a low profile and draw no unnecessary attention to himself in public, he was a very different man in private. And she could attest to that! There was something sneaky going on aboard the schooner and Coleman Douglas Hollister the Third was no apathetic dandy!

Finally, Stephanie's thoughts circled back to Cole's remark and she flung him a pointed frown. "You used to be more diplomatic and tactful before we wed," she chided him. "Your rough edges are beginning to show." A melodramatic sigh tumbled from her lips as she recklessly tossed her packages atop the pile. "Ah, how quickly the newness wears off this marriage that was created in heaven."

"Heaven?" Cole hooted, and then glared at Stephanie when she sashayed over to the liquor cabinet. "Madam, I can say beyond all doubt that the devil had a hand in this wedding." When Stephanie poured herself a drink and swallowed it in one gulp, Cole's eyebrows shot straight up. "Now what do you intend to do? Celebrate your spiteful shopping splurge?"

Stephanie did not dignify his sarcastic question with an answer. Her actions spoke for her. She sloshed another drink into the glass and raised it in defiant toast. After she had downed her third drink, she wandered back to the bed to unwrap one of her purchases. Hastily, she stepped behind the dressing screen to peel off her dress and wriggle into the first garment.

Cole nearly fell out of his boots when Stephanie emerged in her new purchase and spun around to face him. The daring décolleté left little to the imagination. The emphasis on her generous display of bosom and the small indention of her waist, provoked by the yellow brocade gown, had Cole's eyes bulging from their sockets. Sweet mercy! If this stunning beauty took to the streets dressed so provocatively, she would be mauled. Men would be trailing after her, literally fighting for her attention.

"Don't you think that is a mite too revealing?" Cole grumbled as Stephanie pirouetted in front of him.

Stephanie looked herself over with a critical eye. Then she shrugged nonchalantly, causing the scooped neck to swoop even lower. Cole strangled on his breath when she came dangerously close to spilling from the bodice of her gown. He didn't know whether to call the daring bodice a neckline or a waistline. It was that low!

"You look like a strumpet peddling her wares," Cole exploded, even after he had counted to ten twice.

Stephanie burst into a beaming smile, as if he had just showered her with the greatest compliment. "Why, thank you, my love. How very nice of you to say so. Since your ultimate purpose for marrying me was to provide yourself a permanent whore, I should like all the world to know in exactly what capacity I am to serve you."

Holding a tight grip on himself, Cole remained silent. Stephanie was intentionally trying to annoy him and he was not going to permit it. Damn, but this wildcat tested his self-restraint as no other woman had. Every moment spent with her served as practice in poise and control. Cole was constantly torn between the desire to take her in his arms and squeeze the tantalizing stuffing out of her and the urge to shake the orneriness out of her. Judging by the revealing gowns and her reason for purchasing them, this vixen was overequipped with both!

After Stephanie returned to the dressing screen, she shrugged off the yellow gown and wiggled into one that was even more daring than the first . . . if that were possible. Cole ground his teeth until they were smooth. He was trying to control his tongue; he truly was. But the vision of this green-eyed witch flaunting herself in front of his crew and the male population of Boston was simply too much!

He managed to hold his temper until Stephanie had pirouetted in front of him and then returned to the dressing screen to doff the risqué gown. His craggy features puckered in a frown as he glared at the upper half of Stephanie's torso that was visible above the screen. "If the rest of your new wardrobe is as bold as these creations, I will not allow you to set foot in public while you are wearing them," he told her in no uncertain terms. "I will not have *my* wife looking as if she had just wandered out of a bordello!"

Stephanie tilted a rebellious chin and Cole growled, disgruntled that she wore the expression so well. "If you don't approve of my purchases, you can cart them back to the various shops and select garments more to your liking," she sassed as she swept across the room to retrieve her wineglass. Her hand folded around the crystal goblet and she inhaled another drink. "I simply don't have the time this afternoon. I intend to be *waxed* by sunset. And when I am, I plan to scale the mast to view Boston by starlight."

And with any luck you will kill yourself during your ascent, thereby saving me the trouble of strangling you for your mischievous pranks, Cole thought. Then a more sensible idea darted through his mind and he smiled slyly. Let this ornery leprechaun think she had inconvenienced him. It would be the perfect excuse to journey into Boston. After he exchanged the gowns, he would attend the patriot rally. Stephanie would be wobbling about the schooner, stashed away from any trouble that might result from the meeting at the old State House. Cole wouldn't have to fret over her, wondering what had become of his fiery rebel in the midst of a mob.

Stephanie would be kicking herself if she knew she had played right into his hands, Cole thought delightedly. "As you wish, madam," he countered with a lackadaisical smile. "I will see to the matter of your clothes while you continue to punish me for what I did or didn't do last night."

While Cole was wrenching his arm to pat himself on the back for his cleverness, Stephanie was silently applauding herself for *her* resourcefulness. News of the upcoming rally had spread like wildfire. Stephanie had overheard several citizens talking of the protest against the Stamp Act. Knowing Cole as she did, she concluded that he was trying to hide the public meeting

305

from her while he sneaked away to attend. But Stephanie had every intention of being on hand when history was being made.

After Cole left the schooner with her stack of packages, she would march right off the gangplank and make her way to the old State House. Cole could continue to exclude her from his affairs if he wished, she thought generously. But one day all of his careful calculating was going to come back to haunt him—just see if it didn't! He wasn't going to shove her aside, tucking her safely away when she was just as much the patriot as he was.

After Cole scooped up the boxes and struggled out the door, Stephanie parked herself in a chair and meditatively sipped her wine. She could not help but feel a mite insulted that Cole refused to include her in his secret business meetings with the founders of the Sons of Liberty. Her family had depended on her to protect their secrets for years and yet Cole didn't trust her with his. Stephanie reminded herself that Cole was a private man who saw women as objects for his pleasure and nothing else. That thought stung her pride. It hurt to care about a man who couldn't return her affection the one time in her life when she felt inclined to give it.

When depression threatened to close in around her, Stephanie helped herself to more wine. The liquor would take the edge off her sensitive feelings, she diagnosed. By the time she departed for the rally, she wouldn't care what Coleman Douglas Hollister the Third thought of her. Let him think he had eluded her, she mused. Let him believe he had outfoxed her. He could feed his arrogance if he wished but Stephanie was far too aware of him not to notice that he was up to something.

Men, Stephanie mused with a frustrated sigh. Only

God knew what made them tick. Aye, she could understand why Cole felt the need to lead a double identity, why he passed himself off as a peace-loving, dignified aristocrat. He was smuggling in products from foreign ports, ones that could cost him heavy fines or a sojourn in jail. He was supporting the Sons of Liberty who were gathering force to defy the Crown.

And all the while Cole portrayed the role of the well-mannered, complacent gentleman so he would not be suspected of conspiring against Britain, he was in the thick of things. But what Stephanie couldn't understand was why Cole refused to confess his involvement to her. Was it because of that foolish pact they had made before their whirlwind wedding? Was he doing this just for spite? Or did he simply believe she would be more hindrance than assistance to his noble cause?

Stephanie expelled a melancholy breath. No doubt the latter was the reason Cole extricated her from the patriot cause. There had been more than one occasion when he had declared that her middle name was trouble.

Impulsively, Stephanie hurled her glass against the wall, watching the liquid trickle into a puddle on the floor, amidst the shattering splinters of glass. Well, she wasn't going to mope around feeling sorry for herself because her husband had little use for her. Dyer had stated that she was a rebel looking for a cause and she was going to hold true to form. Cole might be annoyed with her for attending the public meeting, but she was going to be there, shouting chants of liberty with the rest of the patriots!

After Cole returned Stephanie's purchases and selected a sensible wardrobe, he sent the carriage back to Hancock Wharf to be unloaded in his cabin. Taking a brisk walk through town to North Square, Cole found the area was brimming with citizens and tradesmen who were bustling about the marketplace just before dusk. But Cole paid little attention to his surroundings. His eyes were fixed on the modest, peak-roofed home that fronted the square. After he descended the steps that led to Paul Revere's gold and silversmith shop, he knocked on the door and waited an impatient moment.

A greeting smile pursed Paul's lips as he stood back to allow Cole inside his shop. "Are you prepared for the evening?" he questioned quietly.

Nodding affirmatively, Cole returned Paul's grin and gestured toward the package that he had clasped in his left hand.

Paul indicated toward the curtained door at the rear of the shop. "You can change clothes in there while I fetch your horse."

Without delay, Cole shrugged off his expensive garments and fastened himself into the same garb he had worn to lead the marches in Mystic and several other communities. A low chuckle rumbled in his chest as he tied the black cape around his neck and fastened the badge around his black hat. He was thinking of the evening in Mystic when he had implied that Stephanie knew the mysterious rider black-clad far better than anyone else realized. The Wakefields had assumed it was Stephanie who was gallivanting about town, inciting the patriots to harass Brice Reynolds. And since they had their hearts set on believing the black sheep of the family was up to her old pranks, Cole saw no reason to disappoint them. But in truth, he was one of the darkly clad express riders of the Sons of Liberty. Inconspicuously, he traveled about the countryside during the darkness, handing out pamphlets and communicating messages between the patriot leaders

308

of the colonies.

Tonight he would masquerade as Joyce Jr., the watchman for the Boston rally. Cole hoped to keep the crowd from degenerating into a destructive mob. Sam and John Adams wanted this to be a peaceful protest against the Crown. But Sam had cautioned him that feelings ran high in Boston and Cole mentally prepared himself for trouble.

At least Stephanie was safely tucked away, pouring down her wine, Cole consoled himself. When the rally was over, he would shed his garb, step back into the strappings of a gentleman, and return to the schooner. She would never know the patriot rabble-rouser who had appeared in communities up and down the coast was her sophisticated husband.

A tingle of excitement shot through Cole's veins as he emerged through the back exit to find Paul waiting with a jet-black stallion. It felt good to shed his gentlemanly garb and revert to his old ways for a few hours. Here was life's challenge, he reminded himself as he swung onto the saddle. He may have been forced to play the gallant to pacify his father, but part of him would always yearn for those days when he was truly free and alive. Cole could never completely sacrifice the man he used to be. Although he felt a fierce obligation to his father because of the past, Cole still thrived on death-defying challenges. It was these occasional tastes of excitement that helped him survive the role he was forced to play.

That was why he was so magnetically drawn to that feisty she-cat he had married. But just as he felt the need to keep his dark identity a secret, he also felt compelled to protect Stephanie. Capable and resourceful though she was, eager though she would have been to wave the flag of independence in the Crown's face, Cole could not permit it. There may come a time when he was hauled off to prison for instigating riots and stirring public opinion against the British. And if that time came, he did not truly wish to see Stephanie tossed into the cell beside him.

"'Tis for her own good," Cole lectured himself as he reined the black stallion toward the old State House. Humming that positive tune, Cole made his way through the alleyways to monitor the crowd while the eloquent Samuel Adams presented his speech on the colonial rights and the ever-tightening oppression of the British.

Had Cole known his mischievous wife was also making her way toward North Boston, his nerves would have resembled tangled twine. But Stephanie had outfoxed the fox. The dark rider who sat upon his gleaming stallion didn't have a clue that he had been outmaneuvered by his green-eyed leprechaun. Indeed, Cole was laboring under a false sense of security that Stephanie was stashed in the captain's cabin, drinking herself into a witless stupor. And before the night was out, Cole would find himself wishing he had *locked* his independent wife in his cabin for safekeeping!

Chapter 19

Wearing a smug smile that would have had Cole cringing in apprehension, Stephanie stepped from her rented carriage. Her discerning gaze swung to the large crowd that milled about the old State House. Although it was an unusually warm night, a group of Negroes and boys had built a bonfire in front of the building. The rebel leaders, including Sam Adams, had offered words of inspiration to the crowd.

Stephanie had not arrived in time to hear the speeches, but she was on hand to add her voice to those who were chanting for the abolishment of the Stamp Act and the protection of colonial rights. As the crowd of thousands marched through the streets in protest, Stephanie found herself swept up in the flood of humanity that poured toward Judge Storey's home. The judge was put to flight, his house ransacked, and his stock of wine confiscated from the cellar. After Storey took refuge from the unruly patriots, the crowd surged toward the home of Mr. Hallowell, one of Boston's custom commissioners.

When the second home was broken into and its wine stock depleted, Stephanie had the sinking feeling that this was not going to be one of Boston's *peaceful*

311

protests. Some of the rowdy mob leaders, who were even more dangerous with liquor fogging their heads, yearned to do more than threaten men who sided with the Crown. They had already run two British officers out of their homes and they were just gathering steam.

Although Stephanie knew it would be wiser to cut her way through the crowd and return to the schooner, she was trapped in the throng of patriots who had crossed the bridge from North Boston. Stephanie became frantic when more liquor was passed among the crowd. The mob had reduced itself to a dangerous state and Stephanie feared it was about to become a full-fledged riot.

Her grim prediction proved to be correct. By the time the crowd, shouting and jeering, reached Lieutenant Governor Hutchinson's grand home, Stephanie knew she was part of a keg of gunpowder waiting to explode. When she tried to push her way through the mob to protest senseless destruction, she was grabbed around the waist and pulled against a man's bulky frame.

Two bloodshot eyes bore down on her as Kent Langdon ogled his prize. Tipping up the bottle he carried in his free hand, Kent guzzled another drink. "Maybe you and me can have a little fun of our own once we send the gov'nor scamperin' for his life," he chuckled.

"Unhand me, you oversized brute," Stephanie snapped as she tried to pry his stubby fingers from her ribs. "This rally has gone far enough. Vocal protest is one thing but destruction of private property is quite another!"

"My, ain't you the high and mighty one," Kent snorted, readjusting his firm hold on the wriggling bundle of satin. "I might just have to take some of the starch out of you, lass."

His idea of unstarching Stephanie came in the form of a bruising kiss that reeked of wine and perspiration. Repulsion riveted through her when she was forced to endure Langdon's embrace. In a burst of fury, Stephanie shoved at him with every ounce of strength she could muster. A surprised squawk erupted from Kent's lips when he was forced backward, tripping over a pair of feet.

Stephanie spun about, hastily searching for a pigeonhole in the suffocating mob. Her ears were ringing with the chants to pull Hutchinson's house to the ground. As Thomas Hutchinson's sons appeared on the doorstep to defy the unruly mob, Stephanie found herself thrust toward the ground.

"You ain't gettin' away from me, wench," Kent growled. Bounding to his feet, he yanked Stephanie with him. "You may not be anxious to see the gov'nor's house come down around him." A jeering grin displayed all his teeth. "But that won't be nothin' compared to what I got planned for you."

Dragging Stephanie along behind him, Kent elbowed his way toward the back of the crowd. Stephanie's screams of protests drowned beneath the roaring chants of destruction. People were pushing and shoving each other to make their way to the governor's doorstep and Stephanie felt as if she were being assaulted from all directions. While she was fighting to elude Kent Langdon, Cole was sweeping the perimeters of the crowd, attempting to discourage violence.

Although Cole was not alone in his effort to hold the boisterous crowd at bay, it was next to impossible to control them in their drunken state. Two dozen men would have not been a match for these unruly ruffians who raised their axes and improvised clubs and charged toward the governor's home.

Cursing in frustration, Cole watched Thomas Hutchinson's sons retreat into the house when the first wave of rioters clambered up the steps to chop the front door to pieces. As the mob swarmed through the foyer in pursuit of the fleeing lieutenant governor, Cole swore under his breath and turned his head away from the impending destruction.

As Cole reined his horse toward the opposite side of the destructive mob, he spied the young woman whose head was capped with red-gold curls. She was writhing to escape her captor, who was dragging her toward a nearby alleyway.

Nay, it couldn't be Steph, Cole reassured himself. She was drinking herself silly on the schooner . . . wasn't she?

"Let me go!" Stephanie shrieked as she dug her booted foot into Kent's toe.

Cole's breath lodged in his throat. Damn! That was Stephanie's voice all right. That minx! She had selected one helluva time for her nocturnal prowlings. What the devil was she doing in the middle of a riot, for God's sake? She should have had more sense than to venture out alone at night in Boston. Confound it, Cole had warned her.

Curse that woman. Cole glared at Stephanie and her captor through the holes of his black mask. Didn't he have enough trouble on his hands without rescuing that minx from disaster?

The yelling and howling that was coming from inside and outside the Hutchinson house pierced Cole's ears, reminding him that he was battling a lost cause. Cursing a blue streak, Cole aimed his steed toward the fleeing hooligan who dragged Stephanie in his wake. Cole felt like a fish attempting to swim upstream as he wove his way through the mob that had closed in around him. His heart thumped at a frantic rhythm when Stephanie was yanked into a dark alley. Cole

314

swore he was moving in slow motion in his attempt to reach his misplaced wife.

Meanwhile, the hellish crowd was in the process of surrounding the house and ripping it to shreds. Family portraits and furniture, too large to be stolen, were being toted outside to use as kindling for yet another bonfire. Rugs, clocks, and china were being carted away as treasures. All the cash Hutchinson had on hand was stolen, along with his jewels.

Like an army rejoicing in its victory, the mob retrieved all available liquor from the cellar to further their celebration. While some of the men drank their fill, others climbed onto the roof to beat down the walls and strip the shingles. The fruit trees were picked clean and the garden house became bare in a matter of minutes. The house was gutted and the fire on the front lawn blazed higher. It was as if the entire crowd had gone mad.

Lieutenant Governor Hutchinson had become the scapegoat for all ill-feelings toward the Crown. Although the governor and his family escaped to seek refuge in his sister's home, his house and all his cherished belongings were stolen or destroyed.

Although the Sons of Liberty had hoped the march would remain orderly and peaceful, it became a tidal wave of destruction. Cole had given the mob up as a lost cause, as had the other watchman who had been on hand to attempt to control the crowd. Foremost in Cole's mind was locating his wife and carting her back to safety. But he was beginning to wonder if he would also meet with failure in that endeavor as well. The pitch black alleys that were known only to tomcats and other varmints that prowled the night was like a hopeless maze.

With the sudden uproar from the riot, it was difficult to single out a voice. Cole pricked his ears as he urged his reluctant steed through the narrow passages. And then a sharp cry pierced the night to intermingle with the mob's chants. Cole's body tensed as he reined his steed in the direction of the sound. Cursing a blue streak, Cole weaved his way through the clutterd maze. Damnit, if Stephanie's molester didn't kill her, Cole was going to. She had invited trouble by attending this rally and now she was getting a full dose of it.

Kent Langdon scowled menacingly when Stephanie warded off another rough embrace by clawing at his face. "Bitch," he hissed as he pushed her back against the wall. "I mean to have you, one way or another . . ."

With her arms pinned at her sides, Stephanie glared at the stubbled face that inched toward hers. She had fought off unwanted advances in the past, but never in her life had she been confronted by such a ruthless ruffian. His manhandling evoked her fury and Stephanie was too angry to be frightened. If this brute raped her, she swore he would have a full-blown fight on his hands.

When his lips clamped over hers, Stephanie bit into them and simultaneously kneed him in the groin. But her attack was like provoking a lion. Kent let loose a string of curses that would have singed the ears off a priest as he backhanded Stephanie across the cheek. Before she could scrape herself off the ground and regain her bearings, Kent grabbed the bodice of her gown.

A horrified shriek burst from her lips when her dress was ripped, exposing the swells of her breasts. But Stephanie had no time to fret over her immodest appearance. She was fighting for her life! Her doubled fists pelted Kent's jaw and cheeks as he sought to press himself against her. Another flood of revulsion splashed over her when his stout body meshed into hers. Making her sickeningly aware of what was about to happen.

And then like a bolt out of the blue, Kent was snatched up off the ground and launched through the air. Stephanie blinked in relief when she spied the darkly clad stranger who had leaped on Kent before he could clamber to his feet.

The sound of flesh pounding into flesh splintered the night. Shaking her head to clear her dazed senses, Stephanie glanced hurriedly about her to locate a makeshift weapon. Her hand folded around the whiskey bottle Kent had carried along with him. While the two men continued to batter each other with punishing blows, Stephanie crept forward, waiting to level a blow on her assailant. But the darkly clad avenger needed no assistance. Murderous fury sizzled through Cole's veins, the same brand that spurred him into action the night Brice Reynolds attacked Stephanie. All he could visualize was Stephanie mashed against the brick wall, suffering the mauling touch of this digusting ruffian.

It was only after Kent Langdon lay unconscious in the alley that Cole regained some degree of sanity. When Stephanie stalked over to clank the bottle against Kent's head for good measure, Cole found a smile returning to his lips.

"If your intent was to render your molester senseless, I fear you are too late," he drawled, projecting an accent that was totally unfamiliar to his unsuspecting wife.

After satisfying her thirst for revenge by breaking the whiskey bottle on Kent's thick skull, Stephanie drew herself up to stare at the caped stranger. She appraised the black mask that disguised his features. All she could see were holes where his eyes, nose, and mouth should be, giving him a most forbidding appearance, especially since his full cape concealed his form. The man who came to her rescue could have been a phantom for all Stephanie could tell in the shadowed alleyway.

Although it was too dark to discern whether or not the mysterious patriot had noticed her gaping bodice, Stephanie self-consciously covered herself as best she could. When her thoughts finally circled back to his question, Stephanie broke into a mischievous smile that even the shadows couldn't hide.

"'Tis no matter that this scoundrel was unaware of my retaliation," she declared saucily. "What is important is that I feel better having cracked his head after what he tried to do!"

A low rumble of laughter rattled in the region of Cole's chest. "Forgive my bluntness, Miss . . ." Cole paused as if he didn't know her name.

"Mrs. Stephanie Hollister," she supplied as she smoothed the tangled strands of hair away from her bruised face.

"Stephanie . . ." He dragged out her name like a lingering caress. "The streets of Boston, during a riot, are not the place for a lady. I don't know why you were alone and unchaperoned in the midst of that mob, but you should have expected no less than you received for your foolishness." The full cape rustled about him as he strode forward to tilt her shadowed face to his. "When a woman is as attractive as you are, she should anticipate a man's attention, welcomed or not."

Instead of pulling away from his touch, Stephanie held her ground. Her lips parted in another radiant smile that glowed like a beacon in the night. The fact that Stephanie was allowing a stranger to stand so close annoyed Cole. Damn this minx. She was behaving as if she would not reject his kiss if he were so inclined to give it.

"Does Mr. Hollister approve of your swarming the streets with the mob, madam?" he inquired, attempting to control his mounting irritation.

"Mr. Hollister has permitted me free rein," Stephanie informed the darkly clad stranger. "I do what I wish . . . with whom I wish."

She allowed her remark to dangle in the air, permitting him to draw his own conclusions. And Cole didn't like the insinuation this curvaceous vixen was presenting. As a matter of fact, he was furious with her for subtly suggesting that she had no aversion to continuing this encounter! If Cole hadn't been so intent on remaining with the secrecy of his disguise, he would have given Stephanie a sound shaking for appearing so . . . so . . . available for a man's affection.

For God's sake, he was becoming jealous of himself! Cole realized. He was the husband they were discussing as well as the mysterious stranger Stephanie had made not one move to reject! Double damn her. Just what did she think she was doing anyway? Was she still spiting him for the incidents of the previous night? How far was this hellion willing to go to have her revenge?

That question brought Cole a step closer. His eyes flooded over the ripped gown that displayed an immodest amount of bosom. "If Mr. Hollister is so generous with his lady, I must assume there is no love lost between the two of you," Cole murmured as his head moved deliberately toward hers. He kept hoping that at any moment Stephanie's conscience would get the best of her and she would slap his face and send him on his way. But to his dismay, she continued to stare at his concealing mask, awaiting his kiss. "It seems such a waste . . ."

To Cole's utter astonishment, Stephanie's arms slid around his shoulders. As she pressed closer, she tilted

319

her head back, causing the renegade strands of red-gold to cascade down her back.

"Mr. Hollister has no time for a wife," she told him, her voice like soft velvet. "And I could never forgive myself if I didn't properly thank you. I owe you my life, sir."

Petal-soft lips melted against his. Anger and desire were fighting to gain control of Cole's emotions. Part of him reveled in the feel of her luscious body moving familiarly against his. The other part of him was downright furious that Stephanie was being so bold with a perfect stranger. She was offering a kiss that burned hot enough to ignite another bonfire and Cole wasn't sure he wanted to know how far this vixen would go to have her revenge on her husband. And yet, he had to know . . .

His arms slid around her waist, bringing her ripe body into intimate contact with his. His mouth slanted across hers, savoring the taste of her. Cole consoled himself by rationalizing that it was the overabundance of wine Stephanie had been drinking that caused her to respond with reckless abandon. If she were in full command of her senses, she would never have behaved so brazenly. And once she returned to the schooner to contemplate what she had done, she would be ashamed of herself for even considering cuckolding her husband.

Reluctantly, Cole dragged himself away from an embrace that gave every indication that it could have continued for several more minutes. "I think 'tis best that I take you home, madam," he insisted, his voice ragged with desire.

Stephanie was in no hurry to leave. She was satisfied right where she was. Between the stranger's tantalizing kiss, the wine she had consumed, and the harrowing events of the evening, Stephanie was in one of her reckless moods. For once she could enjoy a man's arousing attention without feeling it necessary to protect her pride or her innocence. Cole had stolen her innocence and the wine had taken the defensive edges off her pride. She could surrender to the pleasure of being in the company of this dashing stranger and she fully intended to make the most of every moment . . . at Cole's expense. Besides, she reasoned, it was Cole's fault that she was alone in the first place. He could damned well stew in his own juice for all she cared.

"I don't want to go home," Stephanie murmured as she toyed with the strings of his cape. "I prefer to be with you."

Cole clamped his sagging jaw shut after it dropped wide open. Damnit, where was Stephanie's conscience? Drowning in wine? She had damned well better hate herself in the morning! The nerve of this green-eyed elf, he silently fumed. She was propositioning a man she had only met, a man whose identity was unknown to her!

Perhaps he could frighten her back to her senses. Maybe if he returned her seductive advances, she would turn tail and run. Chomping on that mischievous thought, Cole scooped her up in his arms and strode toward his stallion.

"Whatever you wish, Stephanie," he drawled provocatively. "I have always prided myself in accommodating a lady when she requests my undivided attention."

When Cole settled her in front of him on the stallion, Stephanie leaned back in the strong circle of his arms, accepting the protection he offered. And that made Cole all the more irritated with her. But he was determined to see how far she would allow this tête-à-tête to go before she reminded herself she had a husband. And it had better be quickly, Cole seethed as he set about to push Stephanie into an uncomfortable situation that would test her loyalty to her husband.

Boldly, Cole guided his free hand along her thigh. To his frustration Stephanie made no move to stop him. But when his hand wandered inside the bodice of her torn gown and Stephanie held it there, Cole was being torn apart by ire and desire. Stephanie should not have allowed him to take such privileges! And he should not have been so aroused by what was transpiring between them.

Lord, he was suffering nine kinds of hell knowing his wife was being unfaithful to him, knowing he was craving what she so freely offered. Cole had suddenly become the cuckolded husband, as well as her mysterious lover. He was being hounded by a jealousy that was tearing him to pieces, bit by excruciating bit.

But even while he was silently cursing her indiscretion, his male body was rousing to the feel of her shapely curves in his arms. Instinctively, his hand began to caress as he bent her into his hard contours. His mouth swooped down to devour the taste of her and Stephanie matched his ardent kiss with a passion that threatened to burst the night into flame.

When the steed shifted uneasily beneath him, impatient to be on his way, Cole nudged the stallion with his knees. But for the life of him he couldn't force himself to withdraw from Stephanie's alluring embrace. Allowing the steed to pick his own way through the alleyways, Cole continued his enticing exploration while Stephanie shamelessly responded.

Cole could have strangled her for putting up not one iota of resistance. And he would have if he hadn't been so caught up in the heat of the moment. Cole kept telling himself that one of them should have shown a little sense and he also reminded himself that it should have been *Stephanie*. After all, she was the one who was being unfaithful to her husband. Confound it!

How much wine had this minx devoured before she sneaked off to the rally?

Cole paused the steed just before they reached the street. Inhaling a steadying breath he peered at the dwindling bonfire and the tattered remains of Lieutenant Governor Hutchinson's home. The mob had scattered with their treasures, and the only sound to reach his ears was the accelerated thud of his heart.

His eyes were magnetically drawn to Stephanie's lovely features while she rested against his shoulder. She was staring up at his disguised face, her lips still swollen from his hungry kiss. The firelight glowed across the exposed swells of her breasts and cast enchanting shadows on her alabaster skin.

She was a vision no man could resist, Cole mused as his gaze seared her curvaceous figure. If he wouldn't risk having his identity known, he would have reversed direction to search out some secluded niche to make wild, passionate love to her. God, what man could resist this high-spirited beauty? he asked himself. She was what dreams were made of. He wanted her in ways that made him ache and she looked up at him as if she wanted him too. And *that* observation burned Cole to the quick!

"I don't even know your name and I cannot even see your face," Stephanie whispered, totally mesmerized by what had transpired between them in a moment of moonstruck madness. "But, 'tis no matter. You stir something in me . . . something that defies rhyme or reason. I find you wildly exciting, intriguing . . ."

Now Cole was *seriously* contemplating placing a stranglehold on her lovely neck! Stephanie had never uttered such professions to her own husband and here she was, making overt advances toward a man she had just met, for heaven's sake!

Despite his inner turmoil he murmured, "And you

323

have bewitched me."

Stephanie lifted parted lips and drew his head ever closer to hers. "Never in my wildest dreams did I believe I could fall in love so quickly. But 'tis far more than gratitude that I feel for you. I have this unreasonable need to remain in your arms, even when I know I should return to my husband. Take me away with you," she pleaded as her lips drifted over his. "My husband has no need of me. I am only another of his many possessions. I would stand beside you and your cause. I could give you pleasure to satisfy the both of us."

"Ah, er, well," Cole stuttered, frantically trying to formulate a suitable response. But it was damned difficult when her provocative kisses were turning his mind to mush.

"Don't you find me desirable, my dark knight?" she questioned just before her lips melted against his, making him crazy with the want of her.

"Very much so," Cole rasped when he finally came up for air.

"Will you meet me tomorrow night?" she implored.

Cole clamped his teeth shut before he yielded to the urge of biting her head off for making such a bold request. "I have other obligations, Mrs. Hollister, and I'm sure you have commitments to *your* husband."

Her tapered fingers swirled across the dark mask that disguised his face. "Perhaps the following night then? You are the only man who matters to me. I long for you to take me in your arms and kiss the world away," she whispered back to him.

How was a man supposed to reject such a titillating suggestion, especially when this minx's adventurous hands were tunneling inside his shirt to make stimulating contact with his bare flesh? He couldn't. The words tripped off Cole's tongue before he could even think to bite them back.

"Aye, meet me near the Liberty Tree an hour after dark," he breathed raggedly. Helplessly drawn to her inviting kiss, Cole drank his fill, adoring her and hating her all in the same moment.

As the steed plodded along the abandoned streets of Boston, Stephanie surrendered to first one kiss and then another. Between embraces she gave directions to the schooner that sat in the bay. Her thoughts were centered around this daring stranger who rode with the Sons of Liberty and who could melt a woman into a liquid pool of desire. There was no reluctance in her kisses and caresses, no pretense. She responded without restraint, luring him ever closer to the fire that threatened to burn out of control.

When their moonlight ride came to an end, Stephanie pressed one last kiss to his sensuous lips and then slid to the ground. "Until our next rendezvous . . . May it be the first of many," she murmured as she stepped back to view the cloaked figure who sat upon his black steed. And then she had the gall to blow him a kiss that fanned the fires of Cole's temper. "I will be counting the hours, my love."

Cole sat there smoldering. He couldn't believe the things Stephanie was suggesting. He was *her love*? Hell's bells, they had only just met! That damned fickle woman! Cole scowled under his breath.

As the dark stranger reined the stallion in the direction he had come, Stephanie pivoted toward the gangplank. Despite her attempt to contain her giggles, they burst free. She wondered how Cole was faring, knowing that his wife was becoming romantically involved with the mysterious patriot. She hoped he was completely bent out of shape after she had thrown herself at the darkly clad rabble-rouser. If she hadn't gotten Cole's goat, the man didn't own one, she

325

chuckled mischievously.

Cole didn't know that Stephanie knew his identity, but she had no doubt that it was her husband the instant he had laid into her assailant. Only one man could make his entire body a lethal weapon when he engaged in battle. Only one man could take her in his arms to kiss her and leave the stars spinning in the sky. Just because he assumed a phony drawl and lowered his voice an octave couldn't throw Stephanie off track. Didn't he realize he was the kind of man a woman would recognize under almost any circumstances? Well, she would soon discover just how stupid Cole thought she was, she mused on another ornery giggle.

Stephanie had given Cole every opportunity to disclose his true identity. He could have ripped off his mask and scolded her for her attempted seduction. She had done everything humanly possible to rile him, but still he refused to expose himself. Let him play his little games, she thought as she strode across the deck. Let him think she was falling in love with a man she knew only by touch.

It serves him right, Stephanie reassured herself. First Cole had incited riots against Brice Reynolds and allowed her family to think *she* was responsible. Now Cole was purposely excluding her from his life and his thoughts. Before she was through with him, he was going to regret his attempt to hoodwink her with his disguise. And all the while, Stephanie could express her love that she harbored in her heart.

Stephanie had always been honest in her feelings toward men. But that was before she had fallen in love. It was one thing to confess that she liked a man, that she enjoyed his company. But it was an entirely different matter to express her deep emotions for a man who used her to satisfy his lusts. But when she was in the "unidentified" stranger's arms, she could truly be

326

herself. She could allow the pent-up emotions to pour out. And if Cole never came to love her, it wasn't because she hadn't tried to win his affection.

The mischief drained from her face when she closed the door to her cramped cabin. But what if Cole felt nothing deep and lasting for her? What if the woman who had jilted him still had a strong hold on his heart? The thought depressed Stephanie. She knew the time would come when she would be forced into competition with the woman from Cole's past. If the fragile bond between them hadn't strengthened, she risked losing Cole forever. And then what would she do?

A despairing sigh tumbled from her lips as she crawled into bed. If she couldn't burrow her way into Cole's heart, there was naught else to do but leave him. Stephanie was not about to suffer a marriage to a man whose soul was chained to another woman. It had to be all or nothing between them. If this passion that brought them together had not evolved into love, Stephanie resigned herself to the fact that she simply was not woman enough to take Cole's heart and that he was too cynical of love to risk his pride and dignity.

Aye, she was hopelessly in love with Cole. She longed for the rough-edged rogue she had known in the darkness to emerge. Beneath that veneer of self-control and polished manners was a man who stirred her as no one else could—the man who garbed himself in black, who created the craving for freedom in the hearts of his fellow countrymen. Stephanie yearned to earn the love of the man who had sent her sailing from mast to mast and had made wild love to her as if there were no tomorrow.

There was a distinctively different personality lurking beneath Cole's tailor-made clothes. *That* was the man Stephanie had come to love. She didn't understand why Cole was so determined to suppress that other dynamic personality, but she had come to believe the darkly clad patriot who went by the name of Joyce Jr. was the *real* Cole Hollister. And Stephanie was going to be with him again soon. For those brief hours of darkness she was going to do all she could to earn his affection. She was going to prove to him that what they shared was rare and special.

Chewing on that determined thought, Stephanie allowed the effects of the wine and her whimsical dream to draw her into the depths of sleep. While she was drifting in a world of fantasy, Cole was in his cabin pacing the floor, beating a path from wall to wall.

After Cole had returned the steed to Revere's shop and changed his clothes, he stomped back to the ship. His first impulse was to storm Stephanie's door and rake her over the coals for dallying with a total stranger. After giving the matter a moment's contemplation, he veered toward his own cabin. He would accomplish nothing by confronting Steph. She would discover his carefully guarded secret. And knowing that minx, she would demand that he allow her to join the ranks of the Sons of Liberty.

Cole expelled an agitated breath. The entire evening had evolved into a disaster that soured his disposition. He and the other patriots had hoped for a peaceful demonstration. But there had been no controlling the drunken mob that had wrought destruction to Hutchinson's home. And when he saw Stephanie being dragged away, he had very nearly split apart at the seams. He was frustrated by the chain of events that lent a bad name to the Sons of Liberty. And then came the crowning glory for an incredibly discouraging evening. Stephanie had thrown herself at him, unaware that she had seduced her own husband!

Cole sank down on the edge of his bed to ask himself *why* Stephanie had become instantly attracted to the dark stranger. It hadn't taken but a moment to discern the answer to that question. That feisty minx thrived on excitement and challenges. She saw the mysterious patriot as a man after her own heart—a free spirit who defied law and order, a man who roamed the darkness, just as she had always done when she became restless.

How many times had Stephanie referred to him as a stuffed shirt? How many times had she mocked him for his self-control, his impeccable manners? Most women would have complimented his gentlemanly behavior, but not Stephanie. That minx was cut from a different scrap of wood. She preyed heavily on the man of Cole's past, but he couldn't go back. Damnit, he had made a solemn vow to his father and he owed a debt that would take a lifetime to repay. Aye, he could shrug on a black cloak and take to the highways and streets to spread news from the Boston Committee of Correspondence. But come dawn, he would forever be called upon to portray the gentleman and Stephanie had little use for the man Cole had been forced to become.

It was all too obvious which personality attracted his high-spirited wife. The fact that she had surrendered to the caped patriot disturbed Cole more than he wanted to admit.

Blast it, she was just like Rachel, he mused bitterly. Stephanie had defied her marriage vows by allowing another man to kiss and caress her. Well, at least *he* was the other man in her life, Cole reminded himself. But it was hollow consolation and damned if he knew how to proceed from here!

If he continued to play the charade with Steph, he would be fighting the battle of self-conquest. How was he supposed to resist his wife's charms? He knew how easy it was to forget himself when she was responding to his touch.

Cole let out his breath in a rush. Was he going to

allow his wife to fall in love with another man? A tormented groan tripped from his lips. He should be pleased that *he* was the other man she was attracted to. Yet how was he going to discourage her advances when he was his own worst enemy? And what was going to happen when they launched the ship and set sail for Maryland? Would Stephanie pine for the man she had met in the alleys of Boston? He knew that same man would be prowling the countryside of Maryland within two weeks. If she caught sight of him, would she be satisfied to leave her husband and follow after the mysterious stranger?

Cole stretched out on the bed and slammed his fist into his pillow. Suddenly everything was a complicated tangle. Nothing had gone according to plan. The British would be outraged by the recent riot. Before long, those responsible for ransacking the governor's home would be rounded up and herded to jail. The Sons of Liberty would be forced farther underground for fear of being imprisoned for treason. And to make matters even worse, his wife was contemplating having an affair with a masked stranger!

Cole massaged his aching head, chagrined to realize he had developed a five-foot-two-inch headache. He would have been much better off if he had confessed his identity. If he told Stephanie the truth now, she would be furious with him . . . as furious as he had been with her earlier that evening. God, he couldn't imagine having made a greater mess of things. Even while he was cursing Stephanie, he was anticipating making love to her in some private niche that was shrouded with darkness. She would never see his face or learn his identity if he avoided the light. Now was that crazy? Hell, of course it was, common sense shouted in response to his question.

Perhaps Cole could resolve the matter by retrieving his pistol and turning it on himself. Nay, that wouldn't work, he decided. Then Stephanie would never know what had become of the man she intended to meet at their late-night rendezvous.

Why are you even running these tormented thoughts through your weary head? Cole asked himself. He was already sporting a throbbing headache. What he needed was sleep, not compounded frustration. Once he had rested, he would sit himself down and carefully calculate his next move. He would proceed in a methodic, logical manner. And *then* he would shake the stuffing out of Stephanie for allowing him to take such outrageous privileges with her!

That firebrand was driving him toward an early grave. She had him meeting himself coming and going. She was forcing him to yearn to be the man he had buried almost three years earlier. But the ghost of the past was haunting him and Cole wondered if he would ever again be satisfied playing the refined aristocrat, as his father expected. Stephanie was slowly but surely bringing that other personality back to life, unearthing emotions that Cole had learned to control.

Damnit, this was all Stephanie's fault, Cole breathed as he closed his eyes. He had resented the man he had become since the day she breezed into his life and turned it upside down. If he knew what was good for him, he would leave her in Boston searching for her mysterious lover, while he sailed from port. That green-eyed leprechaun was pulling at him from a thousand different directions. Each day that passed found Cole more frustrated than he had been the previous day. Why, by the time they docked in Maryland, he would be a raving lunatic if he and Stephanie hadn't come to some sort of logical understanding!

After Stephanie dropped into her chair at the

breakfast table, Cole flung her a scrutinizing glance. Her demeanor gave nothing away, Cole mused disgustedly. Guilt should have been printed on her forehead in bold letters. If he didn't know better (and he most certainly did!), he would have presumed Stephanie innocent of any wrongdoing. Her smile was, as always, radiant. Blast it, she should have at least *looked* shamefaced when she confronted the husband she intended to cuckold!

Allowing ample time to compose himself, Cole sipped his coffee. "Did you enjoy having the evening all to yourself?" he questioned blandly.

Stephanie shook out her napkin and smoothed it over her lap. "Aye," she assured him. "There is something to be said for solitude. It revives the spirits." She whittled at her ham and eggs and then tossed Cole another bright smile. "Thank you for returning the gowns. The dresses you purchased in their stead were dignified and proper—a true credit to the man who selected them."

The remarks, coming from anyone but Stephanie, would have been considered compliments. But Cole knew Stephanie meant the comments to be pure satire. And, no doubt, her strategy was to divert his attention to the subtle jibe rather than focusing on her activities the previous evening. But Cole wasn't to be distracted, not when he had fumed and stewed half the night.

"While you were consuming a good portion of wine"—he ground out the lie with the most civil tone he could muster—"the mob demolished the lieutenant governor's home. 'Tis most fortunate we both returned before dark or we might have found ourselves amidst a riot."

Stephanie's face registered concern. "How dreadful. Such actions will give the Sons of Liberty a bad reputation. Aye, 'tis fortunate that neither of us were caught up in a violent demonstration. I would have been unduly distressed if something had happened to you."

Like hell she would have, Cole grumbled to himself. His discerning gaze narrowed on Stephanie's features. "Why, Steph, it seems you have somehow managed to bruise your cheek. One might think *you* were injured by the rowdy Boston mob." Now he had her cornered, Cole thought smugly. Let her talk her way out of this one!

Stephanie mustered a sheepish grin as she touched her discolored cheek. "I am embarrassed to confess that I tried to walk through a wall. 'Tis one of the hazards of overindulging in liquor. One begins to see things that aren't truly there and one also overlooks objects that are right in front of one's nose."

She uttered the explanation with such conviction that Cole might have been prone to believe her if he hadn't known she was lying through her teeth. Damnit, she was trying to play him for a fool and he couldn't contest her lie without exposing his duel identity.

Still fuming, Cole sought another approach. "I think we should make a fresh new start, Steph," he declared as he stabbed his egg and allowed it to weep all over his plate. "I would like to take you to the theater to celebrate our truce. Boston boasts one of the colonies' finest opera houses. Perhaps I could purchase tickets for tomorrow night."

Stephanie knew what he was trying to do. He wanted to watch her squirm in her seat and fumble for an excuse. But she didn't hesitate with her response. "'Tis terribly considerate of you, Cole," she insisted, and then stared at her silverware with a repentant smile. "I know I have been pouting like a spoiled child because you have had so little time for me. But while I was sitting there drinking, I did some serious thinking.

You have a myriad of duties to perform when you dock to sell your merchandise. If I accepted your invitation, I would be dragging you away from the tasks demanded of you." Stephanie looked so sincere that Cole wanted to strangle the lying minx. "I do appreciate your offer, but I couldn't live with myself if I accepted. You just go about your duties and don't fret over me. I will bide my time until we reach Maryland. Then we can enjoy the arts Annapolis has to offer."

Cole was sitting there smoldering. His well-disciplined countenance was about to melt. How could he argue with that sweet, unselfish rejection? He couldn't, he told himself resentfully.

While he was stewing in his own broth, Stephanie gracefully rose from the table and batted her enormous green eyes. "Now, if you will excuse me, my dear husband, I have planned to spend the day sightseeing in Boston while you make connections with other merchants."

When she swept out of the room, Cole expelled a wordless growl. How was he supposed to compete with that kind of feminine finesse? She had bested him with her wily charm. That sneaky little vixen. She had declined his offer so she could spirit off with her mysterious lover—a man she wouldn't have recognized if he had been sitting directly across the breakfast table from her (which he most certainly had been!).

Confound it, he had to devise a way to terminate her reckless affair. But *how?* Cole frowned pensively. Something had to be done. But *what,* in heaven's name? Perhaps he should allow some other man to garb himself as Joyce Jr. Then Cole could catch his wayward wife red-handed. A wry smile rippled across Cole's lips. Let her talk her way out of that one! Or maybe he should consider . . .

While Cole was wrestling with several possibilities to

resolve his frustrating dilemma, Stephanie was bounding up the steps to the main deck, grinning like a Cheshire cat. Cole had attempted to outwit her, but she had the supreme advantage over him. *He* didn't know that *she* knew what was going on.

Try to keep *her* in the dark, would he? Stephanie sniffed haughtily. She had been blessed with a sixth sense that enabled her to perceive what most people overlooked. And men were the world's worst about taking women for granted. Men labored under the ill-conceived notion that those of the female persuasion were empty-headed dolls. Well, Coleman Douglas Hollister the Third would never take her for granted ever again, she vowed firmly. When she got through with him, he would recognize her as his equal and he would be sorry he ever allowed this charade to continue as long as it had!

Chapter 20

Sam Adams ran a restless hand through his prematurely gray hair. Although he suffered from a mild form of palsy, it was apprehension rather than his affliction that caused his hand and voice to shake as he spoke to the solemn congregation. "What happened after the rally last night was inexcusable," he breathed in frustration. "Ruffians and vagabonds have given the Sons of Liberty a black eye with their senseless destruction. Our cause is much too noble and important to be lost because of the drunken mob that evolved from our rebel demonstration."

"'Tis impossible for a mere handful of men to control a disorderly crowd," Cole grumbled. "The mob refused to listen to reason. If we are going to employ future demonstrations to vocalize our griefs against Parliament there must be a great number of respectable citizens traveling in the march."

John Adams smiled faintly. "It sounds as if you have thought this matter through, Cole. Have you a suggestion of how we are going to place these noted citizens in the crowd without fearing their arrest? Every face recognized by the Hutchinson family has already been rounded up and thrown into jail." John eased back in his chair to survey the somber group. "Rumors are spreading that the British are tightening their defenses and organizing night patrols. If one more march evolves into a violent riot, we could face a massacre on the streets of Boston. The British will probably pay even higher prices for the services of spies and informants. Before long, the Tories will be raiding our private conferences, refusing to allow us to meet at all."

"After what happened we have no choice except to go underground," Revere interjected. "Our meetings will no longer be *semi-secret,* but instead, they will become parleys held in the strictest confidence."

"But no matter what alternative actions we take, we must not detour from our cause," Samuel Adams declared firmly. "Since we are not allowed representatives in Parliament, the mob is still our best political tool against the British."

Restless, Cole unfolded himself from his chair and paced the Long Room that sat above the printing presses where the Sons of Liberty met in conference. "I suggest that the familiar faces of upstanding citizens be disguised beneath caps and homespun clothes when the mob takes to the streets. The respectable citizens of Boston will not have to risk being ostracized or imprisoned by the British. Their identity will remain unknown. If their numbers are great, they can exert positive control over the unruly crowd and prevent the kind of senseless destruction we witnessed last night."

A pensive frown plowed Sam's brow. After a moment he nodded agreeably. "I think you have hit upon a useful tool, Cole. The mob will be better trained to suit our purpose if a better sort of man is in its midst." A wry smile replaced his frown. "If we handle the mob like an army, marching them back and forth in military procession, handing them a few slogans such as 'Liberty, Property, and No Stamps,' it will better serve our purpose."

"And if we add to that a few free feasts and harmless fireworks, combined with marching to build up the feeling of power and unity, we can ensure the rally will not become so destructive in the future," John Hancock suggested.

Sam Adams broke into a relieved smile. "I do believe we have come up with a workable solution. We have no wish to offend the conservative merchants who oppose the Stamp Act by allowing the Sons of Liberty to earn a disrespectful name in the colonies. Yet we cannot afford to lose the rowdy crowds whose very numbers suggest power for the cause. *Peaceful* demonstrations will solidify the alliance between the less vocal patriots and those responsible for last night's violence."

A wry grin pursed Cole's lips as he came to stand at the head of the table. "I have been toying with another idea I think will ensure that the merchants and businessmen, as well as the rowdy ruffians, realize that the Sons of Liberty have taken a more dignified stand against the Stamp Act."

The Loyal Nine listened intently as Cole unfolded his plan, one that had taken most of the night to formulate. After he presented his detailed proposal and cited its practicalities, Sam Adams chuckled delightedly.

"I like your ingenuity, Hollister," he complimented. "Your plan will further the cause for rights and liberty."

Once the group of men agreed on when and where to put the suggestions into action, Cole inconspiciously made his way back to the schooner. Although his plan would serve the best interests of the patriots, he still had another matter to resolve. The Loyal Nine would be able to restore some degree of order, but Cole was still faced with Stephanie's romantic involvement with the dark rider of the Sons of Liberty.

Cole did not wish to find himself in competition with *himself* for his wife's affection. He had spent the better part of the day deliberating on how to solve his dilemma with Stephanie, but he was still in a quandry. Damnit, what am I going to do about my unfaithful wife? he wondered as he meandered his way through the streets of Boston. What he wanted was to teach Stephanie a lesson about unfaithfulness that she would never forget!

Cole strode across the deck and lingered by the taffrail to stare at the brilliant stream of moonlight that spilled across the sea. A quiet smile touched his lips. He had thought the two tropical storms he had endured the previous month were torment. But now he realized they were nothing compared to the turmoil he faced in his dealings with that misdirected hurricane named Stephanie. But once we launch the ship and set sail for Annapolis, Stephanie and I are going to begin again, Cole told himself determinedly. They had been at cross-purposes since the night he had proposed marriage. But once Boston was behind them, Cole was going to devote his time to wooing his stubborn wife back to his arms.

Aye, there would still be nights when he would be forced to sneak away to confer with patriots in the southern colonies and to complete the chain of communication for the Sons of Liberty. But Stephanie would never have to know he was deeply involved in the crusade for rights and liberty. They could share a peaceful coexistence . . . somehow. But no matter what, Cole would never risk having Stephanie involved in the secrecy. She was too much the rebel as it was.

Heaving a heavy sigh, Cole spun around and descended the steps that led to his cabin. When the door closed behind him he stared musingly at the blank wall of his quarters. He did not like deceiving Stephanie. She had come to mean a great deal to him, more than he cared to admit. The greatest favor he could do for her was protect her, to ensure that she didn't become entangled in the patriot cause. But he would compensate by allowing her all the freedom she desired (under his watchful eye, of course) when they reached the plantation. His first and foremost concern was to keep that green-eyed leprechaun out of trouble. That in itself would be a full-time job, Cole reminded himself as he collapsed in bed. But the first thing he had to do, if they were going to enjoy any sort of marriage at all, was to discourage her from fantasizing about the dark patriot.

If Cole had been blessed with the gift of prophesy, he wouldn't have lost any sleep that night fretting over the problems with the Sons of Liberty and his rambunctious wife. He would have known he was wasting his time trying to tamper with fate. There were times when one disaster led to another and it wasn't humanly possible to change the course of destiny. And Cole was to be reminded of that fact the following evening . . . just when he thought he had resolved his problems for all concerned!

A muddled frown creased Stephanie's brow as she stepped from the rented carriage to await the arrival of the mysterious stranger. There was no sign of the man she had expected to meet. Had Cole decided to leave her standing in wait until only God knew when? Was this to be his way of solving the problem of the other man in her life?

Impatiently, Stephanie tapped her foot and stared at the shadows that hugged the dimly lit street. Tonight she had intended to draw Cole out into the open once and for all, to force him to admit that he was leading a double identity. She had fully intended to push him until irritation got the best of him and he revealed himself. Once he had scolded her for attempting to have an affair with another man, she planned to disclose that she knew who he was all along and that she had deliberately tried to seduce the dark patriot in order to bring the *real* Cole Hollister from hiding.

Perhaps her methods were a bit unethical, but she wanted to prove an important point. If there was no trust and confidence in this marriage of theirs, there need be no marriage at all. Either Cole wanted her to share his life or he didn't. Tonight they would come to terms or they would go their separate ways, Stephanie decided. She was tired of being shuffled out from underfoot and treated like a child who needed protection. If Cole refused to confess his involvement with the Sons of Liberty and his duel identity, then she would know beyond all shadow of doubt that her only purpose in his life was to provide him physical pleasure.

Stephanie was aware that she stood to lose a great deal, but she refused to continue on the same rocky course. She and Cole should have been standing on the same side of this crusade for liberty. They should have been working hand in hand to promote the cause of colonial unification.

The sound of voices stirred her from her pensive musings. Stephanie peered down the street to see a congregation of ruffians following the darkly clad rider. Damn, she muttered under her breath. The last thing she wanted was to be caught up in another unruly mob. She had hoped for a few private moments with the dark patriot. But it appeared she would be forced to share him with a crowd.

As the procession marched down the street, chanting

341

for liberty, another caped figure stepped from the alleyway to confront them. The dark patriot raised his hand to halt the crowd and then eased his horse forward to confront the intruder alone.

"Stand aside, friend," the masked rider commanded. "We wish no trouble with you. Our protests are directed toward the British sympathizers and the King's men."

"Nay," the intruder roared. "You, Joyce Jr., have become the evil spirit that *hinders* our cause instead of *promotes* it. Violence only begets violence." In fierce accusation he thrust a gloved hand at the darkly clad vigilante. "You have taken what is noble and good and transformed it into wicked destruction. You are no friend to the Sons of Liberty! You have become a detriment to our cause. Because of you, all patriots will suffer the wrath of the British. Because of the wickedness and destruction you have come to represent, the Sons of Liberty and their followers will all be considered traitors to the Crown. In order to restore organization and strength to our cause, *you* and the evil spirit of the mob must perish!

The crowd hung in stunned silence, digesting the words of the unidentified orator who stood in harsh defiance. After a tense moment, a peal of laughter rang through the street. Joyce Jr. nudged the steed ever closer to stare down at the man who had spoken out against the mob's violence.

"Our protests will be heard around the world, my friend. In this instance, the *end* justifies the means. The manner of our protest is not as important as the protest itself," he countered, purposely voicing the opinions of the unruly members of the mob who were more inclined toward destruction, *with or without* purpose.

"Ah, but you are wrong," the man parried with a bitter snort. "If we project ourselves as violent mobsters, the Crown will deal with us accordingly. Our demonstrations must be civil if we expect them to be recognized as a just and noble complaint. A man does not pat the head of a snarling beast whose intent it is to maim and devastate." His arm swept in a wide circular motion, indicating the crowd that followed their darkly clad leader. "Your mob has become a monster and it must be destroyed for the sake of our righteous cause!"

Stephanie stood in horror as the intruder reached for the flintlock that he had concealed beneath his cloak. Her shocked scream died beneath the sudden explosion of the weapon. As the masked vigilante clutched his chest and tumbled from his steed, his assassin dashed into the alley to disappear from sight. Stunned, Stephanie watched the mob swarm in around their fallen leader and listened to the frantic murmurs that rippled through the crowd.

"He's dead! Joyce Jr. is dead!" someone shrieked.

It took a moment for the words to soak in. Stephanie's heart was pounding in double time. The world was spinning furiously about her and she felt as if an invisible fist had collided with her midsection, forcing the wind out of her. When her legs threatened to buckle beneath her, she braced herself against the lamp post.

The whole town had gone mad, she mused dazedly. First had come the destruction of the lieutenant governor's home. And now the patriots were squabbling among themselves. Those who had been outraged by the violence of the previous rally had dealt severely with the darkly clad patriot. They held him personally responsible for the eruption of disaster. But he was only a man behind a legendary costume. Joyce Jr. had not been able to control the rowdy mob. It wasn't his fault that drunken ruffians had transformed the demonstration into destruction. Damn them all! They had wasted a man's life . . . Cole's life . . .

Cole was dead? Assassinated in the streets of Boston? Nay, this was a lifelike nightmare, she tried to convince herself. Stephanie shook her head, forcing back the soul-shattering thought that riveted through her mind. Nay, it wasn't true. It couldn't be true! God, not Cole, not the man she loved!

While Cole's limp body was being carted into Paul Revere's silversmith shop, the members of the mob fled to contemplate what the assassin had said before he aimed his pistol at the patriot rebel in black. For what seemed forever Stephanie watched the citizens scatter like ants abandoning their den. When her paralyzed mind began to function, she found her footsteps taking her toward the procession of men who were carrying their vigilante leader away.

With hot tears rolling down her cheeks, Stephanie elbowed her way through the cluster of men. They had laid the lifeless body upon a workbench and then stood back to stare somberly at their fallen leader. Unconcerned that she was making a scene, Stephanie flung her arms across Joyce Jr.'s chest, very nearly squeezing him in two in her anguish.

"Nay, it isn't fair," Stephanie wailed as she clung to his limp body. "He shouldn't have been held responsible for the mob's destruction. It isn't fair!"

"Who the devil is this woman?" Sam Adams questioned bemusedly.

His second cousin, John, shrugged in response. His eyes were fixed on the melodramatic scene. John Adams was also at a loss to identify the young woman who was mourning the death of Joyce Jr.

Cole lay as still as a corpse, pretending to be as dead as everyone thought he was. But he was silently cursing Stephanie's fond attachment to a man she barely knew. He had expected her to be upset when she witnessed the

344

staged assassination, but she wasn't supposed to be carrying on like this! My lord, one would think Stephanie had fallen head over heels in love with the image of rebellious recklessness. It wasn't the *man* she cared for, Cole consoled himself as Stephanie bled tears on his chest. She was simply bewitched by the position the semi-mythical hero had held.

"I loved you," Stephanie said brokenly as she buried her head against his masked face. "And now there will be no chance for us . . . Cole . . ." His name burst from her lips on a choked sob and she held on to him as if the world were coming to an end.

Cole inwardly flinched when Stephanie not only murmured his name but also confessed her affection. Stephanie had known who he was all along? Had she attempted to seduce the masked rider just to annoy him? Had she purposely thrown herself at Joyce Jr. in hopes of tying Cole in knots and depriving him of two night's sleep?

Why, that ornery little minx, he thought furiously. But before that thought could take root, a wry smile crossed his lips. Unfortunately Stephanie was too busy saturating Cole's cape with a bucket of tears to notice the grinning corpse.

The day had finally come when Stephanie admitted she loved him. The saints be praised! She *did* care for him. Armed with that encouraging knowledge, Cole's shoulders began to shake in amusement and a bubble of laughter burst from his lips.

"For heaven's sake, woman," he chuckled. "Can't a man die in peace without having some teary-eyed female crying all over him?" Swiftly, Cole removed the mask and flashed her a taunting grin.

Watching Cole rise from the dead shaved ten years off Stephanie's life. She bolted back as if she had been lightning-struck. Her eyes bulged from their sockets when her not-so-dead husband propped himself up on one elbow to fling her another devilish grin.

The color drained from Stephanie's cheeks. She had suffered the shock of her life when she saw Cole tumble to the ground, a victim of assassination. She endured an even greater jolt when Cole came back to life. She was relieved and furious all in the same moment. He was laughing at her, that miserable vermin! She had confessed her feelings for him and he had laughed *out loud.*

It was one thing to make a complete fool of oneself, but quite another to have someone else do it. Stephanie had never been so humiliated in all her life. Even the public ducking was nothing compared to blurting out her love for this devious, two-legged rat!

Impulsively, Stephanie doubled her fist to smear that infuriating grin all over Cole's lips. Cole braced himself for the oncoming blow, recalling just how devastating this she-cat could be when she delivered a furious punch. Prepared though he was, the force of the blow sent his head snapping backward. Cole clutched his stinging jaw with one hand and used the other as a shield when Stephanie, in an explosion of mortified fury, attacked him again.

Before Stephanie could fully satisfy her craving for revenge, she was grabbed from behind. "Easy, Stephie," Ben Hogan snickered. "The poor man has just been shot to death. You need not add insult to injury by beating him to a pulp."

Stephanie swiveled her head around to see that Ben Hogan was garbed in the identical clothes the assassin had been wearing. Ben had crept in the back door of Revere's shop after he had fled from the street. When the realization of what had happened finally soaked in, Stephanie growled under her breath. Confound it, the entire scene had been staged! She would have bet her fortune that Ben's pistol was loaded with blanks and there was not an ounce of blood spilling from Cole's body. Damn them for not telling her what was going on! Not only had she made a blundering idiot of herself in front of this cluster of men, but she had confessed her feeling for a man who could have cared less what she thought of him.

"Gentlemen, may I present Stephanie Hollister, Cole's wife," Ben proudly announced to the group, who had been grinning at the confrontation between Cole and this lovely spitfire.

Stephanie was well aware that the whole lot of them were amused by her hysterics and her tantrum. Oh, how she wished the floor would open up and she could drop out of sight.

"Madam, we did not intend to distress you," Sam Adams reassured her after he recovered his composure. "We naturally assumed that Cole had explained our scheme to you. In hopes of gaining control of the mob, we found it necessary for Joyce Jr. to meet his demise. Staging the death of the legendary hero of Pope's Day was our attempt to restore order to the mob. The rowdy crowd has molded our purpose into something evil and destructive. We had to dispose of that frightful misnomer and grant the Sons of Liberty the respectable reputation it deserves."

"The mob must realize that the dark patriot is not one of the ghouls or goblins that has come to be associated with what some colonists term as Halloween. He is the noble inspiration of colonial spirit," Paul Revere chimed in. "We wanted to emphasize that violence only begets violence."

Slowly, John Adams came forward to offer Stephanie a comforting pat. "After the mob witnessed the assassination they will think twice before they revert to displays of destruction. You see, my dear, Joyce Jr. had

347

to die to give rise to a nobler realm of protest."

"'Twas time the surly members of our group realized they, too, could face life-threatening situations if they persisted in destroying and stealing personal property from Tories. It was never our want to kill pro-British sympathizers or demolish their homes. Our purpose is to voice our objections to taxation without colonial representation in Parliament. Since the bullet struck so close to home, we hope the unruly mob will conform." John Hancock offered her an apologetic smile. "Unfortunately, you were caught unaware, Mrs. Hollister. But your reaction ensures us that we have made a strong, lasting impression on the mob of Boston."

"I must admit I was surprised when Cole suggested having himself murdered," Paul inserted, along with a gentle smile. "But with Ben Hogan masquerading as the assassin, it all worked out splendidly. The killer will not be apprehended since your schooner sets sail at dawn." His gaze swung to Cole and his eyelid dropped into a wry wink. "When a man is leading a double life, it can't hurt to have one of him shot. Indeed, I thought Cole handled his demise superbly and effectively. If I hadn't known 'twas all an act I would have been taken in when he made his spectacular fall from his steed. Cole certainly looked dead from where I was standing. 'Tis no surprise that you believed what you saw, Mrs. Hollister."

The attempt to console Stephanie was a waste of breath, especially when her eyes darted momentarily to Cole. He was regarding her with a gloating smile that made the hair on the back of her neck stiffen. Aye, it had worked out splendidly all right, Stephanie fumed. The Loyal Nine had shocked the mob back to their senses and Cole had heard the confession Stephanie would have taken to her grave to protect her pride.

Totally frustrated, Stephanie flung herself from Ben's captive arms and darted toward the door. She was not going back to the schooner to suffer Cole's taunts. She wanted to be a thousand miles away. And if wishing would have made it so, Stephanie would have blinked her eyes and transported herself to another continent!

"Steph, come back here," Cole called out the uninjured side of his mouth. But Stephanie never broke stride or looked back. She was out the door and in the street before Cole could bound off the workbench to pursue her.

When Cole stalked after his infuriated wife, John Hancock clutched his arm to detain him. "You can't go back into the street! You are supposed to be dead," John hastily reminded him.

"And if I don't catch my wife, there is no telling what will become of her," Cole muttered as he shook his arm loose.

Paul stepped in front of Cole to block his path. "Change your clothes and take the back exit," he suggested. "I'll keep watch to determine which direction she takes."

Grumbling, Cole began peeling off his garb while he stormed through the shop to collect his clothes. Just what was he going to say to that fiery vixen if and when he caught up with her? he asked himself. The entire incident had backfired in his face. Stephanie was irate that he had played such a wicked trick on her. But hell, how was he supposed to know that she knew who he was all along? All this time he thought he had killed two birds with one stone—shot Joyce Jr. to gain control of the mob and to put an end to Stephanie's infatuation with the mysterious vigilante. Well, his scheme had partially succeeded, he reminded himself. The wicked spirit of the mob was dead, but there was no fury like that of a woman who had been deceived and mortified in front of an audience. Damn, it was going to require all the water in Boston Harbor to cool Stephanie's flaming temper, Cole reckoned. And he was absolutely right!

But at least she loves me, Cole consoled himself as he rounded the corner to reappear in the street. Or at least she felt something for me until I humiliated her, he amended. After Paul thrust the horse's reins into his hands and gestured south, Cole took flight. He squinted to study the swaying shadows but still there was no sign of Stephanie. And then, when he was about to decide she had somehow reversed direction and eluded him, he spied a rider darting in and out of the trees that lined the creek. Cole didn't know where or how Stephanie had managed to procure a horse at that late hour, but the fact was that she was astride a steed and she had every intention of putting miles between them. Gouging the stallion into his swiftest gait, Cole wove among the trees, determined not to lose sight of his fleeing wife.

Stephanie was an accomplished equestrian and she had no intention of being caught. The moment she heard the thunder of hooves behind her, she began devising a plan of escape. Before Cole could close the distance that separated them, Stephanie wheeled the horse into the creek. As the steed stretched out to paddle toward the far bank, Stephanie slid from his back and took cover in the gnarled tree limbs that hugged the stream.

Cole heard the splash but he hadn't seen Stephanie dismount and swim to cover. Following the sounds, he forced his mount into the creek and swam past Stephanie's hiding place, unaware that she was only a mere ten feet away.

When Cole thundered off in pursuit of the riderless

horse, Stephanie pulled herself upon the limb. Inhaling a relieved breath, she inched her way to shore to fumble along the rivulet. There was naught else to do but hike down the road and pray there was a wayside inn where she could spend the night. The following morning Stephanie intended to catch a ride on the next coach headed south and make her way back to Connecticut. And if Cole Hollister dared to show his face near her father's estate, she would make certain the next pistol that was pointed at his chest was loaded with gunpowder! He wouldn't rise and strut away a second time, she vowed vindictively. When she shot that rascal down, he would remain down . . . permanently.

Feeling reasonably safe, Stephanie veered back toward the road. She swore she had walked for an hour before she spied the lights in the distance. Breathing a thankful sigh, she quickened her step. She was anxious to shed her damp gown and climb into a soft bed.

A startled squawk erupted from her lips when a shadow leaped out at her. To her dismay she found herself entrapped in the last pair of arms she ever wanted to feel squeezing her in two.

"Let me go," she growled as she kicked Cole in the shin, evoking his pained grunt.

"'Tis time you and I had a talk," Cole insisted as he dodged another punishing blow.

"We have nothing to say to each other," Stephanie hissed, straining to escape. "I'm going home."

"We have a great deal to say to each other," he contradicted as he backed her against a tree to restrain her. With Stephanie pinned to the bark, Cole deflected her angry glare with a rakish grin. "You don't just tell a man you are in love with him and then spirit off into the night. It isn't polite."

Stephanie gritted her teeth. She should have known he would throw her words back in her face in an

351

attempt to humiliate her a second time. "I don't love you. I despise you and your polished manners, your impeccable self-control," she snapped at him. "You made a fool of me and I will never forgive you for it."

A wry smile parted his lips as he clasped both of her wrists in one hand, freeing the other hand to sketch the defiant features of her face. "Admit it, minx. You are in love with me." His voice was like a stroking caress, meant to destroy her defenses.

"I was upset," Stephanie muttered resentfully, twisting her face away from his touch. "I didn't know what I was saying. I thought you were dead and I—"

"But you uttered the words just the same," he broke in, flashing her a smug grin.

Stephanie's green eyes were spitting fire. "You also said you loved me the night you partook too heavily of Connecticut rum," she shot back. "Shall I hold you accountable for what you said when you were swimming in liquor?"

Cole did a double-take. Had he truly said that? Was that why she was so aggravated with him, why she had set out to spite him? Was that what he swore to her that he would never forget and then completely forgot?

"Let me go home," Stephanie choked out, fighting like hell for hard-won composure. "I can't bear being a responsibility. You don't want me to be a part of your life. You never have and you never will. I have no wish to endure this mock marriage." Her voice crackled and an unwanted tear slid down her cheek. "The man I *could* have loved, the man I once risked my life to defend, no longer exists. You killed him tonight."

Lord, she was bewitching when she was in a fit of temper, Cole mused. He was mesmerized by the emotion in her exquisite features, by the misty green eyes that dominated her face.

"Just what was there about the man that intrigued

352

you?" Cole queried as he tilted her flushed face to his. "Was it his impulsiveness? His reckless daring?"

His sinewy body pressed into hers, forcing Stephanie to tolerate their intimate contact, forcing her to experience sensations she didn't want to feel. She was humiliated and furious and she had no intention of surrendering to desires of the flesh when her pride would have to be sacrificed. It was all she had left and she felt the need to cling fiercely to it.

"Were you fascinated with him because of the way he touched you . . . the way he responded when you set your hands upon him to introduce him to a wild unique dimension of passion . . ."

Stephanie was not allowed the chance to reply. But it didn't matter. The moment Cole became his living past, Stephanie fell in love with him all over again. Cole's craggy features were no longer an unreadable mask. She could see the fire of desire flickering in those pools of ebony. She could feel his body rousing in response to hers, feel his heart's acclerated beat.

"Do you want him back, Steph?" he murmured as his moist lips seared across her cheek, fanning the flame into a raging fire. "His spirit still lives and breathes. He still wants you the way he always has. The dark rider had to die to drive home an important point to the unruly mobs of Boston." His mouth drifted across hers, his breath ragged with barely constrained passion. "But you, my feisty leprechaun, can perform miracles. You can resurrect him with your mystical kiss . . ."

Cole was no longer chaining her against the tree. His arms had enfolded her, clutching her so close that not one part of their bodies remained separated. His gaze was glued to the tempting curve of her lips, studying them as a starving man would visually devour a feast.

As Cole drew her down onto the lush carpet of grass,

353

Stephanie surrendered in wild abandon. Passion burst forth like a roaring waterfall tumbling from its towering heights. And in the fine mist lay the arc of a rainbow, its colors blending one into another. Cole could feel himself losing every ounce of self-control. His body moved instinctively toward Stephanie's silky flesh like a river surging through its channel, touching all within its turbulent path. There could be no gentleness in these raging emotions. Passion had converged upon him, evoking primal needs. His craving for this lively goddess became a monstrous hunger that defied restraint. Only when the need had been satiated would tenderness come. But for now there was naught else to do but tumble with the flow of passion that was as turbulent and overwhelming as a sea besieged by a storm.

Mindlessly, his hands and lips devoured her soft flesh, making her his total possession. A tormented groan escaped his lips as he caressed her and she responded by returning his eager touch. His kisses savored her with cherished impatience and she offered back each ragged breath with such ardent passion that Cole feared he would go mad with pleasure. It was wild and spontaneous and sweet and it was no longer important that they had resolved nothing. No matter what else was between them, there was a slow burning fire that nothing could extinguish. And once it burst into flame, there was no controlling it.

When Stephanie arched to meet his hard thrusts, Cole clutched her to him, fearing he would crush her and yet unable to contain this fierce, illogical need for her. He could not seem to get close enough to the inner driving force that haunted him. He was like a traveler pelted by wind-driven rains. He was running blindly for shelter. The force of passion was at his back and desire's haven was just beyond the storm. He was racing at a frantic pace, his heart galloping, his body taut . . .

As Stephanie's satiny arms enfolded him, he found his haven from the storm and flood. She had taken him to her, sheltering him in a world that knew nothing but exquisite ecstasy. And for that space in time there was no reality, only the satisfying side effects of fulfilled passion. Cole was bobbing on a crystal clear river, basking in the warmth of rapture. There was no past or future and Cole didn't care if he ever regained his senses. He was drifting on a feathery cloud, content to sleep in the arms of this wild, sweet angel.

Stephanie heard Cole's quiet breathing and she willed herself to remain by his side until she was certain he was sound asleep. A trickle of tears rolled down her cheek as she gazed up at the stars that looked as if they had become entangled in the low-hanging branches.

As much as she loved the man who emerged from the shell of infuriating self-control to send her soaring to castles in the air, Stephanie knew she would only cause herself heartaches if she remained by his side. Cole would forever exclude her from his life because he didn't truly care enough about her to allow her to share his private thoughts. If she stayed, she would become frustrated, and in time, her bitterness would spoil what she felt for him.

That troubled thought provoked Stephanie to quietly ease from Cole's side. It was all or nothing and . . . A mischievous grin formed on her lips. Since there could be *nothing* more between them, Stephanie decided to emphasize the point. She scooped up her clothes, as well as Cole's. She would make certain he couldn't pursue her, she thought wickedly. A naked man couldn't give chase and that was exactly what he would be when she confiscated his garments, his boots, and his steed.

As Stephanie led the steed away, she tittered softly. She was the one who had enjoyed the last laugh. Cole Hollister wouldn't dare come back to Mystic after she had thoroughly humiliated him. Cole had played a rotten trick on her by pretending to be dead and he deserved this ornery retaliation. He had offered her passion but he gave little in the way of explanation. Her dramatic exit should be self-explanatory, she assured herself. If Cole refused to take her into his confidence, she would take her leave, once and for all.

Although Stephanie would have preferred to cuddle up on a soft bed, she didn't dare stop at the inn for the night. She intended to be miles away before Cole awoke and found her gone.

A strange emptiness gnawed at the pit of her stomach as she thundered cross-country on Cole's steed. She was never going to see those dark, penetrating eyes again. She was never going to feel those sensuous lips drifting across her skin.

Stephanie flung aside the sentimental thoughts. If she intended to forget Cole Hollister ever existed, she could not torment herself by remembering the pleasure they had shared. This was the time to list Cole's annoying faults. And that was exactly what Stephanie did as she threaded her way through the darkness. And by the time she reached Mystic, she would not be able to think of one nice thing to say about Coleman Douglas Hollister the Third. He would be a closed chapter in her life. The only problem was—how was she going to explain her appearance to her parents?

Stephanie frowned thoughtfully. She would invent some excuse before she trudged up the steps of the mansion, she encouraged herself. But for now she had her hands full trying to convince herself she had done the right thing by leaving Cole to his cause for freedom, one she wholeheartedly supported, one he refused to discuss with her. And that was the first and foremost reason why she should put Cole out of her mind forever.

A man who refused to share his private thoughts and his commitments with his wife didn't need a wife at all. If all he wanted was a soft body to cuddle up to, any female would do. And it wasn't going to be her body, unless he was prepared to accept the feelings and emotions attached to it. Stephanie had her pride after all. Cole Hollister was not going to take her for granted. Indeed, he couldn't take her at all because she was going to be long gone . . . for good!

Chapter 21

The peaceful silence of dawn was abruptly disturbed by an enraged growl that resembled the cry of a panther. The birds fluttered from their perches in the overhanging trees. Cole had awakened to find Stephanie gone, along with his clothes and his mount.

"That mischievous witch," he scowled as he rolled to his feet.

Infuriated, Cole glanced about him, wondering how he was to return to the wharf in his present state of undress. Stephanie had left him with nothing except his dented pride. Damn her, when he caught up with her, he was going to strangle her!

Cursing a blue streak, Cole stalked toward the river, deciding it best to cling to the underbrush for protection. How he was going to traipse across the wharf in broad daylight without being noticed was a question he hadn't quite puzzled out. But Cole was forced to deal with the problem when he crept closer to town.

Although Cole was so irate he was seeing the world through a red haze, he clamped down on his temper. He could solve his dilemma if he carefully plotted it out, he reassured himself. After giving the matter calculated consideration, he scanned the area. A relieved smile mellowed the stern expression on his face when he spied a pile of discarded feed sacks. Within a few minutes, Cole had tied the cloth together in an improvised toga. Mustering his dignity (all that could be had when one was forced to parade across the wharf, bare-legged and barefooted), Cole stalked toward the gangplank. He gritted his teeth when the longshoremen assaulted him with wolfish whistles.

Shock registered on Ben Hogan's weather-beaten features when he realized who was receiving all the attention. Although he knew Cole was going to be in a fit of temper, he could not control the snicker that rose to his lips.

"Don't you voice one word, damn you," Cole scowled as he dropped to the deck and stomped toward the steps. "Fetch some hot water for a bath. These sacks itch like hell!"

The moment Cole set foot in his cabin, he fought his way out of the sacks and hurled them against the wall. A string of unprintable curses tripped off his tongue as a pixie face and sparkling green eyes materialized before him. Damnit, were they always to be at odds? They constantly tormented each other. Even though Cole lectured himself that it was best to turn the other cheek, stubborn pride got the best of him. One mischievous prank gave birth to another. That was how it had always been between him and Stephanie. Well, if that feisty witch thought he would allow her to have the last laugh, she had another thing coming! She had not seen the last of him. And, by God, when he got his hands on her, she would sorely regret this last madcap prank. She was going to compensate for every humiliating step he had taken during his trek back to the ship!

While Cole was feeding his vengeful thoughts, Ben

rapped on the door. Although Cole anticipated a taunting, Ben's expression was stone sober when he appeared in the doorway.

"Paul Revere is on deck," Ben announced grimly. "He has a message for you. I know it isn't going to help your disposition but you better hear what he has to say before we set sail."

Cole snatched up a pair of breeches and pulled on his clothes as he ascended the steps. Fear shot through him, wondering if Paul had a report on his missing wife. Cole kept envisioning Stephanie being attacked by highwaymen, her mutilated body tossed beside the road.

Paul surveyed the disheveled captain who looked as if he had dressed on the run (which he most certainly had). "I'm afraid I am the bearer of discouraging news," he began with a deflated sigh. "We have just received word from our contacts in Connecticut that Brice Reynolds has been released from prison." He was interrupted by Cole's muted snarl. "The British have quietly effected his release. With so many patriots protesting the Stamp Act, the British must have decided they could use every Tory who was willing to sell his soul for his freedom. We cannot say for certain in what capacity Reynolds will serve the British, but I would guess he is to become a hired informant."

Cole didn't doubt it for a minute. But what disturbed him most was Brice's personal vendetta against Stephanie. "Do you have any reports on his whereabouts?" Cole inquired somberly.

Paul gave his head a negative shake. "All we know is that the governor of Connecticut granted him pardon and that he was released from Newgate last week."

"Damn!" Cole swore vehemently.

"If we receive any more information, one of the express riders will contact you in Maryland," Paul

360

assured him faithfully. "'Tis not an unusual occurrence, I fear. Only those who commit crimes against the Crown are left to rot in prison. British sympathizers seem to have a way of evading the debts owed to colonial society."

If that was meant to console Cole, it didn't help one iota. He was outraged that a convicted criminal had been released, especially when it was the very man who had attempted to kill him and Stephanie.

Before Paul turned away, Cole retrieved the coins in his pocket to reimburse his friend for the steed Stephanie had taken. When Paul disappeared onto the crowded wharf, Cole scowled under his breath. Knowing Brice Reynolds was on the loose heightened his apprehensions. If he didn't get to Stephanie before Brice did, there would be nothing left of her. Because of Stephanie, Brice had lost everything. He was not likely to forget what she had done to him and he wouldn't be satisfied until he had disposed of her.

Mulling over that unsettling thought, Cole ordered his crew to open sail. He had intended to make a leisurely trip along the coast, distributing pamphlets from the Boston Committee of Correspondence. There were just over six weeks left before the Stamp Act was to go into effect. The Sons of Liberty had hoped to frighten off every tax collector in every community of every colony before the first day of November. But with Brice running around all over creation and Stephanie only God knew where, Cole didn't dare waste a minute. Once he located Stephanie and put her under lock and key, he would distribute the pamphlets.

Confound that high-spirited sprite, Cole muttered as he glared at the waves that rolled before him. She had selected the worst of times to strike out on her own. Cole expelled a harsh breath. Perhaps if he had included her in his plans, she would not have

361

abandoned him. But damnit, there were risks involved in what he was doing for the patriot cause. The British would love to have the colonial rabble-rousers corraled and contained in one city. If officials discovered how closely he was working with the Adamses and Hancock, they would be following behind him like kittens on the trail of fresh milk! And if a woman was suspect, there was no telling what the British would do to dispirit her. Cole hated to even speculate what lay in store for a feisty beauty like Stephanie if she was caught passing patriot pamphlets. . . .

"Are you going to tell me why we sailed from Boston without your wife and why you returned to the ship in a feed sack?" Ben questioned, jostling Cole from his distressing thoughts.

The inquiry further soured Cole's disposition. "She ran away," Cole snapped more harshly than he had intended.

Laughter rumbled in Ben's chest. "Let me guess," he insisted between snickers. "Stephie wanted to ensure you didn't follow her so she took your clothes, as well as the mount you borrowed from Paul."

"Aye," Cole acknowledged on a bitter note. "And for that I would dearly love to choke her, but I may never be granted the chance if Brice Reynolds gets hold of her first."

The remark erased the smile from Ben's features. "Do you truly think he means to harm her?"

Cole burst into an incredulous laugh. "He would kill her, given half the chance. Stephanie stripped Reynolds of his wealth, his position, and his pride. Reynolds is the kind of man whose arrogance will demand fierce retribution." His dark eyes smoldered as they swept the choppy sea. "Brice Reynolds will never be satisfied until one or the other of them is dead," he grimly predicted.

Hushed silence fell over the quarterdeck. Ben's gaze shifted to study the strained expression that captured Cole's features. "The way the two of you have been going at each other the past two weeks I was beginning to wonder if you had married that minx just to spite Rachel." Ben propped his forearms on the rail and followed Cole's gaze across the ocean. "But you care about Stephie, whether you will admit it or not."

"Why should I care about a female who spites me at every turn?" Cole grunted, fighting to hide his emotions behind a mask of indifference. "If I had any sense, I would let Reynolds have that troublesome misfit."

Ben scratched his head and grinned wryly. "You know, that's the strange thing about the plague of love," he stated philosophically. "When it strikes, a man's common sense begins to decay. Love has nothing to do with thinking. It has to do with *feeling*." Ben sized up the captain and then nodded affirmatively. "Aye, I would say you have a severe case of the plague that has tormented man since the beginning of time."

"I am *not* in love with that green-eyed hellion," Cole loudly protested. "All she has given me is one five-foot-two-inch headache after another!"

"That's the first symptom of the disease," Ben tittered.

Cole was in a foul mood and he had no intention of being harassed. He had fallen in love once and it had ended in disaster. And with a woman as fiery as Stephanie, love would be hell's torment! If that minx thought for one minute that he was truly vulnerable to her, she would trample him into the ground.

"I took a wife because my father insisted upon it," Cole argued defensively. "Love has nothing to do with it."

"Then why are you so concerned about Reynolds getting his hands on Stephanie?" Ben countered, grinning smugly.

"Why don't you jump overboard, old man?" Cole growled irritably. "I have a ship to run and I haven't the time for your probing questions."

Ben shrugged lackadaisically. "You can fight it if you wish, C.D. But when the love bug bites and you're struck down with the plague, you might as well admit you're suffering from the disease."

Cole's frayed temper was coming dangerously close to snapping. "I'll admit to nothing until I come down with the accompanying rash!" Cole bellowed and then snapped his jaw shut when the entire crew paused from their chores to determine what had caused the eruption of their captain's temper.

Ben surveyed the red scratches that were revealed by Cole's gaping shirt. With a stubby finger he indicated the noticeable rash. "Then comes the deliriums," Ben taunted unmercifully. His hand brushed across Cole's forehead to confirm that he had contracted a fever that nothing could cure. "Aye, 'tis just as I thought. You're suffering all the symptoms of the plague."

Cole slapped the lingering hand away and glared daggers at Ben's teasing grin. "The next thing I know you will be pronouncing me dead."

"Somebody did last night." Ben sent Cole a wry wink.

Growling in exasperation, Cole stalked off the quarterdeck to seek refuge in his cabin. Stephanie's life was in danger and he was too frustrated to tolerate Ben's mocking. Besides, what good would it do for him to fall for that minx? She might not be alive by the time he caught up with her, not if Brice Reynolds had his way! And even if he did love Stephanie, which he most certainly didn't, she would never be satisfied until the man of his past replaced the well-disciplined aristocrat.

That couldn't happen. He had made a vow to his father. Cole owed the old man a debt that would take forever to repay.

Stephanie was asking the impossible. The man who aroused her passions was a ghost, a shadow of himself. What Stephanie wanted Cole couldn't give her, not without sacrificing his sacred vow to his father. Blood was thicker than passion, Cole reminded himself bitterly. But Stephanie couldn't understand because he had never bothered to explain his past. Hell, he hadn't bothered to explain anything to her and that was why she left him with *nothing* . . . because that was exactly what *he* had offered *her*.

That revelation caused Cole to groan in torment. He should have known better than to marry that high-strung vixen. She would always want what he couldn't give. Cole had to lead a methodic life and Stephanie defied rigid regulations. She would constantly prey upon his hidden emotions, poking holes in them until they drained out like water trickling through a sieve. Bit by bit, Steph would break him down until he reverted to his old ways. Then he would be in conflict with his father all over again.

Muttering, Cole slammed his fist on his desk. Why hadn't he been the one to die three years ago? It was a cruel twist of fate that he should have been the one to survive the ordeal. It was Clay who should have been managing the Maryland plantation. His younger brother possessed all the impeccable manners Cole had spent three years imitating and perfecting. Cole had tried to become his brother to appease his bereaved father. Cole had sacrificed his own reckless freedom to repay the debt. He had lost touch with happiness . . . until Stephanie stumbled into his life to remind him of all he had forsaken to become the man his father wanted.

"What the hell's the use," Cole scowled disconcertedly. His marriage to Stephanie was bittersweet torment. By keeping her with him he could see a little of himself each time he stared into those enormous green eyes that sparkled with deviltry and irrepressible vitality. And yet his growing attachment to her brought another brand of torment. When she left him, she had taken part of him with her.

"Damned woman, I can't live with her and I cannot live without her," Cole sighed disgustedly. "She represents what I want in life and ironically she represents what I know I can never have."

So why was he so dead-set on finding Stephanie and forcing her to return with him to Maryland? Because he had to protect her from Reynolds, his practical mind replied. But deep down inside, Cole knew there was more to it than that. Losing Stephanie was worse than tearing off an arm. In fact, it closely resembled having one's heart plucked out of one's chest and demanding that one go on functioning as if nothing extraordinary had happened.

She had cast her spell upon him. She had touched each and every emotion known to man and she had turned his organized world upside down.

Now she had spirited away and he felt empty and dead inside. She was a habit that was difficult to break. Now Steph despised him and she wanted nothing to do with him. Cole heaved a heavy sigh. Well, it didn't matter what she thought of him. She was going to accompany him to the plantation. And if she didn't tow the line in his father's presence, he would throttle the life out of her . . . *if* there was any left in her by the time Brice Reynolds satisfied his vengeance.

Lord, what a mess, Cole mumbled, raking his fingers through his raven hair. He couldn't have the woman he wanted because, for his father's sake, he couldn't be the man he wanted to be. And he would live in constant fear for Stephanie's safety as long as Reynolds was prowling around the colonies. To compound the problems, Cole had only six short weeks to organize unified resistance to the Stamp Act in the middle and southern colonies. Damnit, there weren't enough hours in the day to see to his duties, stand as posted lookout over his restless wife, and begin a search to apprehend Brice Reynolds.

Laboring under the dismal philosophy that if everything could go wrong at once it would, Cole slumped in his chair. He should revert to his old ways, kidnap Stephanie, and sail off into the sunset. But blast it, he couldn't do that. There would be no freedom for anyone if he didn't continue the fight against Parliament. And to make matters worse, he would be constantly glancing over his shoulder, wondering when Reynolds would strike. There was also the matter of his father, a man who had never been the same after he had lost his wife and then his second son. And there was Cole's broken engagement with Rachel Garret to smooth over. . . .

Cole refused to wallow in those depressing thoughts. The first thing he had to do was reach Mystic in record time. Once he had Stephanie under his protection, he could rest easier. But until that time, Cole feared he would be prowling the confining decks of his ship like a caged tiger. And he did. He wore a smooth path from stem to stern, grappling with a myriad of disturbing apprehensions. The days required to sail from Massachusetts to Connecticut were the longest and most agonizing of his life!

Inhaling a courageous breath, Stephanie stared at the front door of her father's mansion. It had taken her longer than she had anticipated to return home and she looked the worse for wear after her week-long journey. Apprehensive about facing her parents in her frazzled condition, Stephanie had stopped in Stonington to purchase a gown to make herself look more presentable. Dressed in respectable fashion, Stephanie aimed herself toward the estate.

For a week Stephanie had sorted through various and sundry excuses as to why she had returned home without her new husband in tow. Stephanie had pondered dozens of inspirations and discarded all but one. She would simply announce that she and Cole proved to be incompatible and that they had decided to have their vows annulled. It was her hope that her father would not instantly accuse her of wrongdoing since he had a bad habit of laying the blame on her, no matter what the circumstances.

Pasting on a greeting smile, Stephanie sailed into the foyer. The smile slid off her features when the last man she ever wanted to see appeared at the door of her father's study. Damnation, she had ridden like a bat out of hell, making her way alone, attempting to outrun the memories. Her efforts were for naught. The moment she stared into those craggy features, the memories came flooding back to torment her.

Although Cole had been tearing out his hair wondering what had become of his vagabond wife, his facial expression did not register relief. His countenance was calm and deliberate, as if nothing out of the ordinary had happened. His gaze drifted down her shapely figure, amazed that Stephanie could endure what had to have been a long, tiring week and appear in Mystic looking as fresh as a daisy. She was a witch, Cole concluded. No other woman could make that rugged, cross-country trip and arrive looking as if she had just stepped out of a fashion boutique.

Stephanie ground her teeth, annoyed by the mocking grin that spread across Cole's bronzed features. "What are you doing here?" she demanded curtly.

Cole pushed away from the door frame, where he had been lounging, and swaggered toward her. "Where would one expect to find one's husband?" he questioned, his tone carrying a caustic ring. "Standing stark naked on the road to Boston perhaps?"

Stephanie could not suppress the impish grin that tugged at her lips. The picture of Cole storming cross-country, without a stitch of clothes, was a spitefully satisfying vision. Before Stephanie could fully enjoy the speculation of Cole's embarrassing predicament, his hand snaked out to shackle her wrist.

"I did not find your prank the least bit amusing," he bit out.

"Nor did I find humor in seeing you shot down in the street," came her crisp rejoinder.

One thick brow climbed to a quizzical angle. "Why? Because I didn't die by *your* hand, my loving wife?"

Stephanie wrestled her way from his chaining grasp and straightened the sleeve he had twisted around her wrist. "You may be many things, most of which I do not approve, but you *are* astute. I would like to be the donor of the bullet that has your name on it."

Cole's mouth thinned into a grim line. "The feeling is mutual, my dear wife. But unfortunately, Brice Reynolds has been freed from prison. I imagine I will find myself standing in line to get a shot at you."

To further emphasize his remark, the sound of a musket exploded in the distance. Before Stephanie could react, Cole had shoved her to the floor. The heavy weight of his body forced the wind out of her. Since Stephanie had failed to close the front door, she was in full view of the sniper. Before Cole could swivel around to kick the door shut, another musketball ricocheted off the wall to shatter the vase that had once sat regally on the nearby table.

"You have made yourself a mortal enemy," Cole growled as he dragged Stephanie with him.

"Where are we going?" Stephanie managed to get out as Cole whisked her down the hall.

"Back to the schooner." Cole yanked on her arm, maneuvering her in front of him. "I already informed your family of your arrival and of Reynolds's release. Dyer dashed off to notify the sheriff and took several of his servants with him into town to protect Wes and Natalie."

Stephanie kept silent as Cole hustled her along the path that led to her father's private wharf. When Cole scooped her up to set her upon the gangplank, another shot pierced the air.

"Stay down and get below deck," Cole hissed and then sucked in his breath as he shoved her ahead of him. He had no intention of allowing Stephanie to know he had been hit. If she lingered for a split-second, Reynolds would have the opportunity to reload, take aim, and drop her in her tracks.

Stephanie scurried across the plank, watching the sailors who were simultaneously diving for cover. Never looking back, she scrambled down the stairwell. Her breasts heaved in an attempt to catch her breath. Another shot splintered the oak planks, and Stephanie instinctively ducked away. She waited an agonizing moment for Cole to join her, but he didn't come.

Craning her neck, Stephanie peered around the corner of the steps to see Cole crawling toward her. Her eyes widened in shock when she spied the blood stains that drenched the side of his waistcoat. Upon further inspection Stephanie realized Cole had been hit not once but twice! He was feeling his way across the deck because he couldn't see where he was going. Blood was trickling from the wound on his forehead, blinding him.

"Cut her loose!" Ben yelled at one of the sailors. When the man shrank back in his safe corner, Ben snarled several epithets to the crewman's name. "Damnit, cut her loose before we are all picked off like flies!"

The young sailor inched his way along the deck to free the schooner, setting her adrift in the bay. But the sniper was relentless in taking pot shots at the stairwell where Stephanie was hiding. She was pinned down but that didn't stop her from slithering toward Cole, who by then had fallen unconscious.

When the ship was out of range, she scrambled to her feet and dashed toward him. She should have known something like this would happen, she reminded herself as she dabbed away the streams of blood. When a man dared to tamper with fate by staging his own death, it should come as no surprise to see disaster recoiling on top of him.

A low growl emerged from Brice Reynolds's lips as he watched the schooner float out to sea. He wasn't sure if Cole Hollister was dead or alive, but he knew for certain that Stephanie had escaped unscathed. Scowling in disgust, Brice darted through the clump of trees that rimmed the shore. His attempt to dispose of Wes Beacham had been thwarted by the threatening number of guards Dyer had posted around the inn. Now his attempt to seek revenge on that green-eyed bitch had also met with defeat.

But Brice wasn't giving up his personal vendetta. He had spent three anguishing weeks in Newgate's hell hole, warding off rats, working hard labor, eating scraps a dog would turn his nose up at. Although Brice had promised his soul to the British if it would gain him freedom, he intended to have his revenge before he became an informant for the Crown. The British magistrate who had hand-delivered his pardon for his crime had ordered him to take up residence in another colony to begin spying and delivering information about the network of rebel conspirators. Brice vowed he would do as he was told, but he had detoured back to Mystic to satisfy his thirst for revenge. Even though he detested the fact that Wesley Beacham had been granted the rights to his property, Brice still held Stephanie personally responsible for every ounce of his misfortune. Until she had been sufficiently repaid for the hell she had put him through, Brice couldn't and wouldn't rest.

A satanic smile brimmed Brice's lips as he swung into the saddle to make his escape. Aye, he would take the pouch of coins the British had given him upon his release and he would make his way to Maryland. That was where Cole Hollister lived and that was exactly where Brice was going. He didn't know exactly where Hollister's plantation was located but he had learned that Stephanie had become Cole's wife. Brice was going to find that troublesome vixen if it was the last thing he ever did!

While Stephanie was fussing over Cole, Ben and two other sailors rushed over to retrieve his limp body and carry him to the cabin. "He's hit bad," Ben muttered as he surveyed the wounds. After he sent the crew scurrying to fetch hot water and bandages, Ben eased down on the side of the bed to remove Cole's coat.

Stephanie had never considered herself squeamish, but the sight of Cole's wounds turned her stomach. He had once been the epitome of fitness and vitality. Now he lay in a deathlike trance. His breathing was so shallow and erratic that Stephanie was beside herself with worry. The solemn expression on Ben's face did nothing to encourage her.

"He needs a doctor," Stephanie said blankly.

"Hell, of course, he needs a doctor," Ben grumbled irritably. "But we don't happen to have one and I'm not about to steer into Mystic with that maniac sniper on the loose!" His eyes lifted to Stephanie's whitewashed face. "How good are you at sewing, Stephie? If I do the cutting, somebody is going to have to stitch him back together."

For the first time in her life Stephanie chided herself for her lack of interest in stitchery. "My needlework is barely passable," she informed him.

Ben expelled a frustrated breath. "How ironic," he grunted bitterly, "considering Cole is *barely* alive. If we don't do something quick, he'll be as good as dead."

The grim diagnosis spurred Stephanie into action. The moment the sailors barged through the door with heated water, Stephanie saturated a sponge and set to work cleansing the wounds. Try as she may, she could not stop her hands from trembling as she helped Ben locate and extract the buckshot that was imbedded in Cole's side. It seemed endless hours before they were satisfied that they could stitch him back together without leaving any gunpowder to poison his bloodstream.

When the primative surgery was completed, Stephanie collapsed in a chair. There was no guarantee that their humble skills had saved Cole's life. And while she sat there staring at his expressionless face, Stephanie wondered if she would ever be allowed to peer into those magical, cocoa brown eyes again.

One tear and then another burned down her cheek.

Perhaps her father was right about her, she mused dispiritedly. Maybe she was a jinx. Everything she touched seemed to turn to disaster. Cole had been managing quite nicely until she fumbled into his life. He never truly wanted her there, not really. Only God knew why he had decided to marry her. And if not for her, Brice Reynolds would never have taken a shot at him. She was responsible for every ounce of grief Cole had suffered.

Heaving a tremulous sigh, Stephanie leaned out to trace her fingers over Cole's colorless lips. It seemed impossible that this was the same man she had come to love. Stephanie's heart twisted in her chest. Damnit, there was no justice in the world. She should have been the one lying motionless, her body riddled with bullet holes.

As the shock wore off and she came to grips with what had happened, Stephanie wept like an abandoned child. She had never been prone to tears. She had always prided herself in being strong and capable of bearing up to difficulty. But seeing Cole hovering between life and death was simply too much. Stephanie had told herself she could face an existence without Cole, because she knew he was alive and well when she fled Boston. Imagining a world without Cole in it was incomprehensible. The Sons of Liberty looked to him for guidance and assistance. Stephanie knew enough about his activities to know that Cole was an integral part of the chain that linked the colonies together in their battle for the preservation of individual rights.

No matter what the personal sacrifice, Stephanie would stand in his stead. She would become the rabble-rouser who delivered pamphlets from one community to another. And even if Cole didn't love her, she was going to love him, to devote herself to him in exchange for his life, one that was at that moment literally lying

374

on the line.

Stephanie prayed nonstop until weariness overcame her and she drifted into tormented dreams. And each time Cole roused, groaning in pain, Stephanie was there beside him, whispering words of comfort. But never once did he open his eyes to acknowledge her presence. He kept mumbling barely decipherable sentences, as if his life were passing before him. Stephanie listened with agonized helplessness, learning the dark secrets of his past. Cole was spilling his life story as if all the deep-seated emotions were pouring out of him, as if he meant to bare his soul before he went to meet his maker.

And when he finally collapsed in exhaustion, so did Stephanie. She had fitted the pieces of his life together and had begun to understand why Cole led a double identity, why he had transformed from the daring vagabond who had sacrificed his adventurous life on land and sea to assume the responsibilities of his father's plantation. When Cole mentioned his brother, Stephanie was reminded of the stories Ben had told her. She realized now that it was Cole whom Ben had been talking about when he spun his wild yarns. Cole was the man who lived life at a reckless, death-defying pace, the renegade who had performed all those daring raids during the French and Indian War.

Stephanie cursed herself for taunting Cole about his polished manners. He had his reasons for becoming a man of respectability, for shedding his daredevil ways. Although Stephanie resented his father's demands, she understood why Cole felt the fierce obligation.

As dawn's light spilled into the cabin, Stephanie studied Cole with meditative deliberation. At last she had come to understand this complicated man. And with that knowledge came a deeper, more sensitive kind of love. Stephanie thought she knew what love was, all the emotions it entailed. But oh, how very wrong she had been. It had taken a tragedy to open her eyes and unlock her heart. She could only hope Cole would recover. She longed to shower him with the affection he deserved, to teach him the meaning of selfless love. Perhaps he would never come to care as deeply for her, but it didn't matter anymore, Stephanie mused as she brushed a cold cloth across his perspiring brow. It was no longer all or nothing with Cole. Even *nothing* would satisfy her as long as he was allowed to live, as long as he allowed her to remain by his side.

Cole wouldn't recognize her, she thought with a faint smile. She would become a completely different woman. Never again would she spite him or torment him. She would become the model wife of a wealthy plantation owner during the day and deliver his messages for the Sons of Liberty at night. If he requested that she move heaven and earth, she would see it done. If he wanted the moon, she would retrieve it for him. And when it came to passion, she would offer herself to him, heart, body, and soul. She would be everything he expected of her and she would ask *nothing* in return.

Determined in those thoughts, Stephanie remained by Cole's side, listening to his ravings, consoling him, loving him. Each day that ticked past gave her hope that he would survive. And Stephanie lived and breathed for the moment when Cole would open his eyes and peer up at her. Yet her hell on earth was that for four days and nights he continued to hover on the doorstep of death without regaining consciousness.

Stephanie detested the suspense and the depressing thoughts that avalanched upon her. But she was relentless in her nursing duties. The only time she left Cole's side was to deliver pamphlets to the seaboard communities under the cloak of darkness. Stephanie followed Ben's directions, dropped off the patriot correspondences, and then rushed back to the schooner to check on her patient.

Each night when she returned from her excursions ashore she prayed she would find Cole awake. But he simply lay there in lifeless silence. Yet even in those dark, anxious hours when Stephanie wondered if Cole would survive, she poured out every ounce of love she felt for this magnificent man who had been trapped between two identities.

Chapter 22

Cole lifted heavy eyelids to see the face of a pixie poised above him. A gray haze feathered the perimeters of his vision, but Cole did not mistake those purely elegant features. He couldn't swear where he was or *if* he was. But one thing was for certain—he would be forever staring into those expressive green eyes that danced with living fire.

As much as Cole would have liked to lift his hand to caress that exquisite face, he couldn't. He felt incredibly tired. The most reflexive of movements seemed to require thought and excessive strength. Indeed, Cole wasn't even sure he was breathing since his entire chest felt numb, as if there were ten pounds of lead inside it.

"How are you feeling?" Stephanie whispered in concern.

Her voice was soft and silky and Cole melted farther into the mattress—or whatever was supporting him. He licked his bone-dry lips and attempted a smile but even that demanded concentrated effort. "Miserable," he murmured in belated reply.

Sensing his discomfort, Stephanie lifted a glass of water to his lips. Adoringly, she combed her fingers through his tousled hair. She was so relieved that Cole had finally regained consciousness that she wanted to shout it to the heavens.

A muddled frown knitted Cole's brow. His vision was blurry and his body felt as if it weren't there at all. Was he dead or dreaming? Why was Stephanie bending over him, smiling at him with that special smile he was rarely allowed to enjoy? He usually awoke and awaited her greeting of insult before he went about his business. Had he stumbled into someone else's dream? Things were different now. Stephanie was behaving as if she was happy to see him.

"Why am I receiving all this tender attention?" Cole questioned curiously.

Stephanie's smile deepened to affect every delicate feature. "Because I love you," she told him simply.

Cole's eyes narrowed into a skeptical frown. The last time Stephanie had uttered those words, she had been hysterical and she presumed him dead. Was she patronizing him now because she knew he was about to die?

Of course, she was, his dulled brain assured him. Stephanie had little use for him. She was only accommodating him because his hours were numbered. Stephanie was undoubtedly surprised that he had lasted this long and she was trying to be nice to him before he was removed to a higher or *lower* sphere.

What she had truly meant to say was "I pity you," Cole told himself sensibly. Stephanie didn't love him. She felt sorry for him because he had been shot all to hell.

Stephanie's smile drooped when Cole continued to stare at her without changing expression. Hadn't he heard what she had said, or didn't it matter? Willfully, Stephanie bandaged her wounded pride. Just because Cole didn't return her affection was no reason for her to abandon her faithful vow. She had resolved to love

379

and cherish Cole, no matter what, and that was exactly what she was going to do!

Masking her disappointment, Stephanie busied herself by inspecting Cole's wounds. "Do you feel up to eating something?" she inquired, her gaze monitoring her task of replacing the bandages on his ribs. "You need to regain your strength by taking some nourishment."

"I'll eat if you will spoon-feed me," Cole breathed wearily. "I don't think I could lift a spoon if my life depended on it."

"Your life depends on the fact that you *don't* overexert yourself," Stephanie stressed emphatically. After pressing a kiss to his peaked forehead, she turned toward the door. "More than anything else, I want you back on your feet. But it will take some time before you recover, and the less energy you expend, the better."

Cole would have reached out a hand to detain her if he could have moved that quickly. But he couldn't. He lay flat on his back, watching Stephanie disappear into the gray haze.

What the devil is going on around here, he asked himself. Cole swore it was Stephanie's face and her voice that visited his dream. But that was *not* the Stephanie he had married. Where was the feisty firebrand who defied him for the mere sport of it?

Ben Hogan eased open the portal and poked his head inside. A wide grin stretched across his leathery features. "Stephie said you were awake." He tiptoed toward the bed. "For a few days it was touch and go, C.D. I wasn't sure you were still with us."

"I'm still not sure I am." Cole sighed wearily.

Ben sympathetically patted Cole's limp hand. "You just rest. The men and I will take care of the ship. We've been cruising into ports to drop off the bundles of pamphlets to all your patriot contacts. I gave Stephie the names and she—"

"What!" Cole croaked. He would have come straight out of bed if his body weren't dead weight. "Damnit, I don't want her involved and you know it!"

"You are in no condition to throw a tantrum or even attempt to stop me from doing what I want to do," Stephanie interjected as she breezed through the open door with a tray in hand.

When Cole opened his mouth to complain about her sneaking around the various communities after dark, Stephanie poured a spoonful of broth down his throat. "You know I strongly support your crusade and I cannot think of one good reason why I shouldn't be allowed to use my time and efforts to further the cause. 'Tis for certain that you will be incapacitated for several more weeks."

Cole detested being flat on his back. And what's more, he despised the pitying glances he was receiving from Ben and Stephanie. But each time he tried to scold them, Stephanie stuffed more broth down his gullet. It was only after Stephanie had emptied the entire bowl of soup into his belly and exited the room that Cole was allowed to say his piece.

"Why didn't *you* take the pamphlets ashore?" Cole demanded of Ben. "You know a woman traipsing around along at night is easy prey."

Ben chuckled at Cole's accusing glare. "That fiery little sprite has a mind of her own, in case you haven't noticed. The moment we pulled into port she came waltzing across deck looking like your double—black cape, black breeches, black mask. I told her you wouldn't like it and she said I could run and tattle to you if I thought it would do any good . . . which it wouldn't have since you were delirious with fever."

With considerable effort, Cole eased onto his side. "I don't want her to make any more trips ashore," he ordered weakly.

"Then you better discuss it with Stephie," Ben insisted, rising to his feet. "I gave up trying to reason with her. She's a stubborn, headstrong woman."

How well I know, Cole thought resentfully. There was no stopping that leprechaun when she had made up her mind to do something. And Cole was in no position to physically force her to do his will. Hell, he couldn't even lift his head without becoming dizzy!

Giving way to that queasy thought, Cole closed his eyes and groaned. He was a helpless invalid and the only way he could remedy his situation was to rest. When he regained his strength, he was going to take that rebellious minx over his knee and thrash her for gallivanting around the countryside at night, doling out pamphlets *he* should have been delivering.

For two days Cole allowed himself to be coddled and pampered. He obeyed his nurse, who refused to allow him to venture out of bed for more than a few minutes at a time. After forty-eight hours, Cole could tolerate no more. To add complications to his injuries, he was suffering a severe case of cabin fever. He swore he would go mad if he didn't remove himself from his cramped quarters. Although the soul was willing, the flesh was weak. It took tremendous effort to ambulate toward the cabin door. Once Cole had inched down the companionway, he propped himself against the wall to catch his breath.

Gritting his teeth, he hoisted himself up the steps to greet the glorious sunset on Chesapeake Bay. But even more enchanting was the sight of Stephanie leaning against the rail, her face uplifted to the sea breeze. The pastel colors of twilight framed her enticing silhouette, making her pale blue, off-the-shoulder gown glow as if it were weaved with translucent thread. The waning light sprinkled through the thin fabric, sketching her curvaceous figure as Cole yearned to do. She reminded him of a siren who lured unsuspecting sailors off course. The brilliant red-gold tendrils sprayed away from her face as if some unseen hand had lifted the strands to marvel at their luscious texture. Everything about Stephanie was enchanting and Cole breathed a sigh, not from exhaustion but from the sheer pleasure he derived from staring at her.

It seemed a lifetime ago that Cole had taken Stephanie in his arms and inhaled the intoxicating scent of her, reveled in the unrivaled passion that ignited when they touched. If wishing would make it so, Cole would have begged for enough strength to appease the enormous craving her bewitching image evoked.

Stephanie drank in the magnificent sight that Chesapeake Bay represented at sunset. The immense gray-brown waters captured the sunlight, glistening like beads of silver and gold upon the cresting waves. Low-lying islands that were crowned with wind-bent trees lay silhouetted against the striking spectrum of the sky. Bright green marshes laced with meandering streams sprawled out in all directions. Tall, sun-dappled pines pierced the splendorous array of colors that had been painted on the horizon. The warble of waterfoul as they dived and swam in the lush coves and streams of Tidewater country serenaded the sunset.

Stephanie adored Maryland on sight. Since the moment Robert had steered the schooner into the broad bay, Stephanie had been glued to the rail, marveling at the awe-inspiring view. The decks of the ship were quiet. Most of the crew had adjourned to the galley to take their evening meal. Except for the helmsman, Stephanie had Chesapeake Bay all to herself and she was thoroughly enjoying the serenity of the moment, the fiery splendor of sunset.

Her mystical mood was shattered when Robert gasped in surprise. Stephanie spun around to see Cole shuffling toward her, white as the sheet he *should have been* sleeping under!

"You had strict orders not to rise from bed," Stephanie scolded as she rushed over to lend a supporting arm.

"Lying abed was damned dull without you in it," Cole complained grouchily. "I was bored stiff."

A becoming blush stained Stephanie's cheeks. She braved a glance to determine if Robert had overheard Cole's suggestive remark. He had and he was grinning wryly. When her gaze darted back to Cole, she found him staring down at her with hunger in his eyes—not the kind that could be pacified by a bowl of steamy soup. A tingle skipped down her spine. It pleased her that he still found her desirable, even in his condition (one that might worsen if he didn't retrace his footsteps to bed).

"You really shouldn't be up on deck," Stephanie declared as she turned to direct him to the stairwell. "We cannot risk having you catch a chill." When Cole remained rooted like a tree, Stephanie shot him a condescending frown. "Must I summon assistance to carry you back to bed?"

"I wish to view the scenery," Cole stated stubbornly. "The walls of my cabin are shrinking and I do not relish being squeezed to death."

Stephanie opened her mouth to counter his remark, but the look on his face tore the words from her tongue. The golden light clung to the raven beard that rimmed his jaw and caught in the dark, entrancing eyes that bore down upon her. His thick, curly hair lay in ruffled disarray, like a mane that sorely needed to fall beneath a pair of barber shears. Although his complexion had paled during the days he had been confined to bed, Stephanie stood mesmerized by the speculation that this was the picture of the Cole Hollister of the past. He looked rough around the edges and he made no attempt to disguise the frustration he was feeling. A great deal of his sophisticated polish had worn off while he was flouncing in bed and Stephanie liked him better without it.

She found herself wishing she had known Cole five years earlier. This rake would have stolen her heart the moment she laid eyes on him. She had always been attracted to the reckless side of Cole's nature. Perhaps it was because she shared the same craving for adventure, that quenchless thirst for living. Cole had tormented her with his impeccable manners. But the truth was that the rogue who lurked just beneath the surface was purposely annoying her. He was well aware that she had no use for unblemished refinement of aristocracy. Aye, the man who was presently staring down at her was the man she adored. How she wished this devil-may-care rogue would return to take full command of Cole's life.

Impulsively, Stephanie pushed up on tiptoe to press an adoring kiss to Cole's lips. He responded eagerly, devouring the taste of her, losing himself in the feminine fragrance that was so much a part of her. It was a long, tantalizing moment before Stephanie found the will to retreat to a respectable distance. Their kiss had instilled a craving that had long been neglected.

"I love you," Stephanie whispered, staring up at him with her heart in her wide green eyes.

Cole frowned in frustration. "I wish you would stop

saying that," he grumbled resentfully. "What you are feeling is pity and 'tis the last thing I want from you."

Stephanie gave her head a contradicting shake, sending the lustrous strands of red-gold rippling over her shoulders. An impish grin traced her lips when she flung him a wry glance. "We both know what you have always wanted from a woman, but you are hardly in condition for such strenuous activity," she teased him.

Cole countered with a roguish grin. "And most fortunate it is for you, my lovely leprechaun," he growled provocatively. "Otherwise, you wouldn't be allowed to spend so much time on your feet."

The renewed sparkle in those pools of ebony was like the glimmer of long-awaited sunshine. Cole was going to survive, Stephanie assured herself as she allowed him his whim of ambling around the deck.

"I will permit you to view the scenery if you promise not to tire yourself," she bartered. "If Ben discovers you are out of bed, he will be hopping up and down with irritation."

"I promise," Cole hastily vowed. "I would promise anything to avoid those four walls for even half an hour."

Leaving Cole propped against the railing, Stephanie scampered down the steps to retrieve a chair and some quilts. She returned to ease Cole into his seat and then wrapped a blanket around him. Once he was comfortably situated beneath a quilt, Stephanie curled up at his feet like a contented kitten.

For several moments they sat in silence while Stephanie asked herself if this was the time to question Cole about his past. His ravings had offered bits and pieces of information that fed her curiosity, but Stephanie was anxious to learn all there was to know about Cole Douglas Hollister the Third.

"I have discovered a little about your past life, but—" she began, only to be cut off by Cole's derisive snort.

"Did Ben tell you? Damnit, is nothing sacred? A man finds himself unconscious and helpless and he becomes the victim of vicious gossip," he scowled.

Stephanie could not suppress the grin that blossomed on her lips. It amused her to see Cole throw a tantrum. It was so unlike the cool, calm aristocrat who rarely showed emotion. "Nay, it wasn't Ben who divulged the chronicles of your wayward youth. 'Twas you who told me," Stephanie informed him.

Cole's brows jackknifed. "Me? I don't recall ever—"

"The fever freed your tongue," she gently explained. "Part of your babbling was unintelligible, but some of it was very revealing." The expression on her lovely features became somber. "Is it so wrong for a wife to want to know all there is about her husband? You are warring with yourself, Cole. I have sensed that since I met you. I would like to fully understand why."

A frustrated sigh tumbled from Cole's lips. He should have known that anything he might have said in his fevered ravings would pique this inquisitive nymph's curiosity. Well, perhaps it was time to confide in Stephanie, he told himself. By the following morning they would be cruising into the Hollister's private wharf and she should be prepared for what she would face. It would be infinitely easier for her to cope with the uncomfortable situation if she knew what to expect.

"You have always considered yourself the black sheep of the Wakefield brood, but none comes blacker than the man you seem so determined to draw from my past," he began, and laughed humorlessly.

Stephanie's lashes swept up to study Cole's rugged face. To her, there was nothing dark or formidable about the man she loved. When Cole let his guard down and expressed his emotions, he seemed more human than the stoical aristocrat. Cole was full of life and vitality, but for too long he had contained his feelings instead of allowing them to flow naturally.

"I was always a difficult child, at least I was told that on numerous occasions," Cole began as he sank back in his chair to stare across the silver-capped waves. "There was something in me that demanded fulfillment, a craving that made me restless. When my mother's brother offered to take me on as one of his crew, I begged my parents to let me go." A faint smile brimmed his lips. "Ben is my uncle. I think he understood me better than my own parents. He knew I would never be content just to follow in my father's footsteps without seeing all the wonders of the world. It took a great deal of persuading, but Ben finally convinced my father to broaden my education by going to sea. Ben captained a ship that transported merchandise the world over, one that was owned by the West Indies trade company. I came to love the challenges of the sea and I might have forsaken my formal education if my father hadn't demanded that I return to land after two years of touring foreign ports."

The sparkle dwindled in Cole's eyes. "My father held a tight rein over me when I returned home. He hired private tutors to instruct my younger brother and me. There were times when I thought I would go mad without the taste of freedom. Each time I ran away, my father dragged me home to lecture me on my responsibilities as a plantation owner's son."

Absently, Cole massaged his tender ribs. "'Tis the custom in Maryland that when a boy comes of age he must venture into the wilderness to test himself, to prove himself worthy of manhood. Although my father was wary of allowing me out on my own again, he felt a strong obligation to comply with tradition and custom. He is, and always will be, a firm believer in regulations and tradition," he added meaningfully.

Stephanie breathed a thankful sigh. At long last the confession began to pour out. She knew there were family conflicts, but Cole's wandering ravings had failed to provide all the answers. Without posing any questions to distract him, Stephanie quietly listened while Cole unfolded the story of his youth.

"I struck out for the wild, rugged country of western Maryland. I was entranced by the hills and rounded mountains of Blue Ridge, the swift icy streams that thundered down the rock gorges. Though the land was not suitable for farming, it was rich in furs and thick with Indians. My life consisted of tracking between the crude trading posts that sat among the dense forests, and facing life-threatening situations that sharpened my wits." Cole sighed as the memories of the past converged on him and then he chuckled softly. "In that wild part of the country a man has to be as tough as rawhide and as wily as a fox to survive. He has to learn to deal with the creatures and the savages or he sacrifices his scalp for his lack of resourcefulness. There, in Mother Nature's domain, life is a constant challenge, the greatest of adventures. I came to love the open spaces where the only rules set down were the laws of nature, not the rigid, unreasonable ones my father tried to impose on me."

Stephanie rather thought so. She had perceived that lively vitality about Cole from the beginning. He had tried to suppress his true spirit, to downgrade the rugged masculinity that exuded from him. As of yet, Stephanie didn't understand why Cole was intent on projecting that false image of indifference and impassion, not when he was the essence of passionate emotion. But she had known all along that there was more depth to Cole Hollister than met the eye. Indeed, there was a lot of man bottled up and kept under the strappings of a sophisticated gentleman.

"For more than five years I roamed the wilderness, refusing to return to the plantation until I had had my fill of freedom. I hunted and trapped with men who shared my quest for adventure. But the French and Indian War erupted on the outposts of civilization and we found it necessary to defend our boundaries against the French."

Cole paused momentarily. A hint of pain flashed through his dark eyes. The discomfort was not caused by the injuries he had sustained, but rather by memories that could never be forgotten. "My younger brother, Clay, longed to join me in the wilderness, to taste the same boundless freedom of the unknown. But my father insisted that he remain on the plantation to undertake the responsibilities of a wealthy landowner. He had lost his grip on his oldest son and he had no intention of sending a second one out to test his wings, never to return. The more my father sought to hold Clay back, the more determined my brother became to break free of domination. Despite my father's volatile protests and fiery demands, Clay sneaked off to join the fighting on the western front. But he had been overprotected too many years and his lack of experience proved fatal."

A mist of unshed tears clouded Cole's eyes. He inhaled a steadying breath and forced himself to continue. "I tried to teach Clay to follow his instincts, to develop his sixth sense. But time was so short." Cole's fingers clenched around the arms of his chair until his knuckles turned white. "Clay was too inexperienced. In the heat of battle he froze like a timid rabbit that crouches and hopes disaster will pass him by." His voice quivered with emotion, and for the first time ever, Cole reached out to clasp Stephanie's hand as a friend would cling to another in a time of grief. "Clay died in my arms. But there was no regret in his last words to me. He thanked me for opening the door to the kind of freedom and excitement he feared Father would never allow him to experience. He insisted that the quality of life was far more precious than quantity.

"When I returned home, carrying the grim news of Clay's death, I learned my mother had died of the pox during the winter. My father was devastated by the double blows. He had been a fierce, dominating figure of a man and he became embittered by his losses. He held me personally responsible for Clay's death and indirectly responsible for Mother's demise. He contended that she had worried herself sick over her two neglectful sons who had forsaken their family for the lawless freedom of the wilds.

"Through a flood of burning tears my father cursed me, declaring that I had killed Clay, just as surely as if I had fired the flintlock rifle that felled him." Cole expelled a ragged breath and clung tightly to Stephanie's hand. He felt the need to touch her, to hold on until the bitter memories subsided. "My father has never been the same. He is bereaved and bitter. There are times when he loses himself to the memories of the past. I felt obliged to assume the responsibilities of the plantation and to become the son he had lost, the one he had groomed to follow in his footsteps. 'Tis only when I sail off to trade our produce that I reclaim a taste of freedom, the only time I can reach back into the past, when I am not constantly reminded of the long-standing debt my father demands that I pay."

Stephanie scrutinized Cole's craggy features. Now she fully comprehended why Cole was torn between two distinctly different personalities. He had become his brother to pacify his father, even if his heart and soul still longed for the freedom to live and react as he pleased. Cole had sacrificed happiness and he was like a wild animal caged in civilization, longing for what he couldn't have, what he *refused* to permit himself to have.

"For more than three years my father has hounded me to take a wife. To satisfy him I tried to select a woman who would meet with his approval, a woman from a respectable family." Bitter laughter rumbled in his chest. "The family was above reproach, but the daughter wasn't. The week before the wedding I learned Rachel was more the rake than I was. She wanted the security of a proper marriage but she had no intention of releasing her stable of studs after she took the vows. The wedding would have been a cover for her promiscuity." Cole grumbled resentfully when Rachel's image rose from the sea to taunt him. "If my father ever learned how pretentious that chit was, how unfaithful, there is no telling how he would have reacted. I'm sure he would have taken it as a personal insult since he had handpicked Rachel as my perfect mate. My father is unstable and if he had discovered Rachel wasn't living up to *her* responsibilities . . ." Cole shuddered to think what would have happened if his father had lost his temper with that devious witch. In his mental state, Rachel may have received far more than she had bargained for by wedding into the Hollister family.

"Without informing anyone of my plans, I collected my crew a few weeks early and set sail for New York and then the Indies, leaving Rachel to rope another husband and allowing myself to look the culprit."

"You allowed your father to believe the worst about you when it was Rachel who was guilty of spoiling your wedding plans," Stephanie surmised.

It was inconceivable to her that any woman would turn to another lover when she could have had this irresistible rake all to herself. Stephanie knew very little about Rachel, but she knew for certain the woman was every kind of fool.

Cole sighed heavily as he unlaced his fingers from Stephanie's hand and stared off into the distance. "I'm sure my father will rant and rave at me, declaring I have reverted to my old ways. He will proclaim that I shirked my responsibilities to my fiancé." His gaze dropped to Stephanie's bewitching face and he mustered the semblance of a smile. "I hope you can employ your mystical powers to convince my father that I have taken a wife of quality, one who will credit the Hollister name. 'Tis important to him. Indeed, 'tis his obsession. All he has now is his monumental pride and distorted sense of duty and obligation to the upper crust of society."

"You wish me to project the image of genteel nobility?" Stephanie chortled incredulously. "You know very well that I resent the pretentiousness of aristocracy."

A wry smile bordered Cole's lips. Tenderly, he reached out to tilt Stephanie's face to his. "I realize that is asking a great deal of you, little misfit. But I would be eternally grateful if you would aid in smoothing over the incident with Rachel. It would ease the conflict if you would charm my father out of his boots. 'Tis bad enough that I have to sneak behind his back to deliver messages for the patriots since he holds firm with any policy made by the Crown. But if he disapproved of the wife I have toted to our doorstep, he will make life miserable for the both of us."

Stephanie came upon her knees to press a kiss to Cole's sensuous lips. "I would much prefer to work my magic on his son," she admitted softly. "But to please you, I will mind my manners while your father is underfoot."

Cole felt his heart melt all over his tender insides. Lord, this transformation in Stephanie's attitude toward him was baffling and yet very satisfying. There was a time when she spited him at every turn. Now she was exceptionally agreeable. And he had not battled for one kiss since he had awakened from the dead. Indeed, he had but to *look* as if he might enjoy a few kisses and Stephanie was showering him with them! She was still the essence of lively spirit and undaunted determination, but she no longer treated him as if he were an aggravating thorn in her side.

"Would you mind telling me what I did to deserve this loving affection?" Cole questioned point-blank. "If you are showering me with all this gratitude just because I took the bullet meant for you, I think you must have forgotten that I owed you one, little leprechaun."

A giggle burst from her lips as she cupped her hands around his drawn face. "'Tis because you have been honest with me for the first time since we met, because I find you wildly fascinating, and because I love you . . ."

That did it. Cole was tired of hearing "love" substituted for pity. *That* was why Stephanie was catering to him. "Will you stop pampering me, for God's sake," he exploded. "I have decided I am not ready to die so you can cease with this guilt-ridden compensation for all the ornery pranks you have pulled on me. Do not ply me with one more confession of eternal love when I know damned well I have done nothing to earn your affection. I may be seriously ill, but I am not stupid!"

My, but he was cranky when he didn't have his nap, Stephanie mused as she dropped her hands from his scowling face. Cole would never believe she truly cared for him as long as he was so cynical of love. It was going to require time and patience to convince him that she was sincere. And after what Cole had told her about his father, Stephanie foresaw serious complications while she was battling for the affection of the man she had come to love more than life.

It was during Cole's outburst of temper that Ben emerged from the stairwell. He was annoyed that Cole was out of bed and further irritated that his nephew was chewing on Stephanie for a between-meal appetizer.

"Is that any way to speak to the woman who nursed you off your deathbed?" Ben scolded sharply as he stalked up behind Cole. "The lady says she loves you. If you weren't so damned mistrusting, you would be thanking high heaven that you have her, instead of biting her head off for admitting any kind of affection." He threw up his hands in a gesture of frustration. "What she sees in you is beyond me, Cole. You've had the disposition of a rattlesnake since we sailed from Mystic to Boston. And your injuries have turned your moods pitch black!"

Cole sat there glaring at the waves. "'Tis none of your business, Ben. You are poking your nose in places it doesn't belong and you are risking the possibility of having it chopped off!"

When Ben puffed up to spout off several more spiteful remarks, Stephanie rose to her feet, casting him a silencing glance. "'Tis no matter." Forcing a smile, Stephanie disguised the hurt of rejection. "Cole *looks* like a grizzly bear. It should come as no surprise to hear him growling like one." Grasping Cole's hand, Stephanie urged him to unfold himself from the chair. "Ben, if you will kindly fetch some of the sugar you smuggled from the Indies, we will soak the good captain in it while he takes his bath. Perhaps that will sweeten his sour disposition."

Cole's mood was growing darker by the second. It was one thing for Stephanie to embellish him with confessions of misinterpreted love and quite another to be led around like a poorly behaved child. "I will decide if and when I wish to bathe," he snorted as he yanked his hand away. "Quit doting over me. I will not tolerate all this sticky sweet pity. It makes me nauseous."

As Cole hobbled away on his own accord, Ben tossed Stephanie a sympathetic smile. "I hope you possess the patience of an angel, Stephie. You're going to need it to tolerate C.D.'s temper tantrums. His wounds and his loss of mobility have put him in an irascible mood."

Stephanie knew why Cole was being so testy. She had suffered the same frustrated impatience while she was recuperating from her injuries. It was difficult for someone who thrived on independence to cope with being incapacitated. She had found her convalescence intolerable and Cole wasn't adjusting to it any better than she had.

Arming herself with the tough hide of a rhinoceros, Stephanie followed in Cole's wake. She was determined to see him through this crisis without losing her temper with him. Cole needed her compassion whether he wanted it or not. He was going to be bathed, shaved, and put to bed for a decent night's rest, no matter how long or loudly he protested being ordered about!

Humming that positive tune, Stephanie approached the wounded lion whose scraggly mane was sorely in need of clipping. There were subtle ways of cornering contrary creatures. What she had in mind would not require the use of a chair and a whip. A woman had to resort to her own resourcefulness if she wished to outfox a fox and Stephanie's brain was buzzing with a plan as she aimed herself toward the injured beast who was looking to chew on anyone who dared to come within ten feet of him.

Chapter 23

Cursing his lack of energy, Cole braced himself against the balustrade before attempting the tedious flight of steps. It galled him to feel so incapable, so (heaven forbid) inferior. When a man found himself married to a woman with Stephanie's endless vitality, he was constantly being compared and challenged. It was damned humiliating to endure her pity when he was in no condition to match her determined will and sharp wit.

Exasperated, Cole rubbed his aching head. How could he ever earn her true affection when he was hobbling around like a man twice his age? Cole was suffering an identity crisis and he detested what he was feeling. For the past few years he had kept his emotions under lock and key. No one had infiltrated his cold, calculating facade. He had even endured his father's tirade of insults without exploding in a fit of temper. He had become the bulwark of self-control. But Stephanie... Cole heaved a dispirited sigh. Stephanie evoked every emotion. She was slowly but surely transforming him into the man he used to be, a man who laughed in pleasure and who growled when he was frustrated, a man who threw temper tantrums to release pent-up emotions. She was bringing his past back to life and it would surely lead to conflict with his father.

When Stephanie curled her hand around his arm, Cole jerked away as if he had been stung. "I managed to navigate my way to the deck all by myself and I can damned well find my way back in the same manner!" he snapped, giving further evidence that his temper was sitting on a short fuse.

Stephanie displayed an indulging smile. "I'm—"

Cole refused to permit her to utter more than one word. "And don't you dare tell me you love me one more time or I'll scream the sails down upon us!" he threatened, glaring lances at her.

Biting back an amused grin, Stephanie watched Cole draw himself up to proud stature and descend the steps. He couldn't exactly *strut* since his wound was paining him, but he made a noble attempt to mimic a peacock. Cole was changing by degrees, Stephanie mused as she studied his broad back. His sophisticated veneer had buckled and cracked. He was no longer the polite and distant aristocrat who weathered each storm without becoming ruffled. He was exercising his emotions and instincts, lashing out at his situation and anyone who got in his way. It did her heart good to witness Cole's tantrum. It assured her that he did feel something, even if it wasn't love for his newly acquired wife.

After what Cole had revealed to her, Stephanie realized that he had decided to marry one of the Wakefield sisters on the rebound. And if it had not been a Wakefield, it might have been any other female of good standing. Cole hadn't been particular, just desperate to pacify his mentally ailing father. He had taken a wife not for love but for necessity. Cole didn't really want her love; he wanted a figurehead to serve as mistress of his plantation.

Stephanie had faced impossible odds in numerous instances and she was not the type of woman who folded up at the first sign of trouble. Nay, she loved this difficult, complicated man. One day he would feel something for her, Stephanie consoled herself. He had shown signs of needing her when he clutched her hand for compassion. It had been only a small display but it was a start.

With meager encouragement, Stephanie followed the steps to Cole's cabin. The real Coleman Douglas Hollister the Third had begun to emerge from his rigid cocoon. It wouldn't be long before he could no longer abide the role he had been playing. All the bottled emotions were beginning to pour out. When Cole became angry, everyone knew it. And when he became passionate, he no longer resented his inability to control what he was feeling.

Aye, the life-loving renegade had shown his face and Stephanie was relieved by the transformation. She only hoped Cole's father was reasonable enough not to force his only son to go on pretending to be something he wasn't. He had manipulated Cole for more than three years and Cole had allowed it because of his own feelings of guilt. But the day was rapidly approaching when Cole would shed the last of his polished shell and demand his natural rights, just like the ones he was fighting to protect from the oppressive arms of Parliament.

Glancing up from her pensive deliberations, Stephanie found Cole glowering down at her. It was obvious he wanted to be alone to sulk, but Stephanie would not permit it. A warm bath would soothe his taut nerves and muscles and it would do wonders for his frazzled appearance. If he hobbled to the plantation looking as if he had just slithered out from under a rock, his father would most certainly reprimand him and accuse him of backsliding to his old habits.

"I am not going to bathe until I'm good and ready so you might as well cancel the order for hot water and remove yourself to your own cabin," he told her, a distinctly unpleasant edge on his voice.

Stephanie was undaunted. She understood what Cole was feeling far better than he comprehended it himself. The world had caved in on him and he was fighting his way out of the rubble. And just because she loved him with all her heart did not imply that she had sacrificed her feisty spirit. Cole was due for a soaking and a shave. And, by God, he would have them before the schooner docked at the Hollister plantation.

Wordlessly, Stephanie scurried about the cabin to retrieve the soap, sponge, and towel. Cole scowled under his breath as he watched her openly defy him.

"Damnit, don't pretend you didn't hear me. I want to sit here and *sulk,* not soak. And I *prefer* to do so in private!" he bellowed at her.

When a stream of sailors trickled into the cabin, toting buckets of steaming water, Cole ordered them to retreat or risk his wrath. But Stephanie countered his command and the crew did her bidding, much to Cole's outrage. He was about to express his displeasure with the situation when Stephanie locked the door. As she pivoted to face him, she began to draw the pale blue gown from her shoulders. Unclad, Stephanie recklessly tossed the garment toward a nearby chair, uncaring that the gown missed its target and fluttered into a crumpled heap.

Cole's narrowed gaze widened when he was granted a view of her skimpy chemise. The undergarment left just enough to the imagination to tantalize the savage beast within him. Cole wasn't sure which ache was more bothersome, the one in his ribs or the one in his loins.

401

Stephanie looked positively bewitching standing there, her skin glowing like honey in the lantern light. The toss of her head sent the red-gold tendrils cascading over her shoulder to curl temptingly against the swell of her breasts. Bare arms and shapely legs protruded from the edge of the gossamer garment and Cole scrutinized every well-proportioned inch of her like a starved shark eyeing his intended feast.

Her tactic of distraction proved to be one hundred percent effective. Cole couldn't remember what he had been ranting about the previous moment. He yearned to touch what his eyes boldly caressed. He ached to lose himself in the luscious scent that could fog his mind and numb his pain.

Her green eyes twinkled and her lips parted in a dazzling smile. Stephanie sashayed across the room to unbutton Cole's rumpled shirt. When her hands tunneled beneath the fabric to ease it from his shoulders, Cole's flesh burned each place she caressed.

"I've waited a long time for this moment," she whispered against his hair-matted skin. "You were so gravely ill. I feared I would never be granted another chance to touch you like this . . ."

Cole swore his muscles had turned to jelly. When her hands drifted across his belly to unfasten his breeches, Cole felt his knees buckle beneath him. Aye, she was a spell-casting leprechaun, he confirmed. She touched him and he melted in puddles. She had never been able to match his strength but the technique she employed to subdue him was stronger than masculine force.

When Stephanie had carefully divested him of all his clothes, she continued her tender assault. Her kisses and caresses hovered over his flesh, bringing an exquisite kind of pleasure that erased pain. And while Cole was lost in a fog of rapturous anticipation, Stephanie led him to his waiting bath. Cole had wandered so deep into sensual fantasy that he failed to realize Stephanie had not *forced* him to take even one step in the direction she wanted him to go. Like a fool he thought he had gone voluntarily to his bath, even when he had loudly protested taking one several minutes earlier.

"I've always wondered what it would be like to play the handmaiden," she murmured as she knelt beside his tub. "Will you indulge me while I try my hand at it, m'lord?"

How was a man, totally distracted by a pretty face and even more preoccupied by a dimpled smile, to reject the request? Willpower had its breaking point and Cole's had broken the moment he was allowed a view of Stephanie's well-sculptured figure. Cole didn't have to say yea or nay. The look in his eyes said it all. Dark fires flickered inside the fringe of black velvet lashes and Stephanie could feel the intense heat radiating from them.

Her soapy hands skimmed his chest, plying him with fragrant bubbles. Her caresses were like a gentle massage that eased the stiffness from his muscles. And while her skillful hands cleansed his skin and ironed the wrinkles from his soul, her lips skimmed his mouth ever so lightly. Her words were full of compliments, assuring him that she found him irresistible and arousing.

Cole swore his tub had sprouted wings to set sail among puffy white clouds. Never had he considered a bath to be such a tantalizing pastime. But then he reminded himself he shouldn't be surprised that this bewitching elf could change a man's entire perspective. She had always been able to transform the mundane into an adventure.

His breath lodged in his throat when Stephanie's wandering hand dipped beneath the water's surface to make titillating contact with his sensitive thighs. It was sweet agony to sit in the cramped tub, allowing her to rediscover every inch of him, allowing her to weave his desires into a tangled web of unfulfilled frenzy. His heart hammered against his tender ribs, but Cole was feeling no pain. All he experienced was exquisite splendor.

When her gentle hands receded to fetch the razor, Cole laid his head against the back of the tub to stare up at the bedazzling nymph who was hovering over him. Her ministrations had caused water to splatter down her chemise. The garment clung to her bosom like an extra set of skin, revealing the roseate buds beneath it. The steamy bath caused ringlets of red-gold to curl around her flawless face, its warmth provoked a rise of color in her cheeks. She was absolutely stunning in her damp garb and Cole breathed a sigh of masculine appreciation. Stephanie had mesmerized him, bedeviled him, and he was her willing pawn.

"'Tis the first time I've attempted to shave a man," she confessed as she lifted the razor. A pixielike smile brimmed her lips. "I advise you to sit very still, m'lord. I should hate to shave off something you might prefer to keep. You might look a bit odd without an ear or nose."

Cole heard her teasing remark but he was too entranced by the luscious picture she presented when she bent over him to digest her words. He was enjoying the full view offered by her gaping chemise.

When she completed the task of removing the stubble from his face, Cole nuzzled his cheek against her breasts. His warm lips scaled the tempting swells, spreading delicious fires Stephanie was hard-pressed to ignore.

A sigh of pure pleasure rattled in his chest when Stephanie eased away to remove her soggy chemise. When she came back to him, her smile inviting his caresses, Cole swore he was in the middle of a fantastic dream. The taste of her skin was like drinking his fill of wine. The side effects were sweet intoxication and he could not seem to get enough of her.

While Cole spread exquisite rapture over her pliant flesh, Stephanie's hand glided over his skin, returning the pleasure, touch for touch. Their explorations of each other were tender and inquiring. They were totally aware of each other, cognizant of needs that had lain dormant for more than a fortnight.

Cole's brain had turned to mush and he could not recall the exact moment it had ceased to function. Neither could he say for certain when and how he had risen from the tub to return to bed. But suddenly he was there and Stephanie was stretched out beside him. His body was heavy with pleasure, so much so that he could find no strength to move. And when Stephanie began to spin her provocative spell about him once again, Cole felt himself sinking, as if he had been entrapped in quicksand.

Her gentle caresses rolled over his chest like waves lapping against a shore. They ebbed and then advanced, again and again, until Cole was drowning in mindless ecstasy. Never had he allowed a woman such privileges with his body. Never had he laid back to become passion's slave. But Stephanie's tender domination of soul and flesh was unconquerable and Cole had no fight left in him. What she was doing to him defied physical pleasure. She was unveiling new dimensions of rapture, discovering his ultrasensitive points and creating sensations that aroused monstrous cravings.

The fires she had kindled became an intense blaze of desire. Cole wanted her so badly he would have sacrificed his last breath to have her. She had driven all logic from his mind. and when he swore he could tolerate no more of this delicious torment, Stephanie moved above him, settling intimately against him.

A muffled groan erupted from his lips when she made him her possession. Stephanie was making wild, sweet love to *him*. She was cautious of his wounds, but inescapably aware of their need for each other. Even the sweet memories of their previous nights together could not compare to the sensations that riveted through his body. He felt whole and alive and hungry for that which could not be supplied by nourishment alone. Nay, there was only one kind of feast to break this famine. Cole craved that which this beguiling sprite alone could offer. Her lovemaking compensated for the endless days he had endured, the anxiety of wondering if Reynolds had caught up to her. Her embrace indemnified the agonizing hours he had lain abed recovering from his critical wounds.

Her supple body caressed his, easing the hunger for passion. Wild, uninhibited yearnings unfurled within him. The sensations blended, one into another, taking him higher and higher still. Cole felt dizzy and lightheaded. His male body eagerly responded to hers. Primal instinct engulfed him. What had been the essence of tenderness became a fierce tempest. He felt Stephanie's petal-soft lips upon his, felt her luscious body matching the hungry, impatient cadence of his. There was no sanity in passion's realm, only sublime sensations that burned away time, emotions that billowed and crested in sweet satisfying release.

As exquisite pleasure spilled over him like a river surging from its banks, Cole tumbled with the flow. His breath came in ragged spurts. His heart throbbed against his ribs as if it meant to leap out and abandon him.

Though he had made love to his fair share of women, there was something mystical about the techniques of this unique woman. Nay, not a woman, Cole silently amended as his hand absently stroked Stephanie's back. She was a mythical creature who could change men into frogs if she had a mind to, transform baths into showers of ecstasy. She was a wee bit ornery, a wee bit nice—a product of her grandfather's feisty Irish temperament. And when she chanted her incantations around a man, he was rendered defenseless. Her potion for passion beat anything Cole had ever seen. It excelled all he had ever experienced.

When the haze of desire parted and Cole's water-logged brain began to function, a deep skirl of laughter resounded in his chest. Stephanie propped up on one elbow to smile curiously at him. Gone was the stamp of disapproval on his features. When he broke into a grin, his dark eyes crinkled with amusement. Cole was finally at ease and Stephanie basked in the warmth of his smile.

"I just realized I've been had," Cole chuckled as he flicked the tip of her nose in light admonition. "Shame on you for taking advantage of an invalid."

An unrepentant grin cut becoming dimples in her flushed cheeks. "You've been had twice," she corrected on a soft, tantalizing breath of laughter. "And nay, I'm not the least bit apologetic."

Cole lifted a hand to comb the red-gold strands away from her face. He adored the feel of the lustrous tendrils on his fingertips. It was like caressing fine silk. "You maneuvered me into the tub and then into bed, knowing full well no man could complain about the methods you employed to—"

The abrupt rap at the door interrupted Cole and he glared at the offending portal. "Go away!"

There was a slight pause. "Uh . . . I was just wondering if our patient was cooperating," Ben called from the other side of the bolted door. "Do you need any help, Stephie?"

Stephanie's adoring gaze was focused on Cole's handsome face. "Nay, Ben, our patient's mood has sweetened considerably. We won't need the sugar. The captain has been bathed and bedded down for the night."

Ben muffled a snicker. With that resourceful nymph in command of the field, Ben could well imagine what technique she devised to tame her roaring lion. No doubt Cole had been purring like a contented kitten until he was interrupted.

As the footsteps receded, Stephanie's lips feathered across Cole's in the slightest breath of a touch. "Good night, m'lord. I wish you sweet dreams."

When Stephanie tried to withdraw, Cole's hand folded around her wrist. "Don't go," he beseeched her, his voice husky with emotion. "I want you here with me all through the night."

Indecision etched her brow. Their ardent need for each other had already cost Cole considerable strength. His wounds were still tender and she would never forgive herself if she caused him further discomfort.

When Stephanie demurred, Cole curled his hand around her neck, guiding her lips to his. "It seems like forever since I've felt you beside me. What we shared was bliss but I crave even more." His kiss melted her better judgment into senseless puddles. "Humor me, sweet nymph, I'm not a well man and I want you with me."

How could she reject his request when he put it to her like that, Stephanie asked herself. She couldn't refuse him anything when he stared up at her with those entrancing chocolate brown eyes.

"As you wish," she sighed. "But I think you have had enough physical exertion for one day. We should avoid all else but sleep unless you relish the thought of having me sew you back together again."

"Were I in perfect health, you wouldn't sleep a wink," Cole assured her as he wrapped his arm beneath her breasts, molding her curvaceous body to his.

"And when you are granted a clean bill of health, I shall hold you to that promise," Stephanie teased as she dropped one last kiss to his full lips.

"When the time comes, you won't find it necessary to prompt my memory, madam."

His voice trailed off when Stephanie wiggled away to snuff the lantern. The scar on her shoulder caught in the waning light and Cole grimaced when he was reminded of Brice Reynolds. Lord, how he hoped that lunatic had been apprehended. The moment Cole had returned to Mystic, he had informed Dyer that Reynolds had been granted pardon. His intention was to gather Stephanie, stash her on the schooner, and depart before Reynolds had the opportunity to dispose of her. Dyer had promised to send word when Reynolds was rounded up, though there was no guarantee the man wouldn't be released in the same fashion again.

The apprehension of wondering if Reynolds had managed to harm Nattie or Wes unnerved Cole. But the nagging fear that Stephanie was Reynolds's prime victim was unbearable. Reynolds would derive demented pleasure in seeing Stephanie lying in a pool of blood.

The thought sent a snake of fear slithering down Cole's spine. He couldn't imagine the world without that green-eyed pixie in it. She was the essence of sunshine and moonlight, the personification of spirit. When Cole found himself scraping the bottom of frustration and despair, Stephanie was there to revive him. When he hungered for passion, she satisfied his every whim. She had become a part of him that time couldn't erase, the sweet memory that inflamed his dreams.

A quiet smile touched his lips when he felt Stephanie snuggle up beside him. Life wouldn't be easy for either of them when they reached the plantation. There would be his father to contend with and the looming fear that Reynolds might have escaped arrest. Cole promised himself then and there to carry a knife and pistol at all times. He would be fully prepared for trouble.

But it didn't matter if he and Steph were on a collision course with catastrophe. It didn't matter what obstacles they were forced to confront when destiny clasped the fickle hand of fate. When darkness enshrouded them there would be no conflicts, only the insatiable desire they felt for each other. The silken bond between them would grow stronger. And in time, Cole prayed Stephanie's pity for him would evolve into something deep and lasting, an emotion that would always bring her back to him, no matter how far she wandered to appease her free spirit.

Cole had come to depend on Stephanie's bright, mischievous smiles. Her companionship, her laughter, and her zest for living had become his inspiration. The magic between them would be enough to keep him satisfied, Cole reassured himself . . . as long as it wasn't mere sympathy on Stephanie's part. Cole could endure anything but that. He suddenly found himself wishing Stephanie did love him, totally, completely.

A soft sigh escaped his lips as he closed his eyes. He had considered love to be a waste of time, but that was before Stephanie happened along to turn his world upside down. Worse things could happen to him besides becoming enamored of this spirited lepre-chaun, he consoled himself.

And worse things were about to happen. If Cole could have foreseen the future, he would have ordered

Ben to turn the schooner around. But he was laboring under a false sense of security while Stephanie was lying peacefully beside him. Little did he know that all hell would break loose the moment he set foot on the plantation. And if he *had* known, he wouldn't have slept a wink this night!

Part III

And yet I might quickly arrive
Where my extended soul is fixed,
But Fate does iron wedges drive,
And always crowds itself betwixt.

As lines, so loves oblique may well
Themselves in every angle greet;
But ours so truly parallel,
Though infinite can never meet.

Therefore the love which us doth bind,
But Fate so enviously debars,
Is the conjunction of the mind,
And opposition of the stars.

Andrew Marvell

Chapter 24

Stephanie's mouth dropped open as the entourage approached the spacious mansion that sat amid the numerous outbuildings of Hollister plantation. She had considered her home in Connecticut to be an elegant manor, but it did not begin to compare to the three-story, T-shaped monstrosity Cole called home! The house looked as if two rectangular homes had been joined together to form this gigantic structure of brick. Chimneys jutted off each wing, rising high to scrape the sky. The gambrel roof provided gracious space for rooms on the third floor and huge windows provided light and ventilation for the grand plantation home.

The estate appeared to be a self-contained community with its private wharf, shops, servant quarters, and immaculate gardens. Never had Stephanie seen anything quite so spectacular as the acres upon which Cole's plantation sat. It resembled a king's palace.

"I'm impressed," Stephanie declared when she poked her head back inside the coach Cole's father had sent to greet the schooner. "If you have managed to keep this operation running smoothly during the months you have been away, you are a most incredible man!"

Cole chuckled, but carefully. His innards were a mite tender after all his physical exertion the previous day. "I hired an overseer who makes my duties infinitely easier," Cole explained as he squirmed uncomfortably on the seat. "The man's efficiency makes me look good. I have but to tell Goodson what I want done. Though I'm sure I face an avalanche of paperwork when I set foot in the office, the operation of the plantation will not have suffered during my absence."

Stephanie was listening, but her eyes were darting out the window to survey the tall trees that formed a tunnel leading to the marble steps of the mansion. This was to be her home? She simply could not fathom herself puttering about this elegant estate without getting lost. Why, she would need a compass to navigate her way back to her room.

When the carriage lurched to a halt, Cole winced in pain. The rough ride was enough to scramble his insides and he was anxious to stretch out in bed once again. He thought certain he had regained a reasonable amount of strength. But to his chagrin, he realized he had just set foot upon the road to recovery.

With the groomsman's assistance, Cole unfolded himself from the coach and started up the steps. Although he was discomforted, the expression on Stephanie's bewitching face distracted him. For years this mansion had been like a gloomy sepulcher. But Cole had the distinct feeling all that would change when Stephanie became mistress of Hollister.

The sound of footsteps on the veranda drew Cole's immediate attention. Forcing a smile for his father, Cole raised his eyes. His greeting grin slid off his lips when he spied Rachel Garret poised above him and his father glowering down at him.

The implications of Rachel's appearance knocked the wind out of Cole. "Oh my God," he choked out.

Stephanie froze in her tracks when her gaze landed on the sultry brunette. Rachel was the essence of statuesque beauty and poise. Her classic features would have been an artist's dream. Her dark, silky hair was curled atop her head and garnished with flowers. Her gown was made of the finest royal blue silk and complimented the creamy texture of her skin and the deep blue color of her eyes, which were laced with long, thick lashes.

Stephanie could understand why Cole had fallen in love with this graceful beauty . . . until Rachel broke into a smile that was a mite too triumphant to be pleasant. Even if Rachel hadn't been her competition, Stephanie wouldn't have liked her. Something shimmering in those sapphire eyes warned Stephanie that, in Rachel's case, beauty was, at best, skin deep.

Rachel purposely wrapped her arm around the elder Hollister's elbow, as if to subtly claim her position in the family. But it was not the fact that the young woman was clinging to Cole's father that upset Stephanie. Indeed, Stephanie hardly noticed the gesture. Her wide, tormented eyes were flooding over the empire waist gown that left the discreet, but haunting impression that Rachel was expecting a child! Stephanie needed no introductions. She already knew who this lovely creature was and it didn't take a genius to surmise who had fathered her child.

Stephanie felt sick inside. All of her dreams of making a new life with Cole shattered in a thousand pieces. She couldn't remain at Hollister, knowing Rachel would bless Cole with a child. Their ill-fated marriage was over as quickly as it had begun, Stephanie told herself deflatedly.

Cole's father was staring down his nose at her. His dark eyes were curious, speculating on the reasons Stephanie had accompanied his son home. The expression on his hard features assured Stephanie that she wasn't welcomed. And Rachel was pretending Stephanie wasn't there at all. Her blue eyes were keyed on Cole, as if he were the sun that had just returned to brighten her bleak and dreary days.

The moment Rachel realized Cole had been injured, she floated down the steps, wedging herself between her fiancé and Stephanie. "Cole, what on earth has happened? My poor darling, we must get you right up to bed," Rachel cooed as she fussed over him.

When Cole's father wheeled around to bark orders to the servants, Stephanie watched the flood of humanity pour from the mansion and swarm about like a hive of bees. She was shoved aside and left standing on the steps while Cole was virtually carried into the house and settled in bed.

Cole's voice boomed through the foyer with Stephanie's name attached to it. Rewinding her unraveled composure, Stephanie drew herself up and walked into the hall to follow the sound of Cole's beckoning call. Although it was difficult to produce a smile when her heart was shriveling up inside her chest, Stephanie made a valiant effort. Despite the fact that Rachel had eased down on the edge of Cole's bed as if she belonged there, and Cole's father was towering over the opposite side of the bed looking as unapproachable as a disturbed bull, Stephanie entered the room.

"Steph, this is my father, Doug Hollister," Cole introduced begrudgingly. "And this is Rachel Garret. Father, Rachel, I would like you to meet my wife."

The news was as well received as an exploding cannonball. Doug Hollister's aging features blanched and Rachel proceeded to wilt on top of Cole, eliciting his pained grunt.

"Get her off me," Cole groaned when the limp bundle collapsed on his injured side.

Servants with gaping mouths and bug eyes scurried to remove Rachel to the adjoining bedroom and fetch the smelling salts. Doug stood there, his fist clenched around the bedpost, his eyes stormy with irritation.

"How could you have possibly taken a wife when you were engaged to Rachel, the woman who carries your child?" he scowled disapprovingly. "I have already accepted Rachel into the family after you practically left her standing at the altar! All of Annapolis was awaiting your arrival so the two of you could be married! Damnit, Cole, I thought I could count upon you to honor your commitments and responsibilities. You took a leave of absence and leave of your senses when you sailed off three and a half months ago!"

Cole's mood was as grizzly as his father's. His weakened condition only served to turn his disposition as black as pitch. He knew what Stephanie must think of him. He could see the hurt in those misty green eyes, feel the tension that hung in the room like a suffocating fog. Stephanie's pride had been wounded, his father was outraged, and Rachel . . . Cole grimaced in pain and exasperation. Life had seemed so pleasant the previous night while Stephanie was cuddled next to him. But the dawn brought disaster and Cole hadn't enough strength to fight it. Blast it, this was no time for him to be ailing!

"I had no idea Rachel was in the family way," Cole breathed acrimoniously. "If I had . . ."

"Well, you most certainly will accept your responsibility for the child you have conceived!" Doug roared, glaring at Stephanie as if she were responsible for bedeviling his son and leading him astray. "This hasty marriage of yours will have to be annulled and this wench will have to be sent back wherever the hell she belongs. She most certainly does not belong here! Your first obligation is to Rachel and to your position as lord and master of Hollister. We cannot have this scandal soiling our good name. You must honor your first commitment."

Doug had resorted to his booming voice, the one he employed when he wanted to gain control of the conversation. He was not about to allow his wayward son to have his way in this matter. Cole had simply been bewitched by this little tramp. He had married her in a moment of madness and Doug fully intended to post the necessary papers in the courts of Annapolis to see to a hasty annulment. If news of this preposterous marriage leaked out, the Hollisters would become the laughingstock of Maryland. Doug refused to tolerate such a catastrophe. His honor and pride were at stake, as well as Cole's.

When Doug stormed over to shuffle Stephanie out of the room, Cole propped himself up on an elbow to protest. Before he could utter a word, Doug wheeled around, his face twisted in a hateful sneer.

"Don't you dare defy me in this matter," he scowled at his son. "I have lived more than a decade with your devil-may-care attitude and I will endure no more of it. You made my life hell when you killed Clay and broke your mother's heart. Now you have disgraced our family name by neglecting your responsibilities to your fiancée. Rachel swore to me that she carries your child, that you compromised her more than once before you were to take the vows. How can you continue to disappoint and humiliate me after all I have done for you, all I have given you?"

Again Cole attempted to debate the issue, but Doug held up his hand to forestall any disrespectful outburst. "The servants have orders to keep you in bed. And that is where you will stay until you have regained your strength and the good sense I have tried to instill in you since you were just a child. You will not disobey my wishes, Cole. As long as I'm still alive, *I* am still the ultimate authority of Hollister. And my will shall be done!" he bellowed in outrage.

Stephanie found herself in the grip of a man who was virtually trembling with fury. There was a strange look in Doug's eyes when he glowered down at her. It was obvious that he had hated her on sight, and touching her repulsed him. But Douglas tolerated their physical contact until he had hustled Stephanie down the steps and locked the study door behind them.

Once they were behind the closed portal, Doug jerked away as if he had been handling a hot branding iron and could not wait to free himself from it. "Seat yourself, woman," he growled as he stomped around to park himself behind the desk. "Now, how much do you wish to be paid to forget this fluke marriage? Five thousand pounds? Ten thousand?" His fuming gaze narrowed on Stephanie. "I am prepared to be generous, but do not test my temper. If you will not gracefully bow out and take the money I offer, you will force me to take drastic measures to rid my family of you."

For a moment she sat in her chair, her mind buzzing with several suitably nasty rejoinders. In the past she had made no bones about expressing herself and her opinions, but that was before she had Cole to consider. Although she was crushed that Cole's dalliances with Rachel had spawned a child, she remembered the pleading look in his eyes the previous night when he had explained his past.

Cole was hounded by his guilt and he had dutifully obeyed Douglas because he was his father. Douglas relished the supreme power he held over Cole, and come hell or high water, the man wasn't relinquishing his dominating position of patriarch. Douglas was still

421

ruling the roost and he had no intention of allowing Cole a choice in the matter of marriage. Out of respect for Cole's ticklish situation, Stephanie swallowed the snide remarks that stampeded to the tip of her tongue.

Her thoughts were in a quandry. She loved Cole and it was not her place to defy Douglas. And yet, Cole was in no condition to do it. Even if he were, there was little he could do, considering the condition Rachel was in.

The prospect of leaving the man she loved while he was still wounded and vulnerable had a disquieting effect on her as well. And there was the unborn child to consider, Stephanie reminded herself dismally. She recalled how frantic Nattie had been when she feared her child would arrive before she could announce to the world that she had a husband. No doubt, Rachel was experiencing the same mental anguish.

Suddenly, Stephanie found herself in the corner of the eternal triangle and Douglas Hollister wanted her out! Did Cole feel a sense of obligation to Rachel, even after she had been unfaithful to him? Or would Cole denounce the child as not being his own, knowing Rachel had been indiscriminate? And how could Cole convince Douglas that he wasn't the only man who had shared Rachel's bed when he had never bothered to divulge the reason he had put out to sea in the first place? Cole must have felt something for Rachel or he would not have protected her reputation, Stephanie reasoned. Whatever was between them was still there. Cole still cared for Rachel, even if she had betrayed him.

The past few days, Stephanie had attempted with both words and deeds to convince Cole that she loved him. But he wouldn't believe her, didn't want to believe her because his heart still belonged to Rachel. He thought Stephanie pitied him. He *wanted* to believe that was all there was to it because, deep down inside,

422

Cole had never truly recovered from his attachment to the sultry brunette.

What good would it do to defend her marriage against this tyrant who was glaring mutinously at her? If she stayed, she would only make life hell for Cole and cause volatile conflicts between him and his father. Cole had already warned her that Douglas's moods swung like a pendulum. If the man was unstable, this confrontation could only make matters worse.

Stephanie felt as if the weight of the world were pressing upon her shoulders. She had suffered these identical sensations when she had been caught in the middle of her own family crisis. It was as it had always been, she told herself ruefully. It was up to her to solve the problem, not to become an addition to it. But where could she go? If Brice Reynolds was still prowling around Mystic, she didn't dare return home. And Douglas wanted her out of Maryland just as soon as he could make the arrangements to have her spirited off his plantation.

"Well? Have you decided upon your price, woman?" Douglas demanded impatiently. "I have a wounded son to attend to and a future daughter-in-law to check on . . . one who is carrying *my* grandchild. If you cannot see what a problem you have created by bewitching my son, you are a selfish, spiteful woman." His tone was meant to cut Stephanie to the quick and it would have if Stephanie hadn't deemed Douglas to possess those two contemptuous qualities himself. "Name your price and be gone. I will see to it that you can live quite comfortably until you have lured some other unsuspecting man beneath your wicked spell."

Stephanie looked at him squarely in the eye. "I pity you, Mr. Hollister," she said levelly.

Douglas snorted derisively. "I hardly need your pity, woman."

"Ah, but you do," Stephanie contradicted, forcing a tight smile. "You are trying to manipulate your son's life. You failed to control him in his youth and now that you have something to hold over him you employ the device to make him dance like a puppet on a string."

"I do not have to sit here and listen to your degrading insults!" Douglas spouted indignantly. "You are nothing but a cheap tramp who is looking for the wealth and security my son can provide."

That did it. Stephanie had tried to hold the reins on her temper, to make a crucial point before she walked out of Cole's life. But Douglas was making it damned difficult to be sincere and pleasant all at the same time. If she was forced to leave (and the situation gave indication that she wouldn't last another minute before Douglas summoned his servants to throw her out), she wasn't leaving until she had unloaded a full round of ammunition on this domineering old goat. After all, she felt no respect for a tyrannical man who wanted control of his son, just so he could proclaim that he was the all-powerful patriarch of his kingdom! Damn the selfish man. He didn't give a whit what Cole wanted. He never had. It was his intent to lead his guilt-ridden son around by the nose.

Stephanie catapulted from her chair to lean over Douglas's desk. "I am not a tramp. My father happens to be one of the colonies' most noted shipbuilders and you are not worthy of my respect, much less your own son's. You are pious and self-centered and a miserable excuse for a father. If you hadn't smothered Clay and attempted to mold him in your own image, he would still be alive. Cole didn't kill him. His lack of experience did, experience *you* refused to grant him. You wouldn't let him become a man who could handle adversity with experienced ease. You didn't allow him to trust in himself. He was to be your puppet, your strength when you lost yours, the figure head through which you ruled this kingdom of yours. You planned to live forever through Clay."

This witch's perception unnerved Douglas. Aye, he had envisioned his son as an extension of himself. But never had he voiced those private thoughts. This chit had sized him up so quickly that it made his head spin. It was no wonder Cole had been bewitched, Douglas told himself. There was something rare and unusual about this green-eyed sorceress. Her defiance was dangerous. She threatened Douglas's authority and challenged his position. If she remained on the plantation, she would spoil everything Douglas had tried to accomplish since Cole had returned from the wilderness to assume his obligations.

"Get out of my home!" Douglas screeched, brandishing his fist in Stephanie's face. "You cannot talk to me like that!"

"You hold no control over me, Mr. Hollister," Stephanie sniffed defiantly. "And the only reason you have taken offense is because you know I speak the truth. You have failed to ask Cole what it takes to make him happy. You don't really give a damn as long as he caters to your whims. You want his respect but you have done nothing to deserve it. I pity a man who has to invent devices to ensure his authority is not contested." Stephanie pushed away from the desk and raised her chin to look down her nose at him, employing the same technique he had used to intimidate her on the front steps. "You call yourself a man of honor, a man of tradition—*your* honor and *your* tradition," she tacked on emphatically. "And as near as I can tell, it doesn't amount to a hill of beans!"

On that degrading note, Stephanie spun on her heel to march out of the study. She heard the rustling of desk drawers behind her, but she didn't look back until a pouch of money sailed across the room to collide with the door she was preparing to open.

"My son doesn't know how fortunate he is to be rid of the likes of you," Douglas hissed poisonously. "I'm sure he has never seen this disrespectful side of the woman he married in a moment of madness. Take the money and be gone. I never want to lay eyes on you again!"

Impulsively, Stephanie snatched up the pouch and hurled it back across the room, narrowly missing the side of Douglas's head. A sticky sweet smile glazed her lips as she raked him with scornful mockery. "The feeling is mutual," she assured him airily. "And I'm certain someday you will receive your just reward for being the tyrant you have become. Caesar had his Ides of March. I'm sure history will also record the event of your inevitable downfall as well. I shall read about it with spiteful satisfaction."

Stephanie drew herself up to a proud stature. "And as for your attempt to buy me off, you can keep your money. I don't have a price. My reward will come when you realize what a mess you have made of your life with your bitterness and attempts at domination. When the time comes for you to count your true friends and your *honorable* contributions to society, you will find yourself to be a pauper. Perhaps then your vast monetary wealth will become your only consolation."

When Stephanie reached the bottom of the steps, she pulled up short to inhale a shaky breath. What was she to do now? Where should she go? The tears she had so carefully held in check began to boil down her cheeks, leaving the sediments of hurt and rejection.

Expelling her breath in a rush, Stephanie allowed her blurred gaze to sweep the sprawling plantation that had *almost* become her home. She wondered how Cole would react if he knew her temper had exploded during her confrontation with Douglas. No doubt, he would have scolded her for allowing her tongue to outdistance her brain. Aye, she shouldn't have permitted herself the satisfaction of that disrespectful outburst, she chided herself as she rerouted the tears that scalded her cheeks. But damnation, it had needed to be said. Douglas had sucked the spirit from his son and Stephanie couldn't bear to leave Cole while knowing Douglas would take advantage of his son's vulnerability. Perhaps she had accomplished nothing. But she had felt obliged to try— for Cole's sake.

The thought of never being allowed to tell Cole good-bye caused Stephanie's heart to wretch in her chest. It was over and she had not been permitted one last kiss.

Muffling a sniff, Stephanie marched down the path and seated herself in the carriage. She wasn't certain where she was going. All she knew was that the phaeton was taking her away from the man she loved, away from the tyrant who guarded his castle like a fire-breathing dragon.

By the time Stephanie had made her exit, Douglas was fit to be tied. How dare that bitch speak to him like that! His very position demanded respect. He was entitled to courtesy and Stephanie had not offered even an ounce of it. No one else had ever crossed him when he was determined to have his way! Who did she think she was anyway?

Growling in irritation, Douglas stalked around the perimeters of the study, cursing the vision that kept materializing before his eyes. Well, at least that witch was out of Cole's life and Douglas could begin making arrangements for a wedding that should have taken place months ago.

When Cole had sailed off without a word, Rachel had come to Douglas, crying buckets of tears, humiliated that Cole had abandoned their upcoming wedding. Honor bound, Douglas had taken Rachel into his home, promising to arrange the wedding the moment Cole returned. Rachel had become the daughter Douglas never had. At least *she* respected him and obeyed his wishes. Rachel would be a good wife to Cole, she had given her word. And Douglas vowed to make things right and, by damned, he would!

Douglas massaged his throbbing temples and muttered to himself. Maribeth would be most distressed to hear that her eldest son had reverted to his reckless, irresponsible ways, he mused. And Clay? What would he think of his older brother's foolishness? Douglas made himself a mental note to use Cole's shenanigan as an example of how *not* to behave. He would hate for Clay to make such a tragic mistake with his life. And Douglas promised to speak to Clay on the matter, just as soon as he relieved this atrocious headache.

While Douglas was wearing out the carpet in the study, drifting in and out of the past, Rachel was propped on her bed, smiling smugly to herself. The moment Cole had run out on her, she had aimed herself toward the Hollister plantation. If she had Douglas on her side, she knew she would be safe from mortification. Douglas had been an easy man to manipulate, she reflected as she sipped her cup of tea. He was so overcome by his sense of honor and dignity that he became easy prey. Rachel had but to flatter him, to cater to him, and he was devoted to her cause for life. She had but to pay lip service to all his opinions and convictions and she had him wrapped around her finger. Douglas was arrogant enough to be undermined by his own monumental pride.

Rachel had heard the voices downstairs and she knew Douglas would make fast work of sending Cole's courtesan on her way. Douglas had given his word as a gentleman that there would be a wedding between the Hollisters and the Garrets and his colossal honor would ensure that the deed was done.

It would do little good for Cole to protest, Rachel reassured herself. She had spent three months convincing Douglas that she had been shamed and that she was hopelessly devoted to Cole. Her indoctrination was so complete that Douglas already thought of her as his daughter. Why, she had but to mention a whim and Douglas saw that it became reality. And all the time the foolish old man thought *he* was dominating *her!*

Rachel burst into wicked giggles. Cole would probably resent taking her as his wife, but it really didn't matter. There would be nothing but customary documents to join them together. Rachel would still come and go as she pleased, seeing whom she pleased. A woman of her fickle passions could never be satisfied with one man, not when there were scores of men in the area. Once she and Cole were married she could—

The creak of the door interrupted Rachel's musings. She glanced up to see Douglas's features etched with concern. Determined to milk Douglas of every ounce of sympathy, Rachel conjured up some tears and mustered the expression of the woman scorned and betrayed.

"Oh, Douglas, I'm so upset. I hope I don't lose the baby," she cried into her handkerchief. "Why would Cole do such a thing to me? He knows how I adore him, how I long to become his wife. Now I will never be able to show my face in Annapolis and I will have no father for my child, Cole's child, your grandchild . . ."

Her voice trailed off as she sniveled sobs into her

handkerchief. Discreetly, she shot forth a glance to ensure that Douglas had buckled beneath her melodramatic performance.

"You have nothing to fret over, my dear," Douglas assured her as he eased down to clasp her trembling hands in his. "You are like my own flesh and blood. You understand the importance of honor and pride, even better than my son does. And that is why I will see to it that the two of you are married. You will be good for him."

Rachel wiped her eyes and then batted them at Douglas. "If only Cole realized how fortunate he is to have a father like you," she complimented, her voice seemingly overcome with emotion. "If only Cole didn't have that reckless streak in him that made him rush off to marry the first woman he met when he abandoned me. He did this to punish me and I don't even know why." Rachel heaved a deflated sigh and then clutched her abdomen. "I'm so distressed, but I must get a grip on myself. I have Cole's child to consider."

"You have no reason to concern yourself with this matter. That vicious woman is gone and she won't be back," Douglas informed her. His eyes turned a stormy shade of brown when he recalled the shouting match he had had with Cole's disrespectful wife. "I intend to post the proper documents and have the banns read in court. We will expedite this annulment posthaste. You and Cole will be married as soon as the courts give him his freedom from that belligerent chit."

Rachel flung her arms around Douglas's neck and smiled victoriously to herself. She knew she could count on Douglas to force Cole to toe the mark. "Oh, Douglas, you are so kind to me. I don't deserve your affection and consideration. But you are a true gentleman in every sense of the word."

"You lie back and rest," Douglas insisted as he eased

from her side. "'Tis time I had a talk with my contrary son."

As Douglas exited the room, Rachel broke into a satanic smile. Cole may despise her for ensuring that his little strumpet was out from underfoot, but she didn't really care as long as she had the security of a marriage license. Cole was getting exactly what he deserved for leaving her after she had sent out all the invitations and had made all the arrangements for their elaborate wedding. And every day of his natural life he was going to pay for humiliating her, she vowed spitefully. If Cole ever accused her of being unfaithful, Douglas would never believe him. Rachel had spent three months convincing Douglas that all she wanted was the happiness she could find with Cole. Now Douglas was her champion and her pawn.

Her eyes dropped to the swell of her abdomen. Her appearance and its implication gave her the advantageous edge. Ah, things were working out splendidly, Rachel mused as she nestled on her bed to decide where she would go when she ventured off into the darkness this evening. Douglas hadn't the slightest idea that she had made it a nightly ritual to sneak out of the house. That was also to her advantage. The old man's blind loyalty, once obtained, was like an impenetrable armor of defense, the shield Rachel could stand behind if ever she needed protection.

Chewing on that consoling thought, Rachel closed her eyes to catch a catnap. She needed her rest if she were to carouse after dark with one of her overzealous lovers.

The moment Douglas stepped into the room, Cole's weakened body became rigid. He had tried to tear himself from bed when Douglas shuffled Stephanie off with him, but he had had a fight on his hands. The servants didn't dare disobey Douglas and they refused to allow Cole to hold any position besides prone. Because of the ruckus in his own bedroom, Cole hadn't heard the loud conversation that had simultaneously taken place downstairs.

"Where is my wife?" Cole demanded tartly.

Douglas clasped his hands behind his back and strode forward to stand at the foot of the bed. His features were tarnished with condemning frown. "She realized that your marriage was a tragic mistake after she witnessed the vulnerable condition of your fiancée. Stephanie left the plantation and asked me to tell you good-bye for her. She is going home to Connecticut."

Frustrated rage coursed through Cole's veins. "She didn't leave of her own accord," he growled in accusation. "You *paid* her to leave, didn't you?"

Well, at least Douglas didn't have to lie about that. Not that it would have mattered. He was willing to tell as many bald-faced lies as necessary to dissolve this ridiculous marriage to that fiery-tongued hellion.

"'Tis true that I offered her a pouch of coins to ensure passage home, but she refused to take it. She assured me that she came from a wealthy family and that she had her own funds. When she realized your first obligation lay with Rachel, she thought it best to end your relationship posthaste. She did, however, wish you well in your marriage to the mother of your unborn child."

Cole gritted his teeth and cursed under his breath. He should never have begged Stephanie not to cross his father. She had undoubtedly complied with Douglas's wishes because Cole had requested that she show herself to be a well-mannered lady. And now that Cole was left to recuperate under Douglas's care, there would be no further contact with Stephanie. She wouldn't be back. She had delivered him home and the complications with Rachel had forced her to go her own way.

Cole cringed at the thought of Stephanie venturing to Mystic unprotected. There was no telling what had become of Brice Reynolds. He could be anywhere, watching and waiting to dispose of Stephanie. Cole couldn't rest easily until he received word from Dyer Wakefield that Brice had been apprehended and retried for attempted murder.

"I promised Stephanie that I would see to an annulment as soon as possible," Douglas went on to say. "She wanted to return to Connecticut a free woman." He breathed a heavy sigh as he pivoted toward the door. "'Tis time for you to rest. I have already sent for a doctor to inspect your wounds. When you are feeling better, we will discuss the arrangements for your wedding."

"I'm not marrying Rachel," Cole told him matter-of-factly.

Douglas's back stiffened. How he detested defiance. First he had received a full dose from that green-eyed witch and now from his son. The prodigal son who should never have outlived his brother, Douglas thought bitterly.

Struggling to contain his anger, Douglas swung around to confront Cole's hard stare. But his headache was beginning to intensify and he could barely see straight. "You will marry Rachel, just as you should have done in the first place. You will honor your obligations, as Clay will do when 'tis his time to wed. 'Tis your mother's wish to see you settle down and assume your responsibilities. Maribeth will be beside herself when she learns you have shamed the daughter of one of her dearest friends. There are times when a man has to consider his duties and give them priority.

'Tis the way of things, Cole. When a man loses his honor and dignity, he has nothing. I have been trying to drill that philosophy into your head since you were a little boy, but you constantly defy your obligations."

Cole tensed when he noticed that vacant look in Douglas's eyes and heard the incessant utterances about his family. In Douglas's mind, Maribeth and Clay were still walking the halls of the mansion. Douglas was lost to the past. Cole had viewed that confused expression too many times not to realize that his father was about to fall into one of his senseless lapses. The complications of Cole's return had upset Douglas and he was losing touch with reality.

Douglas's expression became a totally blank daze. "Now, you rest, son," he cooed reassuringly. "Your mother and I will resolve all your problems. I am so thankful you are not as high-spirited and rambunctious as that brother of yours." He sadly shook his head as he turned toward the door. "You are a good man, Clay, and I will ensure that you want for nothing. Mother and I are so proud of you."

When Douglas wandered out of the room and mumbled his way down the hall, Cole collapsed on his pillow. Perhaps it was best that Stephanie had gone her own way, he told himself. Douglas's moments of madness were enough to drive a sane man crazy. There was no reason to subject Stephanie to a life that swung back and forth between past and present like a pendulum! It had been a mistake to marry Stephanie. Her zestful spirit served only to remind Cole of what he had once been, the man Douglas could barely tolerate. To make a life with Stephanie, Cole would have to abandon his father. Douglas was too vulnerable to these incompetent spells to leave him alone for more than a few months at a time. This was Cole's prison and he was confined to it. He had known that, but he had allowed his compelling fascination with Stephanie to overrule his common sense. And now she was gone forever. Cole would never be permitted to gaze into those sparkling green eyes. That lively pixie was a part of the past that he would never be able to recapture. She was his forbidden fantasy, the angel who waited beyond the storm of black clouds that loomed over him, the living memory of secret splendor.

Cole squeezed his eyes shut and tried to tell himself that Stephanie was better off without him. He mentally listed a dozen consoling platitudes to lift his sinking spirits. But his inspirational treatment was not a cure. Hell, it wasn't even a satisfactory medication. Knowing he would never again hold Stephanie in his arms to make that glorious journey through time and space caused something deep inside him to wither and die. Once before, he had tried to imagine what life would be like without Steph. Now he knew. It was like living in an emotional vacuum after he had been touched by every exhilarating sensation known to man or beast. The days would become as dark as the nights because Stephanie had taken the sunshine with her when she left. From this day forward Cole would stumble through the paces of existence without caring or feeling any emotions except regret and despair.

What was life without Stephanie? Cole felt a shudder rock his soul when he landed with a thud on that dismal question. It was no life at all. It was hell on earth. He had been stirred and aroused by that emerald-eyed leprechaun from the moment she had emerged from the pond in Mystic, he suddenly realized. She had touched him in ways no other woman could. Stephanie was the pure essence of life, his thriving spirit, his forbidden love. . . .

Aye, he loved her. But it had been difficult to face that private, heart-felt emotion. And it was even more

435

difficult to put his confession into words. The thought caused a melancholy smile to graze his lips, just before he drifted off to sleep. If reformed devils were granted space in heaven, Cole was going to look up that enchanting goddess when he was removed to that celestial sphere. He was going to tell Stephanie exactly what she had come to mean to him. And until that day, he was going to go on loving her.

Destiny may have conspired against them, but no one was going to prevent him from loving Steph, heart and soul. And Cole would live out his life regretting he hadn't told Stephanie how deeply he cared when he had had the chance. He had wasted the short time they had together by shutting her from his life, refusing to admit to himself that she was the most important part of his days and nights.

Douglas was laboring under the pitiful misconception that honor was a man's greatest possession, but Cole knew different. *Love* was the emotion that enriched the world. *Love* created honor and respect. And without it, honor was hollow and pride was a fake facade. And without Steph's exhilarating smile, the days would become dark and repetitious and there would be no hope of happiness.

Cole's eyes fluttered open to stare at the starlight that sprinkled across his room. Daylight had given way to darkness while he remained imprisoned in his room. But each time Cole roused from sleep, the same thoughts converged upon him. *Stephanie* . . . he could see her reaping vengeance on Brice while she stood covered with mud. She was spiriting off into the night to resolve her family's problems. She was in his arms, responding to a passion that could never be duplicated. In her eyes was that flicker of living fire. In her smile

436

was the breath of spring. Her glorious mane of hair danced with red-gold sunbeams. And within the silken circle of her arms was the quintessence of life and love. She would always be there, Cole consoled himself. He had but to open the memories and she would again become a living, breathing part of him.

"I do love you, little leprechaun," Cole murmured to the empty walls. "Though I can never have you as my own, you will always be my only love . . ."

Although Stephanie couldn't hear his confession, Cole felt ever so much better after he had admitted it to himself. At least he had been honest with himself in confessing his feelings for that spirited pixie. Now he would have to learn to live without her, Cole told himself drearily. He would never be able to stare at Rachel without seeing Stephanie, without remembering what true happiness was really like.

Aye, he was going to pay his penance for each of his devilish faults. And he was also going to atone for sins he didn't even commit. But through it all, he would retain those sweet memories, ones that would last a lifetime.

Chapter 25

Cole stared at the plate of food that had been set beneath his nose. Although he had little appetite, he forced himself to partake his meal. For more than three weeks he had prodded himself through the paces of living. Nothing interested him these days. He tolerated Rachel's presence as a man would endure a buzzing bee, so long as it didn't sink its stinger in his flesh. Cole had listened to his father and Rachel chat through every meal before he excused himself to seek solitude in his own chamber.

The one time Ben ventured to the mansion, Douglas had insisted upon sitting in on the conversation, refusing to allow Cole the opportunity of questioning his uncle about Stephanie or the distribution of rebel pamphlets. Ben had assured Cole that the imports had been unloaded and that all other matters had been completed as Cole had directed. Cole assumed by Ben's subtle comments that the letters from the Boston Committee of Correspondence had reached Annapolis and the surrounding communities.

Although Cole longed to climb atop his steed and set his face to the wind, he knew it was best to bide his time until he had fully recovered. He had strolled the gardens daily to regain his strength, but Douglas hovered over him like a mother hen, virtually holding him prisoner within the confines of his room and the estate. The one time Cole had climbed upon a horse in attempt to make an escape, Douglas had hurried after him, refusing to allow his son to jar his tender insides.

And so, Cole had almost given up hope of fleeing the plantation until he was fully healed and capable of thundering off into the night while his father was unaware of his escape.

"I have heard that another of Annapolis's stamp collectors was dragged into the street last night and threatened within an inch of his life," Douglas muttered resentfully. "I do not know what this world is coming to. There is no respect for the laws of Parliament. Some of these holier-than-thou colonists presume too much. In my day, subversives would have been hauled off to prison for conspiring against the Crown. England has become too lenient with these rabble-rousers."

"Last week one of the King's men was beaten up when he refused to resign his position as tax agent," Rachel added distastefully. "I actually saw a man in a dark cloak spiriting about the street, encouraging some of the less vocal patriots to join the—" She clamped her mouth shut, wishing her tongue hadn't outdistanced her brain. Her encounter with the black-clad patriot had come at night. Rachel prayed Douglas wouldn't question her about where she had been when she had viewed the mysterious rider.

Hastily, Rachel changed the topic of conversation before Douglas began contemplating how and when she had been out and about. "Do you feel up to a stroll this evening, Cole?" she purred. "We did not mean to

439

upset you with this rebel talk. 'Tis best that none of us discuss those pestering commoners who are inciting trouble."

When Rachel's hand folded over Cole's, he inwardly cringed. There was no warmth or sincerity in Rachel's touch. He may as well have been holding a limp fish. Annoyed that Rachel thought she could draw any feelings from him that had died months ago, Cole inched away to take knife in hand and whittle at his steak.

A disconcerted frown clouded Douglas's brow when he noticed Cole's standoffish manner. "How long do you intend to sulk? I realize you are depressed by your lack of mobility but Rachel has made every attempt to show her affection for you."

"I know you resent me," Rachel murmured, her lower lip trembling to give just the right effect of a woman nursing her wounded pride. "But I do love you. I always have. And I will soon become your devoted wife."

Sensing it was time to allow the couple to resolve their differences, Douglas pushed away from the table. "I have decided to go out this evening," he announced. "Perhaps 'tis time for me to voice the aristocrats' opinion on this subject of rebellion. We must put a stop to these evening gatherings that are clogging the streets of Annapolis."

When Douglas took his leave, Cole eased back in his seat to glare at Rachel. "Now that we have finally been allowed a moment alone, I wonder if you would be so good as to tell me who is the father of the child you are carrying," he questioned point-blank.

Shock registered on Rachel's sultry features. This was not the same Cole Hollister she had known the past three years. He had cast diplomacy to the wind. Furious though he had been that night he had caught her with Morris Stevens, Cole had acted the gentleman —outraged and insulted, yet civil. But no longer, Rachel observed. Now there was a savage glint in Cole's eyes. The devilish grin on his face rattled her. She felt as if she was encountering an entirely different breed of man.

Since he had caught Rachel totally off guard, Cole proceeded to pose another taunting question. "Forgive me, dear Rachel," he drawled, his tone not the least bit apologetic. "I see I have upset you in your delicate condition. Perhaps I should rephrase my question by asking if you have the faintest notion which of your stable of studs was on hand the night you conceived."

His rudeness caused Rachel's face to flush crimson red. "The child is yours, of course," she sputtered.

Mirthless laughter splintered the air. "I doubt that even a qualified physician could reach that conclusion," he smirked sarcastically. "Though you have blandished and flattered my father into believing your story of love and devotion, I am no longer fooled by your deceitful prattle." His ebony eyes narrowed on her, drilling into her to pluck out the dark secrets in her soul (if indeed she had one). "And how is it that you could have seen the patriot rabble-rouser when you are so early to bed each night?"

Flustered, Rachel toyed with her silverware, her mind racing to conjure up a believable excuse. "I was—"

"Don't bother to put another lie to tongue," Cole interrupted on a derisive snort. "Knowing you for what you are, I realize you never stopped being unfaithful, even in your fragile condition."

"You have no right to accuse me of wrongdoing," Rachel protested as she slammed her fork against the table. "You left me to explain your hasty departure three months ago. I had to live with the ugly rumors and sarcastic speculations. You have no reason to believe I have been gallivanting about town."

"I have no reason to believe you *haven't* when your past records proves you to be a slut of the worst sort," Cole countered with an intimidating smile.

Rachel vaulted to her feet so quickly that she upturned her glass of wine. "How dare you say such terrible things to me when you know I love you, that I would do anything for you. I should repeat to your father all the hateful remarks you have made. He would see you whipped for insulting and upsetting me!"

Undaunted by her threat, Cole elevated a dark brow to a challenging angle. "If you love me so dearly, I would have proof of this undying devotion," Cole chuckled, delighting in ruffling Rachel's feathers. "You can do me the greatest favor a woman could do for a man."

Rachel eyed him warily. He was still sporting that satanic smile that made her wonder if she could handle Cole as well as she had anticipated. "What sort of proof do you expect?"

His expression changed to a disgusted glower. "If you love me, favor me with your absence and go hound the true father of your child," he requested gruffly.

Her fist hit the table again, rattling the plates. "'Tis *your* child and you are going to marry me because Douglas will hold you to it. You deserve to pay for the mortification I suffered these past months. I did not appreciate your humiliating prank and your total lack of consideration!"

Cole rose from his chair and leaned across the table to breathe down Rachel's neck. "And I do not appreciate your numerous indiscretions. You are as sexually active as a jack rabbit and I will not consent to marry you, even if my father threatens to disown me," he blared into her purple-hued face.

Flesh cracked against flesh when Rachel's temper exploded. "And if you do not follow through with this wedding and give our child his proper name, I will *ensure* that you are booted off this plantation without a penny!" she hissed vindictively. "And don't think I can't see it done. Douglas believes me to be a saint and you to be a discredit to your name."

The muscles in Cole's jaw tightened and it was all he could do to resist the temptation of slapping that haughty smirk off her face. He had never struck a lady, but then he wasn't dealing with one, he quickly reminded himself. If any woman deserved to receive a punch in the jaw, Rachel did. She used her femininity to have her way, to protect her from the violent retribution she so richly deserved.

"Odd as it may seem, I would prefer poverty to flouncing in the lap of luxury with the likes of you," Cole spat venomously.

The malicious tilt of Cole's mouth and the deadly gleam in his eyes startled Rachel. Cole looked as if he would enjoy tearing her to pieces. Clutching her abdomen to remind him of her delicate condition, Rachel backed from the table and sped out of the room before Cole did what he *looked* as if he wanted to do.

Damn him. Rachel fumed as she scurried up the steps to lock her bedroom door. For the past week she had thought him to be passively accepting his fate. But Cole had made it clear that he wasn't going to be a party to her little scheme. And Lord, what would she do if Douglas fell into one of his mental lapses when she needed his assistance and support? He would be no help to her at all. If Cole upset Douglas and he went wandering off into the past, Rachel would be forced to deal with Cole all by herself. That dreary possibility left Rachel shaken. Once Cole fully regained his strength he would become a force to be reckoned with!

Exasperated by her confrontation with Cole, Rachel combed a restless hand through her sable mane and stared at her reflection in the mirror until she had recovered her composure. When she was in full command of her senses she grabbed her cloak and wheeled toward the door. Cole was not going to cow her into clinging to the confines of her room. Maybe he had no respect for her, but there were plenty of men who did, men who would shower her with compliments instead of assailing her with insults.

Mulling over that thought, Rachel made her way down the servants stairway and fled the mansion. And that was exactly what Cole wanted her to do. Indeed, he had purposely inspired her to flight. With Douglas out for the evening and Rachel doing what she did best—doling out free samples to half the male population of Annapolis—Cole could come and go as *he* pleased for the first time in three weeks.

A wry smile pursed his lips as he exited the front door to summon a carriage. The remarks Douglas and Rachel had made at dinner had aroused Cole's curiosity. He wanted to know whose face was behind the concealing mask of the patriot who was keeping emotions stirred in Annapolis. At first he wondered if Ben had climbed into the black garb, but he was stung by the premonition that nocturnal prowling was more Stephanie's style. She had promised him not so long ago that she would act in his stead until he was back on his feet. And if he knew that feisty minx as well as he thought he did, she would be the one striding a black stallion, encouraging citizens to rebel against Parliament's unjust taxes.

For the first time in more than three weeks Cole actually *felt* alive. Tingles of excited anticipation channeled through him, spurred by the possibility of seeing Stephanie again. And if she wasn't the "man" behind the black mask, Cole was going to be bitterly disappointed.

After giving the groomsman instructions that he wanted to proceed in fiend-ridden haste, Cole braced himself on the seat. The carriage lurched forward to speed along the bumpy path that led to Annapolis. His smile grew broader, even though he was being jostled to and fro. If Stephanie was still in the area, this was his one opportunity to locate her. He wasn't returning home until he knew for certain who was disguised in black, leading the crusade for liberty.

A disgruntled frown puckered Douglas's brow as he watched the procession of subversives march up and down the street, shouting their chorus of Freedom, Liberty, and No Stamps. It disgusted him to see such a disrespectful display against the Crown. Douglas firmly believed every rebel should be rounded up and carted off to jail for disrupting the peace. And it was also his opinion that the mysterious rabble-rouser who was notorious for inciting riots should be permanently disposed of.

"This parade is a discredit to the colonies," Douglas declared to anyone who would listen. "I would personally pay to see that rebel taken down a notch."

Those who disagreed with Douglas slowly eased away to follow the procession along the avenue. But the man who had only recently arrived in Annapolis was all too eager to receive pay for disposing of the rebel pest.

Brice Reynolds had made his way through Maryland, searching for the Hollister plantation. His inquiries in Baltimore had gained him no information and Brice had turned south to continue his pursuit of the green-eyed witch who had cost him his fortune. The sight of the dark rider provoked memories of his own harassment in Mystic. Brice would have bet his last shilling that he had located the fiery minx who had caused him so much distress.

"I agree that this tormenting pest should be stopped," Brice proclaimed to Douglas. "And for the right price I might be persuaded to do your handiwork."

Douglas glanced over at the stocky man whose tattered clothes signified that he was greatly in need of coins. Although Douglas rarely stooped to associating with peasants, he deemed this just the type of man he needed to do Annapolis a great service. Once the deed was done, Douglas could offer the man enough coins to take him far away from Maryland's foremost city.

Quietly instructing the stranger to meet him on the abandoned street corner in a half hour, Douglas strolled away. A wicked grin etched Brice's harsh features. His eyes refocused on the prancing black stallion and its rider. He could feel anticipation mounting and his mind reeled with vengeful possibilities. Not only could he collect a fee for disposing of this patriotic pest, but he could demand a ransom from both of Stephanie's families—the Hollisters and the Wakefields. When he had acquired enough funds to venture west to begin a new life, he would rid himself of that meddling bitch once and for all.

The thought caused satanic laughter to bubble from Brice's chest. And when he informed the British magistrate of the patriot's identity, he would receive another reward. But more than the money he gained from spying would come the spiteful satisfaction of seeing the Wakefields and the Hollisters live with the humiliation of having the rebel in their midst exposed.

Luck was riding on his coattails once again, Brice

encouraged himself as he ambled away from the crowd to await his conspirator's arrival. One day soon Brice would be adorned in finery instead of these repulsive garments that were beneath his dignity. He could buy an establishment in another seaport and develop the same thriving business he had built in Mystic.

Brice did not have long to tarry in thought. Within a few minutes, a carriage rolled to a halt near the street lantern. When the man he had met earlier stepped down and ordered the coach to return in fifteen minutes, Brice emerged from the shadows to motion his associate to join him in the alley.

"I do not wish there to be any connection between the two of us," Douglas stated as he retrieved a sack of coins from his pocket. "Nor do I wish to watch a bloody assassination in the streets of Annapolis like the one reported in Boston. I want our mysterious rabble-rouser to disappear, never to be seen or heard from again. If the rebels think they have been abandoned, perhaps it will cool their disloyalty to the Crown and these marches will cease."

"You are absolutely right," Brice concurred. Stephanie would be no good to him dead, at least not until he had used her for ransom. "The rebels of Annapolis might not be as shocked as the mob was in Boston. Marylanders might react with violence instead of stunned silence. But once I have apprehended the dark rider, he will no longer march the streets, encouraging patriots to tar and feather the King's men."

Douglas nodded grimly. "I am thankful you are not a man of public violence. 'Tis grizzly business and we are not looking to create heroes, only to ensure that the patriots lose their inspirational leader." He handed the coins to Brice and then stared him squarely in the eye. "Sufficient funds to pay your way out of Annapolis will be forthcoming. I think 'tis best that you take residence

447

elsewhere when the deed is done."

"My thoughts exactly," Brice replied, stifling a grin. The man was playing right into his hands. "If you will tell me where I can reach you, I will contact you after I have captured the rebel who threatens our society. When I have received traveling money, I will be on my way and we will never meet again."

For a moment Douglas debated divulging his name, but vanity overcame him. Most people sat up and took note when they heard the prestigious name that was well known in Tidewater country. "Send your message to Douglas Hollister and I will meet you at whatever time and place you select. . . . But the designated hour should be after dark," he stipulated and then waited for the name to register on the face of his companion.

Brice nearly fell off of his boot heels. This self-righteous bastard was Stephanie's father-in-law? Ah, this was ripe, he chuckled to himself. The old man would probably keel over when he realized he had disposed of his son's wife. And when he did, perhaps a little blackmail would be in order, Brice mused wickedly. Besides holding Stephanie for ransom, he could drain Douglas Hollister of part of his wealth— enough to ensure that Brice was well established in his new business venture. Cole Hollister would probably pay a ransom for his wife's return while Douglas was paying through the nose to prevent his son from discovering that it was Douglas who had caused her demise.

While Brice's mind was buzzing with possibilities, Douglas was misinterpreting the expression. Proudly, he squared his shoulders and struck a sophisticated pose. "I can see you are familiar with the name. The Hollisters have always been a credit to Maryland society. Though I'm sure we would be praised for our efforts of reestablishing the respect due the Crown and its officers, I am not looking for glowing accolades. A man of honor needs no other reward than to see justice served for the Mother Country." His dark eyes bored into the twinkling gray ones. "I do, however, wish to appease my own curiosity. Before you permanently dispose of the pesky patriot, I would like a look at him. I wish to know what kind of man dares to bite the hand that feeds him."

"You are a true loyalist," Brice bragged, inflating Douglas's self-esteem. "Aye, I have heard the noble name mentioned with the respect it deserves." He swept into a bow. "I am honored to serve as your hand of justice, sir. I will be in contact when the arrangements have been completed."

As Brice disappeared into the dark alleyway, Douglas frowned. He had not bothered to ask his associate's name. Ah well, 'twas no matter. If by some remote chance something went amiss and the man was arrested, Douglas could proclaim that he did not recognize the name. It wouldn't be a lie he gave. After all, he didn't have the foggiest notion to whom he had spoken.

Massaging his aching temples, Douglas waited the return of his phaeton. All this meticulous plotting and scheming had earned him a hellish headache. But he would find relief in returning home to converse with his wife. Maribeth always had a soothing effect on him when his nerves were ajitter, Douglas reminded himself. And, of course, there was Clay, the son who would always do his father proud.

As the carriage paused before him, Douglas glanced up at the groomsman. "Take me home. I'm sure Maribeth is wondering what has kept me so long this night. She never can cease her stewing and pacing until I am safely back within the walls of Hollister."

The groomsman sadly shook his head as Douglas

folded himself inside the carriage. The old man was having another of his addled spells. He had been reasonably normal the past few months but he was back to his old habit of drifting in and out of the past. The driver thought it odd to leave the old man on an abandoned street corner, but there was no sense arguing with Douglas when he wasn't in his right mind. A servant was much better off if he played along with the old patriarch. Arguing with him that his wife and younger son were not in residence at Hollister was a waste of time. Douglas believed what he believed and there was no rationalizing with him in his moments of befuddled confusion.

Cole sat patiently waiting for the peaceful protest to end. There was plenty of marching and chanting and only one stamp agent had been hauled into the street. It had taken very little persuasion to encourage the man to swear he would never sell a stamp and to resign his position as tax collector. The size of the crowd and the fact that his effigy hung above the street lantern was incentive enough.

When the agent had pledged never to enforce the Stamp Act, he was released without harm. The crowd dispersed at the insistence of their darkly clad leader. There were no drunken brawls, no destruction of property. The civil protest was a far cry from the disaster Cole had witnessed in Boston.

While the citizens milled about the streets, discussing their victory, Cole's eyes were glued to the rider who discreetly made his departure. When Cole had climbed from the carriage and ordered the driver to return home, he circled the crowd to pursue the rider. The patriot had dismounted in an evacuated alley. If Cole had arrived a moment later, he would have been unable

450

to make contact before the rabble-rouser vanished into the darkness.

"Sir, I must have a word with you," Cole called out before the patriot became one of the shadows.

Stephanie wheeled around to see Cole striding toward her. The world narrowed to his rugged features. Common sense told her to run but her heart bade her stay. It was impossible to resist the chance of being alone with Cole. He would soon become another woman's husband and Stephanie would have no right to touch him, to stare at him with love in her eyes. That thought caused her heart to wretch with agony. The past few weeks had been the loneliest of her life. She had met herself coming and going, delivering pamphlets to communities in all sections of Maryland. But there had been too much time to think while she was blazing a trail between settlements.

Seeing Cole was like setting a torch to a bonfire. Emotions that had been left too long to simmer engulfed her. Stephanie could have stood there all night preaching to herself that she was asking for more heartache but it would have served no useful purpose. She had not been allowed to tell Cole good-bye. Douglas would have denied her the request if she had dared suggest it.

Clenching the reins in her fist, Stephanie stood feet askance. Her heart was fluttering around her ribs like a wild bird searching for escape from its cage. Her gaze savored the sight of this magnificent man. It was like viewing a portrait that had been hidden from her sight. The memories came rushing back like a tidal wave when the dim light from the street slanted across his craggy face.

"What do you wish of me, sir?" she questioned huskily.

The sound of her quiet voice was the only evidence

Cole required. His pace quickened to match the rapid beat of his heart. Cole had been favoring his right side until the split-second he made positive identification. But at the moment the pain in his ribs vanished. His body was aware of nothing but the woman who concealed herself in a black cloak and breeches. The silence blazed with the fires of longing and Cole couldn't wait to get his hands on her.

Stephanie found herself swept off the ground and swung in a dizzying circle. Her body came alive when it made wild, sweet contact with his. Touching him was the foretaste of heaven. She knew they had no future together, but at the moment it didn't matter. She was in Cole's sinewy arms and all was right with the world.

Cole trembled with pent-up emotion as he tugged the hat and mask from her head. The moonlight caught in the cascade of red-gold that tumbled to her waist. The muted light absorbed into those mystical green eyes that were surrounded with a fringe of long lashes. Cole's hand wavered as he sketched her finely etched features.

"God, how I've missed you . . ." he rasped. "Since you left I haven't cared if I lived. You took the sunshine with you and the days have been as dark as the nights."

Stephanie looped her arms around his neck, stirred by the sincere emotion in his voice. He did care, she realized. The flame he carried for Rachel might have been burning longer, but Stephanie had managed to touch his heart in her own special way. Perhaps it wasn't love he felt for her, but they had endured a great deal together and it had sealed the bond between them. A part of him would always belong to her, even when he took Rachel as his wife. They shared secrets that remained hidden from the world and Stephanie cherished each and every one of them.

When she graced Cole with a dimpled smile, he felt

his body melt like snow on a raging campfire. "And I missed you terribly," Stephanie confessed as she raised parted lips. "Shall I show you how much?"

Cole grinned in amusement for the first time in weeks. But his expression mellowed as his raven head inched toward hers. The moment his lips caressed hers, Cole groaned in unholy torment. He was like a man who had been stranded on a barren desert and who was dying of thirst. He was content to drink the sweet wine of her kiss to compensate for every day of deprivation. His arms enfolded her, molding her curvaceous contours against his hard flesh. The earth shifted beneath his feet when Stephanie offered him a kiss that carried enough heat to set the moon blazing like the summer sun.

His tongue sought out the recesses of her mouth, stealing her breath and then sharing it with her when Stephanie gasped for air. He couldn't seem to get close enough, couldn't ease the maddening hunger that holding her aroused in him. He ached to recapture the precious moments of passion, to unchain his soul and let it soar.

Stephanie was overcome by the same wild cravings that drove Cole to the brink of sanity. She was quickly losing touch with reality. And before she completely abandoned her common sense, she dragged her lips away from a kiss that had every indication of continuing forever.

"I fear we might draw an audience if we stay here," Stephanie murmured, her voice thick with unappeased passion. "Come, I will show you my castle."

Perched on the back of the stallion Stephanie had purchased for her long trips as express rider for the Sons of Liberty, she wove through the byways of Annapolis. When they had ridden more than a mile from the outskirts of town, she indicated the small shack that sat amid a grove of pines.

Cole frowned as he surveyed the dilapidated shanty that looked as if it had been abandoned for more than a decade. "This is your castle?" he squeaked in disbelief.

It galled him that Stephanie was living in this drafty hut while Rachel had pitched her tent on the sprawling estate of Hollister. Damn, there was no justice in the world, he thought cynically.

"My needs are few," Stephanie assured him as she slid to the ground. "I spend most of my time traveling. The pamphlets from Boston's Committee of Correspondence have now stretched to the southernmost colonies. The unified movement that began three months ago is over. Tonight we succeeded in removing the last remaining stamp agent." A proud smile surfaced on her lips. "We have accomplished our purpose, Cole. 'Tis done. Every tax collector in every community of every colony has been ousted from his position. The colonies are unified in one purpose!"

Cole lifted a tapered finger to line the elegant features that were enhanced by the moonlight. "And you, my little leprechaun, are partially responsible for the Sons of Liberty's success. We have accomplished the impossible. We have created a line of communication throughout every town in the colonies. Though our unity will probably be tested again, we have set a monumental precedent. Parliament will be forced to repeal the Stamp Act because there is not even one man in America to enforce it."

After Stephanie entered the cabin to light the lantern, Cole's scrutinizing gaze swept the crude furnishings. Most women of Stephanie's station in life would be horrified to take up residence in such a shack, but Stephanie had made it home. She had restitched one of the gowns he had purchased for her in Boston to serve as curtains. Another dress had become the spread

454

for her narrow cot. Beside the bed, on a nightstand that suspiciously resembled a crate, sat a vase of late-blooming wild flowers. The dining table (if one could call it that) consisted of two upended crates and two rough planks.

"Home," Stephanie declared as her arm swept the cramped quarters. "It isn't much to look at, I know. But it serves my needs." A saucy smile pursed her lips as she ambled over to fetch a bottle of French wine from under the bed. "I think we should celebrate the Sons of Liberty's monumental accomplishments. Would you care for a drink? The liquor was smuggled into the colonies by a most handsome rapscallion. 'Twas the beauty of his guise," she teased, flashing Cole an elfish grin. "He looked to be a distinguished aristocrat, but beneath the lamb's wool was a devout patriot who defies the British with every breath he takes."

Retrieving two glasses, Stephanie poured them both a drink and then extended her hand. "Though this dashing rogue isn't here with me, his spirit lingers." She lifted her glass in toast. "I drink to him. He has become my inspiration."

Cole's eyes bored into hers. She was trying to make light of a frustrating situation. Though he admired her attempt to humor him, the victory of their crusade was the farthest thing from his mind.

"I'm sorry, Steph. I have dealt you nothing but misery. You deserve the world and I have given you only—"

Stephanie pressed her index finger to his lips to shush him. Her free hand folded around his, forcing him to sip his drink. Cole obliged, but there were dozens of thoughts darting across his mind, aching to be voiced.

When they had drained their glasses, Stephanie set them on the table and took Cole's hand. "I know you think this dowdy shack leaves much to be desired, but let me show you the reason I am so taken with it."

Stephanie led him down a winding path to a stream that glowed like a thread of silver in the moonlight. A thick canopy of trees draped across the narrow channel, camouflaging it from the rest of the world. Cole stared at the tranquil setting, reminded of the mountain streams he had frequented in the timberlands of Maryland.

A low chuckle rumbled in his chest as his dark, dancing eyes swung back to Stephanie. "Is this the mystical sight upon which the leprechauns converge for their magic rituals?"

Stephanie tossed her cloak on the ground and then flung her boots upon it. "Aye, and 'tis time to perform one of the ceremonies," she said teasingly.

But Cole wasn't listening. His all-consuming gaze was fixed on the black breeches that slid to the ground to form a pool at her feet. He continued to stare unblinkingly as Stephanie unbuttoned her shirt and added it to the heap.

Moon-dappled skin enticed him as Stephanie ambled to the water's edge. "The ritual is referred to as *bathing,*" she giggled as she sank into the creek and then stretched out to cut across the surface like a graceful swan. "I have spent so much of the day with my horse that we share the same pungent fragrance."

Cole couldn't tear off his clothes quickly enough. What he had in mind had nothing to do with bathing. The temptation of holding Stephanie's naked body against his was overwhelming. Before Stephanie could paddle around to face Cole, she heard his splash. She waited for him to emerge from the dark depths, but she *felt* his presence long before she saw him.

Tingles of pleasure scaled her spine as his hands stole around her waist. Finally his damp head appeared, his hair sparkling with diamond-studded water droplets. Stephanie trembled uncontrollably, not from the cool temperature of the rivulet but from the arousing feel of his hands weaving intricate patterns on her flesh.

And when his moist lips slanted across hers, Stephanie was lost to the tumultuous sensations that burst inside her. She could feel the knot of desire coming unwound. She recalled each splendorous memory of their nights together. Cole had filled up her world, her being. She wanted him. She would have sacrificed her last breath to revel in the ecstasy of his lovemaking.

When he bent her backward to drift upon the water, Stephanie made no protest. She yearned to feel his hands and lips spreading joyous pleasure over her skin. She longed to caress and be caressed by the only man who could make her soul sing and her heart swell with forbidden rapture.

Cole's hand glided over her skin, worshipping the sight and feel of her exquisite flesh. His lips whispered his need for her as they drifted over the peaks of her breasts and swirled across her belly. The memories of the past were mere stepping-stones that led to the sensuous pleasures he unveiled to her this night. For this was the pure essence of rapture. Never had he been quite so tender, so patient. Over and over again, his hands and lips moved upon her, spreading fires that even an ocean couldn't begin to extinguish.

Her body quivered with delight. Her mind was fogged with heady pleasure. And even when Stephanie swore she would go mad with aching, he continued to assault each of her senses until they were overflowing with his taste, his masculine aroma, his practiced touch.

Breathlessly, Stephanie twisted to bring her body in intimate contact with his. Her legs encircled his hips as she arched toward him, aching to become his total possession, to capture that one glorious moment that transcended time.

Cole lost control when Stephanie shamelessly gave herself to him, whispering her need for him. His male body roused to satisfy her craving for passion as well as the monstrous need that overwhelmed him. He drove against her, seeking ultimate depths of intimacy, clutching her to him as if the world were about to crumble around him. His wild desire for this spell-casting nymph created strength, provided energy. It transformed emotion into sensations that he could reach out to touch. Their lovemaking was like being granted supernatural powers for that one timeless instant. Cole was a part of something that defied words and created incredibly tantalizing sensations. All thought and energy converged, driving him to the heights and depths of ecstasy.

Passion burst forth like a shooting star consumed in its own intense heat. Cole felt as if he were coming apart at the seams. With a shuddering groan, he clutched Stephanie against him, burying his head against the rapid pulsations of her neck. A wave of undefinable rapture splashed over him . . . and then another . . . until he was drowning in a sea of fire. The pleasure was so intense that his spent body was numb. It was as if he had sacrificed every sensation, every thought process for that one delirious moment of ecstasy.

Stephanie clung to his hair-roughened body until the overwhelming feelings ebbed and the fog of ultimate pleasure no longer clouded her brain. Love was an odd phenomena, she mused as she set her feet to the riverbed. It created its own unique dimensions in time and space. It opened a realm that was impossible to experience until one was overcome by endless boundaries of love and the limitless horizons of passion.

But the return from love's most intimate of journeys also brought a certain kind of sadness. What she and Cole had shared, no matter how pure and sweet, had no place in either of their lives. She was no longer his wife. Douglas had seen to that. One day very soon the sultry brunette who carried Cole's child would lie in his arms and experience his unrivaled brand of lovemaking.

Dispirited by that realization, Stephanie withdrew to glide toward the shore. She had tortured herself by bringing Cole here. Each time she wandered to the stream bank to bathe, his memory would be here to torment her.

Cole's adoring gaze followed the retreating mermaid to shore. What he felt for this free-spirited nymph could no longer be contained. He had futilely battled his feelings for her from the beginning, knowing it was foolish to become involved with a woman who could set a torch to his emotions. He had tried to convince himself that he could survive without her, but his self-inspiring lectures were empty words that held no consolation.

Whatever the future held, she would know how much she meant to him. If she would consent to venture into the wilderness with him, he would cast all his obligations aside at a moment's notice. He could no longer live for his brother. Stephanie brought out the man of his past so often that there was no way to contain him. Cole had lived through a dozen kinds of hell these long weeks and he didn't give a whit if he had to sacrifice his inheritance, his name, or anything else demanded of him. What good was money when he was only half a man, wanting a woman his father had denied him? What good was his life if he was forced to live it with a vain, deceitful woman like Rachel?

"Stephanie . . ." Cole's voice cracked in the night.

The faint light cast becoming shadows on her enticing features as she turned to face him. "Aye?" Her tone was flat, her eyes misty with tears.

"You can't leave," he told her simply.

A puzzled frown knitted her brow as she watched Cole cut his way through the water, sending silver ripples undulating in all directions. Had she missed part of the conversation while she was immersed in pensive contemplation? What was he mumbling about? She wasn't going anywhere. Cole was the one who would leave *her* to return to his plantation and his fiancée.

"I had only intended to return to the shack," she replied.

"Even that is too far away."

The man had stayed in the river too long, Stephanie decided. His brain was waterlogged and he wasn't making sense. "Would you mind starting over," she insisted as she scooped up her discarded clothes. "I seem to be lost. What are you babbling about?"

Cole stole the clothes she had just retrieved, and he recklessly tossed them over his shoulder. "I am not babbling," he assured her on a soft chuckle. His arms slid around her hips, bringing her full length against him. "Since I have so little experience in this sort of explanation, I'm not quite certain how to broach the subject."

Stephanie pushed back as far as his encompassing arms would permit. My, but Cole was behaving strangely. "I have always followed the policy of speaking my mind," she insisted saucily. "If you are afraid you are going to shock me or upset me with whatever you feel compelled to say, I doubt that you can. There is very little that fazes me these days."

"Nothing?" Cole's thick brow climbed to a quizzical angle.

Stephanie shook her damp head and then tweaked the hair on his chest. "Out with it," she demanded impatiently. "I am inclined to enjoy the full benefits of lying in bed with you before you must go. Every moment you delay is one more moment I will be denied."

Cole was aroused by her candor and by the provocative smile that blossomed on her exquisite features. No wonder he had never been able to resist this high-strung minx. She had penetrated his soul and left her mark. She had him believing in leprechauns and magic spells and . . . love.

Frustrated, Stephanie wormed from his arms and snatched up her clothes on the run. "I will be in bed if you care to join me," she called over her shoulder.

Stephanie would have died a thousand torturous deaths if Cole had not followed her back to the shack. Her need for him was like an eternal spring. Their time together was so short, so precious. She knew Cole was probably taking a great risk by sneaking away from his father's constant vigil. But once more before Cole had to go, she wanted to sail away in his arms, to commit every delicious sensation to memory.

For several anguishing moments Stephanie awaited Cole's arrival. Her anxious gaze was glued to the open door, seeing nothing but the monstrous shadows of the looming trees. Where was he, she mused impatiently. Had she been too forward in suggesting that she wanted him in her bed? Did he view their tryst as a playful interlude before he walked back into the life his father had structured for him?

Cole always had the knack of making her feel special

461

when they made love. Was she deluding herself in believing that he would come just once more? That he would offer her a memory that she could cherish until her dying day?

Damnit! Where was he? She had only begun to tell him good-bye! Before he left her this night, she had intended to emblaze her image on his mind, to become the smile when no one else was around, that soft murmur of love that would long whisper in his soul.

Chapter 26

After several exasperating minutes Cole appeared in the open door. He was garbed only in his form-fitting breeches and he was wearing a rakish grin that would have knocked Stephanie off her feet if she had been standing on them. Though he was marred by a recent scar, Stephanie doubted there was a handsomer man on the planet. The muscles of his shoulders bulged as he negligently propped himself against the door frame to regard her with another disarming smile. The lantern light reflected the sparkle in his cocoa brown eyes and made the broad expanse of his chest shine like copper.

"What took you so long?" Stephanie questioned, distracted by the tantalizing picture he presented.

His mouth quirked wryly. His keen gaze flooded over the thin sheet that concealed her naked beauty. "Stubborn pride, I think," Cole murmured cryptically.

Stephanie propped herself up on one elbow to look Cole up and down. Why did he persist in answering questions she hadn't asked? His response didn't seem to fit her inquiry. "Cole, what is the matter with you? And which one of you am I addressing, for heaven's sake?" she demanded tartly. "The well-disciplined gentleman or the reckless rogue?"

Cole had that devil-may-care look about him, the one she adored. And yet he was plying her with evasive answers that did not encourage any kind of conversation. Damnit, if she lived to be one hundred she would never figure out this complicated man!

"What is the matter with *me?*" he queried on a soft peal of laughter. Cole knew exactly what his problem was. He was totally and hopelessly in love with a green-eyed leprechaun who made him resent the man he had been forced to become. "The question is—what is the matter with *you?*"

Stephanie had generously offered herself to him in the rivulet, holding nothing back. And then, as brazenly as you please, she had invited him back to her cabin to continue where they had left off. Did that sound like a woman who felt only pity for a man? Cole was mending nicely. There was no reason for her to feel any sort of obligation to him now. She knew their marriage had been annulled. She must realize he had no hold over her.

"A lady doesn't just ask a man to join her in bed," he blurted out.

"Nay?" Stephanie tilted her chin a notch higher and the sheet drooped to expose the tempting swells of her breasts. The incident didn't go unnoticed. Cole was all eyes. "Then how is a man supposed to know when a woman wants him there if she doesn't tell him so?"

Her refreshing candor provoked his spontaneous burst of laughter. "Your point is well taken," he acknowledged as he swaggered over to draw the flimsy sheet away from her well-sculptured body. His gaze savored the sight of her alabaster skin glowing like honey in the flickering light. "And since this seems to be a time for honesty, I must confess that I have never in my life seen anything quite so lovely." Cole poised himself on the edge of the rickety cot to run his hand

464

along the satiny smooth curve of her hip and thigh. "And never in my life have I felt so completely out of control when I am with a woman." His dark eyes crinkled when he graced her with a roguish smile. "You, my little nymph, can weave your spell and transform me into a lusting dragon."

His compliments and the husky tone in which he had conveyed them sent a skein of goose bumps flying across her flesh. Stephanie broke into an impish grin. "I happen to like dragons. A woman doesn't stumble upon one just any old day," came her sassy rejoinder. Her arm lifted to tunnel her fingers through the curly raven hair that framed his craggy features. "I prefer a man who has both the qualities of a reckless little boy and an unpredictable beast . . ."

Her voice trailed off when a remorseful thought spoiled her light mood. Cole didn't belong to her, would never truly belong to her. She could have this swarthy rakehell for a time. But before the night was out, he would change forms and walk back into his stolid world of obligations and responsibility.

Cole could read her mind like an open book. When the flicker died in her emerald eyes, he reached beneath her chin to hold her steady gaze. "M'lady, you have roused the sleeping dragon and now you must decide what is to be done with him." The intense glow in those ebony pools startled Stephanie. He had never stared at her quite like that. Although Cole was still talking in riddles, Stephanie was captivated. "I love you and the reason it took me so long to tell you so is because I had to overcome my cynicism and my stubborn pride."

Stephanie's mouth fell open and she gaped at him as if he were a monster that had suddenly sprouted another head. Of all the things she predicted him to say, that wasn't even on the list! "You love me?" she chirped incredulously. "But it's too late now. Your father dissolved our marriage and you are to wed Rachel."

Cole's lips grazed hers, stealing her protest from her throat. "'Tis never too late, not if you feel more than pity for me. Do you, Steph? Do you honestly love me?"

Did he even have to ask? She had told him how she felt a dozen times and he had shrugged off her confession like water dripping down a duck's back.

Stephanie blinked back the sentimental tears that moistened her eyes. "Aye, I love you. 'Tis why I stayed in Annapolis. And each time I set out to spread the word of rebel unification, part of you rode with me." She muffled a sniff and forced herself to continue before emotion deprived her of her voice. "Rachel may soon wear your ring and become the mother of the child I would have eagerly given you. But the wild, reckless part of you will always belong to me."

Cole enfolded her in his loving arms, cursing the complications that stood like mountains between them. More than anything he wanted this lively sprite with the red-gold hair and shining green eyes. He resented the world and everyone in it for separating him from the only woman he had ever truly wanted.

"I can't do it anymore," Cole breathed in frustration. "I can't go on pretending to be the man my father demands of me. And I will never endure a marriage to Rachel without one or the other of us strangling the other." Bitter laughter resounded in his chest. "If you gave me a child, I would know that 'tis ours, but 'tis not so with Rachel. I doubt that even *she* knows who fathered her child. She went out again tonight to meet one of her lovers. That is why I was able to sneak away from that prison I loosely refer to as home."

Cole held Stephanie away from him. His face was no longer a cautious mask that disguised his emotions. "I don't care what sacrifice I have to make. I want you with me and I don't give a damn where we go, as long as we are together. Tomorrow I am going to tell my father that I can no longer abide by his laws of honor and responsibility. If he feels so obliged to Rachel, *he* can marry her. I will no longer live a lie. I love you and I want the world to know it."

Stephanie was too overcome with emotion to care what difficulties they might confront. All she knew was that Cole returned the love she had kept bottled up inside her and her feelings were bursting out all over. Suddenly, she was squeezing the stuffing out of him while Cole was simultaneously squeezing her in two. And as they tumbled onto the cot to express their love for each other, it folded up beneath them, sending them crashing to the floor.

Raising his tousled head, Cole surveyed what was left of their bed and then shrugged carelessly. "Have you an aversion to making love on the floor?" he chuckled before he dropped a kiss to her heart-shaped lips.

Stephanie wrapped her arms around his shoulders and blessed him with a radiant smile. "Nay, your love is cushion enough," she assured him saucily.

Cole's response was a low, provocative growl and a passionate kiss. His muscular leg slid between hers as he crouched above her. "Feed the dragon," he rasped, his voice ragged with barely restrained desire. "If you don't appease his ravenous appetite, he will make a feast of you . . ."

With a welcoming cry Stephanie arched toward him. And when she breathed fire into him, Cole became a living flame. Passion exploded like a crown fire, consuming all within its blazing path. Love fanned their desire for each other into a raging holocaust. Pure, sweet emotion poured from their souls, forging them as one. Sensations boiled between them like molten lava.

Never had there been a time when love and passion had been so intent on making their presence known. Emotion created its own unique storm of wind and flame. It was like a series of internal explosions that sent chain reactions rippling out in all directions. The world teetered on its axis and dangled in space when passion's tempest engulfed the star-crossed lovers.

Cole suddenly remembered hearing Ben declare that love had more to do with *feeling* than with *thinking*. But Cole wondered if even his uncle understood the full meaning of what he had said. Cole had come to realize that there was no pleasure greater than passion embroidered with love and no force more potent or indestructible than the power of love inflamed with passion. The two together formed an invincible bond that nothing could sever. Love created something from nothing. It fed upon itself, growing stronger and even more intense until its power equaled the heat of a thousand suns.

Much later, when Cole's mind cleared and his depleted strength had been revived by rest, he found enough energy to drag himself to his feet. Although he protested taking Stephanie's horse to make his journey back to Hollister, Stephanie insisted. Finally, Cole relented, promising to return for her after he had informed his father of his intentions. Cole was certain it was best to leave Stephanie in her secluded shack until the smoke cleared. There was no telling what Douglas might do when he realized he could no longer manipulate his only son.

Grimly analyzing the best technique of approaching his father, Cole wove his way through the cluster of trees to return to the plantation before dawn. Leaving Stephanie was one of the most difficult tasks he had undertaken, but he consoled himself by thinking it would be the last time he would be forced to leave her.

When next he came to fetch her, he would never let her out of his sight again. It would be like plucking out his very soul, Cole mused as he retraced his steps to the plantation.

A faint smile brushed his lips as he followed the dirt path. He and Stephanie may find themselves sheltered in the very shack where she had taken refuge. But it didn't really matter. As she had said, her needs were few and his need numbered only *one*. If he had that feisty little leprechaun, he needed nothing else.

As Cole disappeared into the thick undergrowth of trees that surrounded the cabin, Stephanie stared dreamily after him. Although their lives were still entangled with Douglas and Rachel, Stephanie's soul was soaring. Their problems didn't seem so insurmountable when she had Cole's love. Somehow, they would make a life for themselves, she encouraged herself.

Sighing whimsically, Stephanie turned back to the collapsed bed and grinned at its shattered remains. Well, there was naught else to do but repair the cot. If only she could devise a way to double its size . . .

The quiet rap on the door stirred her from her musings. Stephanie wheeled toward the portal, her face blossoming into a smile. What excuse had Cole found to return so quickly? Whatever it was, she approved of it.

Stephanie pulled open the door and her smile changed to a look of shock and dismay. Her eyes fell to the flintlock that was pointed at her chest. And suddenly, the world didn't seem quite such a pleasant place. Brice Reynolds stood before her, wearing a deadly sneer that turned her blood to ice.

"We meet again, bitch," Brice snorted triumphantly. He nudged Stephanie backward with the barrel of his pistol. "I was dismayed to see your husband alive and well . . . until he led me to the alley to meet the *mysterious* patriot." His spiteful laughter resounded around the cabin like the foreboding clap of thunder. "You have been a busy little bitch, haven't you, Stephanie? First you turned the citizens of Mystic against me with your charade and your accusations. Now you have come to ruin the lives of every British sympathizer in Annapolis. The Crown will pay a king's ransom to be rid of the devout patriot who has been inciting riots up and down the coast."

Grinning maliciously, Brice dangled a rope before Stephanie. "Though I would prefer to tie this around your neck, it suits my purpose to keep you alive just a little while longer." When Stephanie's eyes darted sideways, plotting a method of escape, Brice grabbed a handful of her hair and painfully twisted it around his fingers. "Don't try it," he advised. "You are worth almost as much to me dead as alive. The coins I might lose may equal the satisfaction I would derive in watching you die earlier than I have planned."

Stephanie was horrified to realize how quickly life could turn sour. The previous moment she had been sitting on top of the world. And now she swore the world was squashing her flat. She didn't know exactly what Brice was planning. But to be sure, there was money to be made or the vermin wouldn't be contemplating it. All that motivated a man like Reynolds was the speculation of wealth and an obsessive need for vengeance. Stephanie had the sinking feeling Brice had been allowed too much time to meticulously plot out his scheme. And she was also harboring the dispirited premonition that although she was worth a fortune to Brice, her life wasn't worth a shilling.

While Brice made fast work of binding and gagging her, Stephanie was praying nonstop. She chided herself for her selfishness. She should have been thankful she had lived long enough to earn Cole's love, but she was bitter that she would not survive long enough to enjoy a future with him. And if Brice was allowed his way (and it certainly looked as though he would be), Stephanie's future was short-termed.

Choking on that dismal thought, Stephanie glared at Brice's gloating smile. After he disposed of her, she was going to come back to haunt him. She would ensure that he paid penance for every cent of his ill-gotten gains—blood money—bought and paid for with her life and her love for the man who had only begun to realize how deeply she cared for him.

Cole came instantly awake after only a few hours sleep. He was hounded by uneasy sensations that made the hair on the back of his neck stand up. He was apprehensive of his confrontation with his father. But there was something more, something he couldn't quite puzzle out. It was a feeling deep inside him, a nagging fear that seemed to bear no definite source, like the feelings he had experienced during the years he had spent in the wilderness.

Shaking away the thought, Cole shrugged on his clothes and descended the stairs to find his father awaiting his breakfast. Inhaling a determined breath, Cole seated himself at the table and poured a cup of tea.

"You seem to be moving about much better," Douglas observed. "Before long you will be able to assume all of your responsibilities on the plantation. But you need not concern yourself with the wedding arrangements. Rachel and I have made all the preparations and the announcements will be delivered to the printers today."

Cole eased back in his chair. "I would like to see the

announcement," he insisted. "There might be a few changes I wish to add."

Douglas beamed in satisfaction. Cole had finally accepted his destiny with Rachel. Their private discussion the previous evening must have aided in ironing out the difficulties between them. At last Cole had relinquished his preoccupation with that green-eyed hellion who had taken up residence in his soul.

When Douglas returned from the study with the announcement in hand, he presented it to Cole. "I'm sure it will meet with your approval. Rachel and I have scheduled the wedding to be held here, followed by a grand reception. The joining of the Hollisters and the Garrets will be a monumental occasion."

Cole stared directly at his father while he tore the parchment in half and then in fourths. Douglas gaped in astonishment as the fragments fluttered recklessly upon the table.

"I am not wedding Rachel," Cole declared defiantly. "I fully intend to remarry my first wife."

Douglas's face flushed with irritation. "We have been through this before," he growled. "You are not marrying that troublemaker. You will wed the woman who carries your child, a woman whose gentle breeding is worthy of your station in life."

Cole burst into bitter laughter. "You have it backwards," he snorted derisively. "Rachel is a tramp and a troublemaker. The reason I abandoned her on the eve of our wedding was because I found her with one of her many lovers. I will not marry a woman who will give me another man's child!"

The color seeped from Douglas's face. "'Tis a cruel, hateful lie," he sputtered. "Rachel has been true to you. She has constantly assured me of her devotion to you, of her undying love."

"You believe a devious woman and yet you deny the truth from the tongue of your own flesh and blood?" Cole scoffed. "Rachel has played you for a fool. Her only reasons for wanting to marry me are to punish me for humiliating her and to grant herself some degree of respectability while she dallies with everything in breeches."

"That isn't true," Douglas screeched, his voice becoming higher and wilder by the second. "She is one of our kind. She holds honor and responsibility sacred. Rachel is loyal to you and she has been a godsend to me during the months you were away."

Cole was becoming frantic. He could see that blank glaze begin to replace Douglas's intelligent stare. This conflict had begun to upset him and he was quickly losing control of his mental capacities.

"It will never work between Rachel and me," Cole insisted. "I love Stephanie. She represents all the qualities I once possessed, the ones you reject and detest. I have attempted to conform to your rigid standards, to repay the debt you believe I owe to you and to my brother. But I am what I have always been and I can no longer live the lie. Rachel has made a mockery of honor. 'Tis Stephanie who bears the noble qualities. I want to remarry her. Stephanie's strength and character put Rachel to shame."

"Nay!" Douglas yelped as if he had been stabbed in the back. "'Tis all a vicious lie, meant to undermine my affection for Rachel. Her feelings for you and for me are honest. She has become like my own daughter! She holds firm in our belief that we are subjects to the Crown. She puts responsibility and honor high upon the pedestal where they belong!"

"Her opinions and beliefs are centered around herself," Cole argued sharply. "She has catered to you to gain your allegiance. Each night while you are tucked in bed, she sneaks out to rendezvous with other men. If you do not believe me, ask her where she went last night after you departed." Cole's penetrating gaze bore into his father's wild eyes. "Ask her how it could be that she saw the dark patriot leading a rebel march when the riots only take place at night. She admitted to it at supper, but you failed to catch her slip of tongue."

The remark took part of the wind out of Douglas's sails. Now that Cole had pointed it out, Douglas vaguely remembered Rachel making the comment. Hastily, he told himself that she had a reasonable explanation and then he uttered that very argument to Cole.

Rising to his feet, Cole gave his raven head a negative shake. "Even her family knows of her indiscretions and I have witnessed them with my own eyes. I also watched her flee the house last night and 'twas not the first time since I returned home that she has sneaked out when she thought everyone else asleep."

Douglas sat perched on the edge of his chair, fervently denying the accusations, becoming more frustrated and confused by the second. His jumbled thoughts were shattered when Cole grabbed his arm and whisked him to his feet.

"We are going to ask Rachel where she was and what she was doing last night," Cole growled as he herded his father into the foyer and up the steps. "I want you to see her face when she fumbles for a suitable lie."

"This is ludicrous, Clay," Douglas muttered. "You are behaving more like your reckless, irresponsible brother with each passing day. A man does not confront a lady with such condemning questions. Why, your mother would faint away if she knew you contemplated such an outrageous breech of etiquette."

Cole scowled in frustration. His father was quickly losing his grasp on reality. He could only pray that Douglas would return to his senses when Rachel was forced to admit her deception.

Without bothering to knock, refusing to waste even a split-second, Cole shoved open the door to Rachel's boudoir. Her startled cry intermingled with Douglas's and Cole's shocked gasps. Cole's eyes sparked mutinous fury when he glared at the barely clad brunette. Rachel stood in her chemise, making preparations to strap a pillow over her flat belly. There was no child. There had never been a child! She had deceived them both, using a pretended pregnancy to ensure that Douglas would force Cole to marry her.

Rachel's face whitewashed when she saw the condemnation flood into Douglas's eyes. Hell and damnation, Cole could not have selected a more inopportune moment to burst into her room. She was caught in a most embarrassing situation and even the best of lies would not redeem her to Douglas's good graces.

All of her careful scheming had been for naught. Rachel had intended to carry on the charade until after the wedding ceremony. Then she had planned to feign a miscarriage. The incident would provide sympathy and strengthen her position with Douglas. He would naturally blame Cole for the loss of the child. Douglas blamed Cole for everything and he had since Clay and Maribeth died.

"You bastard," Rachel hissed at Cole as she snatched up her robe to cover herself.

A wry smile pursed Cole's lips as he swaggered over to scoop up the discarded pillow. Slowly, he turned to present the evidence of Rachel's deceit to his bug-eyed father. "No doubt, half the male population in

475

Annapolis knows Rachel has schemed to hoodwink the both of us. Is this the kind of woman you wish to represent your brand of honor? A witch who agrees with you only to earn your loyalty to *her* selfish cause? She is an accomplished liar and a cheat. She uses her charm to deceive those of us who were blinded by her shallow beauty."

Cole pivoted to face Rachel's murderous glower. "Who were you with when you spirited off last night, my dear?" The endearment resembled a curse and that was exactly how Cole intended it. "Was it Morris Stevens, the same dandy I found you with before I set sail and left you standing at the altar?"

The shock of catching Rachel red-handed jolted Douglas back to his senses, at least momentarily. "You are beneath contempt," he hissed venomously. Douglas pointed a trembling finger at Rachel. His face twisted in an enraged sneer. "I trusted you. I took you in as if you were one of my own. I defended you when Cole spoke against you." Mad fury boiled through his veins. Douglas stalked toward Rachel like a frothing beast cornering his prey. His fingers curled, itching to clamp her neck in a stranglehold. His voice boomed around the room like an exploding cannon. "You lied to me! You used me to get to my son! You . . ."

Cole waited until Douglas had wrapped his fingers around Rachel's throat before he intervened. He felt his father deserved a small portion of consolation after the way Rachel had deceived them. And Rachel needed to know that she could never set foot in this mansion again without fearing for her life.

"Enough," Cole barked as he pried Douglas's fingers loose. "Rachel's punishment will hound her for the rest of her miserable life. She won't dare show her face in Annapolis, not without suffering the mocking laughter

476

of those who know what she is and what she has done."

Still, Douglas refused to be satisfied with only choking *half* the life out of this devious witch. He lunged at Rachel with the vengeance of a wounded lion. Her frantic squawk erupted when she was forced to bound across the bed to escape Douglas's wrath. And for a moment, Cole allowed Douglas to pursue Rachel in circles like a growling bulldog attempting to pounce on a wailing cat. The instant Rachel, who had swiveled her head around to monitor the progress of her infuriated pursuer, stumbled and fell in an unladylike heap, Douglas pinned her to the floor.

"Damn you!" Douglas snarled as Cole pulled him away and held him at bay. "Get out of my sight, woman." He outthrust an arm toward the door. "Get out of my house! If I ever lay eyes on you again, I'll not tarry a moment to consider the repercussions of having you whipped!"

Rachel didn't waste a second in scrambling to her feet. Nor did she have to bother with packing. Like a madman discarding any evidence that she had ever been there at all, Douglas stormed over to yank her elegant gowns from the closet. Within a matter of minutes, everything Rachel had brought with her to Hollister had been heaved out the window. The gardeners, who had clustered beneath the window to eavesdrop on the loud tirade, found themselves beneath an avalanche of pastel gowns and petticoats. The ground and overhanging tree limbs suddenly became cluttered with Rachel's discarded wardrobe.

"You can pick up your belongings on your way out or you can watch them go up in smoke. I will order them burned if you have not retrieved them in ten minutes," Douglas sneered, his chest heaving with outrage. "Get out! G—E—T . . . O—U—T!"

With Douglas's roar nipping at her heels, Rachel dashed out of the room and down the steps as fast as her legs would carry her. The man had become a raving lunatic and Rachel knew Douglas meant what he had said about disposing of her if she ever came near Hollister again. And she had no intention of doing that! Her family had already kicked her out of the house and now Douglas had threatened her life. Rachel decided it was time to take up residence in another community and allow another portion of the male population to enjoy her company. And she would be on the next coach out of town, just as soon as she gathered the belongings Douglas had hurled out the window to adorn the garden and the trees.

When the front door slammed shut behind her, Douglas collapsed into a nearby chair to massage his aching head. He was humiliated beyond words and it was all he could do to face his son.

"I believed in her," he choked out, refusing to meet Cole's unblinking stare. "I was betrayed by my own blind sense of honor and dignity." His shoulders slumped and he expelled his breath in a rush. "I despise Rachel for what she tried to do. But more than that, I detest myself for believing I could manipulate you, that it was right for me to make the decision as to how you should live out your life . . . as if it were the extension of my own."

Cole strode over to lay a consoling hand on his father's shoulder. "I think 'tis time we made amends," he murmured. "You and I have—"

The timid rap at the door caused Cole to jerk up his head. One of the servants moved forward to extend a message to Douglas.

"This letter just arrived, sir. I was told to deliver it to you posthaste."

When the servant took his leave, Douglas unfolded the letter and read its contents. "Well, at least I have accomplished some amount of good," he sighed in consolation. "The dark patriot who has been inciting riots has been taken into captivity and—"

"What?" A shudder of doom riveted through Cole as he snatched the parchment from Douglas's fingertips. His eyes blazed over the letter and then a murderous growl erupted from his lips.

Douglas raised his gray head to peer incredulously at his son. "Surely you can find no fault with that," he chirped. "That rabble-rouser was responsible for ousting every tax agent and stamp collector for the Crown."

"That man was your son," Cole scowled. "Or at least he was until I was incapacitated by my wounds."

"What!" Douglas bolted to his feet. His brows knitted in a bemused frown. "But 'tis impossible. My associate states in his note that he has apprehended the darkly clad patriot. I am to deliver the rest of the coins to my henchman so he can take residence elsewhere. How could he have taken you captive when you are here?"

Cole squeezed his eyes shut as the cloud of impending doom rained down on his head. "Stephanie has been acting in my stead since I was unable to perform the duties as express rider for the Sons of Liberty."

"You are one of the . . ." Douglas wilted into his chair, his eyes bulging in disbelief. His nagging headache was back and it was pounding at his temples like a bass drum. "What have I done now?" he groaned in despair.

Cole's fingers twisted into the front of his father's jacket, giving him a firm shake. "Who was this man you hired to dispose of the patriot leader?" he demanded gruffly. "Where is he?"

Douglas shrugged helplessly. "I only met him at last night's rally. He shared my opinion that riots were not the proper method of protesting against Parliament. The man didn't give his name or his residence. He was only to contact me when he had done the deed."

Cole was becoming more frantic by the second. He wasn't sure if Stephanie was dead or alive and he didn't even know who had apprehended her, for God's sake! "What did the man look like? Had you seen him before? Damnit, tell me everything you know about him."

"I know nothing about him," Douglas insisted. His heart was thudding so furiously he could barely catch his breath. "He was dressed in tattered clothes and he wore a disheveled white wig that had an odd hint of red to it. He was stout. His features were harsh, his ears oversized, and—"

Douglas's voice evaporated when Cole, muttering a string of obscenities, abruptly released him, causing him to stumble back into his chair.

"Reynolds," Cole spat out the name as if it left a bitter taste in his mouth.

Douglas stared curiously at his son. "Do you know the man?"

Cole's jaw clenched with frustrated fury. "Aye, he is the man who had twice tried to kill me, and Stephanie as well. He wants her dead to avenge the loss of his fortune and his prestige." His eyes swung to his father. Again Cole swore under his breath. "The man was granted pardon by the British after his first attempt at murder. Your British sympathizer is an assassin and a spy. His loyalty is not to the Crown you defend but to himself and to his obsession for killing Stephanie."

Douglas's face blanched. "I didn't know," he defended in ragged breaths.

Cole cursed himself for taking his frustration out on his father. Douglas had no way of knowing what kind of damage he had done by hiring someone to dispose of the patriotic rabble-rouser. Exhaling his breath, Cole forced himself to analyze the problem and decide how to deal with it. But it was damned difficult when his emotions kept clogging his thoughts.

"Tell me *exactly* what arrangements you made with Reynolds," Cole requested soberly.

"I paid cash to see the patriot captured," Douglas informed Cole. "Once the man had accomplished his mission, he was to receive traveling money." Douglas swallowed hard. "After I got a look at the rebel, I told Reynolds to dispose of the troublemaker, quietly and discreetly."

Cole groaned in torment as his fist slammed into his hand. His mind raced, attempting to devise a scheme that would ensure Stephanie's safety, if indeed that was at all possible.

"When you deliver the money to the designated place, you must inform Reynolds that you have changed your mind about disposing of the rebel." Cole paced the confines of the room like a caged predator as he put his thoughts to tongue. "Tell Reynolds you have decided to turn the rebel over to the proper authorities so you won't have *his* blood on your conscience. But for God's sake, don't let him know that *I* know what has transpired between you. If Reynolds thinks he can ransom Stephanie to me or to her family, he will have more incentive to keep her alive. 'Tis our only hope of ensuring that he won't kill her immediately."

Douglas nodded grimly as he followed Cole down the steps to gather the money. Absently, he massaged his head, wishing the ache would vanish and grant him peace. Cole noticed the gesture and inwardly flinched at the possibility of having his father wander off the deep end at that critical moment when he confronted the treacherous Brice Reynolds.

The hours Cole had to endure before the designated time to meet Reynolds were literally hell on earth. Cole stewed and paced until his nerves became a mass of tangled twine. The waiting and worrying were far more taxing than any battle in which Cole had engaged. Lord, he would have pulled out his hair, strand by strand, if he hadn't kept his hands occupied by biting his nails. Damnit all, Cole scowled as he spun around to pace in a different direction. The apprehension was killing him, and he hated to think what it was doing to Stephanie, and to his already rattled father.

Armed with a pistol, a musket, and a knife, Cole climbed into the carriage. Cole peered solemnly at his father. "I will do anything you demand of me if you can get Stephanie out alive. *Anything . . ."* he emphasized. "Steph means everything to me. I would sacrifice all else just to know that she walked away unharmed from this nightmare."

Douglas understood what Cole was offering. His son was willing to relinquish his freedom and happiness, his own wants and needs, and even his own life for this feisty female.

A faint smile brimmed Douglas's lips as he crossed his hands over the pouch of money that rested on his lap. "You must love her very much," he remarked quietly.

Cole's heart was in his eyes and the strain of this critical situation was evident in the taut lines of his face. "If ever you have the chance to know Steph, you will understand why," Cole murmured. "She possesses the rare brand of spirit that inspires and exhilarates the most depressed souls. A man cannot help but react to her. There can be no indifference where Steph is concerned."

A soft chuckle bubbled in Douglas's chest. "I cannot argue with that. She most certainly got a rise out of me during our first and only confrontation." A speculative smile settled in his wrinkled features. "She reminded me a great deal of the defiant young man I dealt with a decade ago." His smile faded. "'Tis a shame it has taken me so long to appreciate free, undaunted spirits. And if we all come out of this alive, you need not expect me to make demands on you. I have hampered you too much already. You are your own man, firm in your own convictions. Although I still do not condone your methods or your politics, I have come to respect your right to follow your own heart and lead your own private life. I seem to have forgotten the very reason your grandparents left the Mother Country to settle this colony. It was to gain their own brand of freedom, to enjoy the right of living their lives as *they* saw fit."

"I would sacrifice every ounce of freedom if I could ensure Stephanie's safety," Cole whispered, distracted by the vision that occupied his mind.

Douglas fell silent, cursing his mounting headache. He *had* to keep his wits about him. Cole was counting on him to untangle the mess he had made. Bearing that in mind, Douglas mentally rehearsed his speech to Reynolds, hoping he could sound calm and convincing. If only Clay and Maribeth were here to encourage him. . . . But they were off tending to the affairs of the plantation. Well, he would just have to handle this matter himself, Douglas mused as he toyed with the strings of the money pouch.

Cole grimaced as he watched his father stare blankly

at the purse in his lap. God, grant the man one more hour of sanity, Cole prayed frantically. If only he could devise a way for Reynolds to unknowingly lead him to Stephanie. All Cole asked for was an *opportunity*. He would make the most of it. He had to. Cole doubted he would be allowed a second chance.

Chapter 27

Knowing Cole could have easily retraced his steps to Stephanie's hideaway, Brice had tossed her over the back of his horse and then transported her by boat to a snake-infested swamp. The frightful shack in the marshes made Stephanie's crude shanty look like a mansion in comparison. After he had deposited her on the muddy floor, he had marched off to deliver his message to Douglas.

Brice wasn't certain how much Cole knew about his father's activities and he wasn't taking any chances. His message demanded that Douglas come alone to complete their business transaction. Once he had collected old man Hollister's fee and produced the rebel leader, Douglas would be shocked within an inch of his life. And Brice would bet his last two bits that Douglas would have no qualms about the blackmail money he would be forced to pay to keep his secret. Brice's second order of business would be to contact Cole to make another arrangement for ransom.

Brice hadn't bothered to tell Stephanie that her father-in-law had paid to have her captured and put to death. He should have, Brice mused with a wicked chuckle. Then she would know the hell Cole would endure if he ever discovered that Douglas had indiscreetly killed his own daughter-in-law. That would certainly put a permanent wrinkle in their relationship, Brice thought spitefully. Perhaps he would ensure that Cole learned the truth *after* Brice had collected a few installments of blackmail money. Ah, this was a delightfully ironic situation that would tear the Hollister family apart. And it served them both right, Brice chuckled as he made his way toward his destination. The torture Cole Hollister would endure would be far worse than death.

A smile of spiteful satisfaction curled Brice's lips as he paddled downriver to the abandoned mill where he had instructed Douglas to meet him. The only thing that could have made him happier was if Stephanie had suffered one or two snakebites while she was alone in the shack. And if he hadn't been in such a rush to deliver the message to Douglas, Brice might have been taken the time to round up one or two slimy serpents.

Indeed, Brice would have been delighted if he had known that, at the very moment when he was contemplating the thought, Stephanie was staring into a pair of beady eyes and watching the forked tongue of the snake that had just slithered under the crack in the door of the shack. But the thought *did* provide Brice with another inspiration, one that would ensure his success, no matter what happened with Douglas Hollister. Snickering satanically, Brice turned his mind to the confrontation at hand and mentally calculated his encounter with the arrogant old goat he had met during the previous night's rally.

The instant Brice had made his exit from the cabin, Stephanie had frantically worked the ropes that kept her hands bound behind her back. She had found little in the way of an improvised weapon to slice the ropes. The only device within her reach was the protruding end of a spike that jutted through the wall. Inching herself backward, Stephanie had stabbed the spike against the ropes in hopes of fraying them.

Her efforts seemed futile, but she refused to abandon her attempt to gain freedom. Although her wrists were raw from twisting and grinding them against the spike and her arms were aching, she continued relentlessly. Stephanie didn't know how much time she would be allowed before Brice returned from his mysterious mission, but she was determined not to waste even a moment. Cringing in pain, she leaned forward to raise her hands to the nail. Biting back her agonized cry, Stephanie worked until she had not the strength to lift her arms. After granting herself a minute's rest, she began the procedure again. The feel of sagging ropes against her wrists encouraged her. She had made some progress, though it was impossible to tell how much unless she were blessed with eyes in the back of her head. She couldn't *see* how much headway she had made, but she could *feel* the loss of tension in the rope.

And then suddenly, the binding strap sagged just enough for her to worm one hand free. Relief washed over Stephanie's perspiring features when she tossed the rope aside and removed the gag. Her eyes flew to the door as she climbed to her feet. A muttered curse erupted from her lips when she grasped the latch to find it had been barred from the outside.

Had she worn the hide off her wrists only to find herself imprisoned in this musty hell hole? Since necessity was the mother of invention, it was up to Stephanie to *create* an escape route where none existed. She braced her spirits and carefully scrutinized the empty shack, her mind mulling over the possibilities. The only source of light was the gaps in the thatched roof and the open knotholes in the wooden walls. When her squinted eyes landed on the loose board on the south wall, Stephanie walked over to give it a forceful tug. The board groaned and creaked, but it refused to break loose. Bracing her feet, she clamped her hands around the plank and yanked for all she was worth. When the board finally snapped under pressure, she was launched backward to sprawl on the floor. She had created an opening in the wall but it was hardly wide enough for her to wedge her way to freedom. If anything, she had provided space for the slimy varmints from the marsh to join her in her gloomy prison.

It was while Stephanie was scraping herself off the floor that she spied the intruder that had slithered under the door—the very serpent Brice had wished on her. Stephanie yelped when her gaze locked with the slitted eyes of the viper that was as long as she was tall. And for one terrified moment Stephanie swore the serpent's mate was crawling down her spine. Her heart hammered so furiously against her chest she feared it would trample her to death before the snake sank its fangs in her flesh.

Stephanie didn't take time to contemplate if it would be safer to back *slowly* away when she was staring death in the face or if it was wiser to bolt and run. She chose the latter, quite simply out of instinct. The snake, startled by her abrupt movement, coiled to strike.

Another bloodcurdling scream gushed from her lips as she scrambled to retrieve the broken board she had pried from the wall. As the viper sprang at her, Stephanie countered the attack. The blow stunned the snake, allowing Stephanie enough time to level a second strike. The serpent continued to coil and recoil at her feet, constantly moving, leaving Stephanie to wonder if she had delivered a fatal blow.

Finally, the snake's movement ceased and Stephanie collapsed against the wall to catch her breath and collect her scattered wits. But there was no victory in knowing she had killed one snake when the marsh was crawling with hundreds just like it. *Her* private hell on earth came in waiting and wondering when the serpent's mate would come slinking into her damp cell to learn his whereabouts.

Moonbeams and starlight sprinkled down from the heavens to cast eerie silhouettes on the swamp. Fleeting shadows leapfrogged through the clump of low-hanging trees and dense underbrush that encircled the abandoned mill. The distorted images that were dappled with silvery light lent uneasy sensations to Douglas's already frazzled emotional state. The sound of the unseen creatures that prowled the tidewater swamps left Douglas imagining macabre trolls and spiny monsters that would, at any moment, gather and conspire to gobble him alive.

Nervously, Douglas fussed with the ruffled cuff of his shirt and paced the darkness. He glanced first one direction and then the other, wondering why his associate was keeping him waiting. As Douglas marched back and forth in front of the mill, shooting occasional glances into the thicket where Cole stood as a posted lookout, he saw Reynolds emerge from the wooden structure to lean against the rail on the second story. Relief clung to Douglas's features. He couldn't wait for this ordeal to be over. He was as fidgety as a caged cat.

"Did you bring the money?" Brice called down to the elegantly dressed aristocrat. The first time he met Hollister, Brice had been stung with envy and jealousy. But no more, he thought with a sinister smile. By the time he finished with the Hollisters and the Wakefields, they would respect his cunning and he would have a good share of their fortunes to compensate for the wealth Stephanie had cost him. "I have kept my end of the bargain."

Douglas lifted the pouch of coins for Brice to survey and then tucked it behind his back. "There has been a change in plans," Douglas squeaked, cursing his voice for failing him when he needed it most.

The announcement caused Brice to frown warily. The way Hollister was behaving had Brice wondering if Cole had learned what his father had done. Cautiously, Brice surveyed the dense underbrush. It was a good thing he had taken time to plot how he intended to deal with this haughty aristocrat, Brice congratulated himself. If not, he might have found himself the victim of a trap. Even if Cole was looming in the thicket, Brice would have ample time to fetch his captive and make his escape in the darkness. A smug smile swallowed his harsh features. The Hollisters would never dupe Brice Reynolds, he told himself confidently.

"What change in plans are you suggesting, Hollister?" Brice inquired as his hand dangled near the pistol that he carried beneath his jacket.

"I have a . . . I have decided I do not wish to have the rebel disposed of," Douglas faltered. "I wish for you to turn your captive over to me so that I may make an example of him to the other patriots."

Brice pretended to consider the request. He had the uneasy feeling Cole had learned of his father's scheme. Well, it didn't matter. Brice would have his way because neither Cole nor his father could outguess him. Indeed, they were both in for the shock of their lives, he haughtily assured himself.

"'Tis no problem . . . if that is what you wish," Brice

490

declared to his nervous associate. "After you give me the funds to make my exit from Annapolis, I will return the rebel to you before I leave."

Although Douglas's shoulders slumped, certain Reynolds was unaware he was about to be trapped, Cole's body was taut as a newly strung cable. He stood in the brush, harboring the odd sensation that things were not running as smoothly as they appeared. But he was still helpless to take command of the situation.

Cole muttered under his breath. Reynolds was clinging to the shadows on the outer wall of the mill and Cole could not have winged the wily bastard, even if he'd had a larger target. Brice was too clever to make himself easy prey for a sniper. His short-lived profession as a sniper had taught Brice enough to recall how simple it was to shoot at a sitting duck. (And that was exactly what Cole had become that day in Mystic, in order to spare Stephanie's life.)

Cole detested this frustrated, helpless feeling that loomed over him. But he was wise enough to know that stepping from his hiding place at this critical moment could spoil his chances of locating Stephanie. When Reynolds appeared at the lower door of the mill with his satchel in hand, Cole's silent curses consigned the bastard to the burning fires of hell. The very sight of Brice Reynolds made Cole's blood run cold. If his father had not been standing between him and Reynolds, Cole's trigger finger would have clamped around the flintlock to shoot the bastard's legs out from under him.

While Cole was cursing his father's blunder of placing himself in the direct line of fire, Brice was surveying the dazed expression in Douglas's eyes. The man looked as if he was about to snap.

"You seem upset, Hollister," Brice observed, making

491

matters worse for Douglas. "You do not seem so certain of yourself. Has something happened to disturb you?"

"Nay, I am fine," Douglas insisted all too hastily. "'Tis only that I am most anxious to see this matter done."

Slowly, Brice extended his satchel. "If you will place the money pouch in my bag with my belongings, I will be on my way to fetch the rabble-rouser," he remarked, smiling all too cheerfully. But Douglas didn't notice. He was having too much trouble keeping himself in hand.

Just as Douglas reached forward, it occurred to him that perhaps he shouldn't hand over the cash until Reynolds produced the patriot. Involuntarily, his hand and the money pouch shrank back against his laboring chest.

"Is something else wrong?" Brice questioned cautiously. His gaze drifted to the shadowed underbrush that continued to draw Douglas's attention.

"I think I should like to meet the captive before I offer the money," Douglas insisted. "I see no reason to pay for something I do not have."

"Don't you trust me, Hollister?" Brice smiled like a shark showing off his mouthful of teeth.

"Well, of course I do," Douglas lied as he anxiously shifted from one foot to the other.

"I want the money now." The smile slid off Brice's face. "If not, I will find some other noble Tory to deliver my prize to. I doubt I will have difficulty obtaining a bounty from the British. They are itching to get their hands on the dark patriot."

"Nay, I will pay," Douglas blurted out. The very last thing he wanted was to have his future daughter-in-law in custody. Cole would never forgive him if Stephanie wound up in prison. Having her held captive by the man who had twice tried to kill her was bad enough! "Just don't keep me waiting long. I have an appointment later this evening."

Brice watched in wicked anticipation as Douglas shoved his hand into the satchel to deposit the money. Brice waited for Douglas's shocked cry to pierce the thick silence. When it did, Brice sneered fiendishly.

Douglas jerked his hand from the pouch. He stared in horror at the horseshoe-shaped bite of the coral snake Brice had planted in the satchel. In a matter of seconds the flesh around the wound had turned purple and Douglas was having difficulty drawing his breath.

"'Tis what you deserve for trying to trick me," Brice chuckled sardonically as he clamped the satchel shut. "You know who the rabble-rouser is, don't you? 'Tis why you had a change of plans. But if you want the wench back, it will cost you far more than the trifle of coins you delivered."

Brice watched unsympathetically as Douglas collapsed on the ground and then he stepped back to protect himself from the sniper he had anticipated to be lying in wait. "It would be a pity if you did not survive your snakebite," he sneered. "Fascinating creatures, aren't they? I have yet to see a serpent tried and hanged for murder."

Without a second glance at his fallen prey, Brice scampered through the mill and exited through the back door. He was out of sight before Cole could fight his way through the underbrush to determine what had happened to his father.

"Clay!" Douglas wailed as he stared dazedly at his discolored hand. "Help me! I've been snake-bit!"

Cole cursed a blue streak when he reached his father. His smoldering gaze shot through the back door of the mill to see the canoe send silver ripples through the grassy marsh. Cole felt as if he were strung on a torture rack. He felt obligated to aid his father and yet he feared he would lose Stephanie if he didn't give chase to Reynolds.

Before Cole could sort out the riptide of emotions that tugged at him, Douglas clutched the front of his son's shirt. His eyes were wild, his breath coming in ragged spurts.

"I'm going to die!" Douglas gasped. "Clay, for God's sake, do something!"

The tortured look in his father's eyes lanced Cole's soul. Swearing at irregular intervals, Cole ripped the hem from his shirt to make a tourniquet. When the improvised band was tied above the wound, Cole yanked the knife from his boot to cut open the wound. While his father babbled, lost to memories of the past, Cole sucked the poison from the snakebite and hastily bound the injury.

Forgetting his own mending wounds, Cole pulled Douglas to his feet and herded him toward the underbrush where he had spotted the remains of a skiff while he was standing as sentinel. The vessel looked as though it was only minutes away from sinking, but Cole had little choice. It was the only means of transportation to be found and he was determined to follow Brice to his hiding place.

While Cole paddled upriver with no more than a piece of drift wood to serve as his oar, Douglas lay sprawled in the canoe, fighting like hell to rewind his unraveled composure. The fog of the past began to lift and Douglas peered up to see the grim expression on his son's face, not *Clay's,* but *Cole's.* There was something about the stern set of Cole's jaw, the ruthless look in Cole's eyes that jolted Douglas to his senses. It was as if he were seeing his son for the first time in years. The instincts that had preserved Cole's life while he lived like a savage renegade in the wilderness were etched in his chisled features. The shirt Cole had ripped away to provide a tourniquet and bandage lay open to expose the bulging muscles that contracted with apprehension. Douglas was instantly reminded of a jungle cat poised to pounce. Reynolds had rattled this lion's cage and Douglas was ever so thankful he was not his son's enemy.

Cole looked positively dangerous. His stormy black eyes were focused on the narrow channel that meandered through the reed-choked marsh. A strange sense of pride overwhelmed Douglas as he lay staring up at this powerful specimen of a man. Cole's training on sea and in the wilds had prepared him to deal with every kind of catastrophe. It was not fear that settled in Cole's bronzed features; it was anticipation of the fight. The killer instinct had assumed command of Cole's senses and they were all on alert.

The twilight of understanding registered in Douglas's eyes. He suddenly realized that he had done Clay a grave disfavor by overprotecting him. *He* had cost Clay his life, not Cole. With Cole's guidance Clay would have become as strong and invincible as his older brother.

Here was a man to be reckoned with, Douglas told himself proudly. Cole was a man who had tested his capabilities and resourcefulness to the ultimate limits.

Cole was jostled from his musings when he felt his father's hand fold around the taut muscles of his forearm. He glanced down to see the semblance of a smile hovering on Douglas's ashen lips. His father's gaze said it all. Douglas had a firm grasp on reality and he was staring at Cole with open admiration.

"Don't concern yourself with me," Douglas rasped, his voice gravelly with emotion. "Do what you must do to save that little spitfire of yours. I realize now that she is good for you. She brings out the man I tried so hard

495

to repress, to destroy." His eyes misted with sentiment. "It took a snakebite to open my eyes and see you as you truly are. I greatly admire what I see, son."

Cole glanced down at his torso, noting his gaping shirt and the stains on his breeches. A lopsided smile dangled on his lips as he strained against his improvised oar. "You approve of a heathen who is entertaining murderous thoughts?"

"I approve of the *man*," Douglas said meaningfully. "You are more capable than most." When a wave of nausea washed over him, he fell silent and slumped back in the skiff. "And when you tear that miserable bastard apart with your bare hands, I will be cheering you on."

The smile evaporated from Cole's craggy features. His eyes took on a dark, foreboding glitter. "*If* I am given the chance to get my hands on Reynolds, you had better pray for his damnable soul. I intend to send it to hell . . . in shreds."

There was a deadly ring in Cole's voice, a brooding vengeance in his tone. Douglas had never seen his son in such a state of killing fury. Aye, Brice Reynolds had disturbed a sleeping lion. Douglas doubted that he would like what he saw if Cole caught up with Reynolds. But God forgive him, Douglas could not muster an ounce of sympathy for a man who had wrought such misery with his mere existence. If Cole was allowed half a chance, he would eat Reynolds alive. And, by damned, the bastard deserved it! Douglas decided as he stared at his wounded hand.

Try as he may, Cole could not control the tremors that riveted down his spine. He knew Brice would devise a way to use Stephanie as his shield of defense. Brice was many things, all of which Cole despised, but Brice was not a fool. He would employ any method to save his miserable neck. Cole had to keep his wits about him, had to control his urge to react on impulse. Stephanie's life would depend on his ability to make a split-second decision and put it into immediate action.

And if Brice harmed a hair on Stephanie's head, Cole swore by all that was holy that he would hunt that vermin down and feed his heart to the wolves.

While Cole was wrestling with his overwhelming craving for revenge and his anxious concern for Stephanie's future—or lack of it—Brice was paddling toward the shack. His mind was racing with various possibilities of how he was going to deal with Cole, if he was hot on Brice's heels. The fact that Cole would have to tend to his father first provided Brice with the precious time he required. If luck was with him, Brice could fetch Stephanie and row upriver before Cole located the shack. And if not, he would use Stephanie to protect himself from the Hollisters. Congratulating himself on his ability to foresee difficulty and plan accordingly, Brice eased the skiff into the cove near the hut. With a pistol in one hand and his snake-infested satchel in the other, Brice bounded across the mushy ground to unbolt the door.

A smug grin spread across his face when he spied Stephanie propped against the far wall, her gag hanging around her neck, her arms tied behind her back (or so he thought). Just as he opened his mouth to hurl a taunting remark, Stephanie sprang at him. The snake she had killed earlier was her element of surprise.

And what a surprise it was to Brice when he felt the serpent coil around his neck. Though he had a strange penchant for the slimy creatures, natural instinct made him flinch at the possibility of wearing a live coral snake as a necklace. Brice let out a squawk to raise the dead, allowing Stephanie the opportunity to pounce.

Her arm circled through the air to pound Brice with the board she had pried from the wall. The blow knocked him to his knees while he hastily attempted to untangle the snake from his throat.

Like a cannonball, Stephanie shot out the door. Her frantic gaze flew to the skiff that was half camouflaged by the tall reeds of the marsh. The furious growl from inside the cabin spurred her into a faster gait. But Stephanie had tarried too long in search of her means of escape. As she sped through the thick grass and soft earth, Brice leaped at her, grasping a handful of trailing hair.

Stephanie squealed in pain, but she didn't stop running, even at the risk of having her hair yanked out by the roots. Half-twisting, she struck at Brice with her foot, catching him in the groin. Muffling a curse, Brice made another desperate grasp for the long red-gold tendrils but he found himself holding a handful of muggy air. His arm snaked out again, clutching at the hem of Stephanie's skirt. He clamped onto the fabric like a terrapin wrapping its jaws around its quarry and refusing to release its grasp, no matter what.

Stephanie paid no heed to the rending of cloth. She was only too happy to have the lower half of her ruffled gown ripped away if it would save her from Brice's deadly clutches. And it was to her advantage that Brice's left hand was clenched around the satchel and the pistol. She was sure he would have shot her in the back if he could have untangled his trigger finger from the hem of her torn gown.

"Damn you!" Brice cursed viciously. He tossed aside the useless fabric and maneuvered his pistol to his right hand.

Before Stephanie could fling herself into the canoe, Brice fired. The bullet whistled past Stephanie's outstretched arms to blow a hole in the side of the skiff.

Crouching, Stephanie dived into the canoe and grabbed an oar, determined to paddle her way into the channel before Brice could reach her. But Brice was swift of foot when he was in a furious rage. As Stephanie eased the skiff through the reeds, Brice waded into the water. He latched onto the yawl, dragging it back to shore before Stephanie could put a safe distance between them.

Another frantic squeal burst from Stephanie's lips when Brice's arm clenched around her neck to haul her out of the skiff. Reaching behind her head, Stephanie sank her nails into his face. Suddenly, she was all fire and claws and flying fur, determined to fight this vicious creature with her last dying breath.

Brice released an enraged squawk when he felt the skin being peeled off his face. As Stephanie wheeled to launch her second affront, Brice backhanded her across the cheek. But to his amazement, this she-cat pulled herself off the ground and came at him again. She looked exactly as she had that day at the ducking pond, covered with murk from head to toe. Her enormous green eyes were spitting fire, her fists clenched, her jaw set in vengeful fury. Brice tried to sidestep and snatch up his discarded pistol, but the slippery ground caused his feet to squirt out from under him.

Stephanie dived for the flintlock. Just as her fingers curled to grasp the weapon, Brice yanked her backward. She made one more frantic attempt to reach the pistol, but all she succeeded in doing was knocking it into the clump of reeds and slime. Stephanie stared at her salvation until it sank and then focused her undivided attention on Brice, who was fumbling to retrieve his pouch. Did he have another weapon stored in his satchel? That possibility spurred Stephanie to give chase to whatever Brice was after.

As they wallowed in the mud, each trying to secure the pouch, Stephanie heard a thrashing in the reeds. She glanced up through mud-caked eyes to see Cole appear out of nowhere. But before she could scramble to her feet and leave Brice in more capable hands, Brice hooked an arm around her neck, stifling her. His right hand fumbled to open the satchel. As Cole charged toward them, Brice glanced back and forth between the pouch and his nemesis. The second the coral snake poked its head out of the satchel Brice snatched it up, holding it dangerously close to Stephanie's neck.

Stephanie froze when she stared down at the serpent. Her eyes flew to Cole, who had come to a skidding halt. The silence that hung over the marsh was deafening . . . until Brice chuckled fiendishly.

"Take one more step, Hollister," he sneered in challenge. "I'll give this viper his feast and your wife won't last the hour."

A malicious smile twisted Cole's lips as he appraised the slimy bastard who was sitting in the mud with Stephanie poised between his outstretched legs. "She isn't my wife, Reynolds. Haven't you heard? I had the marriage annulled the moment I returned to Maryland." A low peal of laughter filled the air as Cole trained his pistol on Brice's shoulder, his only available target. "Why do you think this witch was hiding out in that dilapidated shack instead of taking residence at the plantation?"

The remark caught Brice off guard. He was rather surprised to find Stephanie lodged in a hut, come to think of it. But he had been too preoccupied with his scheming to determine why Stephanie had been hiding out in the shack instead of enjoying the luxuries of the plantation.

Another rumble of laughter echoed in Cole's chest when the moonlight revealed the befuddled thoughts that were following each other across Brice's grimy features. "The chit can provide a man with pleasure," Cole assured him candidly. "But she is hardly the kind of woman a man in my position can keep as his wife." His expression sobered, his dark eyes boring into Brice. "It isn't Stephanie I want. She can easily be replaced. As far as I am concerned you are welcome to that troublesome misfit. 'Tis *you* I want for my own personal satisfaction. I still carry the scar from your rifle."

For an uneasy moment, Brice sat there, digesting Cole's words and surveying the murderous look on his chisled features. His gaze shifted to see the elder Hollister fumbling his way through the maze of reeds.

"'Tis true," Douglas chimed in. "When Cole told me who the rabble-rouser was, I had a change of heart. I wanted to be rid of the intrepid chit, but having her murdered seemed a bit too drastic." He stared at Stephanie's grimy face and then turned up his nose. "The girl and I detested each other on sight. I even made the arrangements for the annulment while my son was recuperating from his injuries. But if you think I would trade *her* life for my son's, you are every kind of fool, Reynolds."

Brice felt Stephanie tense at the sight of Douglas Hollister. Now he was thoroughly confused. He had followed his assumptions, certain this green-eyed minx would serve as his defense. But it seemed neither of the Hollisters had any use for her. Brice could kill her and neither man would lament her passing.

Another long, anxious moment passed while Brice tried to decide what to do. And it was during that gap of time that Stephanie clamped her teeth into Brice's upper arm, the one that was wrapped around her neck. Exactly what happened next was anybody's guess because all four bodies were moving simultaneously, each determined in their own purpose.

Stephanie wanted to put a safe distance between herself and the poisonous coral snake. Cole hungered to annihilate Brice. Douglas yearned to compensate for the three years of hell he had put his son through and Brice wanted to be anywhere except in the direct line of Cole's pistol fire.

When Stephanie threw herself away from her captor Brice hurled the snake at Cole, hoping to use the same technique of distraction Stephanie had employed earlier. Without bothering to determine Cole's reaction to the flying serpent, Brice launched himself toward the skiff. Douglas made a sweeping circle to reach Stephanie and then took refuge in the weeds, leaving Cole to satisfy his thirst for revenge.

Agilely dodging the winged viper, Cole sprang into action. Although he had his first clear shot at Brice, he tossed the pistol aside. Brice didn't deserve instant death and Cole was determined to let the bastard pay his penance by extracting several pounds of flesh. With no regard for his tender ribs, Cole lunged at Brice. A pained grunt burst from Reynolds's lips when his body was mashed against the rim of the skiff. Before he could scramble away, Cole grabbed him by the nape of the neck and hoisted him into the air. Brice became a human punching bag, receiving blow after brain-scrambling blow. He fought back as best he could, but he was no match for Cole's superior strength and agility.

"My God," Douglas breathed as he watched his son make mincemeat of Brice's stout body. He had come to realize that his son was a force to be reckoned with, but he had no idea how devastating Cole could be when the killer instinct took control of his mind and body. Douglas had little association with the rough-edged frontiersmen of western Maryland. He had never seen

502

a man totally dominate another in a duel of fists. Cole fought like a tiger, employing both his hands and legs to inflict pain and mutilate his opponent.

"Behold your son," Stephanie murmured, her eyes glued to Cole in open admiration. "This is the man you have too long repressed. If ever there was a *man* you should be *honored* to have sired, this is the one."

Douglas knew what Stephanie was driving at—a subtle jab at his overactive sense of dignity. And Douglas would have apologized then and there, for forcing Stephanie off the plantation, but before he could utter another word, Stephanie vaulted to her feet and dashed toward Cole.

Through a blaze of vindictive fury, Cole felt Stephanie's hand on his right arm, refusing to allow him to deliver another blow to Brice's swollen face. Brice was already unconscious, and if Cole had not been propping him up with his left arm, he would have been lying in a broken heap.

"Cole!" Stephanie's sharp voice splintered his murderous thoughts, bringing him back in touch with reality.

Cole had learned to control his temper, but when it finally snapped, he became a madman, driven by vengeful demons. He kept seeing Stephanie in Brice's clutches, watching the snake that loomed so near her throat. It had taken every ounce of self-control to stand his ground and proclaim that he couldn't care less what happened to this green-eyed leprechaun when, in truth, she was his reason for being. That baldfaced lie and his countenance of nonchalance had cost him every iota of composure.

Once Stephanie was free of this vermin's clutches, Cole had been tormented by a vengeance that surpassed all he had ever experienced. He had wanted to repay Brice for all the pain he had caused, the humiliation Stephanie had endured, Cole's agony, as well as his father's. Cole could have done the world a great service if he killed Brice Reynolds with his bare hands. The man was a menace, a selfish schemer who would have stopped at nothing to have what he wanted.

"Cole . . ." Stephanie's tone was softer now, imploring him to turn to her and forget his murderous obsession with Brice. "Cole, I love you. Hold me . . . I feared I would never see you again."

When Cole unclenched his fist from what was left of Brice's shirt and allowed the man to crumble into a wilted heap, Douglas sank back in amazement. He watched the fury pour out of his son like water rushing over a collapsing dam. But when Cole pivoted to enfold Stephanie in his arms, his dark eyes were as soft as black velvet. He held the muddy bundle of femininity to him as if she were made of fragile crystal. Suddenly, Cole was in direct contrast to the ominous beast who had pelted Brice with blow after agonizing blow.

Douglas sat there watching Cole and Stephanie embrace each other with unrivaled tenderness. Cole had insisted that he cared deeply for this feisty little misfit, but until now Douglas hadn't realized what a dramatic effect Stephanie actually had on his son. What they meant to each other was apparent in their quiet murmurings, the way they touched, the way Cole smiled down into Stephanie's smudged face. The kind of love Cole was experiencing was as rare as the man himself.

A mist of tears clouded Douglas's eyes. Because of his foolishness, his misplaced sense of honor and responsibility, he had very nearly spoiled his son's chance at true happiness. Cole deserved far more than Douglas had allowed him. And it was no wonder Cole had wandered in and out of shallow affairs since he returned to civilization. No other domesticated female intrigued him the way this fiery lass did. She was like the missing half of a living puzzle that made Cole complete. She could fight like a tigress and yet she, too, could be a gentle as a lamb.

Respect dawned in Douglas's eyes for both his son and this incredible green-eyed pixie. Douglas groaned to think he had almost forced Cole to settle for Rachel Garret. She would have made Cole's life a living hell, even if Douglas hadn't managed the feat all by himself.

But things were going to be different, Douglas promised himself. No longer would he interfere in Cole's life. His son would have free rein to live his own life the way he saw fit. At last, the past was in its proper perspective and Douglas would ensure that Cole and Stephanie's future was bright . . . without his meddling, he tacked on.

While Douglas was lost in repentant thoughts, Cole was grinning into the face he had discovered more than four months earlier. But Cole didn't care that her elflike features were smeared with mud. She was back in his arms and he could see beneath that unbecoming layers of grime. He could envision an exquisite face that was inset with the most entrancing pair of green eyes. They reminded him of dew-kissed grass sparkling in the morning sun. They were radiant and alive and he would be content to gaze forever into those breathtaking pools.

Heaving a shuddering sigh, Cole set Stephanie away from him. She had prevented him from fully satisfying his revenge, but he wasn't quite through with Brice Reynolds.

"What are you going to do?" Stephanie questioned as Cole dragged Brice's unconscious body toward the skiff.

Cole offered no explanation as he dumped Brice i

the boat that bore a hole just above water level. Silently, he glanced about him to spy the rope that had once been bound to Stephanie's hands. While Cole went quietly about his chore, Douglas climbed to his feet to stand beside Stephanie.

"What is going on? Aren't we taking Reynolds to the authorities?" he questioned.

Stephanie's shoulders lifted in a shrug as she continued to watch Cole. When Cole began scouring the reeds in search of only God knew what, she was as baffled as Douglas was.

After Cole concluded his tasks, he extended a booted foot to push the skiff into the channel. That accomplished, he glanced toward his bumfuzzled companions.

"Reynolds deserves no consideration," he declared. "But nevertheless, I am granting him the chance to escape."

Frowning simultaneously, Douglas and Stephanie strode forward to see Brice lying prone in the skiff. His hands and feet were bound together. The snake Brice had kept in his pouch was now slithering over his limp body. The rocking motion of the canoe allowed trickles of water to pour through the hole Brice had blown in the skiff when he took a shot at Stephanie.

"When Reynolds rouses, he will have the opportunity to untangle himself from the ropes while he defends himself against his pet viper. When he conquers those two obstacles, he can swim ashore before his leaky tub sinks . . . or he can sit there and rot. 'Tis *his* option," Cole proclaimed.

"I would hardly refer to that as an option," Stephanie smirked. "His chances are virtually nonexistent."

"Reynolds will enjoy the same chances he granted anyone who was forced to deal with him—slim and none," Cole argued. The muscles of his jaw tensed as he watched the skiff drift down the channel. "I am not about to drag Reynolds to court, knowing he will again attempt to bargain for freedom. The bastard sold himself to the devil long ago and I am anxious for Satan to come and collect him."

As Cole strode toward the skiff that had brought them upriver, Stephanie studied his muscular back. Cole was right. Brice was being allowed the only option he deserved, the only option available. Thrice Reynolds had threatened to tear them apart and he would try again if he were granted the chance.

"Let's go home." Cole sighed as he extended a hand to Stephanie and then to his father. "We have a wedding to plan."

Stephanie glanced expectantly at Douglas, who had situated himself at the back of the canoe. A faint smile pursed his lips as he massaged his wounded hand. His expression did not seem as stern as it once had and it gave Stephanie hope that they wouldn't always be at each other's throats.

"You have made a fine choice, Cole," he insisted, casting Stephanie a sidelong glance. "It seems I underestimated your lady, and for that, I apologize." Outstretching his hand, he gestured for Stephanie to join him. "Sit with me, my dear. 'Tis time we became better acquainted."

And so she did. When Douglas insisted that she spill her life story during the journey home, Stephanie proceeded to list her faults, just in case Douglas wasn't aware of all of them. And by the time she finished her extensive self-criticism and confessed that her own father swore she had been born with a rebel's soul, Douglas was chuckling good-naturedly.

"A black sheep, eh?" he teased, tossing his silent son an amused glance. "Then I should like to see an entire flock of them parading through the house."

Cole paused from his rowing to flash his father a sly smile. "I shall see to it that you have your wish." His gaze sketched Stephanie's muddy features and lingered on her comely figure. "I am curious to know how tolerant I will be when my children become as rambunctious and high-spirited as their mother."

"It would be ill-advised to hold too tight a rein on them," Douglas warned, giving Stephanie's hand a fond squeeze. "I speak from experience. Your children will be a handful, just as you were." His expression was soft with genuine sincerity. "Just love them and guide them. Those are the two most important gifts you can give your children."

While Cole rowed quietly toward the mill to fetch the carriage, Douglas confessed the humiliating story of Rachel's deception and then reassured Stephanie that she would be most welcome at Hollister.

Stephanie was relieved to hear what had become of Rachel. She was also anxious to take her place beside Cole, to love him the way he deserved to be loved. No matter what difficulties their future held, they would confront them together.

A contented sigh escaped Stephanie's lips as she eased back to stare appreciatively at Cole. Lord, he was something spectacular to look at. An impish smile pursed her lips as she drank in the arousing sight of him. The moment they arrived at Hollister, she was going to prescribe plenty of bed rest for Cole. He had exerted himself this evening and she would ensure he was fit as a fiddle before she permitted him out of the boudoir.

Cole intercepted the seductive gleam in Stephanie's eyes. It was obvious they were both harboring the same tantalizing thoughts. And the instant they set foot in the mansion, Cole intended to lock himself in with his *former, future* wife. As a matter of fact, they might not emerge from their room until the day of their second wedding. After all, they had yet to enjoy their first honeymoon, he reminded himself. But Cole planned to remedy that oversight within the hour. He was going to book passage on the most intimate journeys. . . .

Chapter 28

Stephanie paced the floor of the room that had once belonged to Rachel. Being directed to this particular chamber was not a premeditated insult on Douglas's part, but that was exactly how Stephanie was taking it. The room was brimming with memories, ones with Rachel Garret's name attached to them.

Her eyes reluctantly drifted to the bed that was covered with a lace spread. Another of Rachel's purchases, no doubt, Stephanie mused resentfully. Grappling with that thought, she marched over to rip the cover from the bed and hurled it into the corner, exposing the pink satin sheets. Stephanie didn't want to think about the times Cole and Rachel had lain in bed together, perhaps not in this one, but in others . . . with pink satin sheets. . . . She squelched the unsettling thought.

Well, maybe Stephanie wasn't Cole's first love, but by damned, she would be the last, she promised herself. She was going to erase every memory of every other woman. She would make Cole forget that conniving Rachel Garret, if only she was granted the chance.

Her gaze focused on the wall that separated her boudoir from Cole's and she muttered under her breath. She knew Douglas wouldn't think it proper for her to share Cole's bed. He was a stickler for custom and tradition. But blast it, she and Cole had been married for more than a month the first time, she rationalized. She was his former, future wife. That fact should allow her a few untraditional privileges, she reckoned. And why should she pretend innocence at this late date? And why was Cole permitting this separation if he loved her as much as he claimed he did? Was he patronizing his father for appearance' sake? Had he taken her reputation into consideration. For heaven's sake, she had never had much of one to protect, or had he forgotten?

Stephanie let out her breath in a frustrated rush. Being so close and yet so far away from Cole was torment, pure and simple. Although Douglas had insisted that she rest after her harrowing experience, Stephanie could not force herself into bed—Rachel's bed. She wanted to be with Cole, to feel the hypnotic magic of his sinewy arms, to reassure him that she loved him beyond all else. How was she supposed to do that with this confounded wall between them?

Impulsively, Stephanie strode toward the double doors that led to the balcony which wrapped around the upper story of bedroom suites. She lingered in the darkness for only a moment before her footsteps took her to Cole's door.

He was probably asleep, Stephanie told herself. Cole had pushed himself to the limits that evening. He had tested his stamina and his strength. Although it had been a month since he had fallen beneath Brice's bullet, Stephanie knew he couldn't have fully recovered.

All the more reason to check on him, Stephanie reasoned. Quietly, she eased open the door, intending to watch Cole sleep, if that was her only alternative. But to her amazement, Cole was lounging at a candlel table, leisurely sipping a goblet of wine. His cream-colored shirt gaped open at the neck, revealing the dark matting of hair and the tantalizing bronze flesh that shadowed his chest. The golden light glistened in his blue-black curls, which lay in roguish disarray. The smile that clung to his sensuous lips caused Stephanie's heart to flip-flop in her chest. He looked so ruggedly handsome that she could have lingered by the door for hours, drinking in the arresting sight of him.

It wasn't until she had devoured him with her gaze that she noticed the untouched glass of wine that sat across the table from Cole. That observation caused a muddled frown to knot her brow. Was he expecting someone? Douglas perhaps? Nay, Stephanie decided. Douglas had retired hours ago. His hand was still paining him and he was exhausted from his own hair-raising encounter with Brice Reynolds.

While Stephanie was assessing Cole, his dark, penetrating eyes roved over the garment that concealed her well-sculptured figure. Since the hour was late when they returned from their fiasco with Reynolds, there had been no opportunity to fetch Stephanie's belongings from the shack. The only clothes at her disposal were Cole's oversized shirts and he was suddenly envious of his own garment. It held what he wanted—a green-eyed leprechaun with red-gold hair. She was the stuff dreams were made of and Cole found himself in the midst of a most arousing fantasy as he surveyed the picture she presented.

The hem of the linen shirt extended just past her derriere, leaving a titillating display of leg. The open neck revealed the luscious swell of her bosom to his all-consuming gaze and Cole felt the quick rise of his blood pressure. The fabric, though not completely transparent, could not camouflage the dusky peaks of her breasts or the trim indention of her waist from his

512

hawkish gaze. In short, the improvised robe did more to *tantalize* than to disguise.

Cole felt the warm throb of desire percolating in his veins. Although he was stiff and sore after his battle with Reynolds, the ache in his loins was causing him the most distress. Cole had but to look at this enchanting bundle of beauty and spirit and he went hot all over.

"What took you so long, Steph?" he questioned in that rich, resonant voice that could transform her legs to limp noodles.

"You were expecting me?" Stephanie chirped incredulously.

How could he have anticipated her intrusion when she had come on impulse? He knew Douglas had hustled off to bathe and rest the moment they had set foot in the house. Douglas had also given Cole orders to recuperate after his exhausting day, she reminded herself.

His husky laughter wafted its way across the distance that separated them to tickle her senses and further heighten Stephanie's awareness of him, if that were possible. "Just because my father confined you to your quarters to rest is no reason for me to assume you would sacrifice your nocturnal prowling," he teased her. "You have never obeyed anyone's commands. I had counted upon the fact that you were holding true to form."

And then it came, that deliciously impish smile that cut dimples in her cheeks and caused her eyes to shine like a beacon in the night. When she took a bold step forward, the pale glow from the hearth sprayed through the thin fabric of the shirt and enhanced the lustrous mane of red-gold that cascaded over her shoulders. The light framed her exquisite physique like gentle hands molded to each curve and swell and created a halo upon her glorious head of hair. She looked positively bewitching standing there and Cole's pulse thumped in rakish anticipation.

"Perhaps your father would consider it scandalous for me to visit your chamber before the marriage, but I have never been able to resist your dark charms," she confessed honestly. "I see no reason to deny the attraction now. 'Tis not as if we have never been intimate."

That was one of the myriad of reasons Cole adored this lively nymph. She was inclined to speak her mind and he was even more appreciative of her candor when he was the object of her compliments.

Cole eased back on his chair and sipped his wine. He studied her for a moment from over the rim of his goblet. "Are you suggesting, shameless wench, that we . . ." His twinkling brown eyes darted toward the bed that had been meticulously drawn back to expose the fresh satin sheets. ". . . that you and I enjoy the pleasures of wedded bliss before we repeat the vows?" Cole clucked his tongue in mock disapproval. "Really, Steph, I am offended that you would even question my integrity, my self-imposed, exceedingly high standards of morality."

That ornery rake, Stephanie thought resentfully. He wanted her as much as she wanted him. She had been able to decode the lusty thoughts that had been darting through those chocolate brown eyes since the moment she had set foot in his boudoir. He had mentally undressed her several times the past few minutes. How blind did he think she was anyway? So he wanted to play games, did he? Well, she had no qualms about obliging him. After all, she was every bit as mischievous as he was.

Her chin tilted, pretending to be offended by his misinterpretation of her reasons for barging into his

514

boudoir. "Nay, of course not," she assured him airily. "I had in mind mere conversation." Her eyes darted toward the blazing fire in the hearth. "But 'tis a bit too warm for my tastes. Would you mind very much if I slipped into something cooler before joining you for a glass of wine?"

One dark brow elevated and his sensuous lips quirked in a smile. "I wasn't aware that you had anything else to wear," he remarked.

"You are mistaken," she insisted as she loosed the buttons of the shirt.

Stephanie presented him with another dazzling smile and Cole felt himself go up in smoke when he caught her intended meaning. The *something cooler* to which she referred was nothing more than bare skin. Once her garment had drifted to the floor, Stephanie pirouetted in front of Cole, allowing him to view the creation from all angles—as if she were modeling a newly purchased gown.

"Do you like it?" she questioned in mock innocence.

"'Tis exquisite," Cole choked out as Stephanie sashayed toward the vacant chair and parked herself in it.

His eyes popped when he was granted a close view of her perfect body, a sight that was having a disturbing effect on him. Distracted, Cole raised his glass to his lips but he missed his mouth. Wine trickled down his chin and dripped on the collar of his shirt.

Feigning concern, Stephanie leaned across the table to wipe the splotches of liquor from his face. "You poor dear," she cooed. "You have overexerted yourself today. 'Tis no wonder your reflexes are not functioning properly." With her task complete, she settled back in her chair to sip her wine. When Cole's mortar began to show signs of cracking, Stephanie snickered to herself. "Now, about the wedding. I think it wise if we wait until winter . . . perhaps sometime after the first of the year."

"Winter?" Cole parroted in disbelief.

Stephanie gave her head an affirmative nod. "I think we owe it to ourselves to fully contemplate this matter of matrimony. The first time we married for the mere challenge of pitting our strong wills against each other. This time we should carefully analyze our reasons, diligently evaluate them, and then decide if 'tis what we both truly want and need to make our lives complete."

She seemed so sincere in what she was saying that Cole stared at her as if her flesh had suddenly become splotched with red and pink polka dots. Was this the same impulsive firebrand he thought he knew? Steph was *contemplating* decisions instead of merely reacting? Wonders never ceased! And how the sweet loving hell was he supposed to sit here and carry on an intelligent conversation when this emerald-eyed leprechaun wasn't wearing a stitch?

Cole had to make a dedicated effort to formulate his question and put it to tongue. "Since when have you become so orderly and methodic?" he wanted to know.

Stephanie shrugged a bare shoulder. "Since I came to realize that method and logic are most important," she informed him nonchalantly. "I also think we should deny our physical attraction for each other until the ceremony. We should concentrate on getting to know one another," she went on to say. Willfully, she smothered the bubble of laughter that threatened to distort her mask of sincerity when Cole's mouth dropped open wide enough for a family of pigeons to nest in.

Somewhere along the way, this encounter had run amuck. He had only been teasing Stephanie. Hell, he knew what he wanted and he didn't want to be sensible. He ached to exercise his male needs until he fell into an

516

exhausted sleep. Surely she knew he had only been taunting her for pure orneriness. After all, he had been sitting here for over an hour, certain Stephanie would come to him. He would have gone to her long ago but he didn't relish the idea of setting foot in Rachel's old room either.

While Stephanie rattled on about her expectations of marriage, spouting pros and cons about wedlock, Cole clanked his glass against the table. The clatter interrupted Stephanie's soliloquy and she glanced over to appraise the stern frown that was stamped on Cole's face.

"You really don't care what I think, do you?" she questioned point-blank.

"At the moment, nay," Cole said abruptly.

"Don't you think it important to decide how many children we want and determine how we intend to raise them?" Her eyes took on a contemplative hue, as if she were carefully deliberating the subject. "I do not approve of strict rules and I have no wish to repress a child's natural vitality. But I am not certain if I have the patience to raise a dozen high-spirited offspring." She slanted him a curious glance, amused by the kaleidoscope of expressions that were appearing and vanishing in the craggy features of his face. "Would you be satisfied with a mere half-dozen children or did you have your heart set on spawning an army of them?"

Cole speared his fingers into the crop of raven hair that capped his head and considered pulling it out, strand by strand. "What does it accomplish to *discuss* children?" he snorted sarcastically. "Talking doesn't produce them. And if you don't garb yourself in something, and quickly, I will not be responsible for my actions!" he all but bellowed at her.

Stephanie flinched at his booming voice. "Would you prefer that I return to my own room?" One delicate

517

brow lifted as she surveyed the scowl that cut harsh lines in his usually handsome face. When he replied with a wordless growl, Stephanie set her glass aside and gracefully rose to full stature. "I had better bid you good night, Coleman," she declared stiffly, tormenting him and loving every minute of it. "'Tis obvious your weariness is affecting your disposition. Perhaps you will be in a more pleasant frame of mind by dawn and we can continue this conversation in a rational, civil manner."

Now Cole had learned the importance of self-control and he had practiced the art on numerous occasions. But there were limits to what he could endure before his glue melted. And it was melting at an incredibly rapid rate.

When Stephanie pivoted toward the door, Cole shoved the table aside and made a beeline for her. "Now wait just a damned minute, woman," he ordered gruffly. "I will not be in a better frame of mind in the morning if you waltz out of here tonight. I want you in my bed and I don't give a whit what is proper or reasonable or whatever else you were rambling on about while I wasn't listening!"

Stephanie looked him squarely in the eye and suppressed her impish grin. "I thought you said you were a gentleman, bound to your convictions," she reminded him.

"I lied," Cole blurted out impatiently. "Are you coming to bed or must I physically put you in it?"

A wry smile pursed her lips, and her eyes glittered like polished jewels. "If that is where you wanted me, why didn't you say so in the first place instead of scolding *me* for making such an improper suggestion? We have already wasted a quarter of an hour, precious minutes we could have been engaging in something far more stimulating than conversation."

Her mischievous smile mellowed his sour frown. "Witch," Cole growled as he drew her unresisting body into his arms. It finally dawned on him that he had been had—*again*. Stephanie had no intention of leaving his room. She only wanted to hear a commitment, a reaffirmation that their second marriage would have a better beginning than the first. He knew better than to taunt this feisty leprechaun. She was the mistress of mischievousness and he couldn't hold a candle to her playful pranks, not when he was out of practice.

"You truly are worth your weight in trouble, minx," he declared, his voice quivering with the side effects of holding her so close. The feel of her body was like a white-hot brand against his flesh. His heart leaped into triple time in response to having her leaning full length against him. "If I knew what was good for me, I would probably reaffirm my vows of *bachelorhood.*"

Stephanie slid her arms around his neck to toy with the raven curls that clung to his collar. "You wouldn't be happy," she assured him confidently. "Not when you love me, despite all my faults."

Cole broke into a broad grin. "You seem terribly sure of yourself."

Her hands began to swim to and fro, scaling and descending his spine, turning bone to jelly, transforming muscle into puddles. His reaction to her touch was proof enough. She could feel his muscular body quiver in response, feel his arousal, hear the quick intake of his breath.

"This time I am very sure," she whispered against his lips. "Twice I have run away from the only man I ever truly wanted, the only man I could ever love, totally, completely. And thrice I have come within a hair's breadth of losing my one true chance at happiness. I won't allow that to happen again."

Stephanie leaned back in his arms to trace the full

519

curve of his mouth. "At first you doubted me when I confessed that I loved you. But there will be no more doubt, no more pretense, no more foolish games to protect my pride. I love you above all else . . ."

A tender smile grazed his lips as he bent to press a kiss to her cheek. "Do you know when I first fell in love with you, Steph?" His soft laughter brushed her eyelids. "'Twas when you emerged from that pond with a handful of mud. You were all fire and flames. It wasn't so much your beauty that attracted me, though I have never seen anyone quite so exquisite. It wasn't the tantalizing sound of your voice that whispered in my soul or the graceful way you moved, though I was instantly mesmerized by both." Lovingly, he cupped her face in his hands, forcing her to look into the hypnotizing depth of his eyes. "It was something far more important, something deep within you."

He gathered her closer to inhale the feminine scent of her, to absorb her softness into his hard length. "'Twas not so much who you were and what you looked like, but rather what you were that intrigued me. You, my lovely nymph, are living fire. And I've been in flames since the first time I touched you."

His sincere words and the husky tone with which he conveyed them sent a hot flood of pleasure channeling through her body. Stephanie would have been content to spend her days right where she was. She was in heaven.

"There is something rare and unique about you," Cole murmured quietly. "You are spirit itself, the treasure of life. You enhance that special quality I thought I had lost. You unleashed emotions that I thought had escaped me forever."

She was stirred by his soft confession and the tender way he held her to him. She felt wanted and needed for the first time in her life. "Cole, I—"

His index finger strayed to her lips to shush her. "I d[o] love you, Steph. But words are not enough to expres[s] all the complex emotions I feel." A hint of a smil[e] bordered his lips as he curled an arm beneath her knee[s] to lift her off the floor. "Fortunately, there are othe[r] more delightful ways for a man to prove to a woma[n] that she means the world to him . . ."

Looping her arms around his neck, Stephanie eye[d] him inquisitively. "Other ways besides all the ones yo[u] already taught me?"

A deep skirl of laughter rumbled in his chest as h[e] navigated his way to bed without ever taking his eye[s] off her. Unceremoniously, he tossed her on the sati[n] sheets and then stood back to devour her with his eye[s]. "I have only begun to instruct you in the ways of lov[e]. And when we have exhausted the limits of m[y] experience . . ." The roguish grin that crinkled h[is] dashing features and the unique quality of his wor[ds] made Stephanie shiver with anticipation. ". . . we a[re] going to invent our own special brand of lovemaking[.]"

Entranced, Stephanie watched Cole's nimble finge[rs] flutter over the buttons of his shirt. When the garme[nt] drifted to the floor, Stephanie studied the wide expan[se] of muscles on his chest, his tapered waist, the sinew[y] columns of his arms. She marveled at this lion of a ma[n] who had become all things to her. When Cole shed h[is] breeches, her eyes drifted lower, aroused by the visi[on] of raw strength and masculinity. He could put [a] Greek god to shame with his virile physique, she mus[ed] dreamily.

A pleased smile hovered on Cole's lips as h[e] stretched out beside her. Stephanie was staring at hi[m] with feminine appreciation and he reveled in the abili[ty] to hold her admiring gaze. He had always wanted to [be] her champion, but more than that, Cole longed to ea[rn] her respect and devotion. The adoring expression [on] her features said that and so much more.

Holding her warm gaze, Cole began to explore her pliant body, slowly, tenderly, until the world around them faded into a breathless blur. When their lips met, all thought ceased. Their kisses and caresses were the sublime expression of what love should be—the caring, the sharing, the joining of one wild heart unto another. And while the fire crackled in the hearth and the candle consumed itself in flame, Stephanie and Cole loved away the hours from midnight until dawn.

Finally they slept, content in each other's arms . . . until Stephanie roused from her dreams to nudge Cole awake. Drowsily, he pried open one eye to see the bewitching face lingering mere inches away from his.

"I have just come upon an inspiration," Stephanie enthused with a sly smile. "One we overlooked . . ."

Cole peered up at her, chuckling at the incredibly mischievous expression that claimed her features. Why would he be surprised that an emerald-eyed leprechaun from Mystic had devised another innovative technique in lovemaking? After all, she possessed magical powers beyond human comprehension, Cole reminded himself. And then caught his breath when her small hand struck out on a journey across masculine terrain, leaving not one inch of his body unexplored.

He caught her adventurous hand in his, detaining her from her arousing investigations. "Don't you think we should take time for breakfast? I'm famished," he told her, his voice husky from the affects of her disturbing caresses.

"I am too," she whispered as her sweet mouth descended on his. "'Tis why I have decided to have breakfast in bed . . ."

Cole was smiling while he returned her tantalizing kiss. What hot-blooded male was going to venture downstairs for coffee and a plate of ham and eggs when

this lively leprechaun was offering delicacies to appeas
the most voracious appetite? Certainly not Cole! H
knew what he wanted, what he had always wante
since this adorable nymph had emerged from he
cocoon of mud to grace him with her beguiling smile
Aye, he had all the nourishment he needed and he ha
no qualms about observing a famine to sample *thi*
delicious feast.

"Steph!" Cole gasped when she began doing in
credibly arousing things to his body. "Don't do that!

But Stephanie defied his feeble protest. Her kisse
and caresses continued to arouse, tantalize, an
explore.

Cole could feel himself losing control and he n
longer cared if he did. "Mmmm . . . do that again,
Cole rasped, surrendering to the tidal wave o
sensations that splashed over him.

This time she obeyed his request and the worl
shrank. All Cole could see was enormous green eye
that dominated a pixielike face. Heaven was just
touch away and Cole reached out to grasp the paradis
that Stephanie's love created. And together the
strolled the glorious halls of the castle in the air—
wondrous, spacious mansion where dreams really d
come true. . . .

Note to Readers

Seventeen sixty-five was a significant year in American History. Waves of discontent rippled through each community in every colony and counter-ripples lapped the seaboard from north to south. The Stamp Act became the instrument that bound the thirteen colonies in a common cause. There were no longer separate entities, but rather one special breed of people devoted to a purpose.

Through the efforts of the Sons of Liberty, a remarkable network of communication was established to coordinate the protest of taxation without representation in the English Parliament. Considering the circumstances and the times, the unification of the colonies was phenomenal. The effective protests and demonstrations during those three months in the late summer and fall of 1765 have become an inspiring example of American spirit.

Although the Revolution was still a decade away, the groundwork of communication and the foundation for liberty and freedom had been established by the tireless efforts of the Sons and Daughters of Liberty. Their fighting spirit and their craving for freedom have made each of us proud to call ourselves Americans.

I hope you enjoyed this adventurous romp throug colonial history. I am always delighted to hear fro readers and I personally answer all correspondence

Sincerely,
Gina Robins

ROMANCE REIGNS
WITH ZEBRA BOOKS!

SILVER ROSE   (2275, $3.95)
by Penelope Neri

Fleeing her lecherous boss, Silver Dupres disguised herself as a boy and joined an expedition to chart the wild Colorado River. But with one glance at Jesse Wilder, the explorers' rugged, towering scout, Silver knew she'd have to abandon her protective masquerade or else be consumed by her raging unfulfilled desire!

STARLIT ECSTASY   (2134, $3.95)
by Phoebe Conn

Cold-hearted heiress Alicia Caldwell swore that Rafael Ramirez, San Francisco's most successful attorney, would never win her money . . . or her love. But before she could refuse him, she was shamelessly clasped against Rafael's muscular chest and hungrily matching his relentless ardor!

LOVING LIES   (2034, $3.95)
by Penelope Neri

When she agreed to wed Joel McCaleb, Seraphina wanted nothing more than to gain her best friend's inheritance. But then she saw the virile stranger . . . and the green-eyed beauty knew she'd never be able to escape the rapture of his kiss and the sweet agony of his caress.

EMERALD FIRE   (1963, $3.95)
by Phoebe Conn

When his brother died for loving gorgeous Bianca Antonelli, Evan Sinclair swore to find the killer by seducing the tempress who lured him to his death. But once the blond witch willingly surrendered all he sought, Evan's lust for revenge gave way to the desire for unrestrained rapture.

SEA JEWEL   (1888, $3.95)
by Penelope Neri

Hot-tempered Alaric had long planned the humiliation of Freya, the daughter of the most hated foe. He'd make the wench from across the ocean his lowly bedchamber slave—but he never suspected she would become the mistress of his heart, his treasured SEA JEWEL.

Available wherever paperbacks are sold, or order direct from the Publisher. Send cover price plus 50¢ per copy for mailing and handling to Zebra Books, Dept. 2254, 475 Park Avenue South, New York, N.Y. 10016. Residents of New York, New Jersey and Pennsylvania must include sales tax. DO NOT SEND CASH.

LOVE'S BRIGHTEST STARS SHINE
WITH ZEBRA BOOKS!

CATALINA'S CARESS (2202, $3.95)
by Sylvie F. Sommerfield

Catalina Carrington was determined to buy her riverboat back from the handsome gambler who'd beaten her brother at cards. But when dashing Marc Copeland named his price—three days as his mistress—Catalina swore she'd never meet his terms . . . even as she imagined the rapture a night in his arms would bring!

BELOVED EMBRACE (2135, $3.95)
by Cassie Edwards

Leana Rutherford was terrified when the ship carrying her family from New York to Texas was attacked by savage pirates. But when she gazed upon the bold sea-bandit Brandon Seton, Leana longed to share the ecstasy she was sure sure his passionate caress would ignite!

ELUSIVE SWAN (2061, $3.95)
by Sylvie F. Sommerfield

Just one glance from the handsome stranger in the dockside tavern in boisterous St. Augustine made Arianne tremble with excitement. But the innocent young woman was already running from one man . . . and no matter how fiercely the flames of desire burned within her, Arianne dared not submit to another!

SAVAGE PARADISE (1985, $3.95)
by Cassie Edwards

Marianna Fowler detested the desolate wilderness of the unsettled Montana Territory. But once the hot-blooded Chippewa brave Lone Hawk saved her life, the spirited young beauty wished never to leave, longing to experience the fire of the handsome warrior's passionate embrace!

MOONLIT MAGIC (1941, $3.95)
by Sylvie F. Sommerfield

When she found the slick railroad negotiator Trace Cord trespassing on her property and bathing in her river, innocent Jenny Graham could barely contain her rage. But when she saw how the setting sun gilded Trace's magnificent physique, Jenny's seething fury was transformed into burning desire!

Available wherever paperbacks are sold, or order direct from the Publisher. Send cover price plus 50¢ per copy for mailing and handling to Zebra Books, Dept. 2254, 475 Park Avenue South, New York, N.Y. 10016. Residents of New York, New Jersey and Pennsylvania must include sales tax. DO NOT SEND CASH.